THE BIRD WATCHER

THE BIRD WATCHER

A NOVEL

JACQUELYN MITCHARD

/||MIRA

///MIRA

ISBN-13: 978-0-7783-6867-0

The Birdwatcher

Copyright © 2025 by Jacquelyn Mitchard

Title page illustration © Shutterstock

Bird icons © stock.adobe.com

For questions and comments about the quality of this book, please contact us at CustomerService@Harlequin.com.

TM is a trademark of Harlequin Enterprises ULC.

MIRA
22 Adelaide St. West, 41st Floor
Toronto, Ontario M5H 4E3, Canada
MIRABooks.com

HarperCollins Publishers
Macken House, 39/40 Mayor Street Upper,
Dublin 1, D01 C9W8, Ireland
www.HarperCollins.com

Printed in U.S.A.

For all my chickadees.
Girls rule the world.

THE
BIRD
WATCHER

I will find out where she has gone,
And kiss her lips and take her hands;
And walk among long dappled grass,
And pluck till time and times are done,
The silver apples of the moon,
The golden apples of the sun.
—*William Butler Yeats, "The Song of the Wandering Aengus"*

And resting on His goodness, I lose my doubts and fear;
Though by the path He leadeth, still one step I may see;
His eye is on the sparrow, and I know He watches me.
—*Gospel hymn by Civilla D. Martin and Charles H. Gabriel,*
 "His Eye Is on The Sparrow"

She walks in beauty, like the night
Of cloudless climes and starry skies;
And all that's best of dark and bright
Meet in her aspect and her eyes:
—*George Gordon, Lord Byron, "She Walks in Beauty"*

ONE

Indigo Bunting

Passerina cyanea. This small cheery singer is a bird on a long journey, migrating over 1,200 miles each way from eastern North America to northern South America and back. The male's brilliant azure color is considered one of the most beautiful plumages; but it's all an illusion, literally a trick of the light. The feathers are not really blue at all but only appear to be because of diffraction around the structure of the bird's feathers, scattering all except indigo, the blue light, resulting in a kaleidoscopic shift from black to blue to turquoise as the angle of light changes. Without the benefit of light, the bird's coloring is as drab as charcoal.

WOMEN ON TRIAL FOR MURDER DON'T WEAR PANTS.

In a simple navy blue shirtwaist dress, Felicity stopped just short of the door of the courtroom as the sheriff's deputy re-moved the shackles around her wrists. If I hadn't been staring at the door, hoping for a first glimpse of her, I would have missed that very real, very ugly moment. By the time she took her seat at the defense table, she looked like the homecoming queen she was once, not like an escort who killed two clients in cold blood. Dark hair brushed her chin in an angled bob. Huge glasses that matched her dress framed her strange amber eyes.

For a moment, I was reminded of what Leo Tolstoy said,

not about all happy families being alike, but about how amazing is the delusion that beauty is goodness. Soon, everyone in this crowded courtroom and beyond would see that this was no delusion. Everyone would see what I saw—that beautiful Felicity was indeed good.

I would make sure of it.

"Please rise," said the bailiff as the judge, a short, buxom woman, her auburn natural skillfully tipped with platinum highlights, swept in. "The court of the Second Judicial District, criminal division, is now in session, the Honorable Maria Brent presiding . . . State of Wisconsin versus Felicity Claire Copeland Wild, cause number . . . Miss Wild is here present in court with her attorney, Mr. Damiano . . ."

I opened the dark pink leather folder embossed in gold with *Fuchsia: The Journal of Culture*. Culture, indeed. Culture at *Fuchsia* was formally designating "captivating coral" as the color of the season. At this moment, being from *Fuchsia* embarrassed me, and that wasn't entirely fair to the publication, which did do serious journalism along with the froth. After all, my editor had green-lighted this story, despite her strong reservations. At *Fuchsia*, we'd run stories about the wage gap, critical issues in women's health, and how sexual harassment wasn't just for twentysomethings. This, however, was different, a salty brew of true crime and memoir for which I would be, as my father would say, punching above my weight. Serious journalism was what I set out to do, like my mother before me, but I slid instead into an easy job, penning marshmallow prose about purses. Felicity had set out to be a scientist, a wildlife biologist studying birds. Like arrows shot in the dark, both of us had gone wide of the target.

Judge Brent told Felicity her rights. "Miss Wild, you have the right to the presumption of innocence, which means the state bears the burden to prove you are guilty of this offense beyond a reasonable doubt, which does not mean beyond any doubt, but beyond the doubt that a reasonable person might have . . ."

I drifted in and out of the recitation, staring at Felicity's attorney, an elegant, compact guy whose bold chin and dark eyes would not have been out of place in that lavish photo feature we'd done about corporate class, and at Felicity, whose calm demeanor astonished me.

"Count one alleges that the defendant on or about December 31 in Dane County, the state of Wisconsin, did willfully, unlawfully, deliberately with premeditation and with malice aforethought kill and murder Emil Laurent Gardener, a human being . . . on or about January 4, did willfully . . . Cary Elias Church."

Judge Brent then said, "The maximum possible penalty on count one is life imprisonment. Miss Wild, do you understand that penalty?"

Felicity murmured, "Yes, Your Honor."

It was just like in the movies. I was just a fashion reporter. I knew nothing about covering a trial.

But I knew Felicity.

She was once my best friend. She had once saved me. Had she not, I would have been sitting exactly where she was now—accused of murder, except that in my case, there would have been no doubt of my guilt. It was irony in the first degree.

Now I would repay that old debt. I would dig deep into her shadowy present life and our shared past. I would find out how the brilliant biology student who seemed poised to take on the world gave up all her bright dreams to become a sex worker. If there was a truth that could set Felicity free, I would find it. For I knew that she was not capable of murder just as surely as she knew that I was.

"The maximum possible penalty on count two, the willful murder of Cary Elias Church, is life imprisonment. Miss Wild, do you understand that penalty?"

Finally, the judge said, "Mr. Damiano, how does your client plead?"

Her lawyer nodded to her, and Felicity, her voice low and assured, said, "Not guilty, Your Honor."

As she spoke, I studied her. She was still so beautiful. But what had I expected? A twitchy, hollow-eyed flat backer with skin the texture of a cantaloupe? She was barely twenty-seven, just like me, and she came of good stock, sturdy, attractive Anglo-Saxons, the sort of generic white people who used to monopolize Hallmark TV movies. We were built to withstand cold precipitation.

A fast flurry of discussion then ensued about setting a trial date, some months out, and then, suddenly, everyone else was standing and gathering up their things. I had no idea that an arraignment for such a serious charge could take fifteen minutes.

"What's going on? Why is it over so fast?" I asked the reporter next to me. She was easily in her sixties, with the face of a grizzled bartender framed by golden Cinderella curls. "People said arraignments take hours." She gave me a withering side-eye and I could hear her thinking, *Loser.*

"They do, usually."

"So why is this different?" I glanced down at the police report secured to her clipboard. I asked, "Where did you get that?"

"I asked for it. Anybody can get one if the cops feel like giving it to you that particular day. It's public record."

"Don't you have to file some kind of request?"

"Only if they try to wriggle out of it. Honey, are you a reporter?"

My cheeks burned. I'd blushed more in this half hour than I had in four years of high school. "I am. But for a fashion magazine."

"Not a lot of material here," she said.

"Nope."

"So?"

"I'm covering this because I grew up with the defendant. We were friends." I added, "She could not have done this."

"Yet here we are," the reporter said. "Still, you're a hundred percent right. She's presumed innocent. You heard the judge." She added, "I'm Sally, by the way."

"Reenie," I said. "Irene Bigelow."

Later, when the older reporter and I knew each other better, I would find out that Sally Zankow was famous. She worked for National Public Radio, and her crime features and commentary were heard all over the country. Having covered crime since her hair was naturally that golden, she knew police and prosecutors all over the Midwest as well as she knew her own siblings. She would teach me the best lesson I ever learned as a writer: Contrary to what you saw on TV, you didn't have to be afraid to ask anybody anything because, most of the time, that person would tell you what you wanted to know. People in and around law enforcement were big gossips. I would also find out that what I initially took for disdain toward me among the rest of the reporters, who grew daily in numbers once the trial was underway, was really something else. The cable TV reporters especially, who were many as rabbits and paid like mice, envied me my pretty clothes—as well as the fact that I would probably never have to stand on the street in a blizzard watching firefighters carry the blackened bodies of children from a firetrap tenement.

"Death threats," Sally said. "That's why this arraignment was sequestered." There had been death threats against the judge, against Felicity, and even against her defense lawyer. Nobody was sure what it was about this case that inflamed so many crazy callers. Arraignments normally took place in batches, with defendants sometimes waiting for hours for their case to come up lest they lose their moment, which would mean starting the whole process over again.

"How long will this take?" I asked Sally.

"The whole trial? Weeks for sure, once it gets going. Could be a month or more."

We'd worked our way to the aisle by then . . . and it was as Felicity, at the door, was waiting for her shackles to be replaced that she glanced around her and finally saw me. Her face opened with a recognition so poignant tears flooded my eyes. She was too far away for me to hear her speak but I could see her mouth move: *Reenie.* A smile ghosted across her face, briefly revealing her enviable dimples.

I had tried half a dozen times before this moment to reach Felicity, but my petitions to visit were turned away, my phone calls refused, my letters unanswered. Now, clearly, she had changed her mind. She was grateful for the presence of someone from home.

So I was shocked when Felicity mouthed the words, *Go away.*

TWO

American Crow

Corvus brachyrhynchos. Crows show remarkable intelligence. An eighteenth-century tale tells of "counting crows," in which a crow proved it could count to five with a logic trap set by a farmer. Crows demonstrate episodic memory, recalling events in order, as humans do. Crows and magpies are curious, prone to stealing bright objects. They recognize their own faces in a mirror, use tools, and engage in play such as midair jousting, which they need to stimulate their intellect. Researchers say there would be more examples of corvid intelligence except that scientists measure only those ways that birds behave like human beings rather than like birds. In folklore, these birds symbolize death.

I STILL BELIEVED THAT FELICITY WOULD TALK TO ME. SHE HAD TO.
After the arraignment, though, I had to admit that the odds weren't great. One thing I knew was true. When Felicity said no, she said it only once.

At the very least, I would be able to tell my editor that I had used every key to try every lock in every door. There's no limit to the number of times you can try the same key in a different lock until that key opens something, even though tenacity and ingenuity are two different things, and I had plenty of the former and not much of the latter. My dad told me once that the number of permutations with the digits one through ten was more than three million and I still don't know what he was talking about. More usefully, my mom used to say that the answer to any question was in the question; the key was finding the right question.

I tried calling Felicity at the jail. Whoever answered told me to hold on, and then, after a minute or so, returned to say that Miss Wild was unavailable. Like she was in a meeting? Or on another call?

I wrote six letters to Felicity, each one different from the one before it.

The first was just a greeting to inquire about her condition in there. Did she need blankets? Was I allowed to send her a better pillow? Felicity was strong and athletic but fragile, one of those people who got strep every year but was so stoic she always waited until she was almost too sick to go anywhere but the ER. I had to believe she was suffering. Dane County jail might not be Alcatraz, but it stifled my breath even to imagine myself locked in a room that was maybe eighty square feet, the size of an average bathroom, with the only window high above my sight line and crosshatched with steel wires embedded in the glass. She had never been a good sleeper: I couldn't count the number of sleepover nights I'd awakened to find her reading or just looking at me in the darkness, her amber eyes like strange lanterns.

The next letter was about the case. That one came back to me inside a larger envelope from Damiano, Chen, and Damiano, Attorneys at Law.

So I wrote again, this time drawing little scenes of some of our old memories, which I thought might give her some comfort. There was the time Felicity agreed to babysit for a squirrel monkey, the pet of the people at her church. Almost all animals were helpless with love for Felicity, but this one, which was named Bushman for some famous gorilla, was the exception. The cage was the size of a Volkswagen and once we got it into the house and pulled off the towels wrapped around it, the creepy little creature peed all over Felicity. Within an hour, we learned that Bushman could pick the lock on his cage too. Of course, he escaped, then proceeded to bite Ruth, then climbed into the pantry to rip apart bags of dried beans and boxes of cereal—I never saw anything without wheels or wings that could move that fast.

Rev. Wild commanded us to take it back. As if we could even catch it. Even if we did, the owners were out of town, like . . . Portugal out of town. By late afternoon, Felicity and I were exhausted. I had to go home for some reason, I don't remember what, but when I came back, the monkey was still at large. The next thing we heard was Felicity's stepfather screaming. Apparently, he went into the darkened downstairs bathroom. There, he experienced the terrifying sensation of tiny hands clutching at his rear end. Felicity heard her stepfather's strangled cries as though he was having a heart attack. Somewhere between hysterical laughter and hysterical tears, she rescued Bushman from the toilet, where he had fallen in and was weakly treading water, for who knew how long?

We used to make each other laugh by making little monkey hand motions across the classroom or the street. And I drew a stick figure of a monkey poking its head out of a toilet.

There was no answer to any of those letters.

Finally, I went to the jail.

According to Sally, arranging a visit was this whole process and she said I might as well take my chances. So I just showed up.

At the desk, I spoke to a wispy blonde woman who looked far too fragile to be a prison guard, although maybe she was just a receptionist. Of course, she asked me if I was expected and made the same face I would have made if someone answered, *Not exactly* . . . Pulling a pen out of her messy updo, she pointed at a metal table where a guy was sitting with his back to me. "Ask her lawyer," she said.

Sam Damiano turned around to face me.

What do you say about a memory like that? The memory of a time when your throat felt filled with glitter hearts or honeybees and would explode if you tried to speak? Watching Sam put the cap on his pen was like watching someone else serve match point at Wimbledon.

I was that bewitched that instantly.

Certainly part of that was me . . . part of my own chemistry. Part of that, I would later learn, was Sam, Sam's effect on people.

"You're her friend," he said. "Reenie the writer. I would be happy for her to see you but she's not going to talk to you or me or anyone else, except maybe Jilly here at the desk."

Jilly nodded. She clearly had such a big crush that if this were a cartoon, little blue birdies and stars would have popped out of her eyes. Did Felicity's lawyer just walk the world like that, among women who threw their hearts at him? Did he even notice? Was it only women? Sam had that thing—presence maybe, or charisma—that made people not only want to be around him but to do what he wanted them to do, probably a useful thing in a defense attorney.

"Could I ask her myself?" I said.

"Sure."

And as if she'd been waiting for her cue, Felicity appeared in the lane between the rows of cells, three on each side . . . even paler and thinner than when I had last seen her, her darting eyes the only living thing in her face. "Reenie," she said. "I thought I told . . ."

I made up things she didn't say next.

I thought I told you to go away?

I asked Sam to tell you I didn't want to talk to you? You especially?

You know that you have a lot of nerve coming here after not even bothering to reach out to me for years, not answering when I reached out to you, and you expect me to throw open the round tower of my soul to you and share everything with you because we were friends?

Felicity jerked her hands up out of the grasp of the guard (not Jilly, a much burlier woman with a grim line where most people have lips), surprising him, who staggered back a little against the bars, grabbing at Felicity and missing as she jerked her whole body toward me. Then, I was the one who shrank back, which I still think of, after all this time. For what did I think she was going to do? Strangle me? Slap me? Take me hostage and threaten to slice everyone else with a sharpened blade fashioned from a pop can? Instead, she whirled and stalked back to the locked doors she had just exited, banging on them with the heels of her hands.

"Felicity!" I called out, and she didn't stop banging. "Felicity! It's Reenie! How can you think that I would ever, ever do anything to hurt you?" But wasn't I already hurting her? Wasn't I already taking advantage of her disadvantage for my own ends? Like my sister, Nell, said?

It was horrible, watching someone actually try to get back into jail. Once she was admitted, she didn't look back.

"So that went well," I said to Sam, to lob in a critical remark before he had the chance to do that.

"Even if she would talk to you, as her friend, she would never talk to you as the press, Reenie."

"I'm not just press."

"Are you writing a story about this trial?"

"Yes, I am, but—"

"Then you are press," he said. "I never called you 'just press.' You said that."

"But what I want to do is try to find—"

"Well, whatever that is, and I'm sorry to interrupt, I usually have better manners, you're going to have to try to find it without her help."

"What about your help?"

"I'd do anything I could to help her or you, but my hands are tired."

"You don't look as though you use your hands that much." We both started to laugh. "I knew what you meant."

"Right. My hands are tied," he said.

"But she must have talked to you about how she would explain that she could not have done this."

"No, she hasn't."

"Why not?"

Sam sighed gustily and went on, "She thinks it's obvious. She thinks that anything she says could make it worse."

"I don't get that."

"Neither do I, but she's afraid of the prosecutor, and rightly so. She's also worried about how she comes across."

I murmured something in agreement. Felicity's appearance belied her true nature: she was shy, but that could read as disdainful. She was practical, but to someone who didn't know her, that could read as cold. She didn't babble about meaningless matters, and her self-possession could seem judgmental. Plenty of people might consider Felicity intimidating, through no fault of her own.

I asked Sam, "Don't you want her to say that she's innocent? In her own words?"

"I do, but I don't think it's likely." He gazed up at the ceiling. "Maybe she's right. Maybe she doesn't seem like the all-American small-town girl next door."

That was, exactly, who she was to me.

"What can I do?"

He gave me a look that, despite the grim nature of our conversation, I felt as a shudder of lust in the pit of my abdomen. "It would be good if you didn't write about this case at all."

This I had not expected. "That . . ." I said. "That's not an option." I added, "I have to. And I want to."

Sam told me he had discussed this with his mother and that it was her opinion that whatever I wrote would not help Felicity. "And could damage her in ways that none of us expected."

I came back at him. "Well, I asked my mom about this also. My mom is an award-winning reporter and she says that thinking of the press as predatory is a common mistake when that's almost never the motive." I added, "And why did you ask your mom about Felicity and me? Why does this concern her? Does she pick your clothes out for you too?"

Here was another question: Why didn't I shut my fat mouth?

"Only for Easter," Sam said. "My mom is the managing partner of this law firm."

I said, "Oh."

Could I ask him if he wanted to have coffee? Or run away with me to Santorini?

Sam got up, sort of bowed to me, and wished me good evening. Then he left. It was a memorable beginning to a memorable friendship.

Not.

Did Felicity see talking to me in the same way as speaking up in court? Maybe. But still, she could change her mind. If absolutely refused, I would write around Felicity. There had to be a way to make it clear to her that my intentions were good. She wasn't wrong to suspect that I just popped up out of nowhere to write about her downfall. That wasn't true, but, after all, we hadn't been in touch for more than two years. She also hadn't said this, but I proceeded mentally as though she had. Her attitude (the one I had no idea whether she had) was mostly my fault. I was consumed by the strange rituals of the tribal world of fashion. I had to keep a straight face while standing on a pool deck to interview naked people as their body makeup was applied. I chased high-strung designers through hotel ballrooms and the backstages of arenas as they wept and refused to discuss their controversial use of metal thread, only to wake me up banging on my hotel room door after midnight, drunk and ready to chat.

So, how would I investigate this? How were all the other reporters doing it? There weren't that many newspapers left and those that were, were mostly in online form, except for those thick Sunday papers, and there were even fewer magazines. But news radio was thriving and TV news was alive if not exactly a bright light. Local TV news thronged the courthouse and their national affiliates were getting into the act. And why? I knew why I was obsessed but why were they?

There were murders more foul, murders more poignant, bad people who killed their children, good people killed by their bad children, second wives who killed first wives, husbands who conspired with their first wives to kill their second wives, hot blood chilled to cold blood by rage or boredom. There was a murder for every purpose, every place, and every day. The accused, however, wasn't often a beautiful, intellectually gifted, and verifiably good young woman who unaccountably switched from studying biology to working it, who unaccountably made a very good living having sex and, even more unaccountably, allegedly knocked off two men for money, with a shit ton of premeditation, men whose only apparent vice was Felicity herself.

That was what drew the cameras: good visuals. And all those artfully coiffed TV men and women seemed to have no shortage of people to talk to—what did they do, pay them? And how the hell did they find them? If I asked, I would reveal myself to be the lightweight I really was. "Lightweight" was probably flattering myself. And yet, I could do this. Felicity and I would support each other as kids when something annoying happened in the linoleum corridors of Algebra II or on those mean streets of Sheboygan, Wisconsin. "Little Biggy Bigelow, give me no shit. You can do this!" she would say. And I would say to her, "Wild woman, shit me not. You can do this!"

It was the awfulness of murder that made it so terrific to read about. Who said that? Quotes and attributions were shooting out of my brain like popcorn.

But not promises. I held on to those.

Wild woman, I can do this.

It didn't help that this story wasn't straightforward, factually or emotionally. It was like those advent calendars, a mystery revealed one little door at a time, each tiny picture changing the larger picture as a whole. That was how the people involved would reveal what they understood as the truth. People loved to talk. I knew that much for sure. The impulse to confide, or even to confess, seemed all but irresistible. Once you got in the door, interviews were mainly gossip, and the allure of gossip was powerful. My mother had the same opinion of history— that, beyond established dates of this battle or that birth, it was mainly people talking about other people reaching a consensus that seemed to explain an actual circumstance that no one could really describe because the people it happened to were long dead.

Whatever I stitched together would only be an impression of the truth, just as a photograph was only an impression of a person or an event. I could only try for the most authentic impression.

I made a verbal list on my phone of people I would talk to. Beyond the obvious, including the families of the victims and the principals of the trial, there were other sources I might try—or try and fail—to enlist. There were Felicity's coworkers at the so-called gentleman's club where she worked for a while as a stripper. And I'd try to find other men who paid for her companionship. Print journalism came with the blessing of a kindly distance that having a microphone shoved into your face for that day's broadcast could not offer; I'd bet my life that the TV reporters weren't snagging interviews on camera with an escort's patrons.

But how would I even begin to find them, or talk them into talking to me if I did? I wasn't afraid of a hostile source. Having to match wits was, in a sense, invigorating. But questioning a hostile source was one thing; it was quite another to question a source who was a ghost. The only people who knew the truth about Emil's and Cary's deaths were ghosts or would surely try to ghost me. I was, after all, just the princess of purses. Why should they trust me? And yet, turned another way, inexperience with this kind of story might be to my advantage. They wouldn't see me coming. Seeming naive was as good an interrogation tactic as any other.

So I would call on my resources. What resources? Who did I know?

For more than one night, I tossed this question around until I fell asleep and it followed me into my dreams. Then in the middle of one of those nights, I sat up in bed.

I did know someone.

Ross Bell taught at UW–Madison. He was in a PhD program in Psychology, and, conveniently for me, one of the things he was obsessed with was personality and how it either was or was not an outward expression of an individual's actual character. I was sure that the news about Felicity had gone off like a bomb at the big U. I was also sure he'd talk to me, and indeed, by the next day, he'd agreed, although a bit anxiously.

He agreed to meet me for a late dinner the following night at Fair Alice, the girliest restaurant in Sheboygan, which tended to drift between fried perch and prime rib. That was Ross's idea. Too many university types might be in earshot at the small restaurants in Madison, so he would come to me. I was relieved.

Between driving to the *Fuchsia* offices in Chicago, up to Sheboygan, where we'd grown up, and to Madison, I was going to put thousands of miles on my geriatric Toyota. Maybe instead of the magazine paying for mileage and inevitable car repairs, I could get someone to sublet my place for a few months and take some modest lodgings in Madison. I heard my interior voice, talking like Miss Marple. Get over yourself, I thought, I was not a real investigative reporter. But then, Miss Marple was not really a detective either. She was just some nosy lady following her instincts.

The next night, Ross and I exchanged hugs and rueful head-shakes. "I still can't believe any of this is happening," he said.

"And yet, here we are," I said, remembering Sally Zankow's words of philosophy.

Ross looked good, trim and gentle and appealing, an elfin guy with a big nose and ears and the kindest blue eyes. He was evidence of how personality and appearance did indeed line up. My dad (him with an aphorism for every occasion) used to say that by the time a man is forty, he has the face he deserves. Ross was barely into his thirties, true, but there wasn't a trace of guile or unkindness on his sweet facade: his face was the outward expression of his equally sweet heart. Why had I never fallen in love with Ross? Was he simply too nice a guy for a woman like me, who seemed to gravitate toward trouble?

Ross had once seemed very grown-up to Felicity and me; when we were twelve, he was an "older guy." And he was a few years older, but time had filled up the spaces between us so he was now not "an older guy" but a contemporary. His parents and mine were close, and there were even photos of me and Ross and his younger brother Warren grinning on the beach in Florida during one of the winter vacations our families took together. Not long before, my folks and his put on a neighborhood "progressive" Thanksgiving dinner. My mom described this about five times as a "Friendsgiving," until Nell deadpanned, "Did you just make that up?"

That November evening was cold, sidewalks sheer with black ice, as we all trooped along, two dozen people having cocktails at one house, then salad at the next house. It was an odd thing to do, probably more impressive in the days when people traveled by horse and buggy. This being Wisconsin, people were getting tipsy by two houses in, people staggering inebriatedly over black-ice-slicked sidewalks carrying covered trays of shrimp toasts and squash rolls, house to house like overgrown trick-or-treaters.

Nell had fantasies of ten houses filled with dirty dishes that drunk people would return to later that night. "This is one of the many, many reasons I don't cook," she said.

"Mom is the best reason," I said. Our mother's culinary efforts were legendary and not in a good way.

After we ordered our drinks and mains, Ross said, "Reenie, I'm not a real man."

Putting on my best faux-psychologist manner and the nice open posture I'd learned from all those counseling visits I'd had the summer after senior year of high school, I said, "How do you feel about that, Ross?"

He grinned and took a sip of his rum punch.

"That kind of drink isn't going to do much to show that you have hair on your chest, Ross," I told him. "All it needs is a little paper umbrella. I'm teasing, I'm teasing!" And then I wondered why I couldn't resist the temptation to needle an old friend who I was trying to convince to spill the beans on his colleagues. "So how did you figure out that you were coming up short in the masculinity sweepstakes?"

Ross said, "I don't know. I thought I was okay with the nerdy academic who wore good clothes and played right field . . ."

"But . . . ?"

"But all these guys my age I knew were hiking to base camp on Mount Everest and biking the Black Mountain Trail in Canada. And my girlfriend can beat me at tennis." He added, "I want to be the kind of guy who can fly fish but also be the kind of guy who doesn't have to bring a bag of taco chips to the Friendsgiving . . ."

"Remember when we had that Friendsgiving that time when there was a blizzard on Thanksgiving and people brought all the things they were going to bring to their family?" I said. "And that one woman brought a chocolate chip cheese ball . . . and we all just stared at it like it was going to catch fire or something?"

"That was Gail Valenti," Ross said. "The woman who worked at the public TV station and would only go out with guys she thought looked like old-time mobsters?"

"Right. What ever happened to her? What kind of person would even think of a chocolate chip cheese ball? It's like mushroom ice cream."

He said again, "Gail Valenti."

For some reason then, my mind wandered back to Felicity and how we'd once organized a Christmas brunch with a couple people our age and their mothers. I pictured us all drinking mimosas and stuffing our faces with quiche, and I wondered if Felicity had already left college behind by that point, which cast a sort of eerie blue glow, like streetlights on an urban corner, across that innocent scene. I tried to recall anything that I'd observed different about her that day, and no, there was nothing I could recall. She was just as she always was: friendly, cordial if a little remote, well-dressed, her manners excellent, her most genuine smile only for me. To my confusion, I felt tears gathering.

Ross was saying something and I quickly switched back to him.

"What would you compare that to for a woman?" he asked me.

"A life crisis?"

"Maybe like an epic passage in a woman's life. I guess having a baby, huh?" This was one of the moments, not particularly unusual, when I had to wonder if Ross, while a very nice guy, was about as thick as the ice in February on Lake Monona.

"I don't know. It could be any number of things. Success. Love. Doing something that matters."

"Do you think what you do for work matters?"

"I don't know. I do think that everybody has the right to know everything they can. We see all the time what terrible things happen when people rely on bad information. So yeah, even though I'm usually writing about purses, I'm writing the truth about purses."

"That's a comfort to me."

"So, Ross, let's talk about Felicity and all this."

He pressed his lips together and nodded. "Sure."

"Are you okay with that?"

"Sure, but . . ."

"You afraid to get people mad?"

"Reenie," he said, his eyes wide. "I'm reluctant because I care about Felicity too. I thought she was a great girl. If this is all true, it's sad, and if it's all a lie, it's even more sad."

I told him I was sorry, and I genuinely was. I'd gotten defensive because of my emotional entanglement and I didn't want Ross to see me as unfair.

He went on. Rumor had it that several other teachers, including one on Ross's softball team, had also known Felicity. Ross stayed only a few minutes but long enough to say that he could never have imagined any of this in his wildest. Felicity always seemed almost prim, self-possessed to an unusual degree for people our age. Had it been anyone else, Ross said, he would have suspected that she'd been the victim of some kind of violence or abuse, but with that family? Her father, Roman Wild, was a minister, and Ruth was our high school chemistry teacher. I was no fan of Rev. Wild's brand of fiery fundamentalist Christianity, and I had not been raised in any religion. But I knew Ruth well and really cared about her. I knew Felicity's two brothers, who were still kids living at home. None of it seemed to add up.

I wanted to talk to him again, at length.

My first task would be to get it in writing that my editor was on board. So I would head to my office for a meeting with my boss, Ivy.

I'd done my research—finding out at least as much as I could about the modern world of upscale vice. It wasn't something I'd ever had a reason to think about before, though of course, trading in sex for money wasn't called the world's oldest profession for nothing. (When my sister and I were kids, my parents offered us each two thousand dollars if we would promise not to have sex before graduating high school. My mother called it the world's second-oldest profession—not having sex for money.)

The language was one big change. Most scholarly writing considered the word *prostitution* to be derogatory now, with its connotation of selling yourself or even selling out. But what else was it? The more accepted term, *sex work*, sounded like digging for sex in a hard hat. Whatever you called it, the sex trade had evolved, especially since the age of the internet. Most of the women were young, of course, but they weren't all by any means desperate teenagers escaping a life of abuse. On a street corner in a red-light district, that might still be the profile, but in the upmarket world of vice, there were college students or new graduates, dentists and nurses and exercise psychologists paying off their student loans, not putting their profits up their noses. They were alluring but also wholesome-looking. They were savvy. Sites like OnlyFans and smaller soft-porn chat destinations purveyed their services in cheerful ways. Many required payment in advance, by card. Virtually all insisted on well-established hotels, or, if they visited a client's home, some took "body buddies," male friends to stand guard in the car or the taxi or the lobby, keeping an eye on the time, staying in constant phone contact.

There were two sides to this: One vocal camp praised sex workers for asserting themselves. Some women involved wanted to see it as a kind of payback, bamboozling men out of big bucks. The other side, equally vocal, said this way of life put people on a collision course with darker forces. Slice and dice it how you would, sex work was still fucking for money. Linnea Noonan, a feminist scholar and writer who'd once supported herself and her infant son that way, said portraying it as some jaunty third-wave feminist twist wasn't entirely honest. She'd created a forum called Council of Whores (COW) to debate these issues online and in person.

"You can say, okay, there's no job where you don't have to hold your nose sometimes. But for every whore who chose this, there are twenty who were pushed into it because they didn't have a better choice." Some of the biggest proponents of destigmatizing the language, naturally, were men, the customers, because it didn't make them seem quite so sleazy. Linnea said that the biggest problem was that, at the end of the day, the body you'd sold was still the body you lived in.

Most women stayed in the life for a few years and then moved on. And when they moved on, this interval would be a secret lacuna in their lives.

But Felicity had gone in the opposite direction, and, presumably, not out of need. Had she continued to be the stellar student she was up until sophomore year, she could have walked out of college debt free.

The question was why? Why everything? What pushed her to change course in the first place? Did that veer have its roots in something that happened long ago? It seemed unlikely that such a white-bread place as Sheboygan, Wisconsin, would give rise to dark deeds, but didn't every true crime show start with

the cliché that said "things like this just don't happen here . . . ?"
I would go to that place where Felicity's family and mine still
lived and talk to the hometown crowd.

And I would talk to my mother.

Miranda was as stunned as I by the news of Felicity's arrest.
She and Ruth Wild were still friendly, if not exactly friends, and
my mom might help ease my way into what would certainly be
an agonizing encounter.

This story was worthy of my mom's attention. Mom was
now a well-paid PR executive for a national organization that
helped women, but twenty years ago, she'd been a newspaper
reporter.

At the old *Milwaukee Journal Sentinel*, my mom, young Miranda McClatchey (now Miranda McClatchey Bigelow), not
much older than I was now, was part of a Pulitzer Prize–winning
team investigating conditions at pricey elder-care facilities. Undercover, she worked as an overnight nurse's aide, watching the
abuse, powerless to stop it, until, with her meticulous and irre-
futable stories, she stopped it in its tracks. Back when Miranda
was a reporter, I was little more than a tot. But I dimly remembered her coming home every morning from her night shift
at one of the awful places, sobbing as she made our breakfast.

So okay, Mom won a Pulitzer Prize. I wrote about the en-
during chic of a vintage Versace clutch compared with a Judith
Leiber. My mom considered me a dabbler. She never said so, but
you didn't have to be a mental gladiator to figure it out. I didn't
care, or so I said. Brokering my journalistic soul seemed a fair
price for not having to spend my life hideously depressed about
things I couldn't change. This walk on the wild side would be
temporary but I wanted it to matter. Whatever it took.

Downtown the next morning, I nearly charged directly from
the train through the (pink-tinted) glass revolving doors into the
Fuchsia offices. At the last moment, I stopped, making a detour

into Latta Java coffee shop next door. Composure, and even a soupçon of detachment, were qualities that my editor respected. I didn't want to confront Ivy with a full head of steam.

I'd decided that, for the moment, I would act as though Felicity had agreed to talk to me—while I implored the universe to send me a justification she would buy into. (If she never came around, I could always later say that she changed her mind.) Convincing Ivy that this piece was worthy of all the real estate it would take up in *Fuchsia*, and all the time I would need away from the wonderful world of scarves, was still an uphill battle. One afternoon last week, I got Ivy's attention by positioning this as a *Vanity Fair*–worthy drama with a third-wave feminist flourish: "This isn't just an ordinary murder story, it's mythic. It's the story of a modern woman's vengeance on the kingdom of men . . . It could even be seen as a sort of dark reverse of the Me Too dynamic, women taking advantage of men's appetites and bamboozling them into paying big bucks."

She agreed, suddenly excited and on board. But the next morning, she started to waffle.

I brought Ivy a skim latte, extra hot. She would know that I was currying favor with her, but Ivy appreciated subtle coercion. It was Saturday, and though we always worked at least half days on Saturday, the voltage was a little lower, a good atmosphere for a chat.

Ivy was always in early. She didn't have to fight traffic, although, given her nature, she'd have been on deck at dawn even if she'd had to mush a team of six sled dogs from Winnetka. As it was, she just took the stairs. Her parents owned the building (and the magazine). Ivy and her family lived in an apartment that occupied the whole seventh floor. Her parents lived in the penthouse above, her two brothers on the two floors below Ivy—the vertical equivalent of a family compound. The rest of the building housed the *Fuchsia* offices and the family business. (Something called Exquisite Enterprise. We had no idea what it did, although we knew it was either fabulously lucrative or a front for a drug cartel, since Ivy's parents and their parents were billionaires.)

No one knew *Fuchsia*'s financial status or even why it existed at all or how long it would last. Her parents had bankrolled it for two years. In an era when once-regal print publications were thin to nearly nonexistent, it was a gambit born of a whim. The whim was not Ivy's, but her mother's. Like many chic and clever writers of previous generations—true stars like Joan Didion and Meg Wolitzer and Mona Simpson—Sabrina Torres had been a guest editor at *Mademoiselle* in 1980, just before that plucky magazine gave up the program. These "college girls" of another era competed by writing essays for the privilege of working at the magazine for a summer in New York, living at the women-only Barbizon Hotel. An idea so antique it was alluring, it evoked a shiny, healthy blonde dressed in an oatmeal turtleneck and green wool "slacks," the kind of thing my grandmother wore at Oberlin College fifty years ago.

I got on board because of a fluke question at a lecture Sabrina gave about *Fuchsia* to Northwestern's grad school, just a month before I graduated.

"I had a lifelong love affair with Sylvia Plath, that brave and beautiful and doomed poet. She was a guest editor at *Mademoiselle* before I was born," Sabrina said. "I wanted to follow in her footsteps . . . well, most of them . . . although I'm not much of a writer." She went on, "People question my sanity, but I see this yearning, as if people are homesick for a place they never lived. Women are going traditional, changing their last names when they get married. Families are using up vacation time to take the children to stay at a working farm." She would hybridize this picture, classy nostalgia with edgy modern views—a demulcent print magazine with advertisements for colognes that cost a thousand dollars an ounce set about with the strongest front-line reporting on women in prison, women in the arts, women in homeless shelters, women in the Senate.

"So why Chicago?" I asked.

"Hometown pride," she replied. "My family has been in Chicago for twelve generations. Came here working on ships, ended up owning the ships. This city has taken so many blows to its reputation. But look what it has! The most beautiful lakefront in the world. The most vibrant art scene. A world-class university. Legendary writing community. And my amazing daughter, Ivy, to head it up."

After her talk, Sabrina pulled me aside and said, "Come work for me when you finish school." I had an offer for a lucrative but brain-rusting job editing the alumni magazine for the University of Illinois Chicago, but this was much more my style. So I showed up at the *Fuchsia* building (indeed, it was a pale shade of fuchsia, thus called "the Purple Palace") the Monday after graduation. I met Ivy (the aforementioned wonderful daughter). She had been a correspondent for CBS morning shows and, later, style editor for *Red*. She didn't confide much about her personal life, but once, out of nowhere, told me that she'd been applying to medical schools when her mother asked her to helm the magazine, for at least the first two years—which might easily be all the years there were.

"Just when I thought I was out, they pulled me back in," Ivy told me, dramatically pulling her fists, Michael Corleone-style, toward her chest.

That Saturday, Ivy was studying mock-ups of possible pages that would feature hats. I'd written the scant amount of copy that went with the photos. Veils were back. Black was back. Not just for Edwardian widows anymore. Mystery, majesty, melodrama, a magical brew (and a lot of alliteration).

Gosh.

It wasn't that I didn't like hats—or at least I didn't dislike them any more than I disliked other really ostentatious clothing—but I didn't really understand them. Although I'd done it often enough, I still didn't entirely get the soul of dressing for ornamental reasons only.

Although she didn't say a word to me, my editor pointed to a space on the counter, far from the photo proof sheets, and nodded her thanks for the coffee. She got out her loupe and peered closer. I gazed over her shoulder, not daring to say a word. Ivy Torres was famous, if not notorious, for her myopic focus on whatever task was at hand. Whether she was interviewing a white-hot celebrity or studying a sandwich menu, she gave it the kind of attention usually reserved for spinal surgery. It was what made her so lethally effective at her job. Interrupt her and she would say something low and slow in her Bryn Mawr accent that you didn't realize had cut you until you woke up the next morning on a bloodstained mattress.

The photographer was no Irving Penn. In one of the shots, a model wearing only a hat had blown her breath on the window glass and written an *F* in the mist. In another, a second model, in nothing except black stockings, had positioned the hat between her spread legs, the brim just covering her concave belly and afterthought breasts.

Ivy straightened up, kneaded her lower back, and reached for the coffee. "Mmm," she said. "You know what, Reenie? We should do a feature about extreme larks."

"Like white-water rafting?" I asked. What kind of accessories would you need to shoot the Colorado River rapids?

Ivy regarded me with an expression I'd only ever seen on the face of a bear at the zoo: curious, dangerous, impassive. People believed that Ivy was all style and no substance when, in fact, she was all substance, including her style. Her own look was so minimalist it made those old black-and-white photographs of Audrey Hepburn look flashy. She didn't wear any makeup at all except a flick of mascara and this sort of tinted balm that made her face look lit from within. I had never seen her eat.

"What I mean by larks is morning people. They call them extreme larks. They get up early, early, like five in the morning. People who live their best lives when it's still dark. Meditate. Write. Pray. Garden. Go running." I pictured a woman jogging through Grant Park in the predawn. Accessories she'd need: An aluminum truncheon, lightweight yet lethal. A can of Mace.

Ivy turned back to the photos.

"What do you think of it?" she said. "It's your story."

"You mean my story about Felicity! I think it's a powerhouse story and I won't write it in a gee-whiz way. I'll ask feminist scholars for their opinions . . ."

Ivy curled her lip. To her, feminist scholars were big butch dames in bad boots. She had no use for them.

"Okay, I won't ask feminist scholars their opinions," I continued, although I intended to do it anyway. "I'll talk to professors who study the role of women in culture, and there's a medical doctor at Harvard who's writing a book about women and revenge."

"I didn't mean that story. I mean this story," Ivy told me.

"It's pretty," I admitted. "But it's weird. Can you imagine yourself really wearing a velvet top hat with a veil? Where would you wear it? And what would you wear it with?"

"Not the point, Reenie."

"Well, it's very pretty."

"Some sort of satin-and-lace slip dress and a long cape. One with a train that drags on the ground."

I said nothing. I hated gowns and coats that dragged on the ground. I could think of nothing except that they epitomized the culture of profligacy. Mulberry silk, a hundred dollars a yard, diaphanous as a butterfly's wing, dragged over pavement, stepped on, spilled on, torn. When I went to the Met Gala last year, and I was indeed required to go to the Met Gala, where I felt like a trout in a tank of black lace angelfish, I wore a black-and-gold Chanel minidress that the magazine had rented for me at a cost that was more than the rent on my apartment. I was so sick with anxiety over the dress that I couldn't eat or drink anything except ice water and moved like a toddler with a full diaper. In my interviews, I confused Jennifer Hudson and Jennifer Lawrence, even though one was a Black singer and one a white actor. ("At least they were both women," Ivy said with a sigh. "It would have been worse if it was Martin Lawrence.") I was ill-suited to my job.

I was ill-suited in all kinds of ways. It would never have occurred to me, in real life, to try to "palette" (a verb) my handbag to my shoes (not "match" it, being too "matchy-matchy" was almost as dangerous as being color-blind). Ever the tutored self, I now had a private skeptic within; I hated having to find something to admire in a Louis Vuitton or Gucci. They were desperately ugly: The clunky chains and clips were to accessories what a garbage truck was to a Porsche Carrera. Why did anyone pay for such garish stuff? Did people really admire them or was it an emperor's-new-clothes thing and nobody wanted to be the first to come out and say it?

Ivy was still studying the images. "It might be pretty, but it should be breathtaking. These pictures suck. I'm going to have the whole thing shot again. Horses, maybe. What do you think?"

I tried a joke. "We'd have to get really big hats for them."

Ivy left the duskily lit photo studio and I followed. She made the kind of noise with her tongue that people make to call a dog, and Marcus Rhinehart materialized as if he'd been crouching under a desk, but a desk with a three-way mirror, wearing a pale blue Loro Piana twill blazer over black jeans from The Row. "This is not working," she told him. "Padraig is so full of himself. Maybe we should call someone else. No, no, he'll do it again and get it right. Find some horses. Same women, not just models. Healthy women who look outdoorsy. I want this done today."

Marcus appeared about to throw up. Where would he find horses on a Saturday afternoon? How would he locate Padraig and face the towering tantrum that would ensue when the photographer was forced to do a reshoot on short notice? As if she could read his thoughts, Ivy told him, "I'll handle Padraig. You get the elements. Wisconsin and Michigan and those places are . . . the fucking Midwest. There have got to be plenty of horses."

"We have to get them here and I have to book the indoor warehouse space again . . ."

"No, an outdoor space, like a ranch or a farm."

"Okay," Marcus said. He angled his eyes at me. I was from Wisconsin. Marcus was from Brooklyn. Surely, I had relatives who got up early to milk the cows? I smiled and shrugged.

"Well, Marcus, if it has to be tomorrow, I mean first thing, daylight, that will have to work, Marcus," Ivy said. She had used his full given name twice. Marcus was on her official shit list, although he'd had nothing to do with the feature story, which was called "Taking the Veil."

Ivy turned to me. "Now about that story. Reenie, as you know, *Fuchsia* is aspirational. This idea of yours feels . . ." She shuddered. "It feels very sordid. This woman is a sex worker. We're about fashion as communication. Issues that face women. This is crime pure and simple, and it could also be seen as voyeuristic."

With intention, I let my eyes rest pointedly on the scantily clad model with the big hat covering her lady parts.

Ivy snorted. "Okay, Reenie. Point taken."

"It's anything but simple, Ivy. The story is in how she got this way, Ivy. When we knew each other, she was admired. She was respected. Even by the teachers and . . . community leaders."

"Maybe she was sexually abused."

"Her father was a minister."

"Well," Ivy said, with some satisfaction. "There you go."

"Even if it were that straightforward, and I'm betting that it's not, last I heard, domestic and sexual abuse and objectification were indeed issues that face women. Those are issues women face throughout their lives, from girls to elders."

Marcus said, "It sounds utterly depressing, Reenie."

I turned on him. "Don't you have to see a man about a horse?"

"I just don't know if our reader is curious about what drives the life of a high-priced escort . . ."

"Oh wait," I said, holding up one hand and peering down at my phone. "I have to get rid of this. Give me a second." I took a few steps away and, in a whisper, voice-texted Marcus: *If you don't stand by me on this, you are dead to me. I will never fix you up with another spectacular woman . . .* Marcus was as straight as the fabled strip of Jean-Baptiste Pointe DuSable Lake Shore Drive where our office building stood, but he was also beautiful and worked for a women's fashion magazine. Surrounded every day by epically gorgeous female creatures, he sometimes protested his heterosexuality too much, and some of those women ended up thinking Marcus really wanted to go shopping with them instead of going to bed with them.

Now, glancing at his phone, he said quickly, "On the other hand, anybody would be fascinated by this. Man or woman. Young or older. Clearly, something profound happened."

I put in, "This isn't a lifestyle piece, Ivy. This isn't a story about courtesan couture. It's a story about a brilliant, beautiful woman, a good person, who left home and started doing this a long time ago, when she wasn't even old enough to drink. Right now, she's barely twenty-seven and she might spend the rest of her life in prison. I'm not saying that I'm sorry for her. But I'm curious. Aren't you?"

Ivy adjusted the lacy bib of her six-hundred-dollar coveralls. Denim would be the next big thing. We never knew whether Ivy created fashion trends or intuited them from cultural clues, like sounds only dogs could hear. But she was invariably right: ten seconds after our story last year about the return of plaid, ("Tartan Is on Trend!"), everyone was wearing kilts.

Ivy said, "I don't think so, Reenie."

"Well," I said and took a deep breath and let it out slowly, "then I'd like to request a leave of absence. To cover this. A few months. Someone will buy it." Ivy slowly shook her head, side to side.

There was a long pause. If Ivy had said just one more word, I'd have taken it all back. In the ordinary run of things, wherever I worked, I would still have had a good year ahead of me of answering phones and bringing people research files before I wrote anything except "Snowball Boosters, left to right, include Hale Shipson III and Ginger Rayburn Shipson . . ." I recalled how my hair smelled after a long night of tending bar and sometimes waiting tables at Angel on the Rock, especially on Thursdays, when the nightly special was fried oysters and onion rings with sauerkraut, and how the head under my hair hurt from the smell of the strong coffee and the sound of impassioned poetry. Just as not everyone who is beautiful is good, not everyone who is earnest is a poet.

This isn't to say that I didn't like Angel on the Rock . . . It's one of a cluster of restaurants owned by the older brother of a friend of mine, all in the Chicago area but each of them themed to represent a different iconic seaside town somewhere in the world. Angel on the Rock is themed after Brighton, in England, a resort town with a huge coastline and boardwalk beach pier where families huddled on the sand. Its chosen art form is poetry. There's one called Seven Gables, that pays homage to the sights of Salem, Massachusetts, where the patrons told ghost stories, often in costume, and he had planned one as an homage to Mykonos, that Greek hillside town with its candy-colored houses and buildings like chunks of chalk, where solo musicians would be invited to perform.

I'd stayed at Angel on the Rock for two years, doing occasional freelance stories ("Ten Ways to Look Like a Diva in Thrift" . . . "Ten Ways to Ace an Interview" . . . "How to Be a Good Parent After a Bad Childhood" . . . "How to Start a Book Club for Serious Readers" . . . "How to Host a Dinner Party for Twelve for $100" . . . "Know Your Physician's Politics") for online zines.

During this time, I lived with Daniel and Steven, married medical students who were having twins by surrogacy with Elodie, another medical school classmate. In the aggregate they were the three most beautiful people probably in Chicago at the time. All that genetic grace and hope had the effect of making me feel dumb and lonely.

So I went to graduate school, figuring on even more onerous student debt but getting a scholarship because the dean was a friend of my mom's, which made me feel like a Hollywood A-lister who bought her kid's way into USC, but in reverse.

I'd had a lucky life. My luck held.

And then, just by chance, right out of grad school, *Fuchsia.*

Mine was not a good job, it was a great job.

And now there was a lot on the line for it, to boot (Louboutin boot . . .).

So when I talked big, I was betting against the house, but I knew that Ivy could not spare experienced staff, even me. Against odds, the publication had lasted a year, and got a ton of attention, but it could either tank after another six months or become the cornerstone of a magazine revival.

"Let's not get crazy, Reenie," Ivy said. "If this story is so intriguing to you and it isn't just because you knew the woman, then you'll do something amazing. Let's get you all the support you need. Write up a proposal."

It took me a full minute to believe that I was hearing Ivy correctly. It was as though I'd been on death row, and somebody came along one morning and said oops, sorry, there'd been a mistake, you were actually supposed to be at the Peninsula Hotel.

All Ivy asked was that I bring our new intern up to speed on what she'd need to dig into for the next issue . . . or two.

"You pulled that out of a hat," Marcus said. "Or out of your ass. I can't believe you threatened Ivy Torres and got away with it."

"Fortune favors the brave, Marcus," I told him, and then I wiggled my fingers at him and retreated to my office.

While I was up there, I would also find that so-cute lawyer of hers. One straight path to Felicity would be through him.

Later that day, for the third time in twenty-four hours, I set out on the same long drive.

When I got home, no one was there. Pure luxury. I made myself a child's meal, peanut-butter toast, scribbled a note, and retreated to my childhood bedroom.

My parents' house was a golden sanctuary of silence.

As kids, we'd come to love our silence. We had no choice.

We had no video games. We had the kind of wireless service you think must be powered by a hamster running on a wheel. We got TV for four hours on Saturdays, period, one classic movie channel. My father watched hockey, football, and reruns of old Westerns. I knew all the words to the theme song from *Have Gun - Will Travel*.

Reading became survival. We'd have lost our minds otherwise. Once you have the habit, if you don't have something to read, you feel like you can't breathe. You'll read an owner's manual. At our friends' houses, TV was like an ever-present loud uncle blatting away in another room. Our friends thought my parents were nuts. They wanted to call social services. But my college teachers were as impressed as my peers were depressed:

One called me the only literate kid he'd ever taught. So at least it got you places with authority figures. Only later on did I discover that a nerdy, pretty woman who could quote from classic books and poetry was considered kind of sexy.

I climbed into bed with one of my mother's prized first editions, Edith Wharton's *The House of Mirth*, which is one harrowing story. But I couldn't concentrate on it.

So, oh well. Sleep solves everything. I decided on a brief nap. I slept twelve hours.

Next morning, in the bright sunlight, I lay quietly observing how not even three coats of Sherwin-Williams Natural Linen could entirely obscure the border of gigantic black roses that I, as a teenager, had stenciled, with house paint, just under the lip of the crown molding. Having surrendered to sleep in the way a human body can do only in the full knowledge of inviolable safety, I was still dazed. In one sense, the trompe l'oeil of ghost roses gave the room a piquant quality, like something from *Masterpiece Theatre*. In another era and economic caste, I'd have rung for tea.

It was a Sunday. Everyone in our small family was around, even my sister, Nell, the golden child. I smelled bacon frying, one of those treats in life you can enjoy only if you don't think too much about it. One of those old songs was playing—"Only you, the very thought of you, the way you look tonight." To be clear, the doors of my childhood home did not automatically open on a pop-up greeting card. Yet, this one weekend, when so much of my consciousness was centered on dark deeds, the gift of good parents with an intact marriage was one of the best pieces of fortune a grown-up kid could be handed. Relative to my friends' parents, my folks were young and strong. Their idea of fun was painting walls together while singing old songs by even older people, like the Eagles. They had been remodeling the house since my earliest memory and, although my father was a builder, it was not much closer to finished. My dad could easily have found someone to finish it in short order, but DIYing it was apparently a big thrill. The dining room, where people ate only three times a year, looked like a set design for *The Great Gatsby*. The bathrooms looked like the "before" segment of *Fixer Upper*.

I sat up, blearily checking my phone for messages, and then heard a sound at the window.

A single crow sat on the outdoor sill, tapping impatiently at the glass, where it probably saw its reflection. Sunlight turned its feathers to shiny onyx. It was also huge, like two feet tall. What kind of monster was this? Were there ravens in Wisconsin? When I was very young, after having seen something on TV about a girl whose parents rehabbed and released injured wild birds, I wanted my parents to catch a crow in a trap to be my companion. I would teach it to talk. They bought me a parakeet, which promptly sickened and went claws up in its cage. I don't remember being sad. It bit viciously and never even learned to say "pretty bird," only "bird."

In fact, I had an old, secret fear of all birds. They seemed to me a violent species, primitive in their disregard, greedily violating the nests of others. Birds were what fascinated Felicity. I thought about crow lore . . . there was something tapping at my mind as insistently as that gigantic shiny black bird was tapping at the glass. What was it? When we were little, Patrick, my father, would read to us from a book of children's poetry that had belonged to his Irish grandmother.

Dad told us that superstitious Irish who spotted a crow or a magpie would say, "Mr. Magpie, how's your wife?" The belief was that magpies and crows should come in pairs, and a lone magpie at the window meant somebody in the house would die.

Nice thought for little kids.

He used to read us this old rhyme from the same book. It

was like making us watch that ancient Disney movie *Old Yeller*, child abuse, but legal. It went, "The crow on the cradle, the white and the black, somebody's baby will never come back . . ."

Somebody's done for.

I remembered a summer night, school just out, maybe in ninth grade, when Felicity and I were sitting in my bedroom in just underpants and T-shirts, the windows open and fans pointed at our heads (Miranda and Patrick didn't believe in using AC until people were sweating through their shirts twice a day). We were trying to watch a horror movie on my laptop, but the wireless was so basic in my house that the movie kept stopping before every jump scare. An ambulance cruised by slowly, running lights but not sirens. Felicity said, "That's how they do it when there's no hurry." I raised an eyebrow. "No hurry to get to the hospital. Somebody's done for."

Now I rapped hard on that same window glass. "Go away," I shouted. "Go away!" What kind of creepy bird ignored a human being waving her arms and shouting and just stared with its jeweled eye?

I ran down the stairs and sort of skidded into the kitchen.

"Reenie!" my father said. "What's wrong?"

To catch my breath, I poured myself a cup of my dad's high-octane coffee and took a scalding sip before I answered. "I slept great, but then I think I had a nightmare."

"No surprise," he said. "I'd have nightmares too if I was writing about a murder committed by my friend. You're either brave or stupid, Irene."

My younger sister, Nell, pounded in from the back porch, lugging a carryall bag and kicking the snow off her boots. She'd been at home all day yesterday but evidently hadn't unloaded her laundry. The old house she shared with other grad students had a murder basement where the washing machines were. It scared her, so Nell still brought her laundry home every few weeks to my parents', whose washer was the size of the Apollo 13 spacecraft despite the fact that they were empty nesters who only ever had two kids. I took Nell's bag so she could shrug out of her coat before laying my warm cheek against her icy one.

I said, "When did it start snowing?"

Nell stared at me. "Midnight? There's a foot of new snow, Reenie."

I looked and yes, there was indeed a foot of new snow, more coming down hard. Had I had an actual nightmare, so real that I seemed to be awake? Did I imagine that big bird, its feathers patent leather shiny in the morning sunlight?

"'Quoth the raven, nevermore!'"

"I swear to you, I looked out the window upstairs and the sky was blue."

"It's a big house," Nell said. "Different climate zone?"

My mom piled my plate and Nell's with scrambled eggs. Her secret ingredient for this was a spoonful of mayonnaise and a dollop of cream cheese, which sounds disgusting but is very good. It was the one dish my mother could prepare without everyone quietly wishing we had a dog. Miranda set out stacks of ice-cold toast with the butter neat and hard as a coat button on top of each slice. Her culinary abilities would have been a smash hit in Scotland. We often told each other that Dad's coffee and Mom's cuisine could be weaponized by the Department of Defense.

"What are you here for?" Nell asked, as if she didn't know.

"The toast," I replied.

"Do you think you're exploiting Felicity and taking advantage of your friendship?"

"Hey, Nell Diablo, what do you really think? Don't hold back!"

"Anything for a juicy story."

"I wish there was no story to tell. Some things are important because they're interesting, not interesting because they're important. They make us think about our own character. Ask Mom."

"You can't compare what you do with what Mom did."

"I'm not."

"So it's not because it's sensational, writing about a killer whore who used to be your . . ."

My mom said, "You might want to confront the apparent contradictions as part of what you write. You don't want to be accused of sensationalism. Nell has a point."

"What is her point? She's being a . . . a goody-goody, and since when? Just because she can read enough Latin to read an old gravestone? To prove that your law-school dollars are being spent?" My parents were paying for law school; I'd refused to let them pay for my grad school. They further assumed that I earned a couple of g's a year, when what I really made at *Fuchsia* would have been a respectable salary in West Shreveport, Louisiana, but kept me awake nights in Chicago.

Nell said softly, "Reenie, I know you care."

"Of course I care. I care about Felicity. I care about the people who died. Not as much, but I care. Plus, who are you going to be when you grow up, Atticus Finch? Really? After a couple of years, you'll be defending corporations for dumping stuff into rivers that causes fish to have three heads and glow in the dark!"

Nell said, "And make in an hour what you make in a week!"

"It's true, it's true. Virtue is so underpaid." I made a prayerful gesture with a strip of bacon still in one hand.

"I'm all about quid pro quo," Nell said. "That's Latin, Reenie. Mom and Dad, ad hoc ergo propter hoc, huh? I learned a little Latin so I'm very, very smart."

"A scholar right here at your kitchen table. A future chief justice." I pointed at her with the bacon strip.

"She speaks nothing but the veritas," said my sister. "About my virtus." We both started to laugh. Then Nell added, "It just sounds so awful and hard. What you have to do for this."

My mom said, "Don't you think some of these people might be not just shady but really dangerous?"

Nell said, "It's not as if she's going to do what you did at the nursing home, Miranda. She won't have to fake being a hooker."

"I might," I added, just to see my mother recoil.

Nell said, "Straight up, just imagine how you'd feel if you were Ruth Wild."

"That's why I'm here. I thought I would try to talk to Ruth."

"Yikes, Reeno, I don't envy you," Nell said, all banter aside.

"Probably not on Sunday," my mom said. "I think they're in church all morning."

"But not all day," I said. It was after two in the afternoon by then.

"I'm sure they get to talk on Sundays if not plow the fields or sew on buttons," my father said. He was confusing charismatic Christians (which Ruth was, as her husband was the founder of the megachurch Starbright Ministry not far from our house).

"Would you come with me? I'm still the kid she knew from high school, at least to her. I've never had to question someone who's a friend about something so awful."

My father said, "I'm sure it's fine, Irene. I'm sure it's not violating some holy order." My dad was an atheist evangelist, if there could even be such a thing. All religion was a scam. He disliked Felicity's stepfather, Roman, on principle. Rev. Wild, a fundamentalist preacher, was the founder of the Starbright Ministry, which started as a country church and grew into an empire on the dime of the faithful. It now boasted its own school, ice rink, gyms, swimming pools, a missionary training center, even a TV studio.

"Ruth couldn't have known what Felicity was getting up to," my mom said. "But yes, back in the day, I used to hate facing people I was scared of but not as much as the ones I was sorry for. Sure, I'll go with you. I could use the exercise." She walked and ran on a treadmill for two miles five days a week. Her fitness was a witness to me. "You brought boots, right?" I had not, of course. But Miranda produced some that "still had a lot of life left in them."

Nell said, "I only go out in snow if there's a ski lodge involved."

So Miranda and I stomped our way through the new powder—for Nell was correct, there was a ton of snow, and what dreamworld had I witnessed from my window?—until we got to the campus of Starbright Ministry.

The place was usually a hive. On Sundays, there were at least three off-duty police directing traffic. And even on days when there weren't any church services, there were always classes and study groups and athletic events for the students of the Starbright Academy.

There wasn't a single car in the parking lot.

We kicked a path through the snow down to the lakefront chapel where summer revivals were conducted in a lighted white tent that extended from the open doors. There was not a soul, pardon me, in sight.

"Let's go over to the rectory," Miranda said, and we did, the heavy fall of snow under the evergreens on the way to Ruth's house needing some real thigh burn to push through.

My mom was curious. She had never seen it up close. Even I had only been inside the rectory once, a memorable unplanned visit. The house was a gorgeous big pile of a Georgian made from lemony brick with dark blue shutters and trim tall casement windows side by side on both levels and a curved pillared porch roofed by a walk-out balcony above. I could hear my dad grumbling.

The walk had not been shoveled. There was no car in the driveway, no snow disturbed by the attached garage. I took pictures with my phone, of the front of the house and a shot down a short rise to the massive, also deserted, tabernacle.

"Come on," I urged my mother. "Let's knock." We used the door knocker, in the shape of a fish. We rang the doorbell. If this had been a ghost story, or a different kind of crime story, the sound would have echoed within, and we would have caught a glimpse of a wraith through the windows flanking the front door.

Instead, no response. No movement. But then, I recalled, it always looked that way: pristine, like a movie set for the home of a good pastor reaping the rewards of the prosperity gospel he preached—for the faithful, rewards on earth, rewards in heaven.

It was so different from the slightly shabby house the Wilds lived in when they were our neighbors on Pine Street. Felicity and I sometimes did our homework at her kitchen table, Felicity helping me with chemistry over her mom's teasing objections. Four or five times a month, we had a sleepover, but now that I really thought of it, I was never invited to sleep over at Felicity's. In fact, I'd only once seen her room, nudging the door open when I went to use the upstairs bathroom. What I glimpsed didn't look as though it belonged to an ordinary girl. There were no posters or piles of clothes or pyramids of cosmetic bottles. Everything was white. On the walls were a few line drawings of birds. The one I remember was of the horrifying cruel face of a shoebill stork, a bird, Felicity later told me, that grows as tall as a small adult human being, that eats baby crocodiles, and is so ferocious that, as a nestling, it kills its siblings to achieve dominance.

"Maybe we should call the police?" Miranda asked me now.

"Wait." I scrambled up on the railing and peered over the café curtains through the clean upper panes of a window. Sun abruptly broke through then, sending a shaft of light into an empty living room. The single piece of furniture was an old ladder-back chair stacked with what looked like a month's worth of mail. I jumped down. "There's no one in there," I told Miranda, and then asked her, "Do you know anybody who goes to church here?"

"To say hi to in the grocery store maybe but I wouldn't have their numbers."

Just then, as if in answer to a . . . whatever, a man and woman in a Jeep with a snowplow scraped into the driveway. We waved. They waved. They made no attempt to get out of the car. I waved again and called, "We need some help here!" Their glacial slowness as they climbed out of the car proclaimed reluctance as eloquently as a sign. As they approached, I called, "I'm Irene Bigelow and this is Miranda, my mom. We're friends of the Wilds. It seems like they're not here. Did something happen?"

After a stretched-out moment, the woman, stern, with chopped gray hair said, "You might say that."

"What happened? Are they hurt?" I thought, *Somebody's done for.*

"Not in the way you mean," she said.

"What then? I need to find them. It's about their daughter, Felicity."

"We know about Felicity. We are praying for her," the woman said, as the man pulled a snow shovel out of the Jeep.

"Are the younger kids okay?"

"They're with their father," said the woman. "We're the Gows, Sharon and Dave. We're the caretakers. I can give the reverend a note if I see him." I handed her a card from the exterior clip of my phone case.

"Tell me how I can find the other pastor, Sara?" I said. "She must be here."

"She's in a conference with the council," said Sharon Gow.

"What happened?"

The man began to shovel the front walk, sending up furious

jets of snow. "It's not for us to talk about," he said. "You can see what happened on the news. There were some camera people out here yesterday."

My mother spoke up. "My daughter is the news. She's a reporter. Please tell us where Ruth is."

"That, ma'am, nobody knows," said the presumed Dave Gow. "You can probably find the reverend, if you can call him that, at the home of Faith Nilson in Fond du Lac."

Bemused, my mother and I quick-stepped our way back to our house.

"I don't know who Faith Nilson is, but I'm not going to give her a chance to hang up on me," I told Miranda. "I'm going to go see her in person."

My mother wanted to come but had her book club that afternoon, so I headed to Fond du Lac alone. The drive wasn't far and because Wisconsin, unlike other places, expects bad weather, the roads were clear, the snow crisp and immaculate. I'd looked up Faith Nilson's address, which was across from a pretty little forested park. There being no other way to announce myself, I knocked at the door and a tall woman maybe five years older than I, with the longest blond braids I'd ever seen on an adult, opened the door.

"Hi?" she said.

"I'm Reenie Bigelow. I'm trying to find Roman Wild. I'm a friend of his daughter, Felicity, and I'm writing a story about her."

"Which are you? A friend or writing a story?"

"Both," I said. "Ruth and Roman were our neighbors. And now Felicity is in trouble and I work for a magazine . . ."

"We don't want any trouble," the woman said. "We have been given enough trouble as our portion." I wondered if English was her first language.

"Are you Faith Nilson?"

"Yes. Roman is my husband."

"I don't understand."

"In the eyes of God."

"I don't understand."

"Go ask him then," said Faith Nilson Wild-or-not-Wild. "He's over there in the park with our children. If you see him, tell him to come home."

I walked over to the low stone wall that encircled the small park. Snow was picturesquely drifting down on several groups of children who had braved the cold to chase each other and stuff the new powdery stuff down each other's necks. Their mothers leaned against the climbing fort, like identical padded pillars of nylon. I pulled on my mittens and my whimsical red Beth Pedicini flat-top hat and began to pace the perimeter of the park's child-sized evergreen maze, hoping that the head-clearing techniques in British novels, where people were always throwing on a mac and heading out for a walk, would literally work.

Suddenly, a voice just behind me said, "Reenie! What are you doing here?"

Roman had to be well into his fifties. But still, he was movie-star handsome. No, that's wrong. He was cartoon handsome, like a Disney prince come to life: oversize square chin, even white teeth, dramatic scooped dark eyebrows.

"Hi, Reverend Wild. I'm actually . . . I'm looking for you," I told him. His carefully concerned frown asked why, but his eyes told me he knew very well. "How are you?"

"I've had better days," he said.

"I wanted to talk to you. I'm writing a story about Felicity. I'm a writer. I don't know if you knew that."

"I haven't seen Felicity in over a year."

"Okay, well. I'm sure you and Ruth have talked about Felicity?"

"I haven't seen Ruth in a long while either," he said, his

tone the deep, authoritative bass he used in the pulpit. "Ruth and I divorced."

"Oh gosh! I'm so sorry."

"Some time ago. I live with my second . . . wife, Faith . . . and our children."

"Your children? You adopted her children?"

"They're my children too," he said.

"Oh." I dropped my bag on purpose but got out my phone and pretended to be checking if the screen was broken, but really switching on Voice Memos so I could record him. Then I decided that there was no reason to hide it: "I want to record what you say in case it's necessary to use anything in the story. I doubt that because this is really just background, but I don't want to make a mistake. I hope that's okay."

I looked up, way up, at Roman Wild, who had to be six-five or taller. Then I looked behind him where two little boys were running around, maybe about four or five—I had no idea how to estimate the age of kids. "If you were married to Ruth? You had two families at once?" He didn't nod. He didn't shake his head. "That's real tabloid stuff for anybody, but a minister?"

He shrugged.

"Reverend Wild, I only came to your church one time. But it's kind of a coincidence that what you were preaching was about honoring your wife and being chaste in your marriage. But you were already with this other woman? Don't you feel like you betrayed the people who saw you as some big role model? And supported you?"

"I betrayed myself and my family—"

"Which one?"

"Very good, Reenie. Very sharp. Anyway, I betrayed myself and my Lord, first and foremost."

I had to take a deep breath and remind myself that in that moment, I was here as a reporter, not as Ruth's friend and Felicity's friend, but it was as a friend that I got mad and wanted to slap that self-pitying look off his face. "And your congregation too," I said.

"They can make up their own minds about that," he said.

They evidently already had. "My mom and I went over to Starbright Ministry. It was a ghost town."

"It's being reconfigured. The county bought most of those buildings, but the church will still be a presence, I think." He told me he had decided to abdicate (his word) in favor of the assistant pastor because of a complex series of issues and misunderstandings. "I was fired. I won't be a minister anymore."

Roman Wild looked miserable. On his cable TV show in the middle of the night, he used to proclaim himself "Wild for the Lord." But now, all that holy exuberance seemed distant as a cold star is distant from earth. "The short version is that I borrowed money from the church that I intended to pay back. I had some significant debts, bills for medical things and some supplies . . ." I thought of my father ranting, after he'd encountered Roman once downtown, in a new Mercedes and a bespoke cashmere suit, about how the vow of poverty clearly didn't extend to Protestants. I thought of that big, luxe, deserted house and the school, the missionary dorms, the auditorium, the gyms . . .

"Was it a lot of money?"

"It depends on what you'd call a lot of money."

"I would call, like, a hundred thousand dollars a lot of money."

He said nothing.

"More than that?"

"We are all sinners," he said.

"Well, I hope you work it out. I just wanted to talk about Felicity . . ."

"I haven't killed anybody," he said.

Just then, the two little boys in identical stocking caps embroidered with leaping red stags ran up and grabbed Roman Wild around the waist. One yelled, "Daaaaaad! I'm too cold! Hot chocolate! Hot chocolate! You promised!"

"Felicity pleaded not guilty," I said.

"I heard."

"Dad!" the second child shrieked. "We have to go home!"

"Reenie, this is Owen the Loud, and this is . . . Roman Jr. We call him Romy." He had no shame. "I should get these rascals back. Faith probably has dinner ready. Anyhow, Felicity's problems have nothing to do with me."

"You sure you want to say that? It sounds cold."

"I don't mean to be cold. But I've lost everything. I am suffering."

I nodded at the two beautiful little kids. I'd met Rapunzel, their mother. It seemed that Roman Wild would land on both feet.

He saw my glance. "Reenie, I did not want to hurt Ruth or my boys, my older boys. They're with me right now, in fact, and I'm trying to explain to them in a way they'll understand. But they'll never understand. Not until they're grown men and they have their own complicated lives. I am mortified." Roman looked like he was strangling, his face purpling. Was he having a heart attack? Or a stroke? "When David saw Bathsheba, he was struck with love for her and lay with her, and when her husband came back, to cover for the pregnancy, which is what happened to me, there was a pregnancy . . ." He spoke as if this baby, presumably Owen the Loud, had fallen from the sky, which maybe, in Roman's mind, he did. "But Uriah didn't want to claim the baby and so David sent him into battle and made sure he was killed."

"Well, right, you haven't killed anybody. And you're not King David." What kind of delusions did this guy have anyway? A defrocked Wisconsin minister comparing himself to this great Biblical prophet . . . or whatever David was?

"David pleaded with God to forgive him. He freely acknowledged his sin. He said, 'my sin is ever before me . . . Against you . . . have I sinned and done what is evil in your sight . . . Behold, I was brought forth in iniquity, and in sin did my mother conceive me . . . blot out all my iniquities.'"

There was always some way to blame a woman. "So you're forgiven if you're sorry?"

"In Proverbs, it says that a man who commits adultery destroys himself, and I am destroyed, at least professionally. If I didn't believe that living a pure life from now on could redeem me, then my life would be meaningless. Scripture says it's better to marry than burn in sin."

"I don't know anything about the Bible but if it says it's better to marry, well, you must be fireproof because you did it twice at the same time."

Unasked, he said that the church council first considered letting him quietly make full financial restitution and go through pastoral and traditional counseling, but when the news about Felicity broke, however, all bets were off. Apparently, a polygamist pastor might hope for forgiveness, but the father of a courtesan killer? Poor Ruth, deserted by a bigamist and then this arrest? I might go into hiding too.

"So Felicity deserves forgiveness too? Even if the worst is true?"

The reverend was quiet for a long time, maybe a full minute, which can seem infinite in the cold. He finally said, "We're all sinners."

I said, "I won't keep you any longer. I just have one question. I'll ask Ruth too when I talk to her. Do you know why Felicity did what she did? I don't mean why did she kill someone, because I think that's impossible. I just want to ask . . ."

"What, Reenie? I don't have time."

"Why do you think she became a sex worker? Did anything happen at home that might have caused her to do that?"

Roman Wild reached down and took a mittened hand from each of his little boys. He did seem like a devoted father. How could he be both things? And yet, wasn't Felicity also? Were all of us two people, one facing outward, one facing in?

"You'd have to ask her."

"She won't talk to me."

"That should tell you something," he said, a trace of triumph tensing his dramatic chin. "My relationship with my stepdaughter . . ."

"Wait. You adopted her, right? So she's your daughter, not your stepdaughter."

"With Felicity. It wasn't close at the end."

I didn't get the sense that Roman Wild was lying, unless he was a stone psychopath. He'd answered my questions. That didn't track with some horrendous abuse situation. Felicity left Starbright Academy, but she didn't leave their house until she graduated. I thought now, she could have come to us, but she never gave even me a hint of any real trouble, except taking off for Madison one day after graduation.

To my shame, that was only something I'd heard by chance, not from her. After a month in upstate New York as a counselor at a fashion journalism camp for high schoolers, I headed to Chicago to a restaurant and bar called Angel on the Rock, which was owned by a college friend's family, who also put me up at their house in Evanston. By night, I waited tables there and learned to tend bar. During the day, I wrote copy for a teen fashion blog called Miss Lead. I was busy morning until night until I left for Missouri. But that was no excuse for the fact that I never even texted Felicity a funny face with tears to say goodbye. Why? Felicity and I used to talk or text daily. Was I ashamed of how well she knew me?

I was.

I knew why. I just couldn't face her. In all honesty, I couldn't face myself and the appalling truth she now knew about me. Even now, in the bone-deep cold, I was pushed back to that June night, just days before we were set to graduate, the breathless wet heat, the flat black surface of the water, the loud, insistent shriek of the crickets. For years, I couldn't hear crickets, a sweet sound for the innocent, without breaking out in a scrim of sweat.

I'd let shame overrule love. Never, I decided on the spot, would I ever do that again.

"About Ruth?"

"Reenie, all I know is that she resigned from her job around Christmas. I wouldn't have even known that except the school called to ask me where to send her things. The boys are worried. I am too. I'm grateful she even wanted me in their lives after everything. I can't exactly call her parents. She used to go and stay there for weeks at a time. They have money, so it was probably a nice setup for her. It didn't help our marriage. I will say that."

To my eyes, his own setup seemed pretty good, at least for a while. But in the end, they had nothing—less than nothing, the house and even their car the property of the church. Rev. Wild would get a small pension from a fund for disabled clergy. He said Ruth had some savings, but that money went for their debts. How unfair that Ruth, in her Mennonite cotton sack dresses, had to share the burden of Roman's spending.

Finally, he sighed and said, "Yes, Reenie. I'm fallen. Are you happy now?"

The question was a surprise. "Reverend Wild, I never wished anything bad for you. And I loved Ruth. Ruth didn't do anything wrong."

Roman said, "No, she didn't."

"I MUST BE LIKE A BIBLICAL PROPHET!" MY FATHER SAID THAT EVE-ning. I was finally back at my parents' house, having restored feeling to my wooden-block hands by sluicing them with warm water at the kitchen sink. Nell pulled out a package of frozen vegetables and began to make rudimentary fried rice, heavy on the soy sauce and scrambled eggs, as I told my family about the soon-to-be ex-pastor. My father said, "Was I right? I told you he was bent."

All three of the women in his nuclear family ignored him.

"So you didn't see Ruth, obviously," my mom said.

"I'll keep trying," I said, adding that, on the drive back, I'd tried to call Ruth's parents, but there was no answer and no way to leave a message. "I know Hal and Alice were not fans of Roman. Once on Fourth of July? Alice said Ruth told her about the Rapture and how everybody would go up to heaven on a big white horse. Alice said her daughter got that right from the horse's ass. That makes sense, they were scientists and they raised Ruth that way. But it was personal too."

Other teachers who worked with Ruth at Thornton Wilder High surely would have had word of her. That night, I would try to reach some of them.

Why would Ruth leave? Even if they lived with their father, you didn't just up and abandon teenage kids. Surely, she would come to stand with Felicity at the trial, no matter what? Or did the magnitude of Felicity's sins preclude even her mother's presence? Would all her family so fully disown her? Was Ruth with her own parents, as Roman suggested? Or somewhere else?

"I think she grew up in the South," Miranda said. "In Florida, if I'm not mistaken. Remember, Hal worked there, on the space shuttle?"

Ruth had not been close to anyone, either on our block or when the family moved to the mansion at Starbright Ministry. She was pleasant and pretty but painfully shy: People didn't catch sight of her from one week to the next. It wasn't as though somebody reported her missing when she missed spin class.

"For the life of me, I can't figure how Felicity's arrest and the collapse of the Roman empire are related, except that they involve the same people at the same time," I told my mom.

My dad came back into the kitchen, his hockey game interrupted by a loud and tedious seven minutes of commercials for dog food and beer. At least, that was his excuse, but he was a horrible liar. We could tell he was eavesdropping. Dad was part owner of a company that built mansions not unlike Roman Wild's "rectory," and in a business where lesser people sometimes padded their pockets by padding your bills, he was known by his associates as Patrick the Pure. He was a little self-righteous. He was actually a lot self-righteous, especially when it came to religious shenanigans. Dad was a card-carrying member of the Freedom From Religion Foundation, the nation's oldest organization of opinionated atheists, founded in Wisconsin. How could he keep silent on such a validating occasion? He had the grace to at least pretend he was just interested in his next cup of coffee. I was always afraid that my father would stroke out one snowy day from his competitive involvement with the Blackhawks or the Packers and his six daily cups of high-octane coffee.

"She must have known all along!" Nell said as we ate. "She's an intelligent woman."

"Not the same thing," my mother said with a sigh. "Roman was always off on TV or preaching at one of those revival things. Maybe she didn't suspect for a long time."

My father snorted, and Miranda gave him the side-eye.

"So when Ruth found out about the other wife, she left him?" Nell asked.

"Well, he kind of left her first," I said. "He's ruined as a minister but, you know? He doesn't seem all that torn up about it. He's got nine lives." The sheer audacity of men was made manifest to me again. Only some men, true, but at that moment, for me,

Roman Wild's was only the most extreme example of the everyday arrogance of the entitled white guy.

With the smug certainty of a second-year law student, Nell said, "Well, now he's going to have to face the laws of the State of Wisconsin instead of just the wrath of God. Dad's right. He'll do time instead of just his penance. He'll be doing Sunday services in prison."

I wasn't so sure. I still thought that Roman might have another trick or two up his sleeve.

"If this isn't proof that Christianity is a racket to make people stop thinking and start obeying, then what is?" my dad said. I suppressed a sigh. We'd all heard it before. "And this God they praise? Cruel? Merciful? Whichever suits Him. But always demanding that people bow down for His glory. And pony up their money."

My mother said, "Pat, settle down. Not all Christians are . . ."

"Sheep?" Nell said. "I believe they are, in the psalms anyhow. Lambs."

"I'm definitely not surprised by any of this," my father said. "Not too unhappy about it either, except for the sake of Ruth and those kids."

"And Felicity," I added.

"Felicity, well, Felicity is . . ."

"What?" I said, biting off the word.

"Another matter," my father concluded, but I knew that was not what he originally meant to say. If even Patrick the Pure was so willing to judge her history, it might be a tall order to find really impartial jurors.

"People have a right to worship how they please, Pat," my mom said.

"And I have a right to my beliefs. All that bloviating about the blessings the Lord bestowed is violating my right."

"That's not their intent."

"If I say that you are fat and I don't mean it as an insult, if I'm giving you a description, then is it okay? Or am I pushing it on you as a fact?"

"It's not the same thing!" My mom had her Irish up now. "You are so tiresome!" Nell and I counted backward: *five, four, three, two, one* . . . for what we knew would come . . . Right on cue, my mother said, "And I'm not fat."

We knew better than to get between them at times like these. They would turn on us like jackals, shouting, in unison, "We are not fighting!"

Meekly, Nell and I went our own ways. I headed back toward my old room, carrying a warmed-up cup of atomic coffee I had tried to tame with half a cup of cream, to muse on all the pieces of this narrative that did not fit.

At the turn of the landing, I looked down the hill of our block, the orderly descent of neatly lighted facades. How many of them were hiding something? Were the people who did not bring shame on themselves the exception?

According to everything I could discern from the police file, which had a lot of inconsistent information, Felicity had been nineteen years old, a sophomore, when she dropped out. The year wasn't even over, which only sharpened the mystery. She gave up pursuing one kind of wildlife to pursue another kind—all that, and she hadn't even been old enough to drink.

My radio reporter friend Sally Zankow had slipped me the name of the so-called gentleman's club where Felicity might have met the men she was accused of killing. When Sally went there, the manager turned her down flat, as had the strippers she tried to enlist for interviews. But maybe I could in fact do something like what my mother did. Maybe I could learn about the world that Felicity entered—how many years ago? Two years? More?—from the inside. I wouldn't have to work there very long, and every place needs a licensed bartender.

I had to keep digging. I needed to follow the thread to the past, and to those people who knew about her present life. I'd only begun to source this thing, and it would have been exciting—finally, a story that would demand all my skills, with all kinds of twists and dark corners!—if it hadn't been so close to my own heart. All I could do was all I could do. I would use all the persistence and courage and style I had, and that would be enough. But what if I pulled the thread and pulled it and it led to a terrible truth? What if my own, my beloved Felicity, really had committed these crimes, for money? What if she had committed these crimes for a more righteous reason, a reason like self-defense . . . that only she knew? Even as I considered it, I knew that no such thing was possible. If it were, she would say it now; she would have said it before. She would be fighting for her life instead of throwing it away.

THREE

American Goldfinch

Spinus tristis. This small bird is prized for its striking plumage and its distinctive call in flight, which some naturalists say sounds like "potato chip!" or "pretty pretty." In folklore, goldfinches were believed to carry the spiritual message of resilience and the need to joyfully accept change. Commonly kept as pets in fourteenth-century Europe, these birds were a favorite of young girls, and a dream of a goldfinch meant that a girl would marry into great wealth. Their small size and relatively timid nature make goldfinches prey for more aggressive larger birds, especially blue jays, which are known to eat goldfinches if they get the chance.

"I'M NOT A REAL MAN," ROSS ANNOUNCED.

I said, "Is that so? Does Amira know?"

Ross had just become engaged to a wonderful woman from Chennai, another psychology grad student, whose parents and older sister, I'd learned at the Friendsgiving, were all tenured professors . . . Maybe Ross thought that he and his parents, who owned a hardware store, were outclassed by this dazzling collective of brainpower.

He said to me now, "Reenie, even a life crisis can be boring. Let me ask you first. How are you, Reenie? How are you really?" What did I expect? He was almost a clinical psychologist.

"We'll get to that later. Your manhood issue first! That sounds intriguing."

"Okay, who was it who said that a man hates himself if he never has his war or his sea voyage?"

"Beats me."

"Come on! You always do that shit! You're a show-off with your whatever . . . oh, I think it was Hemingway who said, I think it was Abraham Lincoln who said . . ."

"Not anymore," I told him, buttering another piece of French bread. I buttered it so thickly that Ross stared. Why didn't I just eat the butter? "I'm going to be one of those writers who says she doesn't have time to read."

Ross smiled up at the server. "Could we have more bread, please? My friend here ate the whole loaf."

The young woman in white-person dreadlocks gave me a sour look. "That costs extra," she said.

"Go crazy," I told her. "Bring two loaves. I'm eating for two now."

"Now she thinks you're pregnant," Ross said. "Are you?"

"None of your business. But why do men disapprove of women who eat?" I asked him then, "Does Amira like food?"

"Oh you bet. She's this crazed cook, trying to learn how to make kimchi now."

"I thought she was Indian."

"She is, Reenie. You're Irish. Do you only cook corned beef and cabbage?"

"So, let's get back to why you're not a real man."

"I just feel like, what have I done? Have I taken risks? Have I proved myself? I've never even been in a fistfight."

"I don't think most people have."

"Maybe I'm too influenced by movies."

I nibbled delicately at my spinach torta, smarting a little from the bread comment.

"You've proved yourself a hundred ways, Ross. Not everybody who went to sea could have learned the things you've learned. Not by far. It's not nothing."

Ross smiled at me. He was so sweet and appealing. Why, I asked myself, not for the first time, had I never fallen for Ross?

"So, you probably think I'm just looking for something to worry about."

"That's incorrect, Ross," I said. "I don't think probably. I most definitely think you're just looking for something to worry about."

I thought of something then that the war journalist Sebastian Junger had said, basically reinforcing what Ross was worried about. I didn't know which of his books he was referencing but he told a reporter, "You know, it's said you're not a man until you've done something really difficult. And war is very difficult." He said that going to war gives young males a chance to find a peer group and purpose to their lives. That's important in a society where a lot of young men don't have either. He also told an interviewer something like that ours was the first culture in history to "actively discourage an intelligent conversation about what manhood should require of men."

It was all enlightening and well reasoned. It was all, also, all about men.

"It was Johnson," I told Ross now, as it had just occurred to me, "who said that about war and the sea."

"Somebody from Wisconsin? The people who make the baby lotion?" I stared at him. "Reenie, you are so easy! I know who you mean. I know who Samuel Johnson was. I do have two brain cells to rub together." He added, "I also know that it's fucked up for me to worry because I'm not fucked up. Maybe it's the tank I'm swimming in. Maybe I think that I'd be more able to understand fucked-up people if I were similarly fucked."

"And who says that first-world problems are silly?" I said. "Come on. Let's talk about Felicity now so I can have the excuse to have two tiramisus."

As Ross talked, I got a clearer picture of how the bomb was going off with the news about Felicity. After all, it involved not only faculty but a former student: one of the victims, Cary Church, was an economics professor.

Ross said that before he went further, he wasn't sure that he wanted his name used in the article, not at all sure about his knowledge of the reactions of faculty members and maybe even if he was only to speak in general terms about personality change—which was one of the subjects we were going to discuss, given that the Felicity we knew, or thought we knew, didn't seem to fit the accustomed demographic either for a woman who sold sex or a woman who did murder.

"So," I said, "you're going to be an expert on something and publish papers on that something and you want to be anonymous talking about it here? Maybe this is your sea voyage, Ross."

"Well, that's pretty manipulative, Reenie!"

"I have my own special talents."

"But I do have some other information too," he said, studying the remains of his entrée. "We should finish up here and go back to the inn." For an instant, I thought he might be making a pass at me, but he was simply worried that we might be overheard here, also. As he settled the bill, Ross gamely put away most of my neglected Caesar salad and all but one bite of my tiramisu. Finally, I chided him that this was not really a social event—not that we shouldn't have a social event, I hastened to add.

Back we went to the bed-and-breakfast inn where he was staying. I didn't have to ask why he wasn't at his parents' in Sheboygan. He didn't feel comfortable in the parlor so we went up to his room. It was comfortable and clean and spacious, with its own little seating area, very girlie, like an explosion in a ging-ham factory (I pictured Ivy's grimace). There was a gorgeous unobstructed view of Lake Michigan. I'd heard that the break-fasts were spectacular, and the proprietor had offered to let me join Ross in the morning, one more reason that I might never again fit into a size six. Or a size eight.

Once we were settled, Ross said, "People are afraid of be-ing, well, outed."

Why would Felicity talk about these guys? I wondered; that made no sense. But Ross meant "outed" by their associa-tion with her in connection with the murders. "She had a fair number of . . . of dates who were faculty or staff. High-profile people. Cary Church was a respected guy. When other instruc-tors found out he was dead, some people literally canceled their classes . . ."

"Imagine that! And just because their colleague was murdered!"

"Come on, Reenie. When you hear that the bridge you drive over every day collapsed, the second thing you think is, oh, those poor people." He got up and paced a bit, then took out two bot-tles of Pellegrino from the room's minifridge, which held no wine, no ginger ale, only fizzy water and an unopened carton of cream, presumably for coffee and tea. Not exactly generous at the price they charged! "They thought, sure, that could have been me. The talk was that this woman was a businesswoman. She might have a heart of glass, but she was dynamite . . . I shouldn't say this." Russ peered through his water bottle.

"You can say it. This part can be off the record."

"It sounds disrespectful to women."

"It's not the sexual rating that bothers me. She was never icy," I said.

"You knew her in a different context. Maybe she changed. I mean, clearly, she changed if she did this."

"It could be a misunderstanding."

"It's probably not. I only know this from criminal psychology, but if they charge you, there's usually a good reason."

That was just what my mother had said.

"Ross, you said she might have changed. You're an expert on this . . ."

"Hardly."

"Do people really change, Ross? Or are they showing faces they hid before?"

"People do change. They change if they have good reason."

"Like?"

"Like if they're sick because of obesity or smoking and they need to change or die. Or they want something in life, and they're going after it in all the wrong ways. But unless there's that kind of big motivation, your personality traits stay pretty consistent. If you're a reserved little kid, you probably won't end up as a drummer in a rock band."

"What if you change for the worse?"

"That usually happens because of some kind of inflicted trauma. An event outside the individual's control . . . You hear these things all the time—he was so loving and affectionate when he was a little boy but then he was abused in boarding school and that impacted his trusting personality . . ."

"Oh damn, Ross, don't use *impact* as a verb. It makes me want to dump that fizzy water on your head."

"Isn't it a verb too?"

"No! At least, it shouldn't be . . ."

"So something changes and it changes the person, essentially."

"Would you assume that she was sexually assaulted as a kid or something?"

"That's definitely one thing that's been linked to that kind of promiscuous behavior. If you accept that it's behavior that degrades the woman, or the man, there are lots of reasons people give for what they do. Some people think it's meant as a kind of vengeance on the abuser . . . look what you made me do! Some people think that it's meant to be a way to establish power for somebody who felt powerless once. Some say it's purely trans-actional: I'll give you this and you give me a lot of money. But lots of people think that it's an unconscious impulse to degrade themselves further because they feel ashamed even when it's clearly not their fault. Maybe it's a little of all those things."

"Who do you think it was? Her stepdad? He's a fundamen-talist minister. You know the Starbright Ministry, that huge campus."

"Sure. I mean, that's classic, maybe too simple. Pedophiles lots of times try to get into situations where they're going to be respected and trusted . . . you know, plausible deniability but also lots of access to the victims." He added, "Look at the cases with Catholic priests. And even when those guys got nailed, half the time the diocese just tried to cover it up and send them somewhere else."

We talked for a while about people we both knew. After a two-year stint teaching in Tampa, Ross was happy being back in Wisconsin, a place he once couldn't wait to leave. I wondered if I would ever feel that way. I still sometimes thought that Mid-westerners were what Ivy called "primitive." I still had strong if fleeting urges to flee.

At last, Ross handed me a card with three names. "I should never have written these down, Reenie. If anyone ever asks you, this intel didn't come from me."

"You can trust me. It's not like I'm going to go to these guys and say Ross Bell, you know the guy in psychology? He said you were one of this hooker's johns!"

Ross looked wretched. Two of them were professors, he went on, one a department head in his fifties, another who'd just achieved tenure, and the third one was university counsel, a specialist in the implementation of equity in women's sports.

Not a good look for him at that moment. He must have been shitting a whole brick factory.

"These are decent guys. I play softball with them. They're worried that it will all come out. She'll expose them."

"I assume they can probably count on that. Won't the police talk to them? So I will too."

"For a story? That could ruin their reputation," Ross said.

"Wait, they're the ones who ruin their own reputation, not me."

"They have families."

"Then they shouldn't have been seeking the services of a sex worker." I got up and stood next to the window, with its cool against my hot cheek. Under a freckled scarf of stars, an ice boat glided across the lake, its hull festooned with a festive string of small lights. It looked fleet as a gull, but I would bet that the pilot was getting his balls pounded by the surface impact.

Ross sighed, then sighed again. "It's not that simple, Reenie."

"It is that simple. If I had a dime for every time a man has said to me it's complicated, I'd never have to work again."

"You've never done anything wrong?"

"I sure have. I've done things that were really wrong, but I never blamed it on my inability to resist biology."

"Apparently, Felicity has some pretty irresistible biology."

I thought of her in court, that pellucid skin, her magnificent reticence. My mind scampered away from a visual of her staring over the fat, freckled shoulder of some grunting bald professor. I'd rather work at the landfill.

I asked Ross, "Did you ever?"

"Ever what?"

"Did you ever sleep with Felicity? Or anyone who makes her living off sex?"

He laughed. "No!" And he added, "I don't have to pay for it."

"And there it is! That's the second thing that if I had a dime for every time I've heard a guy say it . . ."

"But you blame guys who do. I don't. But there's an allure for a man with a night creature like that." He added, "I'm speaking as a guy here, not as a psychologist."

"A creature? Like a vixen? Like an animal? Being with a woman dozens of other guys have slept with?"

Ross said, "No, like she'd have special knowledge. As for the numbers, that's what you're looking at with most so-called nice girls these days anyhow."

"How it's always been for so-called nice men."

"It's more like the ultimate lack of connection, in psychological terms. Pleasure but no strings. No need to think about what she's feeling or thinking or what she'll feel or think later, tomorrow, or next week. Not me, this isn't about me. But lots of men? They want exactly the opposite of what women want. If women really understood that . . ."

"They'd all be gay."

"Reenie! So, you just want to revisit this old friendship for feminist reasons?"

"I want to know what led to this, and that, and the next thing. That's my job."

"I know exactly what you do, Reenie. My girlfriend would never buy a Miaow bag without your advice."

"You mean a Miu Miu bag. Ah, but those are so 2019, Ross." When he didn't respond, I continued. "So what happened to make her quit school? What changed the whole picture? She got straight As. She had a great scholarship. You would think a breakdown, or a death, or a pregnancy, but those things didn't happen."

"Being serious now? Just my gut? If I had to guess, I would say the reason was the money," Ross said. "It's confusing. Felicity always seemed to be almost demure in a way, when I knew her."

"It had to be more than money."

"For a night, four thousand dollars. For a couple of hours, half that. That's what I heard."

Against my own will, I whistled. "Wow."

"I know."

"College professors can afford that?"

"Maybe they budgeted for it, like a car payment."

Even if she worked only ten hours a week, only two weeks a month . . . it wouldn't be long until . . . until what? She would have amassed hundreds of thousands. A fast, if ruinous, track to wealth? Those nontaxable earnings aside, there was also that life insurance money, the supposed motive for her crimes.

Ross said, "I don't know the specifics. Just what people say."

"Do you want to know?"

"Sure."

"You know there were two guys," I said. "Both of them had life insurance policies, one for five million dollars, one for two million, both with her as the beneficiary."

"That's a lot of money."

"It is," I agreed. "The older guy, Emil Gardener . . ."

"The dairy," said Ross.

"Right. In his case, it almost made sense. He was in his late sixties, and he had big issues with high blood pressure. His wife, Erica, some years older, is terminally ill with kidney disease. They had no children of their own.

"The other man, Cary Church, wasn't even forty," I went on. "He was a healthy man."

Ross said, "He wasn't just healthy, he was a fanatic. He was always in the gym or the pool."

"Those insurance policies would have been costly, difficult to conceal from your wife or your stockbroker. And Felicity almost collected on them. But Cary Church wrote a letter to the police, a letter he never mailed," I explained. "The letter detailed how he'd helped Felicity move Emil Gardener's body from her apartment to a snowbank in a forest near the university's golf course, giving an exact location. He wrote two letters, in fact, and in the second one, he changed his mind and said that the defendant was not responsible for Mr. Gardener's death."

"That's crazy," Ross said.

"I have no idea. Almost like he knew he was going to die. But why say two different things?"

"You'd have to ask him, huh?"

"The first guy, they thought died from hypothermia. People sometimes take off their clothes in the last stages of freezing to death. It's called paradoxical undressing. I looked it up. Like those skiers in Russia, a long time ago? Apparently, the way the blood vessels react, you feel too hot?"

"Paradoxical," Ross said.

I nodded. Emil Gardener's clothes were found right beside him.

"That's pretty horrifying, Reenie. I'm like most people. I'm not really into that kind of stuff."

"That actually makes you just the opposite of most people, Ross. Have you ever noticed the sheer number of true crime podcasts? And movies? Sad ones? Funny ones? Ones that are only about murders that took place in national parks? There are specialties and subspecialties. It's nuts."

"I don't think many guys listen to podcasts, Reenie. That's a female thing."

"Maybe. Lots of men make those podcasts, though. Your students are listening right now!"

"So then the professor . . ." Ross prompted me.

Several days later, I told him, Cary Church's wife, Suzanne, couldn't reach him. He hadn't come home. She tried for hours. She called his sister. She called his racquetball partner. They all thought he was with her. Finally, when he didn't show up to take their children to visit their grandparents, she called the police. They found him dead in his own bathtub, naked but with no water in the tub and not a mark on him. Healthy young men in their thirties don't just climb into an empty bathtub and die.

"I heard about the apartment thing from somebody," Ross recalled now. "It was this great apartment because Cary Church had a lot of money, some kind of family trust."

"They were separated," I said.

Ross told me that they were apparently trying to work things out, as their sons were only four and six years old. He asked me, "Didn't it say that in the police report?"

I'd read only the arrest report so far and not the rest of the file I'd obtained, but I told him that I didn't think that those reports detailed the victims' domestic arrangements. In fact, they might, for all I knew. Admittedly, I hadn't yet spoken with police detectives, still fearful, despite Sally Zankow's assurances, that authorities would consider me a lightweight.

The report I'd read did say an autopsy showed no evidence of foul play. One of the forensic pathologists suggested that the victim inhaled a toxin dissolved in the missing bath water—and that toxin would have broken down right away. That was when they exhumed Emil Gardener's body. At autopsy, complete certainty was not possible about the amount and nature of a toxin, but the condition of Gardener's stomach tissue strongly suggested a toxic and corrosive agent. The bruises on his head and shoulders probably came from hitting his head against a hard surface, such as the base of the sink and the toilet during his death agonies. Or maybe someone had hit him on the head.

This had happened over this past Christmas break, during what I now knew were the last days of Felicity's intact family, the final Christmas service that Roman Wild would preach at Starbright Ministry. How long she was there and when she arrived were open to debate, but the visit was her alibi. For how could she have killed anyone from a hundred miles away?

I thought of a previous Christmas, some years ago. The last time I'd had an actual visit with Felicity. It was that brunch that Felicity and I organized with Becky Brompton and Cassandra Sullivan, who had been our high-school classmates. All the guests were female, including a few little kids. We ate too many mushroom-and-chicken vol-au-vents and drank too much cider spiked with too much rum, and laughed that, when we stepped outside, we'd be in Bedford Falls.

After everyone else left, Felicity and I exchanged presents. The gifts she gave me were strange and opulent for kids our age. I loved them. There were simple half-carat diamond stud earrings. After all that fashion blogging, I could spot even the most artful fake and I knew in general terms what they would cost. She also gave me black velvet Saint Laurent over-the-knee boots and a Baccarat crystal paperweight. I gave her a copy of *Fuchsia*'s hardcover "look book" of remarkable photos, an ostrich-leather passport holder, swag from some event, and a gold-plated Montblanc Meisterstück pen we got as a perk from the pen company, which would have cost about five hundred dollars in a store. I figured that everyone likes beautiful pens and I had two of them. Her presents to me would have cost me two weeks' pay. Mine to her were free. Why didn't I wonder how a grad student could afford such things? I suppose I simply accepted that Felicity could pull off the seemingly impossible, as she always had.

She told me she would be going to Canada that summer to work with a professor trying to alleviate habitat challenges to endangered cerulean warblers. She showed me a video of a plump little denim-colored bird with a sweet cheer of a call.

Was not one single sentence of any of that true?

Afterward, I wrote to thank her for the gifts and the party. I wrote a couple of times and tried to call. Felicity never answered the notes and the phone number I had was no longer in service.

As a child at Christmas, I used to stand looking down the

hilly street from our house at a descending necklace of colored lights, pretending I was a princess who lived high in her castle above all her subjects. I recalled Felicity's accounts of her bleak, straitened holidays ("Nothing more fundamental than a Christmas with fundamentalists," she'd say). Back then, the only undecorated house was the Wilds' house. They didn't celebrate a secular Christmas with festive lights, a big tree, and piles of presents, but instead with an austere grind of twice-daily church services from December 1 until early January. As the kind of minister he was, Roman Wild must have felt it was his duty as a minister to set an example of putting Christ back in Christmas. The presents the children received were few and practical. Felicity told me that her parents once gave her pajama bottoms for her December birthday and then gave her the top for Christmas.

"Don't they get that this could backfire, and their children will grow up to hate religion?" my dad said. "Those kids look around them and see all the fun and food and excess other families have, and who can blame them? Puritans must have had more fun!"

Miranda learned from Felicity's grandmother, Alice, who lived not far from my parents, about what happened a few days into the new year, how state police, local police, and police from Madison all converged on the building to arrest a 120-pound girl. (I suppose they thought she could be holed up in there with an automatic weapon.) Alice got there just in time to see her only granddaughter taken away in handcuffs.

Her family had no idea what was happening. For all they knew, it was because of the rigorous nature of her graduate studies that Felicity didn't come home more often. Would my parents have figured out that I wasn't really in school? My mother, of course, was overly inquisitive by nature and training, and further, they helped subsidize my bills and stuff when I got jammed up, so I had very few secrets. Other families were different. Stories of abuse, suffered or perpetrated in secret, were almost ubiquitous . . . *He seemed like a decent guy, quiet, kept himself to himself, I would never have suspected . . .*

When the whole thing transpired, Nell and I were with my parents, house hunting in Florida, in Cocoa Beach, near where my dad had gone to college and where a few of his old fraternity brothers lived. My parents wanted a vacation place, where they would eventually retire, in anticipation of the day when we finally got around to giving them grandchildren. For one hot, creepy week, Nell and I drove every morning to Cocoa Beach past snowmen and reindeers standing on lawns as plush as putting greens. We sat on the sand listening to people's phones playing "Jingle Bells" as the sun smashed down on us. One woman whose mat was next to our towels was so cooked that her skin was the color and texture of a leather boot. She lay there all day, neither reading nor listening to music and not even going into the water to get her ankles wet. How could this feel pleasant? How could she believe the result was attractive? Yet, the oranges were so delicious compared to the ones at our local Woodman's that I ate until my gums hurt. I also actually got sick of eating fried grouper, which, on my first night, was a delicacy.

The condominium our folks decided on was nice enough: two stories, four bedrooms, a pool, solidly built and thoughtfully finished to resemble a little Victorian house. It looked the same as three dozen others in the same planned neighborhood. No matter how old and cold I got, I decided (ironically, as it transpired) that I would never live in Florida.

If I had been home (Where there was snow! Where it was real Christmas!) I might have seen Felicity. We might have had a drink or gone out for lunch. Why hadn't I made the effort to do that sooner and more often? Not that it would have changed anything; that was a foolish notion, but the frisson of guilt was real. It was never that I didn't care for her; of course I did, but life had whirled both of us away—or so I assumed. The age we were, work came first. Study came first. Social life and love were folded into the work of inhabiting the adult role you would have for the rest of your life. You were leaning forward into the wind, into the future, with the past at your back, reliable and recoverable, and sometimes, for the moment, ignorable.

Still, I was aghast in the knowledge that, whatever had happened, it was already underway by then. Whatever she knew, whatever she had planned, if she had done what they said she'd done, the guilt and agitation must have been crushing. How could she go through the ordinary week of holiday rituals, knowing she was on the verge of something so monstrous? It was unsettling to think that, at the time, I knew nothing of something now central to my professional and personal life. At the time, I was stuffing my face with fried grouper sandwiches.

I wondered then, if you were going to do something so grim, why pick such a contradictory occasion for it, a time like winter break when families gathered, that, for the survivors, would stain that supposedly joyous week forever? Or did the murderous not even consider such matters? Was the timing so she could pretend somehow that she was out of town? Was her need for that money so fierce and urgent? Why? Was it just to be safe? Never again to have to rely on men? How did Felicity even feel about men? Did she despise them? Was she gay (not that gay women despised men)? Why did the police just immediately believe Cary's account of Emil's death? Why did no one think that Cary might have killed him?

Why wouldn't Felicity talk to me?

"Do you know where there's a restaurant around here that might still be open?" Ross asked.

I twitched, startled by his voice. Lost in my freewheeling thoughts, I'd all but forgotten he was there.

"I don't. I don't think I'll ever eat again. I feel like I swallowed a bag of doughnuts."

"Well, two loaves of bread . . . single-handed."

"Are you hungry?"

"I'm going to look and see if there's some kind of fast-food place. I'll bring you some cookies or something. Do you want a soda too? We can talk more then. I can't think when I'm starving."

"Sure," I told him, as he shrugged into his peacoat, winding his scarf around his neck. This reminded me that tonight was markedly colder than it had been in weeks. I was in such a hurry to leave that I actually lost time through haste. As my Grandma Nell said, what you lack with your mind, you make up with your feet. I had to go back to get my favorite quilted winter coat, the one she made for me. Despite having seen designers and cutters at work, actually making a coat without a pattern was still a level of textile achievement far beyond my understanding. It was like choosing to knit a refrigerator from steel wool. With the trial still distant, I could go back to Chicago later and pick up more clothing and books. But I would never be without my coat, a confection of white cotton velvet with fringe that Grandma Nell had designed to grow more fashionably faded with every wash.

I'd been inside the tabernacle at Starbright Ministry just one time. My father contemptuously called the place "Six Flags Over Jesus." It was on Valentine's Day, that same year.

Rev. Wild was loud and showy, beseeching his flock. "Husbands, love and treasure your wives! Wives, love and serve your husbands! The love we celebrate today with chocolates and flowers is the merest drop in the ocean of the mighty love of the Lord for each one of you." Calling Ruth "my bride," he passed a Valentine card from the back of the huge tabernacle to the choir, where Ruth stood in the top row, blushing furiously, trying to smile as everyone applauded her.

He was praising her to the skies. And yet, now that I recalled the occasion, it also seemed that he looked down on her.

Plenty of devoted Starbright women might have envied Ruth her marriage, but I didn't. Neither did Felicity. She didn't have to tell me; her face that day was a banner proclaiming hypocrisy. Several women stood up and pointed out that they knew Jesus personally. One of them even beseeched Him for help at the supermarket finding a bargain on pot roast, which seemed to me creepy even in that limited context. I recalled the supposedly joyous songs they sang that instead sounded like a dirge for sailors lost at sea, songs about short and brutal lives, hastening to their close. I remembered as especially gross the ancient tune "Abide with Me" ("Change and decay in all around I see . . ."). There was just one beautiful song, an old gospel hymn ("I sing because I'm happy, I sing because I'm free, for His eye is on the sparrow, and I know He watches me").

When Felicity transferred to the public high school from Starbright Academy the winter morning she turned sixteen, I thought she just hated the school, which she said managed to work Jesus into everything, including math. Maybe there was more to it. There was always more to it, I thought.

I thought of how Ruth Wild, as a science teacher, was good and clear-minded. She did not dodge the bits of science that probably went against her fundamentalist Christian code, or at least her husband's. Being who I am, I appreciated how she managed to style her long-sleeved dresses over leggings and jeans so that they looked more urban hippie than conservative pastor's wife. Felicity's younger brothers, Jay and Guy, were cute little blonds who resembled dark-haired Felicity only in that they were human, since Felicity was the product of Ruth's fleeting college relationship with an absent beau (whom my dad, ever the comic, called "the unsub"). Felicity once told me that she had no idea who her biological father was, beyond his being part Italian, and she didn't care to know. Poor Ruth.

Winding around and around in my memories, I must have fallen asleep. When Ross finally returned with his snack, it was after midnight, and he had to pound on the door to wake me up. It took me a moment to figure out where I was.

I tried to ignore the dismay on his face when, without asking, I grabbed half his beef sandwich. Munching away, I asked, "Do you know how I can convince these guys to talk to me?" Ross shrugged and shook his head. "I won't force anybody to go on the record. But if the police have already talked to them, the reality is that's a moot point anyhow. My call should come as no surprise. I don't care about them as much as I want to know what they saw in her. Why pay a thousand dollars for an hour with her? What would make you agree if you were them?"

Ross said slowly, "I guess if I thought you were going to write about me anyway, then the only thing left would be to make sure you didn't completely trash me, without giving me a chance to tell my side of it." Good point, Ross. Apparently, our long friendship outweighed institutional loyalty . . . or even softball-team loyalty.

"Well, that's what I intend to tell them. But I'm more concerned about what they thought about her and why they paid for her attention. If you were me, wouldn't you wonder? Wouldn't you want reasons? Wouldn't you want to try to trace a visible line that led from here to there? Wouldn't you think, there but for the grace of . . . ?"

"Not you, Reenie. You would never," Ross said. "Apparently, there wasn't a lot of feeling in it on her side. At least, that's what the rumor is."

"You mean she didn't fake orgasms?" I said. "Or she didn't seem to care?" Ross blushed and shook his head. "Would you care?"

Yet I found myself grateful that Ross thought that I would never make such a degrading choice. I was grateful that he said it. I was certain, but is anything truly certain? I knew how disclaimers made in daylight could get lost in the dark. I knew Ross had to be on his way. I'd kept him up so late, and yet hated to part with him. Not only had he given me useful foundational information, virtually being a stand-in for the men I would talk with, but he was also familiar and dear—and very much on my side.

I promised Ross that I would let him sleep and would not, after all, show up at 8:00 a.m. for breakfast. He could leave a note for the innkeepers to pack up something for him, for the road.

"One last thing," I said to Ross. "Then I promise I'll release you. It's not like I need to know how to do an interview. But the kind I'm used to these days is ten minutes if you're lucky, people saying, 'utterly fabulous,' or 'totally trending,' or 'passion for fashion,' or 'OOAK.' Like, once you track them down, you just press the button and out comes the spiel. This is different."

"People will be reluctant."

"That, and I want to ask questions that go really deep. How do you do that? You're the wiz with human communication."

"The thing to do when you interview someone is to listen to everything, not just what they say but what they don't say," Ross told me. "You've heard this before but really think about it. It's not just what people say, it's how they say it. Like a politician who got caught in a scandal. He's saying, 'I'm innocent, I'm innocent, this is all a lie,' but what is he really saying?"

"You mean body language."

"I mean that but content too. Right? Is somebody saying way more than he needs to say? Sixty words when ten would do? You watch for that." That was how I started to train myself to listen for hesitations and gaps in the answers I heard, and especially answers that didn't come, but instead silences, to measure how long those silences lasted and how comfortable the person was during them.

"But is there a technique for asking questions, one way that's better than another way?"

"You have to be patient. You ask and then wait. You resist the temptation to jump in and sort of help the person along."

Ross was entirely correct. I learned just how strong was the impulse to coach people. Waiting is difficult, but silence is a powerful tool. It's accommodating and inviting. A direct answer requires the kind of confidence that somebody with something to hide might lack. I learned to let the froth of their words bubble forth until it ran out. I tried to read the silences. Sometimes silence is its own story.

We hugged goodbye. Ross was looking forward to getting home early to his Amira.

No one waited for me.

That night, I lay awake wondering why I was alone, why I'd had only about a dozen dates since college graduation. Was it down to ambition? Fear? An odd repellent odor? Were my eyes spaced too far apart? Was my mouth too big, in both senses of the word? Was I simply engineered to be lonely?

Or was I alone because I was a bad person, even though no one knew it? Did other human animals instinctively detect something malign and avoid me?

These were the kind of night thoughts that crept out to scratch at the fabric of your pillow. Once one is loose, in scuttle more of them: How would I even write this story?

Yes, I'd gone to one of the best journalism schools on earth. Yes, I'd done straight news . . . but only during summer internships. And even then, what I covered wasn't exactly being embedded with the Eighth Marines in Kabul; it was just how nasty and personal the infighting got on the mayor's office staff, with one man posting photos of his colleague's ass crack on Instagram. Now I wrote whipped-cream prose. I could overlay three square feet of silk, muslin, hemp, linen, copper, indigo dye, nylon, mesh, rubber, steel alloy, and brass with magic. "Sassy but secure, dramatic yet durable, class made comfortable, the Sensational Sandrine sets the standard for satchels and then raises it to the stars." It wasn't wrong, and it was what I was paid to do—convert the unruly details into something scintillating ("We give you the secret lowdown on . . ." "We take you behind the golden doors of the most exclusive . . ." "Why you may gasp at the price before you gasp at the gorgeous . . ."). My painted-on drama allowed readers to leap over the stumbling block of goods made by the hands of children in China.

Would I be tempted to embellish Felicity like a pricey Burberry square? Would I convert the narrative to portray her as much victim as predator? Of course, she was, but only in the strictest sociological sense. And further, I was a romantic. Even if I could keep all the questions in the strike zone, could I later steer clear of tricky tropes and melted melodrama? (Okay, yes, alliteration addiction admitted . . .) By its very nature, any story is the thing itself but also not the thing itself. The event or the issue is framed by somebody else's vision. The descriptions, the quoted speech, the beginning, the conclusion, those are all someone else's choices, not the actual participants' actions. Despite the goal of objectivity, the reporter's own history and personality is folded in, like raisins in a batter.

Long after, I would see how I came to believe my own version of events, then doubt it, then believe it again.

I'd jetted from Chicago to Miami to Honolulu to Rome to cover the debut of the newest microclutch or sculptural crossbody from Alberto or Roberto or Kimiko. But this turned out to be a much longer journey, especially after things combusted between Sam Damiano and me. As the long fingers of night stretched out to tow in the gold morning ribbons through the window of the bed-and-breakfast inn on Lake Michigan, I had yet even to speak his name.

The first time I did was the next day. Tucked up gratefully under a quilt, as exhausted as if the long hours of the previous night were villains I'd outrun, I called his office and asked for him, expecting to leave a message or four or six, shocked when he immediately took the call, his voice a sweet bass, calm and comforting as tea with honey. He offered to meet me that afternoon, but I wanted to reach out to the families of the victims before I got ever more involved with the defendant. I also wanted to talk to Felicity's mother, to the hometown crowd. There was no particular hurry, so we agreed on the following week, after I returned from my visit to Sheboygan. All day long, and into the next night, I thought of the sound of that voice greeting me, telling me, "Hello, Reenie! I've been expecting you to call." I told him that I just couldn't be comfortable with what he'd said during that first conversation—he'd go into detail about his client's version of the deaths if he could. "I would be happy to share her version of those events, if she had ever shared that with me."

"The more I think about this, the more trouble I have believing you."

"Believe me or not, I'm telling you that she won't talk about that at all. I'm not being a crafty lawyer. This is the absolute truth. But she did talk about you. She said it meant a lot to her that you showed up at the arraignment and came to try to speak to her at the jail."

"But she acted like she hates me! She told me to go away!"

"Yes, that's what she wants."

"Well, the trial isn't for a couple of months. Do you think she'll change her mind? Do you think she really wants me to leave her alone? Am I supposed to do that? Is that your advice to her?"

He said, "I'm not sure."

FOUR

Sandhill Crane

Antigone canadensis. Cranes symbolize luck but also
retribution and are often used as a metaphor for witnessing crimes
and bringing culprits to justice. Large water birds, they are long-
lived, the oldest on record first banded in Florida in 1982, then
found in Wisconsin in 2019. Cranes are famed for the leaping,
dipping energy of their courtship dances. The naturalist Aldo
Leopold wrote of their "nobility, won in the march of aeons," and
indeed, a sandhill crane fossil found in Florida was dated at 2.5
million years old. The genus name is shared with the title character
of the play by Sophocles about a brave, loyal, doomed young woman.

I ALWAYS THOUGHT I HAD A VOCATION FOR TRUE CRIME—WRITING
about it, that is, not living it. When you've had a lucky life,
with no significant bad fortune inside or outside the fence, it's
tempting to think you could ace something big and dangerous,
no problem. Now it was freaky to think of meeting people like
no rep from Prada or Burberry ever was.

I knew fuck all about the dark side.

Looking back, I would rather spend eighteen months writing personality profiles of every plumber in the city of Chicago
than ever again talk to the family of a murder victim. The reason most crime stories are about the murderer is not just because

the personality of someone who does wrong is more fascinating
than the mind of someone who gets done wrong (which is almost everyone, at some point, to a greater or lesser degree). It's
because the victim of a crime is usually innocent, sometimes
unbearably innocent. Everything is sad.

When I called Emil Gardener's house, a woman answered
who identified herself as Elizabeth Doll.

I told her what I was doing. She said, "Oh dear."

Gathering my courage, I asked to speak to Erica Doll Gardener. She apologized. "My aunt is literally dying. She's in a coma.
She couldn't talk to you if she wanted to."

"You know about the woman accused of killing Mr. Gardener."

"I do know. And Aunt Erica did too. My aunt was sick even
when she was a young woman. She was so sad that she couldn't
have children. But she really loved Emil. He really loved her
too. Can you make sure that you say that?"

"I will," I told her. I wanted to weep. "I'm sorry for your
loss and her loss. Is there someone you'd prefer me to talk to
instead of you?"

"Oh no! I'm fine. With them, you know how it is when you
love someone, you want him to be happy."

"Not so much as that," I said, without taking time to think,
and immediately repented it.

"He was devoted to Erica in other ways. He read to her every night, for almost forty years. They went to church together
every Sunday, even when Erica was in her wheelchair."

"Can I mention that?"

"Yes, of course you can. I don't blame you, you know, Miss . . . ?"

"Reenie. Reenie Bigelow."

"Reenie, I don't really blame you. I know you're only doing your job. Do you think that woman really killed Emil?"

"It seems the police are pretty sure. But there are so many
questions. The dates don't line up very well. And no one knows

how they died really, except probably some kind of poison or toxin." I asked then, "Can you tell me about Emil?"

He was apparently just like another grandfather to those nieces and nephews, so generous at Christmas that they thought of him as the second Santa Claus. He had no family of his own, an only child whose parents died in their middle years. His wife's family was as dear to him as if they were his own. The Gardeners paid for college for four nieces and a nephew.

"Uncle Em is why I'm a nurse now, and lucky thing, because I can look after Erica." She said then, "Gosh, it probably won't be long now, and she'll be with Emil."

"So she was a believer?"

"She was a churchgoer. I suppose none of us really knows about what happens after we die. That's what you take on faith, right?" I murmured something that I hoped sounded like assent. Elizabeth Doll added, "My mom and my aunts will pray for that young woman as well. Her family must be crushed."

"Thank you," I said and then got flustered, because I wasn't the one needing the prayers, although I'd take them if they were offered. She asked if I needed anything else. Ivy had instructed me to arrange for photos of the survivors, but there was no way I was going to further intrude on these people. Just a photo of the couple, I said, that the magazine could copy. The niece agreed, saying there was a lovely clear picture of the two of them at a summer picnic.

"You know, Erica would want you to find out what really happened. She was a very smart woman. She wanted to be a lawyer but she was the oldest, so she wound up in the dairy business. Wanting to help was in her nature. My brother and my aunts and I, we think it's almost a blessing that Aunt Erica is not aware of all this." She apparently had been in and out of consciousness for months, and no one knew if she understood that Emil was dead—although she sometimes asked for him.

When I finished talking to the niece, I felt as filthy as if I'd been left overnight in an old deep fryer. I wanted to call her back and tell her that I was not the mercenary she probably imagined me to be.

So it was almost gratifying by contrast when Cary Church's wife, Suzanne, barely let me finish saying my name before she ripped me a new asshole.

"I want to say I can't believe your gall but of course, I can. You're a vampire so I shouldn't expect any kind of moral behavior from you . . ." I counted backward from ten, reminding myself that this was a newly bereaved mother of two who'd suffered an additional shock in addition to the death.

"I'm not trying to hurt you, Suzanne. This is something that already happened and I can't change that."

"But you can squeeze it and shape it until it sounds like Cary deserved to die . . ."

"I would never do that. In fact, your perspective on Cary will help people see that there was another side of him . . ."

"What do you mean, 'another side of him'?" she snapped.

"Another side of his character, as a husband, not just as a guy who paid Felicity Wild for . . . companionship."

"There's no proof that he did that," Suzanne Church said. "Just because you can only see the worst, because you're a bottom-dwelling slug . . ."

"Wait! Are you suggesting that he did not have a paying friendship with Felicity Wild? Why else would he take out a two-million-dollar life insurance policy with her as the beneficiary?" Something snapped in me then, and I said, "Cary's death is horrible for your family and a terrible injustice. But I don't see how not writing about it would benefit anybody."

She said then, "I hope the same thing happens to you."

"Being written about . . ."

"No, having your husband murdered."

If this was how Suzanne Church fought, no wonder they were separated. I bit the tongue of my wicked mind on that thought. She was misplacing her anger, that was all, and it was to be expected. "I don't think you mean that. You would never want someone else to have to live with this."

"I would though. I hope your husband dies horribly. Then you'll think of what you put us through."

"Respectfully, the murderer put you through this. And Cary put you through this. Not me." I added, "You can't blame other people for wanting to know how such a strange, awful thing happened."

In the pause that intervened, I could all but hear her gathering her thoughts for the next assault. "Is that what you think, that you're so wise and brave that you'll be able to work out the truth and share it? Or are you just licking your chops to be able to dine out on our grief?"

"Do you want to keep any of this off the record? Like the part where you said you hope someone kills my husband?" I asked her then. That was nasty; I didn't intend to quote her.

"I never said anything like that," she told me. "If you write that down, who do you think people will believe, me or the murderer's buddy pal?"

She hung up. I hung up.

Then, to my horror, she called back. I considered not answering, but I did.

"Why couldn't you even have the decency to come here and look me in the face as you tried to destroy my life?" she said.

"I would be happy to come and see you," I said, and thought, *About as happy as I would be to do bowel surgery on myself in the woods with a stick.*

"You should. I would kick your fat face in."

"Then I should stay right where I am," I said. "Honestly, I feel terrible for you and your children. I am writing this because

I should, but it's not fun. When I think of the ways it involves me too, it makes me sick to my stomach."

Until now, I'd never really grappled with how fragile I would feel if someone else was writing about my biggest heartbreak. I didn't even want to write about that myself. I had the righteous dread of hipster-style first-person "participatory" journalism. Yet, what other choice did I have but to look in the mirror? Would it not have been disingenuous otherwise?

Suzanne Church was quiet for so long I believed that she'd hung up again. Finally, she said softly, "I'm sorry. You're right. This isn't your fault. I'm so angry at Cary but there's no one else except Cary I would tell. I want him to comfort me. I wish we stayed together. Maybe it was partly my fault that he went to that woman."

"No. Don't think that."

"I could have been a better wife."

"I'm sure that you were a fine wife. Who knows why people do the things they do? It certainly wasn't any failure on your part." Then I asked the big question. "You really didn't know anything about this, huh? Not the fact of the woman or the money or any of that."

"I found out when he died. He wasn't around as much as he should have been. I told him I felt like a single mom. But he would ask me, what did I want him to do? I wanted to be with the kids until they were a little older, so he was doing consulting along with teaching and, I guess, this other stuff too." Eventually, Cary came home from some supposed late-night consulting gig and Suzanne confronted him with her suspicions. He admitted everything. She threw him out.

"Maybe it's better in the end that you didn't know."

"It's more than the grief. I feel like a complete fool," she said. She had nightmares of walking into Cary's funeral with her little boys, and everyone started to laugh at her and make kissy noises.

When we ended the conversation, I was exhausted. It was

another one of those situations you think happen only in novels, but here I was in real life, panting and sweating as if I'd run a 10K with a hangover. My T-shirt was soaked through. My cheeks felt as though the skin was scalded. I wanted to tell Nell that it really wasn't worth it. I wanted to run back into the sweet embrace of comparing the merits of scarves cut from silk satin, charmeuse, twill and georgette, or the occasional polyester blend—strictly utilitarian for travel.

If this was what big-league pitchers of writing routinely experienced, I was meant for right field.

Still, I kept trying all the keys I could think of to open the door of Felicity's life after college. Unusual for people of our generation, she didn't have much of a social media presence, except for her own beautiful photos of birds that she sometimes posted on Instagram. I didn't do much in that realm either. Ivy insisted on videos about how to tie a scarf like Mary Berry. I gave Marcus the props, but an intern did the actual tapings. Looping an elaborate scarf knot was for me akin to whipping up a Salzburger soufflé— forget about it. Yet one more way I was ill-suited to my job.

Maybe Nell was right about everything. Maybe this story was just an exercise in voyeurism for well-heeled women readers with secret fantasies about the power to parlay a honeypot into a pot of gold.

If I were Felicity, would I talk to me?

In the true crime podcasts my dorm buddies and I listened to at midnight—Columbia, Missouri, being no more a glitter kingdom of urban nightlife than Sheboygan had been—there were always stories beneath the stories. Women make up most of the audience for true crime podcasts and books, maybe because they have more to fear. My interest wasn't so much in what people did as who they were. In my internship days, I went for what I thought of as the "beforemath," as opposed to the "aftermath."

I thought I knew all about Felicity's beforemath, but clearly

I did not. Her secrets, and the real story, would be in that be-foremath. Even if Felicity was incontrovertibly guilty, there would be a story for me to write—the story of her broken life and my broken heart.

Later that day, for the third time in twenty-four hours, I set out on the same long drive.

For once, I didn't listen to a book.

Instead, I opened the book of the past.

When we were kids, even the stoners and stumblers and art hags and assholes adored Felicity, because she was as noticing and kind to them as she was to the alphas. Was she concealing her meretricious character, handing out smiles, favors, advice, homework help like flowers from a basket? Why would she bother? Life for her would have been easy enough in any case. She hardly needed all that extra goodwill.

So, the corollary question was why Felicity, with so many gifts, didn't have one truly intimate friend? I had other friends, among them girls like bold Chassy Reingold, sweet Cassandra Sullivan, and the gorgeous and ultimately loathsome bitch Molly Boone, who were, if not first-tier females, then definite contend-ers. Felicity did not. Anointed by proximity, I was what passed for a boon companion. It gave me status. It gave me pause.

Not so very long ago, Felicity and I did things like going ice skating on the pond in Bachelor's Woods in the soul-shriveling cold of a purple evening in Sheboygan, Wisconsin, bratwurst capital of the world. One summer day, sweating, swearing, crawling on my stomach over sharp grass quivering with black flies, I helped Felicity drag her camera equipment as we edged closer to the water at Horicon Marsh so she could photograph a majestic sandhill crane and her awkward brown chicks for her senior project in biology and art. I did her updo for the prom. I ate meatloaf at her house, and she ate macaroni-and-cheese cas-serole at mine. She taught me how to swing dance.

She would never tell a lie, not even the small social kind that could be banished by the five-year test (which is, will this even matter in five years?).

One morning in our junior year, just before the organic chem midterm, she gave Marty Mazzoli her meticulous notes. A good student, Marty was on the verge of failing, mostly because he had to work weeknights unloading trucks since his dad was not only a deadbeat but a mean drunk.

When Mr. Styles caught her out, Felicity immediately confessed. Styles was so moved by her charity and honesty that he allowed Marty to do a project to replace the final in the knowledge that Felicity would tutor him through it. They started on a Sunday afternoon. It took them all night. Next morning, when I met Marty coming out of the Wilds' mansion-house "rectory," I heard him say, "That was the nicest thing anybody ever did for me." And he went in to kiss Felicity on the cheek, but she stiff-armed him, patting his shoulder. Marty was embarrassed; he was a cute guy and probably unaccustomed to girls resisting his moves, especially moves as mild and sweet as this one was.

He said, "I didn't mean . . ."

And Felicity replied, "I know. It's okay. I didn't either."

Something about that moment framed it as the first time I ever witnessed anything that made me wonder if Felicity liked boys at all. But it was far from the first time I witnessed Felicity in benefactor mode.

Another occasion had always stayed with me, possibly because of the appalling viciousness of most high school girls. It was at the homecoming dance, where every other girl affected nonchalance in Stella McCartney knockoff slip-sheaths, but Felicity rocked a voluminous tulle princess dress, petal pink, like a birthday cake in the shape of a doll. She wore long black gloves and a cameo on a black ribbon at her throat, all things she'd found at little resale shops in rich burbs like Kohler and Mequon. About an hour after she was crowned the queen, I saw her throw on a long black opera cape, clearly another thrift-shop find.

I called to her, "Felicity! Where are you off to?" Some too-sweet party, I thought, with college kids.

"Home," she said.

"It's nine thirty!" I pointed out. "You're the homecoming queen!"

"My work here is done," she said, twirling that cape in a sort of jokey-regal way, then cutting her eyes at her date, soccer jock Ben Landry. Ben was dancing with Laura Dell-Mason, who'd been in love with him since sixth grade. A bright, kind girl, she was pretty but so painfully shy that no one really noticed her—except, unfortunately, to call her Laura Dalmatian.

On the day Felicity got nabbed for helping Marty Mazzoli, we stopped for coffee on the way home from school. It was stupidly cold, and I again thanked the universe for my coat and my grandmother. I would have that coat all my life. Suddenly, Felicity said, "Reenie, you look like Freya. You look like Freya, if she had freckles."

"Who's that?"

"The Norse goddess of the dead. She was beautiful, with this snow-white skin and a coat made from hawk feathers, driving her chariot pulled by cats."

"Must have been a lot of cats," I said.

"She would lend her magic coat to other gods to protect them in battle. She was really kind, but still, she was the goddess of the dead. So if you had a dream about her, it would be, uh-oh, somebody's done for."

"Somebody's done for," Felicity had said. She'd said that more than once.

It was she who was the fair one, draping her magical coat over those in need—but still the goddess of the dead.

FIVE

Northern Cardinal

Cardinalis cardinalis. Medium-sized red songbirds, cardinals are named after Roman Catholic bishops because the color of the robes those priests wear is very like the bird's plumage. Males are intensely territorial, whistling from a high perch to warn others off their patch. A male cardinal may even mistake his own image on a shiny surface for an invading male and relentlessly fight that reflection. Admired backyard birds, cardinals go bald in late summer to make way for new feathers. Their lifespan is variable, from three to fifteen years. In Native American traditional images and lore, cardinals often symbolize monogamy.

A COUPLE OF DAYS LATER, I STARED AT THE LIST OF NAMES OF FE-licity's purported clients given to me by my friend Ross, starting with the third name only because he lived in Crystal Creek, just south of Sheboygan, and he was a professor, still on winter break, so I might catch him at home.

There was no way that any of these men would happily agree to talk to me. A few times, I'd spent weeks campaigning to snare a few tense minutes with neurotic designers. I sent them fruit and flowers and antique laces, everything except a camel, cajoling them to permit the attention they actually craved but must pretend to despise. Felicity's amours had no incentive at all to give me time. They would not be swayed by books or blooms. So I decided on a direct frontal assault.

On a clear but frigid morning, I located the home of Finn and Briony Vogel, parents to Louis, Levi, and Lars. Theirs was one of those mid-twentieth-century raised ranchers made over into craftsman houses with the addition of a covered porch and a gable, houses my dad hated not because they were bad houses but because they were good houses with good bones. As the lady once wrote, they had stood for seventy years and might stand for seventy more, for about a third of the cost of one of the baby mansions his company put up. The facade was a creamy beige with dark green shutters and a dark red door. I watched as the garage door peeled up and Briony left with tots in tow. Fifteen minutes later, time I used to listen to Finn Vogel's remarks during a radio interview about why scientific knowledge was not always the best guide for public health policy, I knocked on that red door for about five minutes, and I was just turning away when that door swung open and a man stood there. Like Roman, he was intimidatingly good-looking, surfer-boy handsome, his hair shower wet, his toned arms in a crisp white shirt with the cuffs rolled to the elbows.

I had not expected a cute younger guy. What had I expected? Ross's words, *I don't have to pay for it,* bannered across my brain. This story got more curious by the moment.

"Can I help you," he said, not a question.

"I'm looking for Finn Vogel?"

"You found him." He looked me over, head to toe, and leaned into the doorframe.

Though his hair was feathered and his body gym trim, his diction came from a generation decades past. When this young man spoke, I could hear my grandfather, my mother's dad, telling me stories about his college years when he worked summers as a roughneck for the last of the great train-show carnivals, rolling and rattling through the night from one small rural town to the next, playing poker with a woman and her husband who were each only three feet tall. This guy had an accent too. He was . . . maybe Canadian. Or something.

"If you have a few minutes, I need to talk to you."

"Honey," this man said. Honey? Honey? Who did he think he was? "I am a card-carrying member of the Republican Party in good standing, and I've got all the magazine subscriptions and life insurance a man could ever need. So can you tell me what brings you here today?"

I fumbled with my bag as I extracted my business card, culminating in a messy drop that sent my lipstick, pens, comb, and my carefully wrapped cheese-and-pickle sandwich tumbling into the shrub next to his steps. I lunged to recover them and nearly slipped on a patch of black ice, but finally recovered my balance and my card.

"I'm Felicity Wild, from *Fuchsia* magazine," I said.

"You're not Felicity Wild."

Great opening! "Yes, you're right, I'm not," I said. "I'm Reenie Bigelow from *Fuchsia* magazine. Felicity Wild is . . . I want to talk to you about Felicity Wild. For a story that I'm doing."

"Who's Felicity Wild?"

I stared at him, raising my eyebrows.

"Okay, fine. Well, I'm not going to talk to you about Felicity Wild."

"You had a relationship with Felicity . . ."

The man huffed at the word *relationship*, drawing in his chin as if I'd slapped him. "What relationship? That's my own business."

"Maybe it was once, but what if you're called to testify by the prosecution in her murder trial?" I could see from the chase of expressions across his face that he had already been contacted. "And they would just drill down on why you were a client, even though you have a beautiful wife and three little children, and how much you spent on Felicity, and if you ever felt threatened by her, and since mine is going to be an in-depth story, really mostly about Felicity, not as much about what she did for a living, this is really going to be your only chance to share your side of this, whatever that is, to get it right."

"Okay," he said.

It always worked. It worked like a key in a lock, the your-side-of-the-story thing, along with the your-take-on-all-this thing. It was like a magic trick.

"Could I come in?"

Finn Vogel looked me up and down again. I tried to keep my face neutral. I added, "It's ten degrees out here."

Finally, he moved to one side, sweeping his arm in another courtly gesture, and I stepped into the foyer. We sat down by a fireplace bigger than my bed. He brought me some very good coffee. I brought out my little digital tape recorder; the old this-is-for-your-own-protection-from-any-mistakes thing worked as well as the your-side-of-the-story thing. Finn Vogel sighed gustily, the sound of chickens coming home to roost.

"My wife is taking our children to a kids' literature class she teaches with the other mothers. This never should have happened," he began.

You can say that again, I wanted to add. Instead, I only nodded, which a person could interpret as anything he wanted, including understanding. As I recalled, people can't bear silence for long,

"Felicity, she called me that day," Finn said. "I'm not a criminal lawyer but most people, even very bright people, think this is all the same. I guess she thought that too. She told me an old man who was her guest had died of a heart attack and she was afraid and what should she do? I told her to call the police. But she said her mother was coming over, and I assumed that she didn't want her mother to know . . . what she did."

"So you didn't go to her place."

"It was right after Christmas. My whole house was filled with family, my brothers and their kids. My grandparents were here from Amsterdam. I had not seen them in years. I couldn't just walk out of our party and drive an hour. I repeated to her, call the police. But she just started to cry and said that was not a possibility for her." He sighed again. I almost felt sorry for him, although he was a de facto piece of shit, philander, and (I could hear my father's voice) a Republican on top of that. I definitely felt sorry for his wife and little boys; if his marriage had been withering, now it would turn to dust. He could end up alone, which he deserved, except for the fact of the children, who were only innocent.

"Your kids are sweet," I said, gesturing at one of the silver-framed photos on the piano.

"They are terrific. They are scamps," he said. "I wonder if girls are gentler. I will never have a little girl now."

I didn't know if this regret stemmed from a decision not to have more children or the presumptive end of the marriage. Of course, there was no guarantee that he wouldn't have another family, given how forgiving women seemed to be of men and their pasts.

"How did you feel when you found out that he didn't really die of a heart attack?"

"Well, that wasn't for quite a long time," said Finn. "At first, I just felt sorry for her, to have somebody die in her house. Her life was so lonely."

Ugh, I thought. All it took was a death at a very inconvenient moment for Finn Vogel to even consider how lonely Felicity's life would have been. Did he think about the context of her life otherwise, at all? Did you think about what your dentist was doing at a given moment? At that same time, I considered

the timeline: It seemed as though this happened while Felicity
was supposedly at her parents' house, but Finn Vogel had just
put Felicity at the scene of the murder.

"How do you know that she was in her apartment?"

"I didn't really. I didn't even recognize her cell phone number because she never called me . . ."

Even before he completed the sentence, I completed it for
him: *for obvious reasons* . . . The reasons being because if she existed at all, she was supposed to exist in a shadow world from
which she popped up at his convenience. Then, against my will,
I felt a terrible pang for her too, so frightened and friendless on
the darkest night, despite what she'd done, if she had done it,
even more so if she had not, knowing as she did that it would be
so much harder to maintain her innocence. After all, she was a
person who had fallen so far and would now need to prove she
had not fallen still further. I wrote that down.

"Are you quoting me?" Finn asked. "You should have said
that."

"What did you think I was doing?"

"I don't know, background for a magazine story."

"Well, I do intend . . . I do want to quote you on this, not
on anything salacious, Mr. Vogel, but as you know, this could
all come out in court anyhow . . ."

"Well, there are degrees. An obscure trial versus a national
magazine."

"The trial is more notorious than the magazine at this point.
It's captured a lot of attention. One of the reporters I met at the
arraignment was from Quebec," I told him.

"Then I want to review the quotes before you use any of
them."

"You know I can't do that. Maybe you don't know, but that's
not how it works. You can review the quotes for accuracy if you

want, but I'm not going to change the substance." I went on, "Frankly, Mr. Vogel, the cat is out of the bag at this point. The only thing you can really do is tell your side of it."

And yet again, it worked, even on a lawyer, like peanut butter and jelly.

"Well, I thought this man had died accidentally. That wasn't Felicity's fault. The most she could be charged with was not reporting a death, not a felony, not really even a crime, moving or concealing a dead body, yes, a crime, but she might not even have been charged, her motive being the motive of fearfulness . . ." Vogel's English was getting more and more formal; that is, it was deteriorating. "But then, after he was found and the other murder, ah, death, occurred, her problems were snowballing . . ." He spoke about the legal implications of motive, how even killing someone by accident is not a crime in most jurisdictions unless negligence is involved, but of all the motives, money was the worst one.

I asked for more coffee, to buy time. Vogel kept consulting his watch. There was no *oh, honey, I'm a sexy conservative* anymore . . . he was scared. His wife evidently would be due home soon.

"I only have a few more questions," I reassured him, then asked how he and Felicity got started and more importantly, why.

"Oh, I met her at this place where there were nude dancers and these sorts of hostesses, where I went with men I knew."

That place was, of course, Ophelia. What was up with men? *What is the allure*, I wanted to shout at him, *and why do you think it's okay?*

But then he went on, "It wasn't just sex." Of course it wasn't, and there it was again. If I had a nickel for every time a guy said that, as well . . . "She was different. She was beautiful but also just so very smart and . . . an active listener." He explained what he meant. In a marriage, no matter how much love is there,

there are also other matters of consequence: money, children, family members, careers, tension, anxiety, boredom. The love that first combusted flickered, sank. You were lovers, yes, still, but also partners, relatives, best friends. That was if you were lucky, and Finn said he had been lucky with Briony.

But with Felicity, the focus was on him. She relaxed him. She asked questions. She even offered insights, whatever thorny issue was at hand for him in the context of his work environment, like a professor's repeated refusal to see that unwanted flirting was just as serious when the instructor was a woman; she asked how he was sleeping; she bought his favorite tea; she taught him to tie a double Windsor knot, which made him the envy of his colleagues.

I might have wanted to screech, but I moderated my voice and said, "What you're telling me is like some cliché from an old movie, like the whore with the heart of gold . . . who understands when the wife is too busy . . ."

"It's not just that. You know, writing is your gift. It's your talent. Her talent was men."

"How long did this go on, with her?"

"Six months? Eight months? I can't remember exactly. It was summer at the beginning."

As I left the house, Finn Vogel abruptly switched off all the Christmas lights, as well as all the lights inside. How long after the holidays did people leave those decorations up, anyhow? I always thought it was kind of sinister, seeing houses where Rudolph was still prancing across the lawn in February. Finn Vogel didn't need his lights on; it was still daylight, a gloomy daylight— hell is murky—but it reminded me of the way little kids cover their own eyes and then think you can't see them. Once again, I began to tell myself how grateful I was that I had decided never to have children. For the first time, however, I wasn't sure that I was telling myself the truth. Whether or not I ever had children,

I suddenly realized I wanted to love someone enough to mingle our genes.

The next guy on Ross's list was, I recalled, the shortstop, an avid athlete. I'd looked him up on his Facebook. With his mop of still-thick silvered red hair and sprinkling of freckles, he could have played Huck Finn grown up. Pregnant wife named Allegra. Golden retriever named Forbes. His legend proclaimed, THERE IS A LOT OF LIFE IN ECONOMICS AND A LOT OF ECONOMICS IN LIFE. A live wire!

He answered his phone, and I told him my business. "It's about a woman who's charged with murder who was an escort. I think you knew her in that context."

"This is a mistake. I have no idea who this woman is. I never met her. How did you get my name?"

I explained that I asked around, and the information came from another instructor at the university. I couldn't say who it was because I'd made a promise.

"Well, that's the rumor mill for you. People start to believe things that aren't true. Felicity Wild must have a grudge against me because otherwise why would she betray me?"

"Wait, wait. Let's start over. I never said her name, but you do know her name? If you've never met her, how could she betray you?"

"I'm not going to dignify this," the guy said, and the phone went dead.

Call back, I told myself. *Call back if you have even one teaspoonful of guts.* I called back.

"Don't call here again!" he yelled. "This is considered harassment! I could sue you for this!"

"Just settle down a moment. We can speak off the record."

"Listen, you dumb bitch! If you call back again, the next call you get will be from my lawyer."

"I know this is upsetting. I'm not going to necessarily write about you in specific. I won't say anything you don't want me to say. I'm just trying to understand what people are saying about this. People you know."

"If I hear about this from any people I know, there will be consequences!"

He hung up.

Did I need permission to recount this exchange? Would it be nasty to do that, for no good reason? On the other hand, one way to avoid being asked about patronizing an escort would be to not do it. Why did people think that it was not their own fault that what they did caused their public humiliation but was the fault of the press for reporting it?

Needing a palate cleanser, I called Felicity's fifth-grade teacher, who'd also been my fifth-grade teacher.

"She was very sweet and very smart, always the little helper," said Fatima Sharma, who promptly reminded me that I no longer needed to call her "Ms. Sharma." She said, "I had to push her out the door to go home after school." To Ms. Sharma, this fact probably went to Felicity's avid and giving nature, but I made a note to myself: What did it really mean when a ten-year-old little girl didn't want to go home? Her track coach told me that there might have been athletes who had more natural ability, but Felicity anchored her team all the way to state in the two-hundred-meter relay because of her zeal to win. Her coach from the National Science Bee, who was out of the country until March, wrote in an email, **I got this news in Turkey! We are so very shocked and concerned. Did you know that Ruth Wild has resigned? Have you spoken to her?**

I was almost grateful that I couldn't find Ruth to ask her about the supernova created by the collapse of her shining-star child.

SIX

Mute Swan

Cygnus olor. The mute swan, which, unlike the trumpeter swan, has no voice, is a large and very strong bird, five feet long, weighing twenty-five pounds or more, with a wingspread of seven feet. The swan's elegant appearance has inspired ballets and fairy tales, but their voracious appetite for grasses, insects, and tadpoles can disrupt local ecosystems, and they can be very aggressive, even dangerous, to other animals, including humans. The mute swan is often seen as a symbol of love and commitment because they mate for life.

MY PHONE RANG AT 4:49 A.M. IT WAS STILL SO DARK THAT I couldn't even see the window. My first panicked thought went to my parents or grandparents. But then I remembered that I was in my parents' house.

"Reenie?"

It was my editor.

"Ivy?"

"Yes, hi."

"Are you okay?" I said. The air seemed too thin to breathe.

"Why?"

"Because it's not quite five in the morning, Ivy. Are you taking this extreme-lark thing too seriously?"

"No, I was just lounging here making some notes and I got

to thinking . . ." She was lounging among the clouds, or at this hour, the stars, in her apartment-mansion. Even though the *Fuchsia* building was not tall, it was tall enough, and so beautifully situated on the shore that it felt open to the heavens. It would never have occurred to Ivy that this was not quite the right time to call me. After all, she'd thought of it, and whatever was on Ivy's mind came straight out of her mouth—in part because she'd been thinking about it for days and assumed that she had telepathed it to whomever she would eventually tell. "Do you think we should start a sex column?"

"You want to discuss this now, at this moment?"

"I don't really want to discuss it in depth, but what's your quick take?"

"My quick take is that it's five in the morning, Ivy! I was lying here too, but sleeping."

"It's five in the morning where you are?"

"I'm in Wisconsin."

"Oh." Ivy would not have considered the fact that Wisconsin was in the same time zone. She reminded me of that old magazine cover that portrayed the way New Yorkers thought of the rest of the country. Though he was not crass about it, she did not really consider Chicago part of the Midwest that F. Scott Fitzgerald called that "vast obscurity beyond the city, where the dark fields of the republic rolled on under the night."

How could I frame my honest rejoinder to Ivy's question without long-distance insulting her?

"Give me a moment to gather my thoughts," I said. "I'll call you right back."

"Really?" said Ivy.

"Hell is murky," I told her. "I'm referring to the time of day."

"Good good," said Ivy. I thought I'd caught her out. But no one caught Ivy Torres out. "Screw your courage to the sticking place, Lady MacBeth."

I dragged myself to the bathroom and brushed my teeth, which always had a bracing mental effect on me. I tried to contemplate what I would say to discourage Ivy. *Fuchsia* wasn't "that kind" of women's publication, which is to say, a monthly manual for a geisha who daylighted as a stockbroker but really wanted only to pleasure her man. We did stories about the wage gap, teen pregnancy, and mentorship, and, in fact, sometimes features about sex—about women's medicine, sexual health, and sexual dysfunction, not about thirteen ways to give a blow job.

The fact that Ivy had called me instead of someone else was shorthand for her nascent desire to designate me as the presumptive sex columnist . . . and for the second time in a week, I found myself ready to draw a line in the sand. Not only did I believe that the whole premise could be borderline misogynistic—more about men's happiness than women's, about binding that big lug to you with bedroom tricks—but I just wasn't qualified. I didn't really care. While Ivy didn't know this—nobody knew this—I liked sex well enough but I had not yet met the person who could inspire me to feel like one of my college quad-mates who loved sex so much that she told me she was surprised people could think about anything else.

Let Marcus do it.

A man writing for women about their sex lives could either be a great big blockbuster or a great big black eye for *Fuchsia*. Either one would do the magazine good, with great big gossip.

I again pictured Ivy next to her floor-to-ceiling bedroom window, ten feet wide framed in golden lights and tiny blue mirrors. I'd been at her place once, for the holiday party last year. It looked like an ad for *Coastal Style*, everything big and blue and gold and tapestried . . . and immaculate, despite the fact that Ivy had three little boys, aged two, four, and seven. Her sons were actually IVF triplets from a single egg hatch or . . . batch or whatever you called it. I knew this because once, in a

burst of intimacy so rare I don't think I ever summoned a response, Ivy confided, "We didn't want to do the multiples thing
to them, or to ourselves."

Ivy's children were not very well-behaved. On the same day
she told me about their triplet-dom, she also said, "My children
are wild beasts. The only windows that open in our flat are ten
feet off the ground and they need two keys to open them that
we keep in two different safes the way other people keep guns."
Ivy's husband, Telly, was a medical researcher who invented a
widget that revolutionized the accuracy of laser eye surgery.
Neither of them had to work, but Ivy loved to work, so she did.
Her husband stayed home with the children.

I'd sneaked into Ivy's closet for the briefest moment during
our annual holiday party and found it as intimidating as a cyclo-
tron lab. There were the expected high and low rods, drawers,
and shoe cupboards, but also something truly eerie: a photograph
of every piece of clothing tagged with smaller sticky-backed
photos of relevant accessories. This was Ivy's private world and
the importance within it of my so-called specialty was like a
hand around my throat.

I also felt even more keenly the gap between us, six years of
life and six million degrees of privilege.

I was fashionable by fraud. I wore only variations on white—
cream, bone, stone, porcelain, fog, parchment, pearl, seashell—
and I wore the same twenty articles of clothing over and over in
different configurations. My wardrobe included one great pair
of white crepe Alice + Olivia pants, one Khaite Noma midi
dress, one Valentino blazer. People thought it was on purpose.
All my work clothes came from this Lake Forest resale store
called Such Sweet Sorrow (as in parting is such sweet sorrow, as
in *Romeo and Juliet*). Slim socialites went there to consign their
Bottega Veneta boots. I loved the fact that it had formerly been
a bank. I told myself I was traveling light, like a real writer liv-

ing on cheese and whiskey on the Rive Gauche in 1940. I kept my civilian clothes in flat boxes under the bed in my little River North aerie.

I loved my apartment, one partitioned room in a converted warehouse, with a massive floor-to-ceiling steel-gridded window and a network of pipes far overhead. The pipes were at least shiny, though they occasionally belched out terrifying clatters and sighs. The only walls enclosed the bathroom, and they were about eight feet tall, so, no matter how desperate my need, I couldn't use the toilet when anyone else was there. My parents thought that the brutally minimalist furnishings were totemic rather than systemic, that having two chairs instead of four at my aluminum kitchen table was a statement, and it was a statement: the statement was that I couldn't afford four chairs. The big black rag rug with red ribbons woven throughout was a discard from a previous resident, as was my black velvet couch.

It was mine. My name and mine alone was on the mortgage.

I already missed it. I missed tucking it in and saying goodbye every morning. I missed the sweet orange glow when the timer turned the lights on at six each night. I hated to think of anyone sleeping or peeing or having sex or even breathing in my small pristine home. But to completely give myself to this investigation, there was no practical purpose to shuttling back and forth to Madison and Sheboygan from Chicago. I decided to sublet it, preferably to someone who would pay the full tariff, my mortgage plus more, but only use it one or two nights a week. I would be a squatter at my sister's squalid digs, a ramshackle house that looked like the opening scenes of a horror movie, with her three silent roommates, whom my dad called Flora, Fauna, and Merriweather. There was a spare room, albeit with no electricity or heat, where Nell and her silent crew stored boxes. They could put their boxes in that murder basement of theirs, which was at least pretty clean. For a grad student, money was more useful than space.

I remembered the last time I'd been there, to pack up.

Although it turned out to be a more important day, at the outset I thought that my biggest decision would be whether to put my white clothes or my normal clothes in storage. I decided on a little of both, to alternate between dressed and dressed up. (This was something only I would think, despite everything else at stake . . . but I still couldn't forget the dark eyes of Felicity's lawyer, whose photos I gazed at online to a degree that was embarrassing.)

The next time I saw him, I wanted to look good, although he was probably married to his college sweetheart, who was probably a neurosurgeon. There was no mention of his personal life online, which would make sense given the kind of people he had to work for every day. (As my mother reminded me when this all began, most people charged with crimes had done what the police said they did, and *guilty* or *innocent* could be terms for whose story held up best.)

I put an ad on Big Site and my place was sublet within two hours, at a third more than I was paying and with the specification that I was promising four months but could redact that promise with one week's notice if I had to. I drew up a legal document I printed off from a website. I put my few bins of belongings in the storage cage in the building basement, then I packed my car and drove away.

Was all this going to be worth it?

I was still being paid the same thing I'd had two years before when I started working for *Fuchsia*. I didn't know anyone who'd ever received a raise, although perhaps they were sworn to secrecy in case the idea caught on. Writing was supposed to be one of those things you did for love, like being a priest or a ballerina, that required a lot of training in order to make very little money.

Now, however, well before I had proven that I could do anything new, before I had written a single word, was not the time to ask Ivy for a raise.

I pulled the car over. I called Ivy.

I swear she picked up before the ring finished.

I said, "Ivy, we should be having this conversation in person, and I'm sorry that we're not. I need to run something past you. I wouldn't bother you unless it was important . . ."

She exhaled noisily. "I'm waiting, Reenie." A sigh and a peevish first-name dump. Not good. But fortune favors the brave.

"Are you aware that I'm still making the same thing I did when I started?"

"No," Ivy said. "What do you make?"

She didn't know. Well, I wasn't going to tell her. "It is just that I can't survive on it."

"You're asking for a raise?"

I had the impression that no one had ever before used the R-word with Ivy.

I had to swallow hard before I replied. "Just consider it. Maybe, after this story, I can give you more help. I could be more like a writing editor. Steer new projects. Come up with fresh perspectives. Write a column. If you just think it over . . ."

"Don't need to," said Ivy. "Okay. What were you thinking?"

I hadn't been thinking beyond the first sentence. I said, "I'll send you a proposal with a figure."

Ivy said, "Reenie, you know it's never been the case that I didn't think you were capable of writing bigger features. I didn't think you wanted to."

"I always wanted to write bigger stories."

"Why didn't you tell me? Why didn't you ask?"

"I thought you would fire me. I thought that you hired me to be a lightweight, and, Ivy, I don't mind being a lightweight, it's a lot of fun, but it's not all I want to do."

"I understand."

"Well, thank you, Ivy."

I pulled the car over near the first coffee shop I saw and wrote to her proposing a pay raise and a figure for the expenses I would need in coming months, making it clear that the expense figure could get bigger. I was prepared to cry "Psych!" if she got annoyed, but she wrote back right away asking me to keep a running record and copy every receipt that I could. She would put some funds in my next check backdated to January 1. Further, she said, I should make notes about possible longer stories to do when I was back in the office full-time.

Even with an expense account, I made nowhere near what minor-league reporters in New York made, but so far, so good. This was great, great for me, great for my résumé, a giant leap for womankind.

Great, great, great—if you ignored this being perhaps the most distressing work I would ever do in my life. As I headed north again, I thought of what Ross had said about the reputation that Felicity had for being "an ice dolly," a beauty with a cold heart, a transactional thinker.

I was far from being the only one who would say that the exact opposite was true, but no one was ever acquitted of felony murder because people said they were nice in high school.

I thought of a time when I was out walking and ended up near the rectory. At the last minute, in recognition of my friend's legendary insistence on order and privacy, I asked her mother, did she think it would be okay for me to drop in? Uncharacteristically downcast, Ruth said, "I wish you would."

Felicity's bedroom door was partly open. A bright, hooded plant light, like a tiny, blue-toned alien installation, illuminated one corner of her desk. Under the lamp was a nest of three baby birds, all plaintively cheeping, their scrawny, naked necks outstretched, as Felicity fed them from a syringe.

"Oh hi!" I said, as I knocked. Then I noticed that she was crying.

"It's not like they're puppies," she said, hiccuping. "If they were puppies, you could maybe find a home for them, except maybe not in this shitty state where animals are just something you eat or beat on. I called the rehab and they're like, we really only work with hawks and owls. Why? Why can't they care about sparrows? They're so beautiful and they sing their hearts out. They are successful. They adapt. But they're just junk birds. There are too many of them and nobody cares about them."

His eye is on the sparrow . . .

Sitting in my car, I started to cry.

On the drive to Madison, I managed to stop crying only for short intervals, but then a lump in my throat would form and dissolve again. By the time I got to the door of Damiano, Chen, and Damiano, Attorneys at Law, I wasn't even attempting to wipe away the horseshoes of mascara from beneath my eyes. Clearly the receptionist had seen it all, because she didn't even blink when I sat down in the waiting room and pressed the heels of my hands to my eyes and began to sob. That was where I was sitting when Sam Damiano came out of his office.

"I can take it from here, Catalina," he said to the receptionist, who, clearly smitten, lowered her elaborate eyelashes and smiled up at him. "Remember, Monday is a holiday."

"No, Mr. Damiano," she said. "It's not."

"Just Sam is fine. And, yes, you're new, you probably didn't hear. It's a paid holiday for our office."

"Really? That's great," she said. She gathered up her coat and purse and departed.

Sam shrugged into a long cashmere overcoat and turned to me. "Why hello, Miss Bigelow," he said, determinedly ignoring the fact that I was crying so hard that I was gasping for breath and snot was running out of my nose. "Okay. We can go now. Would you like to have something to eat while we talk?"

I said, "Okay." I couldn't remember the last time I'd eaten anything.

"I could cook," he said. "I was going to cook tonight anyway. For myself."

I said, "Okay."

In silence, we drove to his austere, immaculate small house near Vilas Park. He unlocked the door. He turned to me, and I stepped into his arms. We didn't leave that house for seventy-two hours. For most of the first forty-eight, we didn't talk about Felicity nearly as much as I would have imagined. The present seemed to elbow the past and the future aside. We talked about common ground: how disgusting to eat carryout from the carton, even if you used chopsticks, that afternoon naps for adults should have remained a sacrament even after the Edwardian era, that the best historical record was mostly good gossip, that audiobooks were wonderful but did not constitute reading. We drank apple-cider mimosas from his grandmother's blue cut-crystal flutes. We talked about where we would go when this was all over, a verdant somewhere drenched in saltwater and light, maybe Portugal.

Because of a blizzard, the fireworks traditionally held on New Year's Eve had been postponed and then postponed again. Wrapped in quilts the second night on the porch, we watched the fireworks break like falling stars over the capitol dome. I was startled when I heard what sounded like lions roaring. He lived right near the zoo, Sam explained. The lions I heard had been born in captivity, but fresh air was essential to their health, no matter what season, so the zoo had installed heated rocks that melted the snow. The lions liked to loll there even as spiraling snow spattered their coats.

There was nothing sad about this image except insofar as all zoos were sad. And yet I started to cry again, bringing the total of times I'd cried over the past several days equal to the number of times I'd cried during the previous two years. Although these lions would never see the sunbaked savannah where they were meant to live, it lived in them, and they would proclaim their wildness to the night. If I sound like a sentimental fool, I was. I leaned against Sam's shoulder, and he pulled me to him, with me grateful that, although not a particularly big guy, he was taller—enough that I could feel tucked in.

"Are you always this emotional?" he asked.

"Probably. But I don't show it."

"Why are you sad right now?"

He was relieved that it was about the lions. He knew that it wasn't about the lions.

An owl hooted softly, experimentally, as if sending forth a tentative question; from far off, another answered, then the same exchange again, the distant owl moving closer. *Do you want me? Am I the one you want?* The seeking-out of a being by another being, the longing for union and reunion, was not only primal, but it was also not just for primates—and, as evidenced by the owls, we weren't the only ones who talked about it or wrote songs about it. Baudelaire wrote of dark owls "by twos and twos" meditating under overhanging yews. I told Sam this.

"You are the obscure poetry factor. How did you memorize all this stuff at your age? And anyhow, what is your age?"

"Twenty-seven, nearly twenty-eight. I have sort of a sticky memory. Mostly for useless stuff like poetry. But it's sort of seductive. Men like to be impressed—" I ran my thumb down the inside of his hip bone "—by more than big boobs and a . . . lot of energy."

"I think you have a ton of energy. I don't know much poetry, so you can say anything you want and I'll believe it."

I said then, "I have to call my parents."

He raised an eyebrow. "Maybe except that!"

"Only because I'm living with them right at this moment, in Sheboygan, or at least part of the time with them and part here with my sister. This story is going to take months for me, obviously, more research even after the trial. And then the writing of it. My place in Chicago is being sublet."

I told Patrick and Miranda I was staying in Madison with a friend. Any other explanation seemed to require, well, too much explanation.

He was the middle brother of four, two in college in Madison, the eldest a structural engineer in Sydney, Australia. His mother was the senior partner in his law firm. His father was a vet. We huddled on the couch and watched *Arsenic and Old Lace*, which in context, it didn't occur to me until later, was a stunningly inappropriate choice. I could not keep my eyes or hands off him.

Certainly, in Sam, and in the most unlikely circumstance, I had found that person, the one whose body was my anthem, who would make me wonder why anyone ever did anything except have sex. My romantic history, admittedly, rose from dismal and leveled off at uninspiring, and true, that was mostly from lack of trying—but not from lack of caring. I did want the man of my dreams. I devoutly did not want to do all the gruesome things that seemed necessary to find him. I didn't want to speed date, submit a profile to a web sink, or visit a yenta— not even for the magazine, although Ivy had brought this story idea up more than once. I didn't want to be bored, disgusted, disappointed, or worse, required to escape from the romantic equivalent of a house fire.

There had been my doomed, contested crush on Lucius McCool in senior year of high school, literally a couple of half-decent guys in college, and then my grad school classmate, Davis, a music journalist, with whom I briefly fantasized a life of two crowded desks at opposite ends of a vast, sunny Brooklyn living room . . . but that ended when his once-lost true love came back from her posting as a maternal health specialist in South Africa. From that time on, regardless of what Sam suspected, I felt that I was destined for a solo life—and I had further resolved that I would not compromise: If I didn't like the way he chewed, he was out; if his beloved father was a casual racist, he was out; if he believed in the slimmest possibility of extraterrestrials, he was out. And then came Sam. The way Sam's mouth felt on mine— firm, clean, urgent—just the thought made my pelvis clench. My mother would once say that I was "sexually hypnotized," but the truth was that I was hypnotized in other ways as well. Most of the time, I could predict within days when I would tire of a guy or when he would tire of me or when the connection just wasn't robust enough to last. There were times I could predict the finale within fifteen minutes. With Sam, I couldn't see the finale. From the first moment, I never imagined it would end.

And then, immediately, it did.

"We have to talk about this, Reenie," he said.

"I thought we were," I said, adding, "And I thought only the girl said that."

"I mean, we can't do this."

"We can't do this because you're Felicity's lawyer and I'm writing about this, and I'm her friend," I said.

"That's the gist of it."

"I couldn't agree more," I said, although I couldn't see how there was any real impropriety. It wasn't as though I was a lawyer on the other side or even a court reporter or police. "I'm not a lawyer but I don't see how us having . . . whatever this is, could be actually illegal."

"Not illegal at all. Certainly unethical. There doesn't have to be a real instance of impropriety, just the perception of it."

"The perception of some kind of influence?"

"Yes."

I asked him, "If a reporter who knew the defendant gave you some kind of information that might help exonerate her, that would be a good thing, right? Or if you gave a reporter information that would help with a more favorable picture of the defendant? That would be a good thing, and it happens all the time."

"It's more that, if anyone found out, the judge, the jurors, they would wonder about what effect the relationship had on the process."

"You know, we have a code too. Objectivity, or the best attempt at it . . ." No way could I expect myself to remain impartial in this situation. That train had already left the station. My task would be to acknowledge those barriers to objectivity, to leave no stone unturned, no question unasked, no fact unverified, and follow that path wherever it led. "So this barrier would pertain until after the trial, but what if she is convicted? There would be an appeal, not that I would be writing about that because of the time frame . . . Would this perception apply forever?"

Sam said, "No, of course not. I mean, there would be people, if this thing between us continued in the future, who would have things to say, but that wouldn't matter. The only way we can do this is to keep it completely secret, just between us . . . It would be hard to keep this completely secret."

"We can't do that," I said. "We have to end it right here."

"That seems pretty impossible."

"We have to. We have to be adult and recognize that what people see is real to them, even if it's not really real."

Sam laughed. "You can tell you're a professional writer." He quieted then and pulled me to him. "I thought of doing this the first time I saw you." He kissed my eyes and the top of my head in a way that I would be able to summon up fifty years from now, when I was a grandmother, and be able to say to myself, I knew what it was like to feel loved.

"How long do we have? Should I leave now?"

"Tomorrow. It's a risk. But it's not such a big risk. Nobody expects either of us anywhere. I'd love to get dressed up and take you out to dinner, but that's not in the cards."

"And I don't have any dress-up clothes in my purse."

I asked him if whatever we were experiencing was big enough that we would want to resume it months from now. The thought made me so sad I wanted to run outside and leave right then, before I fell further down this ladder of stars.

"I don't know what I feel," Sam said. "Just that I never felt it before." He told me there was no one else, not even a contender, and there hadn't really ever been one.

He said, "We can still talk, right?"

I said, "Not like this."

"But communicate?"

"Not like this."

"You're right," Sam said. "Just business. It will be easier for both of us. Reenie, you can ask me anything you want. I promise that I'll always give you a truthful answer, except if it's about a client and if it would violate attorney-client privilege. Just don't ever ask me a question unless you really want to know my answer."

"Me too."

"I promise," he said.

Very late, we got busy cooking. Well, he did. I don't see the point of cooking, especially when people who can actually cook are getting out of prison every week. As we took turns kneading bread to go with the corn-and-shrimp chowder, I asked, "What's the best thing you've ever done?"

Why did I say that?

Why, when I knew that would mean he would ask me what the best thing I'd ever done was, and then, logically, we'd proceed to ask what was the worst thing?

Sam told me, "I turned a pilot at Logan in for being drunk. I told the police. I saw her at breakfast in the airport, before she was wearing her uniform, and she was drunk, she was having a Bloody Mary, and I recognized her when she showed up in the boarding area. She probably lost her job, but there were all those people, a hundred people, flying to Alaska."

"I meant as a lawyer, but that is so cool, a lot of people wouldn't have had the courage to do that. And I've never been to Alaska."

He said, "Salmon fishing. I ate salmon for seven days straight." I thought of my adventures with fried grouper.

"What's the worst thing?"

"I found a wallet with eight hundred dollars in it and I kept the money. I mailed the wallet back. I was fifteen. I told my dad and he said, 'You'll get no joy from it.' And he was right, I didn't." Sam said, "How about you?"

"Best or worst?" There was no way. There was absolutely no way. I would think later, *You wanted this. You wanted to kick the hornet's nest.* It was too good to be true. "Okay. In grad school, this writer from India went into labor early. Her husband was in surgery, not having it, doing it, and we were in a class. I drove her to the hospital, going a hundred miles an hour, so the police would pull me over, which they did, and I was calling the police at the same time. And they delivered the baby, right there on a rubber sheet on the ground. The baby was fine," I said. "Now you."

"A guy from Iran was charged with shoplifting a kids' watch. He was buying the watch, but his wife called for him and he walked outside still holding the watch, and the owner took a photo. The guy offered to pay three times what the watch was worth, but the owner pressed charges. The owner's sister-in-law had died in 9/11. The guy with the watch was a surgeon in the US on a special visa, and he would have lost that and been deported. The jury found him guilty."

"So how . . . ?"

"The judge overruled the verdict. She said it was an unreasonable verdict. That almost never happens."

The doctor and his family were crying; Sam's mother was crying; Sam was nearly in shock. He'd been a lawyer for about fifteen minutes. A few weeks later, the doctor and his family sent Sam a watch, a Baume & Mercier watch, a modest model that was worth only five thousand dollars. Sam said he wanted to return it, but his mother told him that would be ungracious.

"Do you wear it?"

"At first, I was too scared to. Now I wear it every day." He didn't ask me what the worst thing was. Still, the longing to tell him and be judged thrummed in my chest like an extra heartbeat. Sam said, "What's the best thing about you?"

"I have good manners," I said. "What about you?"

"I'm fair."

We danced in the kitchen to Marvin Gaye while the bread baked. The bread was very good, its crispy crust achieved by spraying the loaf with olive oil and sliding a cake tin of boiling water into the oven. He had majored in biology and knew all kinds of weird things about face blindness and why sphenopalatine ganglioneuralgia (a "brain freeze") is really a dangerous warning. When he asked about my top-five favorite movies, he didn't interrupt with his own list. He asked to see a picture of my sister, Nell, and I had to struggle to find one in which she didn't look prettier.

We couldn't wait to go back to bed.

A LITTLE WORN-OUT BETWEEN THE LEGS THE NEXT MORNING, REally closer to afternoon, I took a bath in the big claw-foot tub, beneath two vast skylights, staring up at the steep blue sky as if it was a sea I could fall into. He washed my hair for me, like a scene from a movie based on a Hemingway novel. I had to re-mind myself that even if it lasted, and it probably wouldn't, it could not always be like this.

I wanted to be clear on one thing. There was a cartoon devil on my left shoulder jumping up and down—*Ask him, ask him, dare you*—while the cartoon angel on my right shoulder wagged a cautionary finger and counseled restraint. *Just don't ever ask me a question unless you really want to know my answer.*

He said I could ask him anything.

The devil always wins.

I asked, "Are you attracted to Felicity?"

Sam didn't answer, a beat of silence more revealing than any answer. Finally, he said, "Yes."

"If I weren't a factor. If she weren't on trial for murder . . ."

"If she weren't on trial for murder, I would never have met her."

"If you had."

"Okay. Sure. Felicity is intelligent and beautiful and unusual. She has a unique way of listening. I wouldn't have been a fan of her work in the slightest. But in another world, under other cir-cumstances, I might have fallen for her. Reenie, wouldn't most men? Wouldn't women be drawn to her too? In other ways? You said so yourself, in so many words." He added, "That's not a factor now. Now that you are here."

He was right, but his being right didn't temper the need for what I wanted him to say. I wanted him to say that the moment he saw me, all other images of all other women exploded like an ice sculpture to a mallet blow and melted away.

"Do you want to get married?" he asked.

Ah-ha, I thought, as the other shoe hit the floor. *He's crazy. Well, good, at least now I know.* Experimentally, I told him, "I haven't really given it a lot of thought."

"Sure, you have."

"You mean, all women do?"

"I mean, all people do. All normal people."

"Okay, so do you mean generally or specifically?"

"Generally," he said. So, he wasn't asking me to marry him. Realizing this, I wished he were crazy enough to have asked. "I want to get married. I want to be happy. Do you know any happy marriages?"

"My parents are happily married."

"Mine too. They had some rough patches. My dad drank too much for a while."

"Veterinarians like to party?"

"Long ago. When we were very young kids. I think money was a big issue for them back then. Not anymore, though. They have separate bedrooms, and they say it's the secret to true happiness. My dad snores like a Cape buffalo."

"I only think of guys thinking about marriage in the sense of trying to avoid it."

He shook his head. "My one younger brother says that women think men are eight-celled creatures when it comes to love, but I always say, hey, who wrote most of those love songs? Men wrote most of those love songs."

My heart kicked up speed, but even I wasn't enough of a romantic to think he meant love in the context of him and me. He meant *love* the word, the way people sling it around, as in true love, a love letter, a love affair, a love story, a love interest, love is a many-splintered thing.

I don't believe in putting off difficult things; I believe in doing them first (that is, I believed in doing them first until I had to interview the families of murder victims . . .). But I wanted to ask Sam for a postponement, for another day . . . even though I knew that this had to stop, if not end, right now.

Then he asked, "So why are you named Irene?"

"After the old song. The great old blues man Lead Belly

sang it. And folk singers, like The Weavers. Everybody sang it. 'Irene, good night, Irene, Irene, good night . . .'"

"Right," he said. "Before my time." He asked then, "Sisters and brothers?"

"One sister, Nell. Eleanor. Named after my mother's mom, who was named for Eleanor Roosevelt. Who are you named for?"

"My grandfather on my mother's side. Samuel Anthony Messina. It spells 'Sam.'"

"Are your grandparents alive?"

"All four," he said.

"Me too."

"So you come from a line of hearty people."

"Yes, my dad used to say that you could tell we Bigelow women, my sister and I, were of peasant stock by our sturdy hips, until my mother told him that if he ever said that again, it would be the last thing he ever said."

"I like her."

"I like her too. Do you like your mother?"

"I am crazy about her actually. She's very funny. She has a very bad temper. She's also my boss, the managing partner at Damiano, Chen, and Damiano."

We settled down to sleep, as though we did this all the time instead of twice. I'm pretty sure he thought that I was already asleep when he wound one finger into the back of my newly washed hair and whispered, "Irene, good night, Irene. I'll see you in my dreams."

He had known all along.

LATE NEXT MORNING, WE DRANK OUR COFFEE. HE ATE A PIECE OF toast and I, suddenly self-conscious, didn't. Soon, I would have to leave. I was packing up my backpack when Sam said, "One more night." I knew that I should go, right then, while things were sweet as new snow, but who knew if this new connection could weather months of separation, not a wall placed between us for the trial, but, worse, if possible, a window. And if it didn't, who knew when love would come again for me? I set the backpack down.

I agreed to leave first thing, before anyone else in the neighborhood was awake.

"Thank you," he said. "It's practically night already, anyhow."

It was not even two in the afternoon, but . . . who cared? Those last few doors within broke open with a force that made them shudder on their hinges, doors I feared I might not be able to force shut again, or if I did, I would always see this light shining around the edges. I wasn't exactly thinking of names for our firstborn son, but I was so far gone that I almost wished I hadn't tasted this thin slice of sublime couple-hood that would make the store brand seem so bland.

Everything that last day and night was lovely, at first. All the urgency of wild love too soon undertaken, too often denied, still pertained. For dinner, I cooked my one dish: my mother's macaroni and cheese with the secret ingredient. Sam pronounced it delicious. We talked more. I told him about our feature story about cat people and dog people and how that preference extended even to the way people dressed, about how my father's grandmother, an Irish immigrant, had four sisters, all of whom were or had been nuns, about how our only pet ever had been a parrot named Rosh Shoshana that spoke only Yiddish and which had to be given away when it nearly bit off the finger of one of those great-aunts. Sam told me about how much he hated dirty jokes, and he thought that Irish women were the most passionate and kind, how he'd once wanted to be a farmer. When it came to sports, he loved only college basketball because, for most of them, their championship season would be the great lyric passage of their whole lives. He didn't think fiction was girlie. One of his brothers wanted to be a writer. He asked me how many books I thought I would write, where I would live if I could live anywhere, if I liked to fish.

It was lovely, yet it didn't feel like a gift, as it should have. It was just a flight delay. We'd been outward bound, and, relieved as we were to turn back to each other, our brains continued to outpace our emotions. Things I had to write down or pick up kept skittering across my mind. My clothes felt old and soiled on my skin. Sam was already lost to me. He had gone deeply into his preparation, like an athlete concentrating on the race, a surgeon on the operation, an actor on the role.

"Can I ask a question?" I said to him finally.

"Sure."

"It's not as a reporter, it's as a person."

"So, off the record."

I gave him a raised eyebrow. "Everything here is off the record, as you say. Very off the record."

If Felicity didn't do it, who did?

"My mother and I talked about this several times, bunch of times," he said. "She thought maybe it was Felicity's mother, because she was this born-again Christian and maybe she lost her marbles and did this to free Felicity from sin."

"Ruth? My chemistry teacher? If you ever met Ruth, you could not be more wrong," I said. "She is such a gentle person."

I could think of only one time that I'd ever seen Ruth lose her shit. I'd forgotten it because it was so subtle but it ended with Ruth required to make a formal written apology to Felicity's and my second-grade teacher.

One morning before school, Ruth was called in. Felicity, it seemed, had changed her answer on a math test. Felicity had, indeed, changed her answer, she told her mom, because kids on either side of her had copied her paper. Ruth explained this quietly. The teacher, Sandy Albertson, was the principal's wife.

Gently, she told Ruth, "Sometimes a child as bright as Felicity becomes a bit of a perfectionist. She just can't bear to have one thing be wrong. We think that's what happened here."

Ruth said, "Felicity told you why she changed her answer. If she said that is what happened, then that is what happened. Felicity doesn't lie. Did you talk to the two kids who copied the wrong answer from her paper?"

"Felicity was seen changing her answer. Ruth, you know that's cheating," said Sandy Albertson. "And all kids lie sometimes."

By then, the first bell had gone off and kids were beginning to file into the room. Mrs. Albertson explained to Ruth that they could talk more later, but we overheard her say that Felicity would receive an F so that it would be impressed on her young mind just how serious a matter cheating was and how accepting just one wrong answer would have been so much better. Ruth, seven or eight months pregnant at the time, with one of Felicity's younger brothers, repeated the reason that Felicity had changed her answer. Sandy Albertson gently shook her head.

"I can't stop you, can I?" Ruth asked. "What you are teaching her is to lie."

The second-grade teacher said, "Ruth, let's talk about this another time."

Ruth picked up her large, handsewn patchwork purse and turned to leave the room. Then she turned back and took Felicity's hand.

Clearly, but not angrily, she said, "Felicity doesn't lie. If you think that she's a liar, then you can't have her anymore. Ask the other two kids which answers they got wrong on their tests."

Everything might have ended peacefully then, but Mrs. Albertson gave a gusty sigh and said, "Ruth, you're making way too much of this." She had turned her back on Ruth and it must have been eerie for her to feel Ruth's breath on the back of her neck.

"Sandy, I don't wish to be unkind," she said softly, and Sandy Albertson jumped, whirling around to face Ruth, who was so close to the teacher that she could have rubbed noses with her. It was a graphic illustration of what *in your face* meant. "I love teaching. I'm a good teacher. The only thing I hate about teaching is that I'm lumped in with terrible teachers like you."

"I need to call the principal's office."

"Oh yes, by all means, call your husband," Ruth said. "Call the big boss. Call security. Call the police. Restore order! No one will have the courage to tell you that you are the epitome of everything that's wrong with education in this country. But I will tell you. You are lazy. You are bored. And you are always right." Ruth's voice was rising, as if she was trying to be heard over the approach of a plane. "If you could listen, you might not be such a silly bitch, Sandy."

The last of the children were entering the room now. They were paying attention, their eyes wide. Felicity started to cry, as did I. We weren't delicate little violets—well, relatively speaking, we actually were delicate little violets, compared to what I've since learned about the way some kids grow up, even on the mean streets of Sheboygan, Wisconsin. But we weren't used to adults talking like that around kids. As Ruth turned to leave, for some reason, I grabbed her other hand and followed her out the door and into the parking lot. She didn't object; she seemed to expect that. She took us home and gave us some worn-out men's dress shirts to put on over our clothes and set out containers of brown sugar and oatmeal so we could make oatmeal chocolate chip cookies. Even I was aware Ruth seemed to be listening very attentively to something far away. It was over an hour before she called my parents and only then when I suggested it. "Oh, of course, Reenie, you're right! But I'm sure she knows that you're just fine with me."

The following Monday, both Felicity and I were in the mixed second-and-third-grade room. My parents, wisely, let the whole thing pass without much commentary, my dad murmuring only that even parents sometimes got overexcited.

So maybe Felicity was as protective of Ruth as Ruth had been of her. Maybe Felicity, like Ruth, was an apparently tranquil bay with a strong, hidden undertow.

I said as much.

"The theory was that Ruth took off because she thought the police would be after her. But yeah, we gave up on that. It didn't seem like that was in her nature. And it was a little too neat. We thought maybe Cary killed Emil and then killed himself." Sam reached for my hand. "But none of those felt right. Those insurance policies were around for nearly a year. Felicity quit at the strip club long before any of this. And one thing is for sure, those guys knew that she wasn't in an exclusive relationship with any of them."

"They still might have been jealous."

"I'm sure maybe they were. But why would it all come to a head right then? Right after Christmas and New Year's, in the middle of the break? It's just too improbable."

"Then who?"

"I think Felicity must have crossed somebody scary without realizing it. Either somebody scary or somebody crazy. There are nutters out there who have whole fantasy relationships with women who don't even know they exist—or who they talked to once at a grocery store, or at a strip club. Maybe it was another client who stalked her and watched other men come and go and then went off the rails."

"If that were true, she would just say that to you. She's private but she's forthright."

"So like you said, the other possibility is a bad guy. She didn't know he was a bad guy until he crossed the line, whatever the line was, and then threatened to kill her too if she ever told. Or maybe after Ruth resigned, this guy abducted Ruth and killed her. I don't know for sure who she is afraid of, but she's so afraid she'd rather go to prison than risk talking about it. And that means giving up seven, eight, ten years of her life, before she can even apply for parole."

We lay down in the darkness.

Once again, I reminded myself it wouldn't stay this way, if it stayed at all. Once again, I thought of the way my mom and dad still danced to "Stardust" in the living room. Once at a party, I'd heard my mother say to my dad, "Let's just go home, it's more fun at home."

Neither of us really slept. Just before dawn, a storm exploded, dramatic and erotic, the kind you never see in winter, white metallic lightning that strobed without even enough of a break for us to count, as Nell and I had when we were children: *one, one thousand, two, one thousand*, booming thunder that shook the windowpanes in their frames. Blizzards and other big storms seem to move your anxiety outside the self, freeing a person to do and say things she might guard more closely in the ordinary world. Pregnancies happen during blizzards and blackouts.

So do murders.

Why did it seem the right time to tell Sam? Did I need to test his devotion? Perhaps in that stormy darkness, I wanted to trust my new beloved with my own darkness, as I had never trusted father, mother, or sister.

How do people get caught for murder? I asked, warming him up. Great detective work? Their own mistakes? Conscience? Some bragged, Sam said. Some couldn't bear the suspense and confessed. Sometimes, years later, police just got a tip.

"Why does anyone think I know much about this?" he wondered aloud. "Why do people think I defend the Boston Strangler?"

"Do you think anybody could kill? You think a normal person could snap?"

Sam said, "They say anyone could if you were pushed far enough. I don't think I could." He added, "My mom used to say that if everyone who ever considered murder or suicide turned purple, this would be the planet of the grapes."

"That's kind of funny," I said. "You never asked me what the worst thing I ever did was."

"Okay, you're on."

"I tried to kill somebody."

"Who?"

"It doesn't matter who. No one knows. Well, one other person knows, besides me." *And now you*, I thought.

"You mean, the person you threatened?"

"No, even she doesn't know. But I didn't just threaten her. I didn't just fantasize it," I said. "I tried to kill someone. I would have done it."

"Why?"

"She humiliated me."

Sam said, "I don't understand."

"My grandmother McClatchey used to say nobody ever died from embarrassment. But they have. Girls killed themselves ashamed of a rape or a pregnancy and boys ashamed of being gay or being weak."

Adolescents were assaulted by each other and by culture, even by school. What makes girls line up together in an open shower, when just a few metal panels would protect them from shame? My mother told me that, in her day, boys were required to take swimming class naked. Why? How could desperately self-conscious boys learn anything, subjected to humiliation like you read about in British boarding schools? How could teachers have forgotten that they were once fragile adolescents? Or were they ever? On a seventh-grade field trip, the phys ed teacher who was a chaperone yelled, "This girl needs a tampon!" Why? Why did she have to shout?

Sam remembered sixth-grade dancing class at Catholic school, budding adolescents shoved together in the guise of a social grace. The foxtrot? The polka? What for? One wedding decades later? Sister Genevieve, the last nun in America, a PE teacher, who looked like Jack Nicholson, demonstrated the twist in her red polyester pantsuit. It was as though this class was designed to make children hate dancing and hate themselves.

Add wildfire social media and cell phones, "Instagram" becoming a verb, TikTok and chat in a snap, all spreading seeds of shame, even as understanding of those consequences grew as well.

"You've thought a lot about this," Sam said. "This is why you tried to kill somebody."

"I was in high school."

"Delinquent," Sam said.

"It's not funny."

"The look on your face is scaring me. I said when we started that you could tell me anything, and you can. But you don't have to."

But I did have to, even though the paint was not close to dry on this thing between us. I wouldn't have told any other guy. It was because of Felicity that I had to.

"I was obsessed with this boy, Lucius McCool. So was another girl, Molly Boone, and he went back and forth between us, week to week . . ."

"Asshole in training," said Sam. "Reenie, I may be immature but I'm not immature enough to be jealous of your first love."

"That's not it! You might not love me anymore."

"Kind of dramatic."

"Okay, so Luke wasn't bad, just skin-deep. Pretty good at most things, funny, he was a great dancer, and you know that any woman would walk through fire for a guy who can dance . . ."

"So maybe my suffering at Blessed Sacrament wasn't for nothing. We can do the cha-cha anytime you want."

"We do that very nicely anyhow," I replied. His effort to lighten the mood turned my heart. But I had to go on. I described Molly, a living doll, five feet tall, ninety pounds, the cheerleader at the top of the pyramid, the good fairy in the school musical. "Molly would walk up the stairs with Luke, just checking to make sure I could hear, and be like, 'Oh, honey, tell me what we're going to do on Friday, and I mean, tell me everything we're going to do. Because I wouldn't do everything. A little rub and grind, but not everything.'"

I was gone then, blown back light as a leaf down the corridor of time, through the angles and circles of the fusty library, where, with just enough late-winter light from the stained-glass windows in the images of Hemingway and Hawthorne to see each other's eyes, we leaned against the yellow hardwood shelves and made out; the cushiony field of lavender behind the field house, a leftover from some former farm, where we lay in the spring evening and made out; the black marble tables in the world-class lab endowed by the estate of Sheboygan's most famous scientist, where he lifted me in my tight jeans and stood between my legs and we made out until my thighs were sore, a bruise my body still remembers; the spangled moonlight on the surface of the reservoir where we huddled in his car; or the woodland park, heavy with the smell of pine, where he pressed me against a tree and we made out. Impressed as he was by the limits I set on our passion, Luke wanted the all of it. He kept asking me why I didn't love him, why I didn't trust him—as though he honestly didn't understand why, although the former was true, the latter never could be. If I gave that to him, would he give up on Molly? Would he be only mine?

"Where is he now?" Sam asked me. "Did you keep in touch with him?"

"He's an orthopedic surgeon, of course, so he doesn't have to ever be nice to anybody—he only sees patients when they're asleep. But then he can enjoy how much they suffer when they wake up."

"So, not a fond memory. You slept with him."

"I never got the chance to."

"I thought you said . . ."

"He undressed me, we were in the field, I was unbuckling . . . and that was when she made the video. Luke was the one to spot her. He yelled at her. She ran. And within an hour . . ."

It was everywhere.

People burst out laughing when they saw me in the hall. They pretended to suck their middle fingers. I wanted to die. Luke was blasé. He thought himself as a real stand-up guy for saying Molly was a bitch. By then, I didn't care if he went back to Molly.

I played sick and then I got sick. I missed two weeks of school, until only finals week was left. I went to Broadway Blooms and begged for dead flowers, supposedly for an art project. I left these on Molly's front steps in the middle of one dark spring night, tied with a black ribbon, with a note that read, "This matches your heart." Next morning, from behind a big Chinese maple across the street, I watched Molly show the bouquet to her mother. They both laughed. Apple, tree, huh?

"We used to go to this granite quarry to swim. This huge place. We called it the reservoir, although it wasn't really that. It was clean, deep, pure water, cold enough to freeze your bones and yet not as cold as Lake Michigan. Kids still go there to swim and make out. My parents even still go there to swim. We would go when the workers were gone, those nights when the heat was like this giant hand pressing down on you," I said. "It was crazy dangerous. No-trespassing signs all over the place, and the police would make noise, but their own kids swam there."

Kids would pull their cars up close to the edge of the quarry and turn on their headlights. Everybody would rush in, the boldest ones naked, screaming when the water hit their vulnerable bellies. It sounds hopelessly 1950s and it was, something out of a James Dean movie. By then, it was late summer, the video of me and Luke still circulating, but he actually did go back to Molly, so much for "love" and "trust." I went to a party where I knew she would be, not with him. She was falling-down drunk. I was sober, the "gin and tonic" sparkling in my glass all tonic. I went up to Molly and hugged her. She jumped. I said, Can we talk it over? I didn't leave things bad between us. She knew that I had every right to hate her guts, and why would I give a shit if she hated me too? But she agreed to come with me.

Was she so conceited she thought people would like her no matter what she did? Did some sliver of her being repent the hell she had put me through, especially since she got the boy?

I slipped a couple of nip bottles of gin into my pocket, along with a lime wedge wrapped in a napkin.

"Let's go," I said. "I'll drive. You're too wasted."

She followed me, stumbling a little on her book-thick platforms as she did. She was so clueless. It was like agreeing to go on a midnight ride with an assassin.

And what about me? Did I tell myself I was only going to off and leave her at the reservoir to call somebody else to bring her home? Maybe to call Luke? It seemed that my choices that night were fated, as though I was steered by a force much bigger than I was, that there was no retreat.

"What happened then?" Sam asked, in a voice so low I could barely hear it.

"Someday I'll show you the reservoir. We could go night swimming maybe." I tried to describe the quarry for him, a strange, still kettle, deep but with no tide, and glittering dark sand all around.

"I have to say, Reenie, not making it sound super attractive. I am not even a little tempted to go swimming in a place where there are probably dead bodies on the bottom."

"That's true of every single body of water except a swimming pool."

"Then thank heaven for swimming pools. I also wouldn't go swimming in my underwear in front of a bunch of buff college guys and girls for a thousand bucks. I'm neither old enough nor young enough for that."

"It was always so dark. Without the cars around the fence and the headlights, it would have been pitch black, impossible to see anything."

Once she was good and drunk, I convinced Molly that I would drive her home in her car and somebody would pick me up. How grateful she was almost stopped me, but only almost. She got into the back seat and promptly passed out. I drove to the reservoir, which, because of the party and because it was still early, before eleven, was deserted. There was one person, apparently scavenging stuff that washed up or was dropped, easily two football fields away. All I could see was a headlamp bobbing along, then that disappeared, a car engine rumbled, and there was the sound of tires popping along the gravel. I piloted the front end of the car into the water, opened the driver's-side door, and began my descent. Water romped into the front seat and finally I could tell that if I got out now, the car would roll on without me, until it sank, until it plunged to the bottom where no light could penetrate.

Then suddenly, Felicity was there, driving my car. She stopped and scrambled over the front seat of Molly's car, somehow managing to shove the back door open, hauling Molly, limp as the corpse she would soon have been. When she huffed at me to help her, I did, tugging on Molly's feet.

She coughed a little but didn't even wake up.

Without a word, we lugged and shoved Molly into the back seat of my car and drove her home. Finally, she moaned, and her eyes fluttered open as we draped one of her arms over each of our shoulders and half carried her up the curved rustic stone front walk, ringing the bell to the right of the huge carved red door, until her mother answered, in pajamas and a robe, her hair flat, her cheeks creased, clearly prepared to be outraged but then abruptly rueful, mortified, and relieved, choking out the words "thank you" as she pulled her daughter inside.

Felicity and I went back to the reservoir, where we tied ropes from my trunk onto the bumper of Molly's car and began to haul it out. We hadn't gotten too far when Felicity stopped. "Let's leave it this way. It looks like she was so drunk she drove too close. And we just got here in time. That's sort of lying by omission, I guess. But I can't figure out anything else." She went on, "I want you to promise that we will never speak of this again."

I began to cry, hard. You didn't hug Felicity, but I grabbed her then, and she allowed it, gently patting my back a little. "I don't blame you if you don't care about me anymore," I said.

"I care about you just as much as I ever did. I didn't do this for Molly, I did it for you. I'm just glad I followed you. I'm just glad you left your keys."

"Why did you follow me?"

"I'm not sure," she said. "Something was strange. It was like when something wakes you up at night and it's not a sound? Like the quietness is the sound? Or like a storm is coming and it's just holding its breath?" I was crying so hard that I couldn't speak. "You're not that person, Reenie."

"I almost was."

"Thinking about it isn't the same as doing it," she said.

We got into my car and went home.

As I talked, I watched Sam. I heard him thinking, as if he had spoken the words aloud, that his hunch might be correct and, despite all the indications to the contrary, Felicity might be entirely innocent—just as I, despite all the indications to the contrary, was very nearly guilty. There was a break in the storm, but the sky was signaling a second act, smears of gray clouds hanging low, lightning flickering in their fat depths, like lamps snapped on and off.

Something was wrong in his face. Something was changing. He didn't say a word. Minutes. A minute is a long time if your life depends on it.

Somebody's done for.

Sam finally said, "That is a hell of a story."

Now he would leave me, I thought. *Now for sure. Could you blame him?* I thought. *If the tables were turned, as it were, wouldn't you leave him?*

"Felicity was right. Thinking about it is not the same as doing it. You would have stopped." He made a tent of his two hands and pressed his index fingers against his eyes. "I just don't know . . ."

The tables have turned, with a vengeance. Whoever said that? Who the fuck cared? I was sick of being the woman with the suitable quote for every occasion. I was losing the only man I ever loved.

How many nights had I asked myself, had I truly wanted to end her life? Or to humiliate and terrify her as she humiliated me? Was my brain back then even formed enough to fully encompass the enormity? A seventeen-year-old still doesn't possess the long view. How smart you are doesn't matter. I still lived as a teenager lives, in dog years, in which each week is a month, each month a season, each season an era. There were nights when I almost forgave myself. There were nights when I was certain that I should never be forgiven.

It was long ago.

But not really. I was still wearing the same Shinola Bixby watch my grandmother bought me for high school graduation.

An anemic sun was out by then. The stolen night, at the end of the stolen weekend, was gone. Sam got up to make coffee. Then his phone rang.

"It's the jail."

"Is it Felicity?"

He didn't answer. But moments later, he was slipping into jeans and a white shirt he left untucked. I admired the curve of his hip as I pulled on my own clothing. He was as beautiful to me as a statue, my own shrine.

He is mine, I thought.

He was mine, I thought.

"Are you okay staying here alone?"

"I'll come with you."

Sam stopped, regarding the screen of his phone like an oracle. "You can't. It would be inappropriate. You're not part of Felicity's defense team. You're just a reporter writing about her . . ."

"I'm not just that."

"You know what I mean, Reenie. You can't go with me to see her unless she asks to see you."

"Will you tell her about you and me?"

"No, why would I do that? Why would that be relevant?"

It wouldn't be relevant, not unless he liked her better. What was wrong with me? Why was I jealous of a sick woman facing a life sentence? A sick woman who had never shown me anything except loving kindness, since the day in first grade when she gave me half her cheese-and-pickle sandwich because Miranda put so much butter on my peanut-butter sandwich that it was like a lard-wich?

"Why does she want to see you right now?"

He tucked his shirt in. "That wasn't Felicity calling me. It was the assistant warden. Felicity had a seizure . . ."

"Can your mom go see her?"

Oh god, I was horrible. I was selfish and horrible.

Sam didn't shout at me but it felt as though he did when he said, "No!"

"What?"

"She's being taken to the hospital. I'm going to meet the ambulance there."

"Let me just ride with you."

"No," he said. "No. It's not a good idea."

"Is it usual to call a prisoner's lawyer if she gets . . . sick?"

"Yes, and the lawyer calls the person's family. But that's not an option. Her brothers aren't even driving age yet, and the father, the stepfather . . ."

"That wouldn't be a great idea. Why would she have a seizure? Did she fall and get hurt?"

"She was outside," Sam said as he gathered up his coat, his keys. "She was in the exercise yard, with her binoculars, and the guard saw her fall. I don't know how badly she's hurt."

"What was she doing?"

"She was watching the swans. In that little marshy place next to the lake, right behind the municipal building? She told me that they had babies . . . signals . . ."

"Cygnets," I said. "That's what little baby swans are called."

"How do you know?"

"Obviously, from the birdwatcher herself. Felicity told me that." I shared the story with Sam, of our one-and-only camping trip.

We were juniors, maybe sophomores, watching swans gliding decorously across Green Lake. She had decided to go camping and dragged me along. We were the only guests at the campground except for a huge trailer with a TV antenna and an awning depicting the Confederate flag. It was so cold and stormy that the guy who ran the office didn't even have the heart to charge us anything.

We somehow pitched the sagging dome tent, then dined in the car on Pringles, power bars, and cold pizza. We were by then soaking wet and too filthy even for a woodsy restaurant, and, between us, we also had a total of seventeen dollars. In the tent, it was as dark as I imagined the outback. After conversation and canned Beyoncé tunes on our phones ran out, for of course, we had no car charger, we wrapped ourselves in sleeping bags that smelled of campfire smoke and mucky little brothers. I woke every hour to bitch about which was worse, the mosquitoes or the ever-damper tent floor.

Then, as often happens, the rain stopped as the dawn broke in breathtaking violet and gold. As she took pictures, Felicity told me that, despite their graceful, nearly mystical splendor, swans were fierce and dangerous, even to humans, especially in defense of their downy, awkward chicks, the "ugly ducklings" of legend that grew up to be creatures of surpassing beauty. She gave me a framed print of one of the pictures she took that morning, a swan just lifting its mighty, ragged wings as it rose up from the still surface of the water.

Felicity. Felicity. Her name meant "happiness."

We rode silently to my sister's house, each of us shawled in our own thoughts. I had no idea what his were: I hoped they were not regrets.

"The seizure was probably from a high fever," he said when he stopped in his office parking lot for me to pick up my car. "I guess she had the flu, and nobody noticed. She didn't complain about it, and nobody is taking your temperature when you're in jail. She's on IV fluids and medication now. I'll have to ask for a postponement for two weeks, so she can recover. I mean, people go on trial when they have cancer, but she would be infectious in a situation like this." He pressed his fingers against the line between his eyes. The silence was like waves in my ears, rising and receding, rising and receding: one wave my empathy for her, the next my fear of losing him.

The binoculars had bruised her face. Even with youth on her side, she would start the trial with a lurid bruise. Those binoculars, as well as the big *Birds of America* hardcover book, came from me. The field glasses were the pricey kind, and now I would have to find new ones for her, if she was even allowed to have them anymore. Clearly, they were breakable and could be fashioned into a weapon she could use to slice her own wrists or a guard's neck. Sam said prisoners could make anything into a weapon, the foil from a candy wrapper, playing cards from a deck, even pebbles from the exercise yard slowly collected and stuffed into a sock for a handy cudgel.

He was saying now, "I need to find some clothes for her before the trial. She's too thin now to wear anything she has . . . Even her underwear is too big."

"I'll help," I said. "I know how to make four things look like ten."

This I was good at. A dress, a natural linen blazer, a Starbaby cardigan in muted green with purple buttons, wide-leg wool-and-linen pants a subtle violet plaid, Moon in June midi-skirt, all from Such Sweet Sorrow . . . nude pumps in the size eight I knew she wore, some sturdy Hanes bras and briefs from Target.

I told Sam, "It won't cost much. Maybe two hundred dollars." He gasped. "You think that's a lot?"

"We don't have much to spend, because Felicity doesn't have much money. She can't even sell her condominium because it's tied up with Cary Church's estate. So we're doing this pro bono," he told me. "Thanks, Reenie."

I assured him that I would pick up the clothing and send the things to his office. He could Venmo me the money. He nodded. He made no response to that either.

"What's going on, Sam? Are you afraid that something is really wrong with Felicity?"

"Not really."

"What then? You're acting weird. Is it what I told you?"

Sam said, "Maybe?"

Hardly breathing, I made a show of rummaging through my big purse, as if I'd misplaced something important, which I had— my heart and my mind. I noticed a piece of linen and remembered that, sometime during the night, I had stolen a pillowcase. How nuts I was by that point, I didn't regret this at all, despite the fact that Sam, precision personified, would probably be looking for it in his laundry for weeks. I said, "We agreed this wasn't right for now." Sam nodded. "But after the trial, we'll try again?"

"I don't know."

"So are you ending this?"

He kissed my cheek. Mourning sculpted the corners of his mouth downward. If my face was a mirror of his, we both looked like tragedy masks. Then, slowly, Sam answered, "I can't say for sure. I'm sorry. Remember that I promised to answer every question you asked but I promised to tell you the truth."

"Okay. I get it."

He drove me back to my car at his office. He murmured that the snow had been cleared; that was good. I made a noise I hoped sounded like agreement. I opened the door and stepped out. He didn't stop me. I closed it behind me. He didn't stop me.

I took a few steps before I turned back briskly and said, "So okay! Back to business! Can you persuade Felicity to see me?"

But he was already gone.

DISTRACTED, I NEARLY GOT LOST DRIVING BACK TO MY SISTER'S. Not even bothering to change or shower, I stuffed some clothing into the first thing I found, a reusable grocery bag. I got into my car. I got lost finding the entrance to the highway and found myself near Sam's house again. Should I go back? No, I couldn't go back. I turned around near the gates of the zoo, where those well-housed but unhomed lions longed for the veldt they'd never seen.

I wanted out of this story. Once I honestly believed that Felicity's connection with me would be my best advantage. Now I was part not only of Felicity's life but also of Sam's life, which made me part of this case, and it wasn't better—it was awful. Never had I doubted my ability to drive my way to the beating heart of a tale. Now I longed to consider the kind of weighty questions I used to consider, like were sunglasses a fashion statement or a quasi-medical device? Were garter belts sexy or slavish? Why did I cast myself into a stew of sex and strippers, plots and poisons? I was worn-out by the prospect of trying to pull all of it together and the trial hadn't even started.

In that moment, then, as if I'd opened a box like Pandora, all my wishes came true. And just as in that myth, they were all bad. The phone went. My editor. I put her on speaker.

"So are you close to finishing your story?" she asked, adding then, "It's Ivy."

"I somehow guessed that."

"So have you finished it? Can I have a look?"

"Ivy, the trial hasn't even started. It'll be weeks. You knew this."

"So much for swift justice."

"It's not as though I've been eating bonbons. I've had to do a ton of background research and I still have more to . . ."

"Well, I need you to take a break and go do this little thing about a vintage Kate Spade event, sort of a handbag swap meet, collectors, nostalgia, all that. You know, the rise and fall and rise of a brand." Ivy chatted on, about how the cool purse right now was SeeSawSo. I hated SeeSawSo clothing, with its stingy little shapes and models who looked like heroin addicts. But Selena

Gomez had gone boldly against trend, spotted just recently carrying a Kate Spade bag. "This is the sort of thing that's right in your wheelhouse. I want you to write about how the sales and prices spiked after Kate Spade's suicide."

"That's hideous," I told Ivy. "No."

She didn't even acknowledge that. Tears welled up in my eyes. How long would the trial be postponed? A week? More? I had no right to refuse. I asked Ivy, "When is this?"

"Tomorrow," Ivy said, "near Milwaukee." I thought, *Milwaukee?* "Just nose around for a little featurette, not about this event per se but about these kinds of fashion swap meets." Ivy pleaded to my better nature. "Nobody writes about this stuff like you do," she said, meaning this as a compliment. Instead, Ivy transformed the handbag swap meet into an objective correlative for my career. My greatest contribution to arts and letters would be my paeans to purses, my deft analysis of how the new geometrics and the influence of the young royals were pushing boho bags off the shelf in favor of sharply structured pocketbooks.

For you will surely get it, I thought.

"I can't," I told Ivy. "What I'm writing about here is life or death and the trial starts . . . tomorrow." This was a big gamble. Felicity's strange case had spread all over the place; Ivy was so delighted by that it bordered on cold-blooded. She could easily turn on her TV and spot the lie. As insurance, I added, "Unless it's delayed." Ivy did not reply, an ominous sign.

"Reenie," she said. Using my name was another ominous sign. "I want you to just pop in at this swap meet. It'll take you a couple of hours at most. See what people are saying about the brand. Then fill in a little history. Five hundred words." She added, "I'm not pulling you off your magnum opus."

I knew when I was beat.

Later that day, back at my parents' house, I observed that

my mother had made herself hours late for work to give me breakfast, as if I were a child. Well, I was her child. She asked me if she should work from home. I said not to bother, as all she would be doing was watching me alternate between sleeping and crying.

"This friend?" she said. "Is he or she making you happy? Because you don't look happy."

"I think I'm in love."

"That would explain not looking happy."

"I think it's already over."

"Even more so. Don't you have too many irons in the fire to start up a love affair?"

"You don't get to pick the time that's convenient, Mom."

"Probably best, though, given the circumstances and suitability of the person."

"I didn't fall in love with an unsuitable person."

"Felicity's defense lawyer?" my mother said, adding, "Hmm."

How did she know that? How on earth did she know that, then? I didn't know then and I still don't know. But what I said was nothing. Fully Mirandized, I struggled upward to my childhood room, where, yet once more, I started to cry.

SEVEN

Mourning Dove

Zenaida macroura. Sometimes known as the turtledove, this attractive gray bird, which reminds some observers of a woman in Quaker garb, is one of the most abundant and widespread North American birds. Doves are often hunted, with more than twenty million birds shot annually in the US, both for sport and meat. Some think the bird's distinctive low call sounds like a lament. In the Bible, John the Baptist referenced a dove to signify innocence. In the second century AD the Roman writer Juvenal said, "Censure acquits the raven, but pursues the dove."

NOW BEGAN THE HARDEST TIME OF MY LIFE TO THAT POINT.

What do police say, the training takes over? I would dress and work and eat and drive and make coffee and brush my teeth and remove my mascara at night because I knew how to do those things. I was used to being alone.

I went to the Kate Spade event alone.

Alone, I walked through a field of flower beds fashioned into an elaborate carpet (there was no way to not walk on the flowers, which made me nervous) toward a series of gilded tents set up just outside the ballroom at one of those cornfield castles on the Wisconsin border, purpose-built in the twenty-first century to look like an eighteenth-century English great house.

Kate Spade was my favorite designer. I often thought about her bright and bold and ultimately heartbreaking life, of her death by suicide and her final note reassuring her adored young daughter that Daddy would explain everything. I wished I could have been there to tell her, hold on, tomorrow could be better, tomorrow could be worse, you can always decide that another day will be your last day.

Depression was something I had never experienced. That day, I understood that I was only sad. People had died of a broken heart, but I would not; I was not that finely strung. In time, I might even be happy, albeit without the astonished completedness I had briefly known.

There was a row of huge easel-backed photos of Kate Spade: flanked by a display of purses, with her arms out to embrace the doorway of one of her retail stores, a close-up of her with her sweet, iconic sixties-style French twist hairdo, her smile both mischievous and demure. Behind the easels were boho flourishes, including a pickup truck overflowing with artfully disarrayed baskets of roses and lavender, each bushel basket adorned with a huge patent leather bow. Risers draped with bolts of pink satin were decked with bags and wallets and totes and shoes in characteristic bright primary colors, decorated with pink carousel horses, teddy bears, cartoon pineapples with faces, hearts, and windmills.

I wandered about, desultorily talking to fans and shoppers, writing down a few of the things they said, spending a few extra moments with a woman who described the worth of collecting accessories, smiling because I knew how to do that. An extravagant array of gustatory delights sat there for the taking, mimosas at ten in the morning, tiny baked brioche egg cups, strawberry flan cake. Waiters offered trays of crab puffs. I bit into a baked brioche, swallowing the single bite with difficulty, dropping the rest into a wastebasket. I drank three mimosas in rapid succession, and the swirl of bright colors around me began to pulse and emit a kind of noise like the far-off siren of an approaching police car.

"I'm eating too much," said Stevie Lan, a casual friend who freelanced for *Vogue*. Carrying a clear plastic sack with five graft purses, he sat down beside me and kissed my cheek. "What's the big word, Reeno? What's the big story?"

Normally I would have teased him and demanded that he give me one of the purses as a present for my mom, who had the best collection of purses in Wisconsin. Puzzled by my silence, he handed me one anyhow. I drained another mimosa in two swallows, then examined the bag for country-of-manufacture tags and a collection label. It was a copy, but an excellent copy; the manufacturer had misspelled the Maira Kalman collection designation, replacing one of the *a*'s in the first name with an *o*. I tried to laugh, but that proved too big a task. "This is a fake. Fathead fraudsters, learn to spell already," I said, showing Stevie the error. "All the great criminals have moved out of town." He said he would keep it anyhow, for his teenage niece, and gave me a white Kate Spade clutch shaped like a seashell.

"So, Reenie, you look a little pale. Maybe pale green."

"I'm temporarily out of pocketbook, Stevie. I won't be back in Handbaghdad for a few months. The gossip is that I'm writing a story about my best friend from home, who is going on trial for murder."

Stevie had the grace to say nothing at all for a full minute. A full minute is a long time, as I have observed. Then he asked, "Was it her husband? Did he beat her up?"

"I don't think so," I told him. "She was an escort. They were clients of hers."

"They?" Stevie said. "More than one person?"

"Two," I told him. "Well, really more than two."

He added, then, slower, as if finally hearing what I had said, "Your best friend from back home was an escort?"

"I didn't know she was. We didn't see each other after high school," I told him. "Just holidays. And once in a while in summer."

On Stevie's face I saw what I was destined to see on the faces of all my party friends—a look that suggested that somehow I was complicit, as it always seems when a reporter befriends a criminal. It occurred to me then that maybe I deserved that. Wasn't my disclaimer of Felicity a kind of betrayal, making her sound like barely an acquaintance? Bye-bye, lovely world! All my new friends were going to be strangers.

Stevie and I watched the crowd stroll past, so-called street photographers snapping photos of well-heeled shoppers and sellers and fashion reporters, slim as pleats and always cold, who wore bright oversize blazers and wispy cashmere ponchos and took only one nibble of a tiny brioche before lighting up a cigarette. I'd watched models eat one bite of rare steak and a gigantic bowl of greens and onions with a squeeze of lemon. That was what you did to make a hundred dollars an hour, less, I thought then, than what Felicity earned.

I didn't want anyone taking a picture of me, in jeans and one of Sam's white dress shirts I had stolen, my hair scraped up into an actually instead of artfully messy ponytail. The last thing I wanted was for Ivy to see me this way, representing *Fuchsia* looking like a college student late for an eight-o'clock class.

I would have to have the shirt cleaned and give it back to Sam. I told myself that I hadn't really meant to steal it.

"Let's take a walk," I said to Stevie. "I think I've had too much champers and sun."

We walked over the flower carpet to a little bridge that crossed a stream, where there were some trees. My dad said really rich clients who built their mansions on former farm fields had full-grown trees installed, for why should they have to wait for nature?

Just after we sat down in the shade, I leaned over and kissed Stevie on the mouth, not a peck but a hungry kiss to which he responded, pulling me against him and lying back so I lay on top. I opened a button on my shirt, then all of them, so he could reach inside, holding the back of his head as his mouth touched my hot skin. Then I screamed when, from somewhere, a hard jet of cold water drenched me. Both of us scrambled to a sitting position.

"What are you doing on my land?" said the beefy blond guy pointing the hose at us.

"We . . . we're at the event," Stevie said.

"This isn't part of the event. Get out of here," the guy snarled. He directed a jet of water at me, soaking my shoes.

Stevie gave me his hand and pulled me up and we ran for the parking lot, with him still dragging his bag of purses. We were laughing at first but then the stupidness of the whole thing got to me.

"Stevie, I'm so sorry," I said.

"Reenie, no reason! That guy was a complete asshole." He added, "I've always wanted to kiss you."

"I'm so sorry I made a pass at you. Really sorry."

My stomach lurched then and I ran for the nearest trash barrel, throwing up all those mimosas and minibrioche. Stevie quickly got a bottle of water from his car.

"Not wanting to kiss you as much right now!" he said. We did honestly laugh then, as I used the water and a roll of paper towels to wash my face and hands. Stevie said, "I get the feeling something's wrong, Reeno."

"I met a guy and fell in love. It was this whirlwind, not even a week. He broke up with me yesterday. And it's all my fault."

"Ouch."

"Yeah. I'll live. Not enthusiastic about that right now but give me time. I have to go and write this story now."

"Call me, Reeno. Maybe you'll want to kiss me when you're sober."

I said, "Stranger things. Thanks, Stevie. Thanks for being there."
I wrote:

The vibe at a Kate Spade "swap meet" north of Chicago,
where collectors of the late, legendary designer's pop styles
met to sip breakfast champagne, munch on baby brioche,
and to buy, sell, and admire vintage pieces, was bright, antic,
and a little wacky. It seemed to reflect the public persona of
Katherine Noel Brosnahan Spade herself, a Kansas City girl
who came to the big city for the bright lights, but who, at
last, couldn't evade the shadows, and who died by suicide
in 2018 at just fifty-five years of age. Those close to her
said she struggled all her life against depression. After her
death, the profile and prices of her whimsical purses, shoes,
handbags, and clothing soared. Those who loved Spade's
work can be forgiven for their desire, certainly meant as
admiration for most, but for others as investment.

Kitsy Murray, a veteran collector, said there was an
inherent dilemma in "collecting" a functional object. "Do
you use a vintage Kate Spade bag you paid $1500 for to
carry a wallet, a lipstick, and some Kleenex? I do, and I
think that if you can afford to, it's okay. It lessens the value,
but I think that Kate would like it."

In the eighteenth century, the Japanese artist Gechu
fashioned from ivory a four-inch carving of a shaggy dog
with her pup, a "netsuke." It had a function, as a fastener
for the belt of a formal kimono. In 2022, that carving
sold at Bonhams in New York, where the sale of ivory is
outlawed unless it is more than a hundred years old, for
nearly half a million dollars.

I got my minifeature approved and sent Marcus the number
of one of the photographers who'd been taking pictures.

It felt like an accomplishment. I could still do that.

Still, it took a toll. Hours later in my childhood room, after I showered and slipped into pajamas I'd had since high school, I laid myself slowly on the bed, as if too abrupt a movement could break me. Against my stomach, I curled the pillow that still smelled of Sam's light lavender aftershave. I placed my phone right beside my head, for wasn't it possible that he was as lonely as I was and might call any moment? Like a ninth grader, I checked my phone ten times a day, tested the ringtone, pushed his number over and over, and hung up before it could ring. Finally, as two days became five became eight, I silenced the phone.

Work.

Coffee and work.

I could do that.

Eating, not so much.

A thesis had begun to take shape: Maybe the puzzle of why Felicity turned to sex work could remain a puzzle. Everyone said she was the last person to have done that. At least in high school, she seemed almost allergic to romantic interest in boys. She was the sort of antislut, a goddess like Diana the Huntress who ran from men. Finding that answer, or not finding it, would be the conclusion, the murder trial part of the exploration.

I wanted to explain it to Sam.

I couldn't, so I wondered, was it because of my past or our agreement that he didn't call? It didn't matter. I willed myself to stop thinking about it.

Fat chance.

And yet (move forward, move forward) I called Ruth Wild's sister, also Felicity, who was called Fay. She lived in Minneapolis and still used her unmarried name, Copeland.

Right away, she said, "Reenie! You remember me from when you were kids. Of course, I'll talk to you. Where are you?"

I confessed that I was currently in Madison but, on impulse, said that I would get a flight next morning so that she and I and the third sister, Claire, could speak in person. I couldn't wait to get away even for a day. I asked, had Ruth contacted her?

"I have no idea where Ruth is. Our parents must be sick with worry though they aren't saying much. They're pretty stoic. I've tried over and over to talk to Felicity, but she won't answer my letters or phone calls. I asked her lawyer, Sam, I think his name is . . . "

"Yes, Sam," I said, as eager to speak the name of the beloved, only to have it sour in my mouth.

"Such a nice man. He told me she won't talk to anyone, but she sends her love. What do you think that's about, Reenie?"

"I'm the wrong one to ask. She won't talk to me either."

"It's crazy. It's just unthinkable. Claire and I are just obsessed with this, that brilliant, beautiful girl, my little namesake, the best of us, why she would do those things to herself . . . ? It makes no sense." Fay sighed. "You must plan on staying overnight, right here with me and David and our sons. Please, it's no imposition, I insist. I'd love to see you again. Of course, I wish it was for a happier reason. It's been years, Reenie, since you were in college."

I arrived the next morning, cabbing from the airport.

Fay, who taught earth science at the local junior college, had rearranged her schedule to accommodate me. ("Don't worry about it, Reenie. There's no greater gift a professor can give than a sign on the door that says class is canceled . . .") Like all mothers, it seemed, she had also assumed that I hadn't eaten for the previous two weeks: She'd made tuna Niçoise salad, a cold cucumber soup, lemonade with mint, croissants, and homemade cinnamon ice cream, which she said was nothing, you just dumped everything in the little machine and pressed Go.

I consumed seconds of everything. It felt safe to eat in the presence of a mother.

We sat on the screened porch overlooking one of the myriad Minnesota lakes, where sailboats tacked back and forth in the distance like bright toys, and presently, the third sister, Claire (Felicity Wild's other namesake), showed up. It was like seeing a composite portrait of features made from Ruth and Felicity. All of these Copeland women had those arresting leonine eyes.

Claire said, "We hoped that you had news. It's been months now, Reenie. We fear for her. To just vanish? I know she's been going through a complete, well, you'll pardon me, a crucifixion. Not only that bastard's disgraceful behavior but taking the boys?"

I didn't have the strength to explain, and it didn't matter in any case. I couldn't yet face the grandparents, who'd lost a daughter and a granddaughter as well—not that Felicity was going anywhere. If she were convicted, they would know exactly where to find her: for a long, very long time at Manoomin Correctional Facility for Women, a forty-minute drive from where they lived.

The elder Copelands were over eighty by now and fully retired. After leaving NASA and then his teaching post at Minnesota, Hal had apparently moved to Sheboygan to be nearer his wife Alice's family and to consult for an aeronautics firm that paid him whatever he wanted for as much as he wanted to do. Alice objected at first; she'd had enough of moving around. She was, however, comforted knowing she'd be able to spend more time with Ruth's family, just down the road. Alice never liked Roman Wild. Hal tolerated him, but they adored Felicity and Jay and Guy and established a fragile peace.

"The truth was, they were his kids, not Ruth's. They were his heirs. They looked like him and they acted like him, and even when they were little, he didn't really correct them when they weren't very respectful to Ruth because she was a woman," said Fay. "It was a different story with Felicity. Felicity was everything to Ruth. She was determined that Felicity would be a shining light, not 'poor Ruth's' daughter. And Felicity was just that. She adored her mother." She added, "When Ruth found out, it must have broken her."

"We hated how meek Ruth was with him," Claire continued. "Remember, Fay, that time you said to him, 'Ruth's not your child, Roman, she's a grown woman . . .'"

"About swearing. Because she said, 'those goddamn creeps,' that was it, about men in show business taking advantage of women."

"And he said, 'Ruth, no profanity!'"

"He didn't allow her to swear?" I asked. "He corrected her in front of people?"

"Absolutely," Claire said. "And not only that—"

Fay said, "Claire! Let her get a word in edgewise!"

Claire ignored her. "Come on. This is Reenie. All of us, Ruth too, we thought Felicity was going to Costa Rica for field studies with her birds. Shock doesn't begin to describe it! I may just be a Minnesota housewife . . ."

"Oh please, Clary, with a PhD and a standing offer from—" Fay began.

Claire, the youngest sister and clearly the favored baby, mother of four-year-old twins, retorted, "Maybe someday, when my boys are older."

Fay said, "Ruthie was the giant brain, the jewel in the crown, even smarter than Claire, until Felicity, that is. There was nothing Felicity couldn't do, arts, math, music, which makes it more devastating . . ."

"Not that we're elitist jerks . . ."

Not jerks, I thought, but certainly elitist daughters of the rocket scientist and the mathematician mom.

"And imagine how it was for them when Ruth was describing herself as a submissive wife."

Then Claire said, "There was that one time," and Fay nodded. I was reminded of Nell and me. Sisters don't need complete sentences.

"What one time?"

They exchanged glances, clearly not sure if they should tell me.

Finally, Fay continued. "He grabbed Felicity by the arm, not hard, but hard enough. She fell. She hit her head on the corner of the door. I will say that he didn't mean to hurt her, he was just so big and Felicity so slight . . . I remember she was supposed to jump right up and clear the table, house rules, but she wasn't doing her chores, she was all excited telling my parents about this birding trip she wanted to take, an Earthwatch trip. The boys were little, just starting grade school. They were big enough to help, but they just sat there, Roman didn't require them to do kitchen work. What was it, Thanksgiving?"

Claire nodded.

Felicity jumped up right away, not really hurt, only upset and insulted. She ran upstairs. Nobody knew what to say. Roman began to apologize.

Fay went on, "But Ruthie's face just went blank. Her eyes, I'll never forget this, were black, all pupils."

"Ruth's face scared me," said Claire. "She followed Felicity upstairs. The meal ended right then. Roman cleared the dishes himself. My mother helped, I guess."

"Was that the end of it?"

"No," Fay said. "Far from it."

I asked, "She was still expected to jump up and clear the dishes instead of the younger kids doing it?"

"She was a woman," Claire said. "It was that kind of house."

That night after everybody else was presumably asleep, Fay remembered that she'd left the novel she was reading in her purse. Unnoticed, she tiptoed through the darkened downstairs hall to the coat closet but then saw that the kitchen light was still on and caught sight of Roman and Ruth. The dishes had all been washed and put away. There was nothing on the counter except the last of the apple pie in a container. Ruth was wearing her robe— their bedroom was on the first floor—and yet she was busy with something on the stove. Retreating, hoping she hadn't been seen, Fay flattened herself against the wall at the turn of the staircase to eavesdrop. Clearly still annoyed, Roman demanded to know why Ruth hadn't come to bed, and why she was boiling water in her big pasta pot at midnight.

"And she said," Fay continued. "She said . . ."

"What?" I prompted her.

"She said, 'I'm going to wait until you're asleep and then pour this on you and kill you.'"

"She said that?"

"Obviously, she didn't mean it."

Claire said, "Of course not. That wasn't Ruth. She doesn't have a violent bone in her body. He crossed a line. She just wanted to scare him, I guess. I think she did scare him."

Fay went on, "But, Clary, you didn't hear her. Because she sounded like she meant it. Just as calm as could be. And the good reverend started to beg. 'Ruth, I said I was sorry, I tried to apologize, I'm sorry, I shouldn't have been so rough with her.'"

Fay remembered Ruth saying, very quietly, "You'll have to go to sleep sometime."

Claire said, "I need to see Felicity. Nothing will keep me from coming down there for the trial."

"Oh, Clary, think of how ashamed she must be," Fay put in.

"Not if she isn't guilty!"

"Even if she isn't guilty, she was a prostitute . . ."

I steered them back to Ruth.

"When he left, she suffered so much. She looked terrible," Fay said. "She got so scrawny, even her Mennonite clothes, those crappy blue cotton sacks, those just hung on her. The good reverend gave her nothing. She got a part-time job at another church as a secretary."

"Was your whole family devout? Is that how Ruth met her husband?"

They cracked up. "Not even a little!" Claire said. "We were awful. We used to sing 'oh, holy shit' instead of 'oh, holy night' at Christmas."

The last person they expected Ruth to fall for was a fundamentalist minister. The last thing they expected her to do was to reconstruct her life as a submissive Christian wife.

"She adored him," Claire went on. "And at first look, you know, he's so good-looking and commanding. We felt guilty for disapproving. My parents kept saying, 'Where did we go wrong?' Like instead of a born-again Christian, Ruthie was a drug addict or a . . ." Claire stopped, turning those big amber eyes on me in grief, and I knew just what she had been about to say, which she quickly amended. "An embezzler or a shoplifter or something."

The marriage seemed to prosper as Ruth gave birth to Jay and then to Guy. "The two boys that every Copeland sister is required to have," Fay said now. Years unrolled, Ruth seemingly content, until it all caved in. Both sisters were horrified on one level, gratified on another, appalled at Ruth's decline.

Fay went on, "Ruth was never strong." Ruth had a weakened heart, consequence of a runaway case of strep she'd suffered as a child. One of the reasons Roman Wild gave for leaving her was because he insisted that they have more children. Ruth refused, sure another pregnancy might kill her. "What if she's sick again? What if she can't contact us? Like, she's in a hospital someplace!"

"I just don't buy that she's too ashamed to show her face," said Claire. "That is not Ruth. In every other way except with the Jesus freak, she was bold. And she was the funniest, most involved mom. She would do chemistry experiments with them in the kitchen instead of making cookies."

The police couldn't treat her like a missing person. Ruth had given evidence of a plan; she'd resigned and withdrawn her savings from an account in her parents' name, something the sisters had just learned. Claire said, "You know he took all the money they saved together!" They'd circulated her photo and description through organizations that help abused women and girls. Nothing.

We talked long into the night. They showed me photos of Felicity as a child, which awakened my own memories of that fragile girl who had the grit of an athletic boy. Did I miss Felicity or my innocent past? Fay allowed me to borrow the photos to copy for the story. I'd forgotten to make my reservation but, to my relief, there was plenty of space on the flight that left at nine. Just after dawn, Fay gave me hard hugs and blueberry scones, but Claire, good as her word, showed up in her Volvo station wagon with her computer bag.

"Are you taking me to the airport?" I asked, confused.

"I'm coming with you," she told me. "The kids are covered."

"You are? Why? It's days and days until the trial."

"I'm going to make it my business to see my niece in jail. If she knows I came all that way, maybe she'll agree. Otherwise, I'll just sit in my bed-and-breakfast inn and work. And sleep. I could use some recreational sleep. For women my age, it's like recreational sex."

So I canceled my reservation and we set out on the four-hour drive, which, the way Claire drove, would probably take ninety minutes.

Partly out of self-defense, so I wouldn't know about the moment we crashed going ninety miles an hour, and partly because I was wiped out and being with someone so take-charge as Claire let me act the child, I fell asleep after about ten minutes. She woke me gently at the exit for Madison. She'd already arranged a room at a bed-and-breakfast. Before I left her there, Claire said, "So you and Sam, you're, ah, friends."

"How could you tell?" Would I someday be a mother and have psychic powers? I kissed my mom goodbye, telling her I had business in Madison and would stay with Nell for at least a couple of days. "We were. But it's over now. I think it's over for good."

"Well, maybe for the best. Too combustible right now."

I told her, "It breaks my heart."

"This is like a movie," Claire said when I explained more about how things had transpired between Sam and me. "I just don't know if it's like a good movie or one of those movies you think, ah, that could never happen in real life."

EIGHT

Redheaded Woodpecker

Melanerpes erythrocephalus. Why does a woodpecker peck wood? The redheaded woodpecker uses its strong beak to drill into wood for diverse reasons: to "call" a potential mate by "drumming," to establish a cave in which to build a nest, and to hunt for insects. An unattached male will drum on anything, even vinyl siding or pipes, to advertise his availability. First described in the early 1700s, these medium-sized birds have a wide habitat range and are busy parents, often hatching a second brood while still caring for the first. They are very territorial about their nests and will destroy other birds' nests and eat their eggs to drive them away.

MY FATHER SENT ME A PHOTO OF HIS FAVORITE TREE IN BLOOM. IT was a red horse chestnut. The sight of the deep rose-colored flowers shocked me. Patrick called the budding of his tree the first sign of spring. So much time had passed. I'd been happy and then miserable. Now I lived in neutral, either staring sleepless as the shadows made their nightly traverse of the ceiling or sleeping so soundly I woke up to find my sister taking my pulse, slightly sick to my stomach some of the time or gorging as if I'd just broken a six-week fast. The seat of emotion is definitely not in the heart, but in the stomach.

Work is supposedly something you can throw yourself into to distract yourself from heartbreak—and that's sure not true. But it does fill up time. And yet, whenever I had a free moment, I concentrated so hard on not thinking of Sam that all I did was think of Sam. Bad memories stung; good memories scalded.

A couple of weeks into that long stretch of time, I remembered a moment from that last, lost weekend, after I'd stated my high-minded intention to swear off him but before I confided my dark past intentions. It was a moment I hadn't allowed myself to relive. I'm not sure why that was, perhaps because I wanted to save it if I ever needed to remind myself that once I was loved.

Sam was standing naked at the upstairs window, his back to me. He was not an Adonis, but his strong, modest body was everything I knew I would ever want to touch, his fierce, tender mind everything I would want to learn. In that moment, I wanted to take it all back, because who cared about any fucking story? The truth was, although I wasn't confused by my feelings for Sam, nothing was ever clearer. I was overwhelmed by those feelings—and by the strangling vines of the case. Multiple tendrils tangled around the case, my past, and my story. I wondered, in retrospect, if I had approached life and love with the emotional maturity of a ninth grader. I said to him, "If it means I'll lose you, then we won't do it. I don't want to sneak around. But nothing is worth losing this."

In truth, we hadn't gone far enough for either of us to feel that way, and I regretted skating so close to emotions that sounded like so much romantic hyperbole. "This isn't something I want to do, Sam. It's the right thing to do. I've had the time of my life here with you! And I love you." It was out before I could restrain it. The next thing I said, after a breathless moment, was "Oh wow, I didn't mean that."

"You didn't mean it or you didn't mean to say it?"

I had to pause again for an additional few breaths while I considered lying. "I didn't mean to say it."

"Good," Sam said. "I love you too."

I thought then that if I had to live the rest of my life on that moment, I would have been able to do that. And as it transpired, it seemed I would.

I plunged back into research of the most granular variety.

The following afternoon, I headed for Ophelia, that "gentleman's club" mentioned by the guy Ross knew, one of those places frequented by actually-pretty-good guys who cheated on their wives with escorts. Or just watched strippers.

The building was unprepossessing to say the least. Entirely windowless, it was a single story of bright pink concrete blocks with no windows, like a lurid bunker. There was a rotating sign on top that featured the silhouette of a naked, buxom woman, and it boasted a huge black wood-and-wrought-iron door that would not have looked out of place on an Italian castle. In the parking lot, which was nearly deserted, I had to sit for a while to calm down, wondering if anyone I knew would see me here, dismissing that thought as about as likely as the sky raining frogs, next wishing I had a wig and a pair of glasses, then thinking about how I'd never seen a wig in a movie, even a spy movie, that didn't look obviously like a wig—and why was that? Surely movie producers had the money. They could hire the best costumers. Did the costumers have horrific taste? Was it on purpose? Ivy had a platinum blond blunt-cut bob wig so realistic that it actually had slightly darkened outgrowing roots and a couple of unruly layers that looked hand-trimmed. Marcus told me that it cost nearly two thousand dollars. I was still thinking about wigs when someone tapped sharply on the window. I screamed and the woman backed away, palms out.

"I'm sorry!" she called. "I didn't mean to scare you. You're Aurora, right?"

"Oh no, I'm Irene, and I'm here to apply for the bartender job."

"We didn't advertise a bartender job." The woman grinned. She had a fake birthmark, like the old-time actor Amanda Blake, the dance-hall girl in the reruns of the 1960s show *Gunsmoke*, which my father loved. (When we made fun of Matt Dillon, he would point out all the famous actors who got their start on that dusty set. "Look, that's Jodie Foster," he would say. "Look that's Harrison Ford. And Kurt Russell.")

"Don't you have a bartender job? Just a couple of shifts a week? I'm a licensed bartender." Every single bar in America had a couple of shifts for a licensed bartender who didn't need to be trained.

"I guess we maybe do," she said amiably. "Follow me."

We made our way around the back, where the setup was pleasingly like a picnic spot at a family-friendly beer garden, with a dozen sturdy metal picnic tables ringed by a low wall of the same pink concrete blocks. A few outdoor fireplaces dotted the area and a graveled path wound through it. Trust Wisconsin to boast a strip club with a spick-and-span venue. Introducing herself as Lily Landry, the woman unlocked the back door and beckoned me in. Even after she flipped on a panel of lights, it was so dark in there that I had to stand still for a while to make sure I didn't trip. *Hell is murky*, I thought. And so it was.

Despite the Brutalist Barbie style of the exterior, the inside seemed to be decorated to look like a medieval banquet room, or a medieval boudoir, or a medieval bordello—but it actually looked like a medieval dungeon. Along the back wall, under a massive mirror, was the most ornate bar I'd ever seen, made of black granite and brass mesh.

"The boss designed it," said Lily. "He loves New Orleans. He loves bars."

On the walls, thick, flocked gold-and-black wallpaper was draped with dark pink floor-to-ceiling puddle curtains held back by gold hardware. In the center of each pair was a portrait of a reclining nude woman, different sizes and styles, probably intended to suggest Modigliani and Botticelli and Klimt, with more enthusiasm than skill. The round stage was surrounded by sequential circles of tables, standard-issue four tops that I knew would be slivery and sticky. It looked like a pretty clean place. Still, the thought of what might go on under the surface of those tables and what might remain on the sturdy carpet (black embossed with gold fleur-de-lis) gave me the crawls.

"The boss doesn't invest a lot in furniture," Lily said. "There's at least one fight a month and the tables and chairs take a beating." I blinked. She added, "It's a shock at first."

"I've worked in bars. I've seen some real brawls. Not just men, women too."

This wasn't true. Angel on the Rock was the kind of place people burst into tears, but not the kind of place they traded blows. Lily handed me an application to fill out. This, I hadn't counted on, but I dutifully placed it on that shiny bar and filled in the blanks. When I was finished, Lily perused it as a few women came in through the back entrance, the most remarkable of them at least six foot two, with curly waist-length red hair, sporting a mink coat the size of a pup tent.

"Hi ho, Lilyloo!" she said, wiggling a hand decked with neon talons the length of the tines on a garden rake.

"Good evening, Archangel," Lily said.

I blinked again, as the amazon woman favored me with a cheerful grin.

When she went down the hall, to where I presumed the dressing rooms were (this, after all, was the undressing room), I said, "Archangel?"

"That's her real name! And here come Dovey and Lolo— they're mother and daughter." At that, I had to sit down.

Meanwhile, Lily was perusing my application.

"Can I ask why you want to work here, instead of a downtown bar or a supper club or . . . ?"

Playing for time, I said, well, the location was convenient . . .

Lily squinted at me. "You live in Chicago."

"Not right now. I'm staying with my sister for a while, to see if I might want to move here," I told her quickly. "Our family's from Wisconsin. I have a new, ah, boyfriend here. My sister's in law school, just a couple of blocks away." For the sake of verisimilitude, I added, "And I thought it might be fun. I'm a writer . . . at least, I want to be. I thought this place would be great for, you know, people watching. Like, working in a bar in an airport. Everybody has a story, right? Way more interesting than a frat bar."

"Right," Lily agreed.

She began to explain how each day and night worked at Ophelia. "The bar sets up at about noon. Can you do that, let's try maybe Thursday and Friday to start, noon to seven?"

I nodded, still speechless over Dovey and Lolo. The place opened for lunch (lunch?) at one in the afternoon; shows began at three. Besides drinks, the bartenders were responsible for microwaving chili and pizzas, serving nuts, snacks, and pickled hardboiled eggs. The cook came in at four, to replenish the chili, and to make the grilled rye-and-beer-cheese-with-sauerkraut sandwiches that the place was famous for. Fried pickles and vinegarfried potatoes made up the rest of the menu. I tried to imagine Ophelia as a dining destination and failed.

The drinks menu was spartan: red and white wine, beer on tap or bottled, whiskey and tequila by the shot. In summer, there were frozen margaritas. In winter, there was Irish coffee.

"When do all the strippers get here?"

"Any minute now," Lily said. "They come in three at a time. Sometimes four at a time. Kitty is always late, here she comes. These girls will finish up at seven. Kitty will change and be out of here like a bullet, she has two toddlers at home. The others might hang around and chat. Three more come at six, three more at nine. We close at one. There is a new person coming to apply, I thought you were her. Aurora."

"How do you apply to be a stripper?"

"You dance for me," Lily said. "And we don't call them strippers. We call them exotic dancers." When I wondered aloud if they were good dancers, Lily assured me that many of them were very good, some of them trained dancers. While every place had a different routine, at Ophelia the "girls" did five numbers each night, about five minutes or less each; the music and choreography and costuming was on them. The more I learned, the more I came to understand that this kind of place was its own specific world, with its own economy. Stripper costumes were dresses and skirts made for easy removal, sturdy, tiny, and immovable bikinis. They all wore high heels, but a special kind of high heels made for dancing. Most of them favored a brand called Pleasers, which also catered to pole dancing.

"Is that difficult?" I asked. "Pole dancing?"

"Very," she said. "You have to be graceful and strong."

That was the beginning of the time when I learned the secrets of a strip club. I loved learning those secrets, and I still love thinking about them. I took notes like crazy. I watched and listened. Someday, I thought, I would write a story for *Fuchsia* on what it cost to be a stripper, financially and in other ways.

High heels could cost two hundred dollars, and they wore out quickly, so most dancers had them resoled at least a few times. Many of them made their own costumes (I pictured a woman in her pajamas at her kitchen table, sipping coffee as she ran up a G-string on her Singer). Each girl got a hundred dollars a night from Ophelia and shared their tips. On a good night, like the night after a football game, or even a summer Saturday, they could still easily make a thousand dollars a night on tips. Three days was the standard workweek. Some of the dancers also were "bottle girls," selling bottles of wine or champagne at many times their real cost and, dressed in costumes that ranged from sparkly miniskirts to cowgirls and soldiers and nurses, doing private dances with minitorches and sparklers for a table.

Club rules were clear: look but don't touch, not even the privilege of slipping a bill into a woman's costume. Ophelia was a topless bar but not a so-called nudie bar. The tiniest scrap of a bikini bottom, which must have weighed no more than a couple of ounces, comprised that distinction.

"How can they?" I asked. "It's like being a . . . a geisha."

"You make lots of dollars for pretty fun work," Lily said. "That's not nothing." If someone misbehaved (or, as Lily put it, "fell in love," and caused a fight with a dancer or another customer) that person was escorted out, out for good, after a quick photo was taken to ensure that their passage would be one-way only. I saw the bouncers arriving—men the size of water buffalo who apparently didn't require coats even in freezing March. Police rarely needed to be summoned. Police, in fact, were steady customers.

Lily said, "The women who work here aren't treated like, well, like lowlife, ah, Irene. They're treated like talent. Like entertainers." She added, "And Ophelia has high standards for them too." They were the cleanest girls in town, she explained, more fully rouged and shadowed, plucked, tweezed, shaved, and scented than anyone. "You can see and smell the girl next door at the office, or at a bar. This is not the girl next door. This is the perfect girl. This is an unattainable girl."

But, my mind spluttered, but . . . but . . . but . . . there was no way around the fact that they were on display . . . for men to ogle.

"I know what you're thinking. It's a weird way to make a living. I'll say what I always say—lots of women put up with sexual remarks and put-downs working at an insurance office."

A brief flurry of icy air snaked into the room and Lily looked up. A very slight blonde woman was standing nervously in the archway. This must be the foretold Aurora. Lily greeted her. She offered Aurora tea or a soft drink. Then she asked what music she would prefer. Aurora chose an old Rod Stewart song, shrugging out of her coat to reveal hip-hugger Lycra and a crop top.

Sotto voce to me, nodding encouragement at Aurora, Lily said, "I myself couldn't get out of that with a crowbar."

Aurora struggled as well. She was a good dancer, limber and agile. As she wriggled away, Lily interrupted her, reminding her to be more subtle. Finally, she texted the woman named Archangel, who strutted out of the back room like a supermodel on a catwalk and, without a costume, wearing just jeans and a fuzzy yellow sweater, proceeded, with an attitude that was somehow covert, even shy, to gyrate, thrust, her face a convincing facsimile of a woman surprised by her own lust. And I was surprised by the pinch I felt low in my pelvis. My sister used to say that everyone was a little bi—and when she did, I thought, *Huh, maybe you are, Nell, but me?* Now I wondered, was I? Or was Archangel just so alluring that she was like an irresistible force? (Her irresistible biology, I thought, remembering my chat with Ross, which now seemed to have taken place years ago.) When she finished, Lily asked the young woman to fill out an application and leave it on the bar; she would be in touch either way.

"So when can you start?" Lily asked me. I shrugged. She suggested, "How about tonight?"

So away I went to my sister's place for a quick nap. I turned off my phone after leaving Nell a message to tell her I was sleeping in the erstwhile closet. But when I woke up, there was still nobody in the house except me. I ducked out for a quick shopping trip and then back for a quick shower, and at six that evening, I was fitting my car into the employee section of a now-packed parking lot, wearing what she told me to wear: black pants and a long-sleeved button-down black shirt.

The first thing Lily did was to hand the floor over to a cocktail waitress and pull me into the back room, where I beheld a hardboard wall with pegs hung with costume headpieces, crowns and cat ears and clown faces. The costumes themselves were arranged in neat racks farther back in the room. Framed like a bookshelf was a library of (very pricey) makeup. Clear instructions were given: "Please use sanitizing wipes on hands and containers before and after use. Replenish cosmetic stocks from the storage bins in the kitchen cool room. Wash or replenish brushes as needed."

"Sit down," Lily said, pointing to one of the chairs facing mirrors ringed in lighted bulbs. I sat, and she began to remodel my eyes and lips in shades of purple with smoky charcoal liner.

Having your makeup applied by another person is a very intimate experience. It wasn't my first time (there had been the Met Gala debacle) but I was very aware of Lily's physical presence in this sanctum of women's bodies. She leaned in close and I smelled her breath, like wintergreen, and the scent she wore, some kind of spicy oud, if I had to guess. When she finished, I looked like an elegant vampire, all cheekbones and deep, mysterious eyes.

"As I said, it's a strip club, not a library. You don't push drinks but you do sell drinks. You offer to top people off. You're a bartender, you know that. And you're pretty, so why not let that work for you? You get a share of the tips from the pool too." She removed my four earrings and gave me a little zip bag to keep them in. "You don't want to have your earlobes ripped off if someone gets into fisticuffs. The dancers all wear clip-ons." She handed me a shiny pair with faux rhinestones.

When Lily opened the door leading back into the club from the dressing room, it was like taking the lid off a box of noise:

clattering, shouting, raucous laughter, an old Billy Joel song about his uptown girl. I scuttled behind the bar and set up as many beers and backs as I could. I was sweating as if I'd run a 5K, not that I had any idea what it was like to run a 5K, but the front of my regulation black shirt was soaked; thankfully, it was from Target. The night went quickly; even six inches of sugary spring snow apparently didn't scare off Ophelia's regulars.

I left a message for my mother, telling her I would come up in a day or so. I left a message for Nell telling her that I would be working nights. I left a message for Sam telling him that I was staying at Nell's. In truth, I no longer knew where I lived. What I did know was that I wished I were back on the stone porch at Sam's house, listening to the mourning in the snow for an ancestral home they'd probably never seen. With a serving of self-pity and a dash of drama, shaken not stirred, I allowed myself to identify with those displaced lions.

The third night, I made drinks for a table of men, one beer and five ginger ales. I watched them curiously. Their conversation was low-pitched but I remembered what Ross had told me and studied the silences. When people converse, they fidget, crack their knuckles, glance around them, maybe even stretch. But these men were motionless as they looked into each other's eyes. When one talked, the others attended, their hands flat on the table. Finally one of them made a fist and quietly pressed it into his palm. He got up. He was handsome, not large but graceful and strong-looking, and I knew his suit had to go fifteen hundred dollars easy. He walked away from the table and spoke to me.

"Hello, Irene," he said. "I'm Jack Melodia. I own this place. Welcome."

"Hello," I said, putting out my hand, which he took. His palm was warm and dry. He held my hand just a beat longer than necessary and raised it slightly, as if he meant to kiss my hand, then released it with a wide white smile.

"Have fun here. Make lots of money. Be careful."

What did he mean by that?

Maybe he referred to those very occasional outbreaks of customer fisticuffs.

Nights passed quickly. I slammed drinks, watched mesmerized as the tongues of patrons literally protruded from their mouths during the shows, and practiced some very inventive dance steps in case I ever wanted to impress somebody with my strut-and-grind capabilities. My hunch that I really had the personality of someone born in 1965 was confirmed by my instinctive response to the disco music. I broke up one fight with a single short bark ("Stop that now!") that I borrowed from my mother, but had to duck under the bar when another brief brawl ensued that required Kelly, the bouncer, to step in, taking hold of two full-size men by the backs of their collars and dragging them to the exit with the ease of a cat moving her kittens.

Still, I found myself physically exhausted, my desk-riding days doing me no favors as I sprinted in my ultrasupportive black leather tennies from one end of that shiny granite bar to the other, as I hunkered down on bended knees to wash glasses and pull beers and replenish ice, and the combination of that workout and cold temperatures was so potent that I got twinges in my ankles and fingers and had to rub them out with Aspercreme. It was worse than my old days as waitstaff at Angel on the Rock, when I'd struggled with sudden leg cramps in the middle of the night, so painful I had to jump out of bed and stretch until they went away—at least until I learned the old hack of self-medicating with a spoonful of pickle juice. Possibly, I was just a wimp.

I remembered then listening aghast to the tale told by two of my grad school friends who had hiked to Everest Base Camp the previous spring. They described the misery of altitude sickness and huddling in all their layers of down as temperatures suddenly fell to zero at night, and that was barely even the starting point! Those same two friends, now a couple, had contacted me not long ago, inviting me to join them on the Kenosha Dunes Trail, which they referred to as a "cute little baby hike." At the time, I agreed, imagining this would be a breeze, but now, taxed even by a few shifts tending bar, I realized this might be the apex of my athletic destiny.

My windowless bedroom at Nell's Victorian hellhole was unexpectedly comforting, as if I were a mouse in the hollow of a fallen tree. My single bed, demulcent with one of my Grandma Bigelow's hand-pieced comforters, was cozy and warm. I fell into bed at night and plunged into sleep, sometimes still fully clothed, with the light still on and my paperback, opened to the single page I'd stayed awake long enough to read, splayed over my face. In the morning, I would often find one of my false eyelashes stuck to the book and an imprint of my lip-sticked mouth, as if I'd kissed the page.

It was more than just unaccustomed physical exertion and the new employment of old skills, of course. It was grief.

I longed for Sam, my desire for him an affliction like a head-ache that crouched in my forehead always waiting to spring. I longed for him, so I made a conscious decision to fill every hour with things that would help me avoid even the thought of him. I was not about to fall apart, especially over a guy. The effort felt like removing the bulb from a light that wouldn't turn off. I signed up for a baking class. With a group from the local chapter of the writer's guild, I volunteered to read a chapter twice a week to elders over lunch. I built all these distracters around my new job.

You can only keep yourself so busy for so long, though.

I was never particularly one for lots of reflection. I told my-self that I did things rather than mulling them over. But now I was forced to admit that staying upbeat, for me, required a hefty daily dose of denial. When it came to deep thoughts about the kind of person I was, my chosen rationale had been what I didn't know wouldn't hurt me. The truth was that it already had.

One afternoon, as I left my sister's house, I got a text from Sam: **Need to talk to you. Personal.**

I responded as though he'd invited me to jet to Bali for the weekend. But I forced myself to hold off for two hours before responding: **When? Where? Why?**

I'll call you, he texted, and my heart went still. Would he call to set up a time for us to meet, during which meeting we would, quite naturally, drift back together (although that would be wrong!)?

Instead, he called nearly immediately. I was struck silent just hearing his voice.

"Reenie," he said. "I heard that you were working at Ophelia. It's not a good idea. I say this as a friend."

The term stung. Was that all I was to him? Was that all I ever was?

Quickly, he recalled for me a moment when I'd asked him if he was ever disgusted by his work, by the people he had to defend. He'd told me that yes, he'd defended people who did what they said they did and he'd gotten them off, but never anyone whose guilt so offended him that he couldn't discharge his duty in good conscience. I agreed that I remembered the conversation, and I remembered asking, "Do I know any of them? Mass murderers? Heartless career criminals?"

"You know one of them," he said.

"You mean Felicity."

"I mean John Marco Melodia, who owns that club where you work. Jack."

"He's just a businessman. And I've barely even seen him. He's not a gangster."

"Well, he is, Reenie, he is a gangster. He doesn't traffic fourteen-year-old girls from third world countries, or import heroin, that I know of. He doesn't get his hands dirty, but he has friends who don't mind. He has a great many friends, including one of my partners at Damiano, Chen, and Damiano, who grew up with him. I didn't work with him directly, but I did indirectly, because I assisted his counsel."

"Well, what could be so heinous, Sam? This is Madison, Wisconsin, not Chicago in 1955."

"You can look up the next thing I'm going to say to you, Reenie, but you can't look up the thing I'm going to say after that. I have to trust in your goodness, and your feelings for me, that what I say will never go any farther than this." I gave Sam my word. This conversation was making me wildly late for work, but although I probably needed the job more than the job needed me, I was still destined to be a short-timer, so I wasn't terribly concerned. I wouldn't be counting on Lily Landry for a job reference, although I wondered what Lily really knew about her boss.

Jack's friends apparently helped their own friends make sure that their places of business never suffered mysterious events, such as surprise fires or floods. But then, a couple of Madison's seedier roach motels burned to the ground, on the same night, no less, in conflagrations so ferocious that trucks from several departments were hard put to extinguish them. It turned out that these properties had been for sale. A developer was interested, but Jack kept hiking up the price, and the blood between the two was getting bad, then downright polluted.

"You won't be surprised to learn that Mr. Melodia made out better with insurance payouts," Sam said. And then that business adversary went somewhere, like Missoula, at least according to his estranged wife.

"Did he really go to Missoula?"

"I don't know," said Sam. "Does anybody?"

"So, all that is a matter of record. He's not going to want to come over and kill me if I mention this in my story, not that I can imagine why I would."

Sam said nothing for a long while. Then he said, "Don't mess with this, Reenie."

I said, "Too late."

Before he could hang up, I asked, "Did you ask Felicity to talk to me?"

"I asked her again. She shut me down right away, Reenie, and I could tell she was mad at me for carrying the water for you. I did tell her that we had been involved briefly and she did smile about that but she won't talk to any press, not just you . . ."

"I'm not any—"

"She knows that. Reenie, in all fairness, I'm afraid for her. She's so thin she looks like she's dying. I try to send food to her, but I have other things I have to do too, and she says she can't eat the jail food at all, and I don't blame her. People who work there say she's quiet and polite but they can hear her crying at night. They almost put her on suicide watch but the night county matron, and yes, they still do call them that, put her in the holding cell full-time, next to her desk, so she could talk to her about books and things. They made sure she has binoculars. A couple of people brought her suet cakes."

"She eats suet cakes?"

"For the birds, Reenie. Somebody rigged up a little sort of feeder from a bent hanger outside her window. She watches the birds and she reads. She walks in the yard for an hour. I'm afraid for her. If the worst happens, if that happens, I don't think she'll survive."

"If she's convicted, well, that's what the punishment is," I said. "I know how that sounds. I've cared about her all our lives, Sam! Much more than anyone else does apparently. Doesn't anyone else come to see her?"

"She doesn't allow anyone, except this one woman, this incredibly tall . . ."

"Archangel. She works at the strip club. She used to be a track star until she got hurt . . . I know her."

Archangel apparently also sent books. "She wrote that woman to thank her for bringing her books. One of them was *Crime and Punishment*. Not too subtle."

"That's a favorite of Felicity's. It was actually a very nice thing for Archangel to do," I said and sighed. "I think Archangel wanted to send her some good meals too. You know the rules are that you can send food to people in jail from approved restaurants, but you can't bring them food you made yourself . . ."

"Yes, no handguns or razor blades in the risotto."

Sam had helped to facilitate some food delivery. "And a minister. He came once, but she wouldn't see him."

"That would be her stepfather, her adoptive father, Roman Wild." I went on, "Her mother is nowhere to be found. She won't see her aunts or me. I feel sick thinking of her being all alone but she's bringing that on herself. Right?"

"I think that she's ashamed," said Sam.

I could, in fact, imagine that very easily. It was all part of that swirling twilight cloud that was Felicity's world, *hell is murky*, where things were neither right nor wrong, but only possible. "So how is this on deep background?"

"The part on deep background is what I haven't said yet. Jack was in love with Felicity. And for a while, from what I can gather, she was in love with him too. He's a charming guy, he's extremely good-looking and . . . what would you call it? Cultured? He's married but only in the Catholic way. And he's very smart, third in his class at Marquette Law School."

"He's a lawyer?" Now he had managed to surprise me. "Jack Melodia is a lawyer?"

"He is. He trained to be an environmental lawyer. I don't

think he practices, but yes, he is a member in good standing of the Wisconsin Bar, having never been convicted of a felony. Or even of a misdemeanor."

When he heard what I was doing for research at the club, Sam said he had to gnaw on his tongue to keep from saying anything. Until now, he had not, figuring it was not his role or his place. Finally, his determination collapsed. "None of this is rocket science, Reenie. All business is based on loyalty because all unity is based on loyalty. And all conflict is based on loyalty. The Union and the Confederacy. The Montagues and the Capulets. The Earps and the Clantons."

"Earp, like Wyatt Earp, was a sheriff or something, right?"

"A federal marshal," Sam said. "Sorry. I was a history major. And my dad watches all those old Westerns. They're his life."

"Mine too. How weird is that? Did you know how many famous stars got their start on *Gunsmoke*?"

"I do. I've heard a hundred times. So please don't tell me."

Sam would probably have gotten along well with Patrick the Pure, if things had gone that far. I told him, "My dad builds houses. He used to tell me that there were a lot of bad guys involved with things that got delivered on trucks. I never believed him. He has a flair for the dramatic."

"Well, there are. I don't mean like in the movies, Reenie. I don't mean like *The Untouchables*. But wherever there's something somebody wants, a Porsche or a carton of cigarettes, there's going to be somebody else who finds a way to hijack that process. Hijack that truck. Make a big profit." He went on, "And it's not two jamokes sitting at a diner on a Saturday night who decide that would be fun. It's someone who has a boss who has a boss who has a warehouse or two or ten."

"Why did she stop loving him? Because he was married?"

Sam paused for a few moments and considered his answer. "No, because he would have divorced his wife for her, even though he's a strict Catholic. Something happened, I don't know what it was, that made her afraid of him. She left the club because she didn't want to be with him anymore but also because she needed to make some big money, maybe off her private clients? I think it was to get away from Jack."

"Could you ever get away from somebody like that?" I noticed that there were blue broken birds' eggs on the asphalt surface of the parking area, a tiny trail of ruined robins, which seemed almost too metaphorical. "In the movies, they always find you. Or people try to come back and get caught."

"Sure, you could get away. People transform themselves all the time, they even change their name and their birth date. That's why there are skip tracers." He could tell the term puzzled me and explained, "They're private detectives who look for missing people. They trace people who skip, who skip town, as they used to say in the old days." If Jack didn't go after Felicity, Sam said, it might have been because he was a man who understood appropriate social behavior, which meant that you didn't track down a woman who had made it clear that she didn't want you anymore. Or for all he knew, something could have happened between them that ruptured the dream for Jack as well. When I suggested that the breach could have occurred because Felicity slept with other men, Sam assured me that Jack certainly would already have known and accepted that. "At least he would have accepted it for the short term. Maybe he wanted her to give that up and she refused. I just don't know. I do know, he would have done anything she asked."

What was it about Felicity?

There were women I knew, pretty women, smart women, talented women, whose boyfriends cut them off because they danced with another guy at a bar. Felicity apparently wrote her own ticket with the men who loved her.

What was it about Felicity?

What earned her not only money, but the dreamy kind of devotion that was almost unimaginable in her role as a paid escort? That was what I needed to know. I was putting together the edges of the jigsaw puzzle: She let men come to her rather than playing up to their vanity; she dressed like an old-money heiress; she listened better than anyone they'd ever met; she remembered the small gestures, the tea, the scent, the double Windsor knot. Perhaps that was it, the entire point. She was present. She was like those old party invitations that you used to get, the ones that urged guests not to bother with gifts, notes that said your presence was your present. I couldn't prove it, but I believed that Felicity, who was analytical, turned away many more men than she admitted into her life. She chose wisely, in that she chose whose needs met her needs and whose means met her needs—or at least, they met her needs until her needs turned terribly real, not just a matter of financial means. But until then, when she was with those lonely men, she exalted them; she made them the focal point. Sure, maybe those guys had no right to feel lonely. Maybe they had everything: loving wives and beautiful children, plenty of money, enviable jobs, secure homes. That didn't matter. Who among us is not longing for the kind of understanding that passes all understanding? That, which Felicity gave them, was her talent. Her presence was her gift. What was that worth to her guests? It was worth big money. It was worth whatever she wanted. I would have bet everything I had on that notion, and I would have won.

Sam and I parted with a cursory farewell. I couldn't tell what he felt, but none of my feelings for him had abated since that lost weekend. If anything, they had intensified.

Can new love be denied? The love cannot but the exercise of it can. I was setting myself a test, setting a test of Sam and me, if what we felt would survive outside the rarefied and undeniable drama of the trial . . . or if that connection, so fragile and new, would be strangled in the tentacles of that huge event. I was doing it for all the right reasons. There would be no romantic pollutants in the story I would write for *Fuchsia*. I would write a story about being me without trying to be his. The fact that it was the right thing to do was no better, and much lonelier.

I woke at night in my maiden's bed with the sheets as sweaty and tangled as they'd ever been when I was seventeen and so madly in love with Lucius McCool that I thought I would go mad—as I had.

"Who's Sam?" Nell asked me. I hadn't told her about him; I knew that she would say some lawyerly thing that would be unwelcome.

"Why do you ask?"

"I heard you say his name in your sleep."

"You heard me say his name from your room?"

"I could have heard you from Denver."

My sister started bugging me then, as she had for days, about my love life, or my now ex–love life, which she didn't really know about, but bugging me more often about my strip-club job, which she did know about. What was it like? Was it disgusting? Was it sexy? Was everyone there a sleaze? Could she come and watch while I worked? I agreed to the latter, because despite how much of a pain she could be, Nell was a sharp observer. My only request was for a little more time to get myself sorted out there.

I wanted to find ways to talk to people who'd known Felicity. As it turned out, that happened pretty naturally.

At the end of the first week, Archangel came to the bar near the end of the night.

"You hungry?"

"I am," I said. I never ate at work, the old axiom holding true; you couldn't eat food you saw made. I used to love chili.

Now, like a kid who craved mint chocolate chip until she got a summer job scooping ice cream, I gagged when I smelled the chili bubbling in the prep kitchen.

"Let's go for breakfast," Archangel said. She had just started working double shifts, short-term, to sock away what she described as her "do-over" stash, money she would use to move to Ireland for a couple of years, see if she could give up the crazy life. She now ate one massive meal on a working day, a pre-dawn breakfast and dinner combined, and nothing but apples and coffee after that. Her appetite was so prodigious that her stomach would protrude during her dances if she ate all that she was capable of eating.

Walking with her into The Eggs-Ham-iner (the sign featured a picture of a newspaper with a giant plate of sunny-side-ups) was quite an experience. The whole joint, which was packed, paused, forks held aloft in hand. Six-two, in full stripper makeup, a crop top, and miniskirt, topped by a fuzzy white fur jacket, which I could tell was not faux fur, she must have attracted those kinds of stares no matter where she went.

Archangel confided, "People think I'm trans. I don't care if they think I'm trans of course. But I'm not. Born this way."

Only her hair, which she freed from the tight topknot she wore onstage, looked the way it would look in the wild. Cascades of blond twists falling past her shoulders, she then looked like a big raw girl, perhaps off a farm, at least off a farm a generation ago, the kind of long-legged, strong-limbed, big-shouldered girl who might have been an athlete. That was exactly what she had been, a track star who could hurl a discus and a javelin like paper plates and vault over a pole as if it were a backyard croquet wicket, all through high school and a single semester of college. Then she wrecked her shoulder, and the scholarship collapsed along with generations of hope for Arch-angel Kolowitz, for her and for all her very tall family, and she slipped into a netherworld of not having planned what else she wanted to do besides pray for the next Olympic trials.

It broke her heart.

For a while, she drank and drugged, but that brought her no relief; it didn't come naturally to someone who'd spent her life in training since she was ten. Now, she was studying sports medicine, with the hope of helping other promising little girl athletes avoid those kinds of career-ending injuries.

"But you don't want to hear about the drama of waking up one day as an over-the-hill twenty-two-year-old former almost-Olympian, do you?" she said, opening the menu. "You don't want to hear about good girls gone bad. You want to hear about bad girls gone worse. Escorts in jail. What a colorful life I lead."

I, meanwhile, was studying the menu, one of those menus that seems to feature every kind of short-order entrée ever created—and a few more. The omelets alone took up a full page—Southwestern, Veggie-licious, Mushroom, Greek, Spanish, Irish, Hawaiian, Tex-Mex, Denver, Philly, Margherita, Grilled Hashbrown, Brie and Bacon, Kale and Cheese, Rosemary and Prosciutto, Salmon and Cream Cheese.

"What's a Mère Poulard omelet?" I asked Archangel.

"Puffy, with crème fraîche," she said. "It's quite good here. I've had them all. The food is actually really good here."

In keeping with that, she ordered what seemed to be the whole left side of the menu: avocado eggs Benedict, French toast with strawberries, oatmeal with currants and brown sugar, extra wheat toast, and a scone. She must have seen the look on my face, because she said, "I'm a vegetarian," and then burst out laughing. "I don't gain weight. I have an insane metabolism and I'm always dancing or practicing or running or lifting or something."

"Could I ask you something?"

"Sure."

"Is yours a chosen name?" This was, I knew and she knew, the polite way of asking if her name was fake, if she'd been born Suzanne or Kathleen. She grinned. She had a startlingly sweet smile; it looked new, as if she'd just discovered how.

"You mean Kolowitz?" Again came the throaty, slightly raunchy laugh. "No, I know what you mean. It was chosen, yes, by my mother," she said. "My mother was a nun. I mean, she wasn't a nun when I was born, it wasn't that big a drama, but before that. She's still very religious. My whole family is." She studied my face again. "My brother is named Saint Joseph Kolowitz, though he goes by Joe. My mom knows what my job is. She doesn't think that I'll be cast down into hell for it, in case you're wondering, and neither does my father or my grandfather." This was curious to me, because I wasn't sure what my own mother, who wasn't religious, would think.

As we ate, Archangel told me that most people at the club were speechless when Felicity was arrested. Felicity was not crafty or violent. Felicity was not greedy or cruel. It had to be a mistake. "Dovey said she was the one more likely to kill somebody than Felicity. Nobody believed it for one second. And then when they found out who the guys were? People said, no way, not possible."

It was at the club that Felicity met Emil Gardener. He was a regular who showed up every Thursday night, heat wave, blizzard, or thunderstorm. A nice man, a shy man, who drank a single beer and ate a sandwich. If he had a second beer, the girls teased him. Cary Church was another matter.

"How?"

"He was kind of a show-off. He threw a lot of money around. He was always giving everybody investment advice and bragging about his big . . ." She laughed at my expression. "His big portfolio! He was going to take early retirement in his fifties and have a full pension and buy a house in Hawaii." She sighed. "So much for that. I don't think he was a bad man. Just one of those guys who knows it all. You could see the way he watched Felicity, as if the two of them were on a date and he was just bored and having to put up with all the other men there."

"And how did she react to that?"

"She gave him some special attention. She smiled and winked. She acted sort of shiny around him." Archangel said, "If I had to guess, I would guess that he gave her things. Like stocks. Or he paid her mortgage. Did you ever see that place?" I shook my head. Archangel gave a low, skillful whistle. The other diners tried not to stare and failed: They really did think she was a trans woman. "That place! The building is just two stories, but her place is the whole second floor. And the rooftop. Three bedrooms. Everything is white or blue or gray except the plants and pictures. Even the dishes were gray. All understated but really comfortable, you know? And her pool, it was tiled in blue glass. Like a wave pattern. Those shaped evergreen trees . . ."

"Topiaries?"

"Yes, shaped like birds. A heron, maybe? A hawk. A swan. She had those trees in pots all around the pool. It was like *Architectural Digest*. It's just exquisite." She reached into her bag. "Wait. I have a picture."

And suddenly, in front of my eyes, there was Felicity, barefoot in jeans and a white men's button-down shirt many sizes too large. In a picture taken from just above her, she was leaning forward, in the act of pouring tea from a ceramic pot, her neutral, pleasant expression one I recognized: It meant she was annoyed but too polite to say so. Behind her on the blue-gray wall were mounted two rows of skulls, masks painted cobalt and lime and bright gold, Day of the Dead masks. El Día de los Muertos, November 2, Felicity's birthday.

"So you have to wonder, why was she dancing at a strip club?"

"There are all kinds of theories but no one can be sure," Archangel said.

The others, she said, didn't know Felicity well enough to be invited to dinner at her place. Archangel was the only one. Felicity was reserved, all business. When she danced, it was almost balletically, to songs like "Bolero" or "Swan Lake." She never stripped down to almost nothing and she used her boas and scarves strategically. The costumes were her own, specially made, like a cape in the shape and colors of a peacock's fan. Her modesty had an ironically erotic effect on the customers, who spoke to each other about her "class" and "femininity."

Archangel continued, "She was in the book club, and got us to read *Crime and Punishment*. I think it was the first time most of the girls read the Russians." She regarded me again, this time ruefully. "What, are you surprised we can read? Do you think we're all middle school dropouts?"

"Not in the least. But you would have to admit it's not the first thing that springs to mind, the Ophelia Gentleman's Club Book Group. It's like the Harley-Davidson Baking Society."

"Now that's funny," Archangel said. "I'll have to remember that one and tell Lily." She hastily assured me that not all the strippers were Rhodes Scholars either. Some of them had come from abuse. Some were runaways or had babies when they were fifteen or lost a battle with drugs or had indeed dropped out of ninth grade. Not many of them had a background like Archangel or Felicity. Every one of them was a striver, though. Every one of them wanted a better life. Not every one of them was doing something about it.

Felicity was.

She didn't drink. She didn't smoke. She ate abstemiously and only healthy food, which she brought from home. She didn't put any of her money up her nose. Her street clothes were clothes she wore repeatedly, simple but stylish, clearly vintage, faded but well-tailored jeans, gray flannel pants, a sleeveless silk shirt, a pumpkin-colored designer sweater, a black wool blazer (and here, a wash of tears ambushed me again, as I thought of that homecoming dress and the cape she twirled—*my work here is done*—and of my own clothing forays, inspired, I realized now, as much by my friend's example as by my own lean means). She wasn't spending money on cheap and current clothes. She had other plans for the money that she made and she didn't dress to lure, but instead to look like anyone else. A grad student. A librarian.

Some of the people at the club thought that she was gay.

It wasn't because Felicity was standoffish or stuck-up, Archangel said, because she was never that! (*I know*, I thought, unreasonably, *she was my friend first!*) It was mostly because she didn't try overly hard to impress the men. They were impressed, probably more, because she didn't try. *The unattainable girl.* No matter how much money they gave her, she was appreciative, but not gushy.

"I knew right away that she wasn't gay," Archangel continued, demolishing her multiple entrées as I watched, almost too captivated by her appetite to pay attention to what she was saying. "I am gay, that is, I'm bisexual, and my gaydar is impeccable. She was different. She never faked any kind of social shenanigans. She liked you or she didn't like you, and when she didn't like you, she wasn't impolite, she simply didn't bother. If some of her fans at the club thought she was gay, that wouldn't necessarily have been offensive to them. Kind of the opposite. Some straight men are very turned on by gay women. Maybe because they've watched women together in pornography or maybe because they think, wow, they could change them . . . you know, if a real man finally got his hands on them?"

She paused, and we both ordered more coffee. I got a latte and more toast because I wasn't really eating my breakfast. At the best of times, I have an uneasy mental relationship with eggs, since I learned in high school that they were only one cell, which seemed obscene. That day, my relationship with eggs took a big left-hand swerve. I thought that if I took one more bite of my Mère Poulard omelet, I would throw up my whole life. The thought crossed my mind then: Could I be pregnant? I'd had an ominous dream the previous night. I was sitting in the passenger seat of a car and in my cupped hands were three tiny naked babies, fully developed but each the size of a shrimp. I had to keep them warm. I had to keep them alive, and I had nothing to cover them, so I held my hands close to my face and tried to blow on them with my warm breath. A man was driving, and although I couldn't see his face, I kept asking him for advice, but he didn't answer. I woke up crying.

Archangel was saying, "Or maybe it's because what women do together is pretty much like what men do with women, whereas what men do with men is foreign, or even scary to them."

What if I were pregnant? Wouldn't that be the coldest drench on the hottest newborn love affair? Sam wanted children, he said. He wanted me. Did he want a whole package deal, instantly? Would I be the only woman in the middle of the twenty-first century who "had" to get married? What was I thinking? I knew I wasn't pregnant, that this was just an idle speculation. On one hand, it was sort of an inverted relief to even be in the position of having to wonder about unplanned pregnancy; on the other hand, it would be a nightmare come true.

As if the outside of my head was echoing the inside of my head, Archangel said that she and her husband wanted to have a baby soon, at least one, probably more than one.

"I thought you were gay," I said. "Didn't you say that?"

"Not entirely. I said I was bisexual. A little of this, a little of that. I think that's true of many people who wouldn't admit to it in so many words. I'm married to my best friend, and he likes boys too, I mean, not boys, but men. That's in the past now. We like each other best of all."

"Does he mind that you're a stripper?"

"No," said Archangel. "He works at the club. You know him. Kelly, the bouncer. Kelly Green."

"His name is Kelly Green?" Of course it was. The sociology of that place!

"He's the gentlest guy on earth when he's not . . . bouncing."

Indeed, Ophelia was a microcosmic universe of alternative love . . . not to mention dining. How many ways did people find to how many kinds of love in how many kinds of places? Who'd have imagined all this drama—sex, scandal, infidelity, murder—in a Pepto-pink place the size of a dental office? There was probably plenty of intrigue at a dental office too, given what Sam had told me about veterinarians living *la vida loca*.

Sated, apparently, with only a single triangle of wheat toast remaining from that entire smorgasbord of proteins and pastries, Archangel leaned toward me. Lowering her voice to a growl, like a fingernail scraped across satin, she said, "One thing I know is true. The last time I saw Felicity, this was a few weeks after she had left the club, it was late fall, and something was wrong." It had been months since the two were together. Every time Archangel called, Felicity begged off: she was late for an appointment; her car was in the shop; she was consumed with a list of pressing chores that she told her had to do with getting back to college. "It just didn't sound right. I could have gone to her. She didn't need a car to meet with me. I would have picked her up. And you can fill out a form anytime."

The last part of the story was this: One late afternoon, Archangel ran into Felicity. Even though she was swathed in a voluminous coat and several scarves, Archangel could see that Felicity was not just slender, she was sunken. She was also rattled, distracted, and that wasn't Felicity. "She started to leave, but I stopped her. I insisted we get a quick cup of coffee. When we sat down, she kept looking out at the street, looking at her phone. I finally said, 'Felicity, what the fuck is wrong?'" That was when Felicity told Archangel that she had to get away, far away. And for good. "It was like . . . I know how this sounds . . . it was like she was being hunted."

As they left the coffee shop, headed in different directions, Felicity suddenly took hold of Archangel's arm, pulling her close, into a tight hug. "And that wasn't Felicity either. She was the person who let you hug her but she didn't initiate it. I had the strangest feeling. It was as if she might never see me again." Archangel pressed her forefingers, perfectly manicured silver talons, to her closed eyes. "That's my theory. That was why she was working at a strip club. That was why she was working as a hustler. She needed all that untaxed, untraceable money. She was going to disappear." She added, "I don't think Felicity killed anybody. But she was scared."

But what Archangel said was only a theory. On the night Emil Gardener died, if Felicity truly thought the old man had a heart attack in her apartment, if she really didn't know he had ingested cyanide, and she had nothing to do with it, why did she call Finn Vogel on Christmas Eve?

Why didn't she call the police instead?

It wasn't because she was an escort. The police couldn't prove that. Mr. Gardener could have been visiting for any number of innocent reasons. She might have been considering the study of dairy science. He might have been her spiritual adviser. In any case, I knew enough to know that women who got arrested for engaging in sex for a fee these days most often paid a fine and went home. The story crossed over to obsession.

Archangel repeated, "You know Felicity didn't kill anybody. I will never believe that."

"You don't want to believe it."

"That's different. I don't believe it. It wouldn't have appealed to her sense of order. She knew how to get what she wanted. Even if it didn't go against her beliefs, she wouldn't take that kind of chance. Not even once, not to say twice."

As we left the restaurant, I asked, "Why is the club called Ophelia?"

"It's the name of Jack's godmother. He has a niece of that name too. He adores her. He wishes she was his instead of his sister's." Archangel told me that she would give Dovey and Lolo the word that it was okay to speak to me. ("Lolo" was short for "Lolita"—you couldn't make this stuff up. They both liked attention, and probably wouldn't mind their real names being used if I wrote a story, although Archangel said that might not be in their best interests.)

I asked why.

"The boss might not be a fan of the publicity."

"The boss . . . Lily?"

"The owner, Jack. You met him. On the other hand, he might not care. It's well-known that she worked there."

THAT EVENING, LILY BUTTONHOLED ME, MOTIONING ME INTO THE dressing room. "I know what you're doing," she said. I said nothing. "I have eyes, don't I? You work at a magazine. You come from the same town as a former employee who's now been charged with murder. I didn't really think you just wanted to try out strip club life for research when you could have worked any number of places. But the real reason is, she mentioned you once."

"She did?"

"I have dreams of writing a novel someday," Lily said and laughed, shaking her head ruefully. "Doesn't everybody? Doesn't everybody think, *Wow, I've lived such a fascinating life, it could be a novel!* And how many times is that actually true? And if it is true, how many times do people have the guts and the talent to try it? Anyhow, I told Felicity this once, and she said, 'You should talk to my best friend. She's a writer, she's a wonderful writer.'" Lily paused. "I thought she called you Ronnie. But when I saw your name, I put it together."

I'm not particularly gifted at concealing my emotions, for hadn't I just not long ago confessed true love to my three-night stand? I looked up at the ceiling and, even though crying was now a second job for me, tried to staunch the tears that flooded the corners of my eyes. When I had my face under control, I told Lily, "Well, I hope you don't think I'm nuts, with my undercover stunt. I didn't know if you'd let me in the door . . ."

"It's okay with me. You can tell the people you're talking to. I would ask them to use their discretion. You're not doing anything wrong. But the boss might be a little unpleased."

"The boss?" I replied, playing it dumb, as if I hadn't already heard the same reference, in much the same words.

"The owner, Jack. John Marco Melodia. He owns a bunch of businesses and apartments, but he hangs out here mostly, and he has his business meetings here. We call him Tony Soprano."

"Is he a bad guy?"

"What does that even mean? I don't know. He's a nice guy really. He has good manners. I guess he's not somebody you want to mess with. Like I said, it's not a library." Lily continued, "She was not well-known here, but she was well-liked. She was modest and kind. She would come in for people who had emergencies or hold a baby for Kitty while she danced." My eyes must have widened, but Lily nodded. "People need to work, especially if they're single moms. Felicity was only here for a couple of months before she went into, well, private practice. What happened hit these women hard."

Lily continued, "I would do what you're doing. If I were you, I'd try to see her context too. But this wasn't her context, Reenie. She was as out of place here as . . . as Princess Diana would have been. Not quite that, but you know what I mean."

Then she told me how Felicity always had a notebook. "And in the notebook were these columns of numbers, sums, like my great-aunt would do with double-entry bookkeeping. And she also wrote down what looked like chemistry, like chemical formulas. She was always working away on something, and you'll think I'm nuts here . . . but I would look over her shoulder and she'd be writing down these odd facts about birds . . . I remember some of them. Like orioles are very social, they want their nests to be like condominiums, so they can visit. Albatrosses go for six months at a time without ever touching ground, just riding the air above the sea. And raptors, like hawks, are the best parents."

"I don't think you're nuts. She loved birds. It was her passion," I said, only then realizing that I was speaking in the past tense, as if Felicity had died. "Birds were what she wanted to study. Before. Before all this."

She headed toward the door of the dressing room, but then stopped. I stopped too. She appeared to be thinking it over before she shrugged and asked, "Did she do it?"

"I don't know. She pleaded not guilty. But everybody always pleads not guilty . . . I thought I would be able to tell, but I can't. And she won't talk to me. At least, not yet."

"Well, you're her friend. She needs friends now. When she does talk to you, will you tell her Lily Landry is praying for her?" My eyes stung again.

Later that night, I said to Lily, "So he named a strip joint after his niece?" Lily shrugged. I asked her, "He's a Shakespeare fan? Does he know that she dies at the end?"

Lily didn't know anything about Jack's reading or theater preferences—or those of his relatives. She did say, "Everybody dies at the end. Not just in Shakespeare."

American Robin

Turdus migratorius. The quintessential early bird that often gets the worm. American robins show up on lawns across North America, as well as in mountain forests and even in the Alaskan wilderness, popular for their warm orange breast, cheery song, and their funny habit of "listening" for worms underground. Robins can produce three successful broods in one year but only a quarter of fledglings survive to November. So while a hardy robin can live up to fourteen years, the entire population turns over on average every six years. Seen as signs of spring, many American robins actually spend the whole winter in their breeding range. In British folklore, robins bring a messenge from a lost loved one.

BY THE TIME SAM CALLED TO TELL ME THAT THE TRIAL WOULD BE-gin a week from the following Monday, of course, I already knew, and I also knew he'd called me just to be able to call me.

My time at Ophelia was up.

It had barely begun.

Lily was correct: I would have loved to write a story about the place, which most people probably thought didn't exist outside Las Vegas.

I still wanted to chat for a moment with the other strippers who'd known Felicity, but since I was running out of time, I let Nell come to work with me.

"I'm interested in the show but what I really want is food," Nell said as we opened the door. She sat at the bar, where I set her up with a beer and some nachos, but it quickly became clear that in the beer-versus-show equation, what Nell thought was exactly opposite to what happened.

She was instantly mesmerized by the sight of Archangel on-stage, which I had become used to, so I didn't remember how startling that could be. Sprinkled in glitter from head to toe and wearing only a sheer black body stocking, Archangel was doing a sort of reverse strip, pulling scarves and boas from a box on a stool next to her while simultaneously removing the body stocking, a task I could not have accomplished even while sitting on the stool, much less dancing in heels to the old Blondie song "Rapture." It was with a start that I recognized how much Archangel resembled the young Debbie Harry, in face if not in stature.

"Do you know that this was actually the first rap song?" I said to Nell. She didn't hear me, so I went off to find Lily and explain that my departure from the club was imminent. Then I took my place behind the bar, replacing a clearly pissed-off Raquel, who paused only long enough to point out the two customers who were already overserved and to add that she was late for her babysitter. "'Now he only eats guitars,'" I sang along with Debbie. I told Raquel, "I'm sorry." She flounced away. I checked the chili, scooping up a cup for Nell, who accepted it gingerly, only after I reassured her that it was prepared under perfectly sanitary restaurant guidelines. She took a tentative bite.

"It's amazing," said Nell, who'd finally turned to the food. "It's so good! The chef could be making this anywhere." I agreed. But I bet that if I had checked, the cook was either probably related to Kelly or Lily or somebody else at the club, or in some other jam. Short-order cooking was one of the top jobs for parolees; I had no idea how I knew this.

The overserved guy asked for a double and I provided him

two frosty glasses of unspiked Diet Coke, betting he was so smashed he would not notice. Archangel left the stage, replaced by Dovey, who continued with the Blondie music.

"'Someone's love had a heart of glass,'" I sang and did a little spin to grab the brandy. I'd convinced Lily to offer a sweet brandy old-fashioned, the most requested drink, easy to fix, and more expensive than the usual fare. I felt a tap at my back and there stood Lolo, in a red spangled minidress and high-heeled red boots.

"Archangel said you might want to talk to me about Felicity," she told me, her smile at once shy and mischievous.

"I do. Are you on the way out?"

"I'm on the way in," Lolo said, jumping onto a barstool in a far corner, away from the men at the bar. "I can talk to you, but I have to get dressed. Can I get a ginger ale?"

"Just ginger ale?"

"I can't have alcohol. I'm not twenty-one."

"I'll be back," I told Nell, who said nothing in reply, seemingly lost in the music and the sight of Dovey on the pole, removing a pin to loose the shining blue-black curtain of her waist-length hair. She seemed to regard Dovey as though the dancer was some sort of rare creature in the wild rather than a very fit fortysomething grandmother. Because Dovey had a daughter older than Lolo, and said daughter had a baby of her own. I just couldn't believe that. I buzzed Lily and asked if she could cover the bar for me, just for fifteen minutes, while I followed Lolo to talk to her, or at least try to, while she changed into her work costume. Not particularly happy about it, Lily agreed. I liked Lily, and I didn't want to burn any bridges. I had always been a short-timer, but now I had to make the most of the little time I had. There was no need for finesse, if I'd ever demonstrated any. Nodding Lolo toward the back room, I told Nell I'd be right back and asked her what she thought.

"I'm trying to come up with what I think. I would never

have thought it was so pretty and artful. And it is sexy too," she said. She pointed to Dovey. "I don't know whether I'm attracted to her, or I wish I was her. I could never do that, Reenie. And I don't mean I could never let myself be seen like that. I mean I could no more do that than I could do a triple flip on figure skates. It seems like that kind of talent should be doing something more in the world."

"Maybe she doesn't think of it the way we do," I said. "Her grown daughter works here too. That's her, the one I'm going to interview."

"Her daughter?" Nell said, with a gasp. "She has a grown daughter?"

In the dressing room, I glanced into the mirror. Lily must have despaired of my clothing and cursory nature-girl makeup, but that day, I just couldn't face the contour stick and five coats of mascara. Lolo was adjusting her hair extension, an elaborate confection of curls, securing it to her long ponytail with clips that looked like dragon jaws. When she had it all in place, it looked like some kind of small monument on her head. "I just want to ask you if you can tell me anything about Felicity that would shine some light on what happened with her."

"Why she killed somebody?"

"Well, yes."

"I don't know if she killed somebody," Lolo said. "But I know she was unhappy. Crazy unhappy. She would sit in the back and eat a whole box of vanilla wafers by herself. That wasn't Felicity. She was Miss Apple Slices and Carrot Sticks. Not like me, I couldn't care less. Give me a box of hot biscuits and I'll make them disappear." For the first time, I noticed that Lolo had a slight Southern accent and a sprinkling of gingery freckles.

"Where is home for you?" I asked her.

"Mom grew up in North Carolina. It's a shithole where she grew up. My grandparents live there, the meanest people in the world. My dad lives with them. They don't approve of my mom being white. So it's much better here. Although there are good things there too. My dad's sisters, they're great. And it's warm."

"How did you end up in Wisconsin?"

"My mom has a sister here."

"Are your parents divorced?" I didn't know how to ask if they were married, and I also didn't know why I would wonder that—was it because both of them were strippers?

"No, they're still married. He just lives there. We go every other month, holidays, all summer." She stuck in one more taloned clip.

"Is it weird to see your mom strip?"

Lolo laughed as she pulled open a bag of fiery hot Doritos. The unmistakable smell assaulted the room. How could something that tasted so good reek so bad? I had seen Lolo eat her meal before. A whole bag of Doritos, a whole pint of tabouleh, a pint of coleslaw, a full-size bag of Famous Amos. She weighed maybe ninety pounds.

"It's very weird," she said. "Especially if you know Dovey and you know that she has a heart attack if you open her bedroom door when she's getting dressed, or God forbid, walk in when she's in the shower. She would really prefer you to pee outside or hold it for twenty minutes while she takes her very long, use-up-all-the-hot-water shower. I have never seen my mother use the toilet, ever." I imagined what it would be like for me to watch Miranda remove her clothing in front of a room of leering, tipsy guys. The image was outlandish . . . However, the thought of my doing the same thing with Miranda standing there was utterly appalling.

"I don't know why I asked that," I told Lolo.

"Natural question. I guess my mom and I are a little bit unusual. You would not meet a lot of mother-and-daughter strippers."

"You never performed . . . together, did you?"

Lolo rolled her eyes. "Jesus Christ, no! That would make me

puke!" She said then, "There is totally nothing in the way of a turn-on about stripping, Renee. It's just working."

"Reenie."

"I'm sorry, sure. For somebody who gets called Lulu all the time I should know better. Anyway, there's nothing sexy about it. It's like going to aerobics class. It's bad enough we work at the same time because we only have one car. And she's always criticizing me."

"For taking too much off?"

"No, for looking like I'm miserable, which I am. You're quitting and I am too. In like a month, when I save enough to go back home. Dovey says she's going to go too. Lily will lose her shit. Not to mention Jack. Jack calls me 'the tulip.'"

It occurred to me that, after standing in the dressing room for fifteen minutes, I hadn't asked Lolo anything of importance. And I'd left Nell at the bar. So I hurried to ask, "Okay, why was Felicity unhappy?"

Lolo began to apply her false eyelashes. "I thought it was because she gained weight. She was miserable about that." She added, "She did gain weight. But she was too super skinny before. She looked really good."

"But it wasn't that?"

"It was more than that. She was all fine one week and then, boom! She didn't show up . . . That was what . . . months ago? And after she left, Lily started acting all nervous too." Guiltily, I thought of Lolo getting a job stripping at Ophelia at just eighteen, when most girls weren't even out of high school or were just starting college. She was a smart kid, so . . . why?

Don't, I scolded myself. *Just don't.*

And then, just as abruptly, I forgave myself for wondering. Why not ask why? Lolo's work wasn't illegal, or particularly dangerous, but it was, yes, it was demeaning. It was pandering, gratifying a distasteful desire. It wasn't really work you'd wish for a daughter to do if you had a daughter, unless, I guess, you did it too. And even if you did, you'd be fighting with all your might to convince your daughter to do something more worthy of her than being peered at by men old enough to be her dad. Yes, I was making a moral judgment on Dovey. But since when was it wrong to make a moral judgment?

I steered my concentration back as Lolo wetted down a sponge and began applying her foundation, the thick, water-proof kind that would stay put even with sweat and hot lights. "Did you ask Felicity?"

"I tried. She didn't answer my calls. I went by her house. She wasn't there." She stood up and began to use body glue to apply twirlers to her nipples, then put on a silver shirt that she knotted under her breasts. She shook out a silver pair of hip-hugger leggings.

"And Lily?"

"I didn't have to ask her. She was weird. Almost like she was scared too."

"Of what?"

"Of whom."

"Okay, of who?"

"She was scared of Jack."

"Okay, let's forget about Lily for the moment. Did you get the impression that Felicity was scared of Jack as well?" Lolo nodded, pressing her lips together for emphasis. "Somebody said Felicity loved Jack."

"She did. She talked like she did. Or at least, she talked like he loved her. She didn't talk about things he gave her, but I know for a fact that he bought that Mercedes for her. And he furnished her condominium. The pool. The landscaping. Have you ever seen that place? The trees in the shapes of birds?" I said that Archangel had shown me a picture of the living room. "But then something happened."

"Do you know what?"

"If I did, I wouldn't tell you probably because I'm not

entirely . . . I guess you could possibly say I'm scared of him too." This went along with what Sam had said, that Jack really was a gangster, that he was capable of the kind of hurt that people assumed went out with movies based on events in the 1960s. "Only one who isn't is Archangel. She's scared of nothing."

"Well, if you don't know what changed, who would know?"

Lolo just shrugged.

"Lily?"

At that, Lolo snorted. "I'm sure! But good luck getting Lily to say anything to you about Jack. Especially now. She knows better than anyone else . . ."

"Knows what?" Lolo shook her head. "Knows what, Lolo? Would he, like, keep your paycheck? Or key your car? Or . . . "

"Key your car? Come on. You think that's what people are afraid of?"

"Can't you tell me anything else?"

"No!" Lolo said, her face slamming closed like a door. "Ask Felicity yourself."

Would that I could, I thought, and remembered my sister. "It really is like porn," Nell said. "You think it's going to be this forbidden delight. But it gets boring after ten minutes."

"Are you going to hang around?"

"For a while maybe," she said. "I can take the car and come back for you later."

"I can get a ride to your house. But I have to let Lily go back to the door. I have to be behind the bar."

"Okay."

"I'm sorry for stranding you behind the bar," I told Lily. "But before you go, give me one moment. Let me ask you just one thing—do you know why Felicity left?"

Before Lily could even open her mouth to answer, one of the guys at the bar quite calmly got up, lifted the guy next to him bodily two feet off the ground, and threw him on top of a nearby table, which broke in half like a dry graham cracker. Immediately, it was team bar against team table, with everyone from scholarly little nerds to bluff neighborhood types to ex–football players gone to fat, along with a few suited wannabe hoodlums, flooding across the room to join the fray.

Until now, the fights I'd seen involved no more than a little bluster, some pushing and shoving, lots of sweating and slurring and swearing. They were nothing like this. Stripped to her undies, Dovey jumped off the stage and vanished. Kelly charged into the melee like Goliath, but promptly ended up on his butt on the floor. I put out my hand to Nell, who jumped up on her barstool. A guy grabbed her by the shoulder, and I picked up my ice water pitcher and threw it in his face. Nell scuttled over the bar and hid behind me. I pulled both of us down onto the floor, which was just what Lily had told me to do in the event. When she said that, during my interview, I thought she was just being dramatic. I glanced up, and there was Sam. What was Sam doing here? Of all times? I was so caught up in the action that I couldn't even compose myself to decide if I should run to him or ignore him.

He was, however, ignoring me. He was mesmerized. Nobody's idea of a street-fighting man, he was clearly as fascinated as I was by the willingness of testosterone-fueled men, ordinary men who had jobs and paid taxes, to go batshit crazy over something that had nothing to do with anyone except the original battlers—if even with them. He would later tell me that he had never been in a physical fight, even on an athletic field, but that he almost admired the complete abandon of the combatants.

They huffed and grappled and bellowed, their faces mottled with effort and booze, throwing wild roundhouse punches, only the tiniest percentage of which landed, and those with no visible harm.

It was fun for them. It was fun for me in all honesty. Nell's eyes glittered. She was getting the full dark-side extravaganza.

It quickly got serious. One guy got hit and went down hard.

He struggled to his knees, a cut on his head and one on his lip that bled histrionically. That guy's friend began to pound the one who threw the punch and soon his nose was a pulp, and he was unconscious on the floor. Two other guys waded into the fray.

"Cut it out!" Lily yelled. "Stop!" In response, still another guy broke a beer bottle and advanced, holding it like a knife, taking swipes at the guts of anyone who came near him.

Then, suddenly, all the overhead lights switched on. It was like pulling a sheet off a corpse. The wreckage of broken glass, blood, smashed food, spilled drinks, stained and dropping wallpaper was exposed. The brawlers stood up straight, or pulled themselves up off the floor, and scuttled away like beetles. Some of them bumped into police who were coming through the door, probably as insurance against the chance that some few customers might want to pursue a drunken beef. One of the uniformed police called out, "Lovely Lily Landry! How are you doing, partner?"

"It's the finest! Better now you're here, Rambo!" she called back. This was evidently a private joke.

It was when Jack came in that I noticed he was handsome in the way that Sam was: compact, dark-haired, not a large man but graceful, immaculate, capable, quietly classy. I didn't know if it was Sam's brief on him that prompted the next thing I noticed, which was that he was also something Sam was not—dangerous. He said to the battlers, who were still wandering around as if they'd just been roughly roused from a nap, "Get out of my club."

A police officer knelt next to the more aggressive of the bleeders, applying pressure with a bar towel. "He needs an ambulance," he said. As if they'd heard their cue, paramedics burst through the door.

Jack asked Lily if she or anyone else were hurt, putting a comforting hand on her wrist when she shook her head. He then turned to me. "If it isn't Irene, a good bartender, a bad fake, a nosy writer," he said affably. "Who is this?"

"This is my sister, Eleanor," I told him. I plucked up my nerve. "I would love to speak with you about my friend Felicity Wild, who as you know . . ."

"Yes. A terrible circumstance. A lovely and intelligent woman. And yes, of course, I'll talk to you. I'm an open book."

I doubted that. Further, I was stunned by his agreeable response. We made a date for coffee the following day, as Sam, clearly astonished, said nothing. As if they'd been waiting outside the door for our conversation to end, a burly crew of cleaners with shovels and buckets and wheely bins rolled in. I overheard Jack say that the club would be open for business at the usual time.

I told Lily that I would return the next day, in the early afternoon, to fill out my last time sheet and turn in my black vest with the monogrammed pocket of the busty woman in silhouette. I told Lily how that vest, which I wore over my black shirt from Target, had drawn some stares at the coffee shop—and that I'd made the mistake of grumpily assuming that people were openly gaping at my bosom. She laughed a little then and turned back to brushing broken glass off the bar.

I then approached Sam and asked, "What are you doing? I mean, I'm glad you're here but . . ."

"I wanted to tell you something, and when you didn't answer, I got scared," he said.

"What did you want to tell me?"

He gestured at the ruin of the room and said, "Well, for some odd reason, Reenie, it just doesn't spring to mind at the moment. And you're obviously okay."

He murmured that he'd be in touch and turned to leave. I wanted to chase him down, but didn't have time because Nell was in full marvel mode.

"Wow," Nell said, as we headed for the door. "Just wow. Gunfight at the O.K. Corral, sister! I was flipping scared off my ass. You just don't imagine a joint like this in a nerdy little city like Madison, huh? And you were just so cool, Reenie, so 'hey, no problem!'" For some reason, I was reminded of times when we were little, awakened at night by one of those Wisconsin thunderstorms where lightning flashes strobed and cymbalic crashes split the air every two minutes, nights when Nell came running to my room, tucking her cold feet under my knees and her cold hands under my back.

Since everyone had fled the brawl, my sister's was the only car left in the lot.

All four tires were flat, not just flat, but on closer inspection, slashed. I wanted to charge back inside and face Jack. But I realized that wouldn't be prudent . . . that this was a message to me. I said as much.

Nell was outraged. She babied her five-year-old Honda Accord, a graduation gift from our parents. She yelled now, "A message to the tune of hundreds of dollars! Those tires are only a year old!"

"I don't think it will cost that much," I said, as, just then, a tow truck pulled into the lot. The driver asked for Eleanor or Irene Bigelow. We nodded in unison. He then asked if it was okay to replace the damaged tires now. As he set about doing that, Nell signed the proffered receipt.

"You ordered new tires?" Nell asked me. "What, did you know this was going to happen?"

"Of course I didn't order new tires! And of course I didn't know this was going to happen. I think it was Jack who ordered new tires," I said. "From the look of them, brand-new tires." I also commented "What the fuck?" or words to that effect.

Nell said, "You were already quitting. What was the warning? Was it about Felicity? And next time, is he going to cut your throat, or my throat, instead of some car tires?"

I didn't answer. I didn't know the answer.

But my mind was also waterfalling with questions. Was there a world in which any of this was even remotely coincidental? And if it was not, how could Jack have predicted or arranged a barroom brawl?

And though I was frightened—of course I was frightened—I was also increasingly flooded with the fury reporters have felt since the first guy walked through the town yelling out the local news: We are only writing about things that happened, not making them happen, so don't blame us when the light turns on you.

Of course, there was no reason for Jack to be in favor of this story. Although it wasn't about him and would touch on his strip club only tangentially, Felicity was an escort who'd worked at his strip club, a brilliant fallen angel, accused of killing two people who were apparently loyal customers. I couldn't prove, and wouldn't write, that he and Felicity had ever been lovers but . . . even if Jack was married only "in the Catholic way," could he really believe that his wife knew nothing of any of these shenanigans? Further, sure, okay, he was a "businessman," but would Jack's kind of business be damaged by a story like mine? That is, could he actually believe that he operated in anonymity, if, as Sam had pointed out, some of the mishaps he was connected to were a matter of public record?

Theories were not facts, of course, but if Jack was so adamant about suppressing a story about Felicity, why had he agreed to talk to me? Was it because he was smart enough to know that refusing to talk to me would make him look even worse?

Neither was the stupidness of my own position lost on me.

Here I was, risking my own life, or at least my sanity, certainly my job, to try to help someone so unconcerned with her own fate that she wouldn't even tell her own lawyer the truth of what happened. If Sam wasn't lying, Felicity refused to cooperate in her own defense. So why was I bothering? And speaking of Sam, even if he had been the love of my life, and who knew if that was true, that was over, and I'd surrendered my deepest secrets and my peace of mind only to be kicked to the curb for my honesty. Emil Gardener and Cary Church were dead. Nothing could change that. The judicial system was doing its job on their behalf, and Felicity was either stone guilty or content to go to jail for something she didn't do. All this was true, so making this my personal crusade for curiosity's sake was curious to say the least.

Rolling along on those fancy new Firestones, Nell and I headed for her place, grabbing some bagels on the way. We then loaded them with cream cheese and sat dolefully at her kitchen table, watching yet more stupid Wisconsin spring snow feather down on the crumbling back steps. Afterward, I went into my closet at Nell's, hit the bed, and fell unconscious for eight hours before getting ready to go back to Ophelia for a final time, to pick up my check and have a last word with Lily.

When I stepped through the door, back at Ophelia, I would not have recognized the place—or rather, there was a hallucinatory quality to how much I did recognize it. It looked exactly as it had looked before the bar fight: spick-and-span and orderly, all the bottles, glasses, and pitchers tidily lined up in their places, the ice bins filled. You could never have detected signs of a scrap, much less what my dad, who loved this word, would have called a "brouhaha." It was only because I knew where to look for it that I was able to find a chip of a couple of millimeters, about the size of a two-carat diamond, in the left lower corner of that vast expensive antique mirror behind the bar. I'd seen that happen when someone nailed the mirror with a full bottle of beer. And still, even with the witness of my own sound memory, I wasn't sure it hadn't been there before.

Lily came out of the dressing room. She looked as though she'd been drowned and resuscitated.

"I'm getting too old for this," she said in lieu of a greeting.

"I was born too old for this," I said.

"You said you wanted to ask me something, Reenie. What was it? Forgive me for being so blunt but I'm worn-out."

"Okay, I'll cut right to it. Why did Felicity leave Jack?"

Lily blew out breath gustily. "Maybe I should quit and get a real job," she said finally. "Except that real job wouldn't come with so much real money, probably. All those lovely tips from the regulars." I didn't say anything else, remembering the power of silence, letting the question sit between us. "You can't quote me on this or even refer to it because I'm one of only three people on earth who knows this."

"Okay."

"Promise."

"I promise. But why?"

"You'll know when I tell you," Lily continued. "She left because she overheard Jack talking to another guy one day."

"She overheard what he said to somebody?"

"I heard it too. It wasn't so much what Jack said as what the other guy said. And it wasn't that so much as the way the whole thing felt." It was early afternoon on a Saturday and Felicity was with Lily in the dressing room. "We were sitting in those big chairs back there behind the costume racks?" I nodded. "We were reading, just us two, when it started. If the door hadn't been open a crack, I never would have known anyone was out there. But I could see this tall, thin, young blond guy and he was sobbing, he was saying, 'Please no, please, Jack, no,' and Jack was showing him a photo. It was a real photo, not on Jack's phone, a color photo about three by five inches." She made a box with her hands.

"Of what?"

"I don't know. If this was a movie, it would have been a photo of the guy's kid swinging on the swing at his preschool. Maybe it really was that, or something like that. Jack was speaking so quietly, just completely calm, I could barely hear him. He was smiling. He said something like, 'You knew better than to try this. I always get what is mine. Always.'"

"How come Jack didn't know you were there?"

"My car wasn't in the lot. It was in the shop. I gave Felicity a ride from her place that day. It was cold, but it was only a couple of blocks, so we walked from the oil change place to the club. We went in the back. He always comes in the front."

"What day was it?"

"I'm not sure of the date. It wasn't really cold yet. I could probably look it up on my credit card bill."

I imagined the scene as the two women listened, as their eyes met, everything clear, no need for a single speculative sentence about what would come next, then Felicity getting up, gathering her things, and leaving, intending to quit not only club, but also leaving Jack, unsure whether he would grasp that, but also how he would take it if he did, if he would try to find her no matter how fast and how far away she went. I pictured Lily staying behind, trying to get her nerves under control. Her position was not nearly so dire despite what she'd witnessed because she didn't have an intimate involvement with Jack, never suspecting until much later that the next time she saw Felicity, nothing would ever be the same again.

What was Felicity's actual plan? Did she intend to get not only out of the state but perhaps out of the country too? How long did she think she would have before Jack realized that she was finished with him? A week? A month? If he had bought the penthouse for her, did she want to sell it? She would have wanted to gather up as much ready cash as she could, to make arrangements (with whom?) to have more money sent to her. She was certainly by then fully entrenched as an escort, with clients of long standing, as Finn Vogel had told me. Did she ask others for help, before all her prospects went dark? Did they all turn her away? I couldn't be sure.

What I was sure of was that, by that point, fate was starting to close in on Emil Gardener and Cary Church.

At last, I began to guess what might have motivated Felicity, which was fear, although that didn't entirely make sense to me.

Did Ruth, I wondered now, do something similar in her own vanishing? Did she believe that she had nothing left to lose? Was her shame so great it overcame her reason? How could such a thing happen, nearly simultaneously, to two women, those women a mother and daughter? Did it happen to one unbeknownst to the other?

TEN

Turkey Vulture

Cathartes aura. Nature's garbage collector, this large species has been around since prehistoric times, using keen smell and sight to find ripe carcasses. Turkey vultures are scavengers that rip apart carrion. Scientists are studying how they can eat rotten diseased carcasses and not get sick and why their droppings are also disease free. Through their digestion, disease is cleaned out of the environment. Despised and unattractive as they may be, often regarded as harbingers of death, they play an important role in protecting other animals and people from contagion.

A FEW DAYS LATER, I SHOWED UP AT THE COFFEE SHOP WHERE I would meet Jack. I still wasn't sure that he would show, and I was ordering my latte when I realized that he was already there. Most people, even people older than me, scanned their phones while waiting for their order, or for their companion to arrive, or for their turn to board the flight. Jack wasn't doing that. He simply sat there perfectly composed without even the social crutch of a cup of coffee to legitimize him. I sat down across from him and fought the inane urge to comment on the weather. He was older, maybe in his early forties, on the other side of that decade in life when so many significant events seemed to occur. He said he had just taken his youngest, who was three, to preschool.

"My wife sees no sense in it. She would just rather keep them all at home. But I see it as socialization. Socialization skills can't start too early. They're the emollient of business. They're the emollient of life."

"Do you have older children too?"

"Four sons," he said with no trace of either pride or unease. "I desperately want a little girl of my own, but the wife says she's done and done, and she won't consider adoption. It just seems like too much of a hassle, for Lucia, I mean. I would do it in a heartbeat," he said. "But you didn't want to talk about my home life." In that moment, I considered the truth that his home life, in a sense, was exactly what I wanted to talk about. "You wanted to talk about Felicity Wild."

"I do but back up first." I turned on my phone and took out my purple leather binder with its tablet of scented notebook paper. "You're a father. Of sons. You own a strip club. How does that square?"

"I own four apartment buildings, two commercial buildings, a couple of small hotels, and a tree farm as well. A whole slew of assumptions come along with that place, and most people think it's a dive that attracts lowlifes. But the customers are ordinary guys out for a laugh. Or lonely. Or bored. Guys who like to see pretty women undressed, which does not mean they are perverts." He rubbed at an imaginary speck on his sleeve and added, "Once in a while, sure, there's a bad actor. Lily never fails to spot him—it's her training—and if Kelly can't handle it on his own, I come over and we convince this person to move on." He smiled.

"I'm just curious though. Why does a family man own a strip joint, because, at the end of the day, a strip joint is not a library, as Lily likes to say."

"I inherited it. It belonged to my godfather . . ." He gave me a wry look to signal that he knew just what he was saying.

"None of his kids was interested, and I love the guy. The price was right—" he made a circle with one thumb and forefinger "—and I was just a couple of years out of law school. It seems like an odd thing, but it's not that different from any other bar."

"Okay."

"So, why are you writing this story?"

"I can only say I'm compelled to. Felicity and I grew up together, we were close friends," I added.

"Do you think she's innocent?"

"I go back and forth, every day."

"She's a terrific person," Jack said. "You can ask any of the girls. Thoughtful and very, very smart. The few times I got to really talk to her, I was so impressed by the way she could assess situations, whether it was a separate parking area for the girls or the problem of a geriatric president, in just a few words . . ."

"So that was what I wanted to know about. You had a relationship with her."

"Well, don't write this down—she was more interesting to talk to than some. She had more life experience and intellectual curiosity."

"I didn't mean the working relationship."

Jack's face changed then, so slightly that if I hadn't been close enough to smell his faintly floral and clearly costly cologne, I might never have noticed. His face realigned somehow, right down to its texture and color, as if he had put on a very flattering mask. He looked not agitated, but even calmer and more composed. He said, with the ghost of a smile, "I never had any kind of romantic relationship with Felicity Wild."

"I thought, I understood that it was . . . " I stammered, feeling my face heat up.

"Who told you that?"

"No one specifically. Really, no one at the club ever said as much. I just had the sense that she, that you . . ."

"A professor told me history is really just gossip. She didn't mean the dates of this battle or that factory fire, she meant personalities. That it was mostly anecdotes, somebody saying this, somebody saying that, and some of those things were wrong." Jack took an old-fashioned hemmed and monogrammed handkerchief from his pocket. I didn't know that men carried these anymore; the idea was both courtly and disgusting. He began to fold the crisp square into an elaborate trumpet-shaped pattern. "So the same information is repeated many times, a consensus forms, and then, from that consensus, a presumption that there had to be something to it."

"Sure," I said.

"But that consensus isn't fact. That's why hearsay evidence is inadmissible, for the simple reason that the person who said it isn't there. Even if there's like a diary entry from the day that something supposedly happened, if there's no corroboration, it's not evidence."

I got up to top off my coffee. As I sat down again, I watched Jack finish his cotton sculpture. He didn't hurry. Everything I knew about the power of silence was now working, from him on me. "Ophelia is a sort of community. A bunch of women, kind of like an old-time convent, right? And I'm the priest, right? Like in the old days, when my father was a kid. I'm not a spiritual adviser but I'm their boss. One of me, twenty of them. They're waiting to dance, doing their nails, reading books, talking, talking, talking, about each other and their customers and me. One little nugget of gold turns into a gold mine. One conversation, one pat on the shoulder, one laugh, one tear, and boom." He smiled. "I want to answer your questions, about the impact this incident had on our little world. But not if you presume that I had an affair with Felicity."

"Even if you did, the story is more about the effect on this . . . well, community."

"Agreed. But I didn't." He added, "People love a good story, including my girls, including your readers. You get your information by what you see and hear and read, and I realize you haven't done this for years, like Miranda, but you can still tell, presumably, when somebody is lying." Then he raised a warning finger. "But what if a person doesn't know she's lying? You wouldn't be able to tell."

He went on to describe the chill that stole over the club when Felicity was arrested. "There's a lot of longing, right after Christmas. People think, another year and what have they done with their lives? The girls thought that Felicity was going back to college. They thought, *Maybe I should do that too.* Then, her real job, the murders, that was a Felicity they never knew." He shook his head. "Everybody caught a cold, not the best look at a place like mine. Everyone coughing, crying at the drop of a hat. Major waterworks! I had to give everybody a raise."

"Did that help?"

"It never hurts. But you can't put a price on an illusion. Although I guess that's what the customers at Ophelia are paying for, an illusion."

"I wanted to ask why you named the club that. Or was it called that before?"

Jack said, "I just liked the name. I have a relative called that. It was a name I thought I would like to call my daughter. Before, the place was called Club Sir. Another illusion, I guess."

"It's a beautiful name but it has a very sad connotation."

"You mean in Shakespeare. Well, yes . . . "

"Naming someone that, isn't it bad luck? Like I never got naming a baby Jonah." It occurred to me then, the truth of what one of my professors at journalism school always said, that the answer to any question was in the question. Ophelia was a beautiful name, but because of *Hamlet*, it would always be sad. Jack might want to make the place over into a diner after the trial. With the same chili for sure.

"I'll bring my kids up knowing that sexuality is just a nat-ural thing. But if it ever gets to where other parents talk about it, I'll peddle the place. Kids have it hard enough fitting in. Are you a jock? Are you a nerd? No sense making it harder." He stood up, smoothing the front of his pants. "Will that do it?"

"Almost," I said. "Oh right, what did you mean about Lily, her training? What kind of special training does a strip club manager get?"

"I meant her training as a cop. Lily was a cop."

"Lily was a police officer? When? Why isn't she still?"

"She left, what, three years ago? She left when she got her twenty years in. She got her pension. She got hurt once too, and I guess that changed her."

"How was she hurt?"

"I wasn't there. That would be hearsay," Jack said.

"Okay, wait . . . just a moment. This story won't appear for months, long after the trial is over, and it won't be as much about a trial as about women's sexuality, and men's perceptions of wom-en's sexuality, at this point in our culture. What I'm saying is, this isn't breaking news, more of a sort of third-wave feminism analysis based on one woman's actions at a particular place in time. And so, I want to ask you, did you ever think of Felicity as someone who could murder people for money? Did you ever think of her as being an escort?" I added, "Just from what you knew of her as someone who worked for you. As an acquaintance."

Jack looked off into the middle distance, as if considering. "I know she was driven. And people who are driven can be ruthless. Just an instinct, but I've met all kinds of people. Still, I didn't know her that well."

That was the last thing I expected him to say. He was, how-ever, correct about my intuition. I could usually tell when people were lying. And he was. As he put on his gloves, he said, "Give my regards to Mr. Damiano. He is that rare thing, a lawyer with a conscience. Are you friends?"

"Yes," I said. "He is a friend."

Not until Jack had disappeared up the street did a couple of things occur to me.

Although he was perfectly relaxed, the way Jack talked was just like the way Ross described people who were lying: He used too many words and gave too many details. And also, how did he know my mother's name?

ELEVEN

Bald Eagle

Haliaeetus leucocephalus. Bald eagles mate for life unless one of the two dies. Their courtship rituals are spectacular, with the birds locking talons, then flipping, spinning, and twirling through the air in a maneuver called a cartwheel display. They break apart at the last moment, just before hitting the ground. Eagles are serious parents: A pair raises one to three chicks each year in a huge messy nest, the largest nest built by any North American bird. Males and females care for the babies equally. Bald eagles have a wingspan of up to seven feet and, if standing on the ground next to an average-sized human, the bird's head would reach about to the height of the person's hip. The female is larger and typically more aggressive. The bald eagle is a traditional symbol of justice, freedom, and the rule of law.

THE FIRST MORNING OF THE TRIAL, I DRESSED CAREFULLY. IT WAS all I could do. When I went to meet some hotshot designer or movie star, my luxe clothing was my only armor. Someone always complimented me "Oh, you made that old brooch into a necklace with a ribbon." It was my ritual, my preps, like things that ER doctors do when they know an ambulance is coming— deep breathing, handwashing, knee bends, eye drops, strong coffee. I power walked in place until I was breathless, then blow-dried my irascible slippery hair into amiable smoothness, then put on my all-white uniform of SiBelle wide-leg trousers and a plain silk shirt covered with a light long-sleeved navy linen duster I'd borrowed from my mother, only a month after giving it to her. I would use this as protective coloration, to fit in with the prevailing press look, which was urban shabby. Like an old-style gambler, I rolled up my sleeves and cinched them with garters to avoid the dreaded ink mark.

In the hall outside the courtroom, the first person I met up with was Sally Zankow, in a black skirt with black tennies and a black sweatshirt, her yellow mane freshly colored. She spotted the garters first thing. "That's a good trick," she said. "I don't know how many blouses I've destroyed with pen marks. Are those like wedding garters?"

"Exactly that," I said.

Then without further small talk, Sally asked, "Do you think she was really sick?"

"Felicity?"

"I wonder about that. I wonder if it was just a defense move to derail the process."

I was about to say that I knew for a fact that she was sick but instead took a neutral path. "She's here now, I guess."

The next person I passed was Suzanne Church, who covered her eyes with one hand. The third person I passed was my mother. I did a real double take, seeing her, walking past her, then recognizing her.

"What?" I said.

"I'm interested," she said.

"Are you going to come to the whole thing?"

"I'm not sure. I took some time off. I hope you don't mind."

"It's a public courtroom," I said, but then I reached out and took her hand. Not only did I not mind, but I was also pitifully grateful for her presence, for the opportunity to talk this over with someone so much more experienced than I was, or ever hoped to be, with such awful things. That touch of hands also said, *I know how overwhelmed you are; I will help you and never offend your fragile, young dignity.*

It said also, *Something else is wrong, but I won't ask.*

When my mother let go, she stared past me, and I turned just in time to see Sally Zankow throw her arms around Miranda, with more genuine feeling than I would have thought she was capable of. "McClatchey!" Sally shrieked. "Did you decide to come back from the dark side?"

"Nah, I like the dark side. I like the devil's money. But, Sally, you haven't aged one single day!"

Sally wouldn't be distracted. She asked, "Come on, Miranda, what are you doing here?"

"Just observing for a few days. This thing, this case . . . You know, Felicity Wild grew up in my neighborhood. I knew her very well when she was a kid," my mom said. "And, of course, this young woman here is my daughter."

Sally didn't know that, and reactions, from a puzzled crinkle to a wide-eyed smirk, galloped across her seasoned face. "Apple, tree, huh?" she said. My mom shrugged prettily.

Then the doors opened, and as we filed into the courtroom, the other press and I heading toward the front, the spectators settling themselves near the back, the first thing I noticed was the strippers.

A cluster of poppies in a hayfield, they were a row of women dressed not exactly inappropriately but as if they'd wandered into a municipal building in the belief that it was a nightclub. There were Dovey and Archangel and a handful of others I had only seen in passing, Rochelle and Marianna and Cheryl, who came from the East Coast and whom everyone called "Boston," in skirts and blazers of bright daffodil and peacock blue, shiny thigh-high boots with impossibly high heels, black taffeta palazzo pants and black silk cowl-neck blouses with decks of gold chains, some hung with a crucifix. I didn't know whether to laugh or cry. It was the worst possible retinue of attendants for Felicity's image as the demure young scholar she had once been, but it was the sweetest possible display of solidarity for a sister in a jam. Shoulder to shoulder, they took quick glances, like sips, at everything around them.

Then the bailiff said, "Please, all rise for the Honorable Judge Deborah Martin . . ." and an older woman, slight, neat, bespectacled, wearing a Ruth Bader Ginsburg lace collar at the throat of her judicial robes, took her seat, inviting everyone else present to do the same.

Into the room came Felicity, shockingly thin, her cheekbones sharp, even more hauntingly beautiful, the green dress with the gathered details hanging loose from her frail shoulders. Only when I studied her closely did I notice that her eyes were as frantic as fish in a bowl, darting from her defense attorney to the jury box, where sat twelve upright people who would decide if she walked out of this place to go home or if she walked out of it to get into a van that would convey her to prison for the rest of her life, or at least for the rest of the best part of it, to a place that would make the Dane County jail look quaint, a place where many of the women would be rough and desperate and even crazy, who would try to befriend her or romance her or destroy her. Felicity was strong and smart, but now she was beaten down. I could not see how she would survive that.

Sam, my beautiful and beloved, pulled her chair out for her, settling her between him and an attractive older woman in a light gray suit. The case called, the counsel introduced, Judge Martin said, "Good day. I need a preliminary word. It has not escaped my attention that this is a high-profile murder trial with some very unusual elements, to say the least. Still, it is an event of the utmost seriousness, with the highest stakes for the families of the men who died, and the fate of a young woman to be decided. This is my courtroom. I will have no shenanigans. Anyone who speaks out of turn or otherwise acts up will be out of here so fast it will make your head spin. I will eject you on the spot and ask questions later. I hope that this is understood. Let's begin."

Since I knew I could obtain the transcripts to make sure that I could quote with absolute accuracy what the participants said, when I took out my dark pink notebook, it was to take down only general observations of the trial's progress, but even more to describe the scene, the behaviors, the temperature of the emotions that transcripts could not convey.

I studied the room as everyone got settled.

The jury was like a photo negative of the strippers, an opposite: eight plain women and four plain men, dressed in the kinds of clothing that would not have been out of place at the Starbright Ministry. Sam said he'd sought out women in jury selection for the exact opposite reason that the prosecution did. The district attorney believed that righteous women would be stern critics of Felicity's life, while Sam and his mother gambled that any woman, no matter how conservative, would have endured and resented criticism from men. Every one of the jurors appeared apprehensive, even frightened, whether of the surroundings, the process, the strippers, or of Felicity, I couldn't say. My mom caught my eye and gave the briefest ghost of a nod: *You're good*, it said. It helped me, and, for an instant, I caught myself wishing that Felicity, guilty or innocent, with much more to lose, had her own mother in her court.

The prosecutor stood. He buttoned his suit jacket as if buckling on his battle shield and said, "Good morning, ladies and gentlemen. I am Israel Ronson, and I am the district attorney here in Dane County. Often, an assistant district attorney would be prosecuting a serious case such as this one, although I would pay very close attention to its progress. However, as the Honorable Judge

Martin has stated, this is an unusual and a controversial case. I am pleased to meet all of you, but this is not a day I looked forward to. On this most beautiful day, a summer morning in the beautiful state of Wisconsin, in the beautiful city where we live and are privileged to live, we are here to do a duty that no one wants to do but that is right and necessary and in all our interest. And that is to seek justice for two people who are here today only in the memories of those who loved them, their wives, their children, their beloved relatives, two men who worked hard and served their communities and loved their families and made people proud to know them."

He raised his hands as though to welcome the jury into a friendly hug. "They weren't movie stars or politicians or athletes. They were just ordinary people, people you wouldn't necessarily remember if you saw them passing you on the street, except if they helped you put your groceries in the car or told you your taillight had a broken bulb." For a moment, he turned away, and then leaned in, confidingly. "They weren't perfect. They had weaknesses. They were tempted by a seductive woman into doing something that no self-respecting man should ever do, paying for sex outside his marriage. Emil's wife was ill. They hadn't had a sexual relationship for years. Cary and his wife were at odds for a long time, and finally at war, although they were working it out. Is that any excuse? No. You might say that they put themselves in harm's way, but so does anybody who rides a motorcycle or smokes a cigar. But most people who do things they shouldn't do aren't murdered for it." He paused, as if struggling to hear a sound in the far distance. "And now, they are gone. They're gone forever."

He talked about how Erica Doll Gardener would die alone. He talked about the children whose dad, Cary Church, would "gradually become a photo on a wall in the hallway growing older with each passing year." They would not have the love and financial support every child deserves from their dad. They would have his life insurance benefits, but so would his killer, Felicity Wild. "If she walks away from this charge, she will get that money. A huge amount of money, millions of dollars. Think about that. She will be rewarded for her evil and greedy actions unless you say no, that isn't fair. It isn't right."

Israel Ronson described the discovery of the bodies, the false starts and final conclusions. He made air quotes to point out how Felicity "didn't know" who'd killed Emil Gardener, how she "panicked" when she found his body and called one of her "many friends" to get that body out of her place and into a so-called "cold and lonely" snowbank.

"We're not talking about a crime of passion. We're talking about a plan by one person to live a rich and easy life and who didn't care whose lives she destroyed to make that possible. In fact, in all my years of being a prosecutor, I've never encountered a person quite so cold and ambitious."

Sam would admit he had to suppress a sigh as Ronson laid it on so thick, but that was a ploy right out of the playbook, exactly what he was supposed to do, an emotional appeal to people who were new to all this and eager to be guided toward doing the right thing.

Ronson was a very good-looking guy, slender and well over six feet, with a close crop of dense curly hair just dusted with silver. Next to him, Sam looked like a kid wearing his new suit for prom. As he wound things up, Ronson gave the jurors a look of surpassing tenderness and then, in what Sam would later tell me was a deliberate piece of theater, stood with his arm resting confidingly on the rail in front of the jury box before he spoke again. He removed his glasses, glanced down at them, and appeared to rub away a speck before he shook his head ruefully.

"That person is here in this courtroom now. She is there at the defense table, Felicity Claire Copeland Wild. No one else.

Look at her, ladies and gentlemen. Her appearance is so lovely that everything I'm saying must be very hard for you to believe. Frankly, it was hard for me to believe. I had to ask myself, Israel, is there another possibility?" He went on to enumerate the uncertainties and then concluded, "There is no other possibility. The evidence will show that Felicity Wild is a very intelligent student of science, who would know that some poisons don't leave a measurable trace." She lived alone, he would say, with few close friends, her only visitors her clients. She could keep her secrets . . . she had the classic triad familiar from TV courtrooms: means, motive, and opportunity. She had, further, behaved in a guilty way. "If you found a friend dead in your bathroom, what would you do? Would you call someone to help you hide your friend's body? Or would you call the police, just as fast as you could? Of course you would. An innocent woman would have called the police. Even if she was a drug dealer or something. Even if she had a meth lab in her backyard." He talked about the confusing letters Cary Church left behind. "Why didn't he just call the police? Or send an email? Very strange behavior, almost as though somebody else wanted proof that Cary was changing his story."

I felt, rather than saw, Sam trying to suppress the impulse to react.

"The state will present four witnesses. They will be Michaela Doherty, the police officer who found Emil Gardener's body in the snow; Karen White, the detective who interviewed Miss Wild and knew something was not adding up; a neighbor, Gray LeMay, who owns the condominium just below Felicity Wild's and used to hear all manner of rather exotic noises coming from her neighbor's place but right around New Year's Eve, heard very distinct sounds of a vicious fight, and then a fall, as if something heavy was hitting the floor repeatedly; and the Dane County medical examiner, Dr. Moira McDermott, who was responsible for ascertaining the cause of death in two very difficult cases."

At last, he concluded with his regrets, of which he had many. Shaking his head more in sorrow than in anger, he pointed out that not only did two good men die, but a young woman with "the whole package, brains and beauty and chances," had wasted her life. He said finally, "My esteemed colleague Sam Damiano, who is just about as gifted a lawyer as they come, will tell you that none of this is true. He'll say there's somebody out there in the shadows who is literally getting away with murder right now. But you already know the truth. Ugly as it seems, Felicity Wild killed Emil Gardener and Cary Church. She did it for money. As intelligent and decent people, you will sadly but rightfully reach the inescapable conclusion and find Felicity Wild guilty of murder in the first degree, for which she should rightfully go to prison for the rest of her life. I thank you for your patience and for your service."

Israel Ronson sat down, slumping a little, spent, having spoken earnestly and without notes for nearly an hour. The judge called for a short recess as the jury, tight-lipped and wide-eyed, filed out. Felicity glanced at the strippers, acknowledging them, and then me, with a smile that got no further than her tired eyes.

I whispered, "Please . . ." and she turned her gaze to the floor.

I ran out to the hall and out the door, where I breathed in lungsful of air. Even city late-spring air with its dank savor of Lake Mendota was restorative after the funk of coffee breath and anxious sweat in the windowless courtroom.

On impulse, as a sort of sorbet for the darkness in my mind, I called my office. Ivy thankfully wasn't in that day, but I left a greeting for her and then talked to Marcus, who caught me up. Things were heating up at *Fuchsia*. There was an offer for a TV show that Ivy was ready to "ink," as Marcus put it, which would go the celeb-model shows one better and do stories that dealt with real society as well as high society. There was, even more interestingly, a possible relocation to Florida. He described Mother Sabrina's vision for the location of the next Purple Palace, in Vero Beach, Florida, a small sugar-sand city on a barrier island across the Indian River Lagoon. It would be a whole purple neighborhood, with restaurants, *Fuchsia*-linked stores, maybe eventually a convention center and hotel.

"Florida? What? The whole operation?" I asked. "A real cultural destination. The next Rodeo Drive."

"It could happen," Marcus said. "Florida is the new New York."

"I couldn't live in Florida. Could you live in Florida?"

"I could live anywhere. I'm adaptable."

"Ivy didn't even send me an email!"

"She didn't want to bother you," he said. "And right, she would normally call you at six in the morning and get mad if you didn't pull over in traffic and take the call. This is Ivy trying to be respectful."

Marcus was working on a story about how famous and beautiful people sometimes fell in love with ordinary and unbeautiful spouses. Just good investigative journalism. "Reeno, I miss you so much! We have no fun here without you. I don't meet hot girls. You haven't called in ages. Why did you call? Are you okay?"

"I don't even know. This case and everything around it just keep getting nuttier."

It felt so thoroughly blessed to natter away about approximately nothing. I promised Marcus a real talk with all the trimmings as soon as I got a break, then ran back up the stairs and whirled through the door, nearly running into Sam. I nodded, and he nodded. He was visibly thinner. I was grateful for that. I'd thought he might look robust and his new girlfriend would be there to observe. Would Nell still get her internship at Damiano, Chen, and Damiano? Of course she would. The two things were not related. Nell was a good lawyer. She was also a good sister, and I hadn't told her that Sam and I were finished. I didn't want to make it real. I almost leaned my forehead against the cold wall, then thought of the desperate sweat that must have soaked into every surface of that place.

When I went back into the courtroom, I saw that someone had taken my seat. I would sit next to my mom—after all, who was I kidding? Sally Zankow already seemed to have more respect for me because I was related to Miranda. As I made my way toward her, I felt a touch on my arm and there was Claire. I had all but forgotten our long journey together. In my continuing parade of things-in-real-life-that-you-thought-were-just-clichés-from-cheap-prose, her face literally was white, her makeup standing out garish as a Pierrot. "Reenie, do you think Felicity is dying?" she said.

"She had flu and she was in the hospital. She's better now. I think it's the food. She can't keep it down."

"Can I send her something?"

"You could give Sam money and he could bring her something?" I promised to help ferry her to the front of the room so that Felicity could at least get a glimpse of her aunt. Just before she turned away, Claire saw my mother. They had probably not set eyes on each other for years. They waved at each other weakly.

All the players in my life were lined up in ways I would not ever have believed.

TWELVE

Peregrine Falcon

Falco peregrinus. Falcons were named from the Latin
for *sickle*, referring to the shape of their claws, by the eighteenth-
century Swedish biologist Carl Linnaeus. Earth's fastest creature, they
have been observed flying at 240 miles per hour. A wild falcon in
myth and sacred tradition represents vision and freedom, but also
greed. This raptor can never be tamed but was trained to hunt other
birds, with extraordinary eyesight nearly three times sharper than a
human being's. In the 1800s, Irish poet and priest Gerard Manley
Hopkins praised the "dapple-dawn-drawn Falcon," pointing to the
majesty of God as "a billion times" lovelier and more dangerous.
Supposedly inspired by a falcon's deadly drop, Shakespeare's Hamlet
said he was only occasionally mad. "When the wind is southerly,
I know a hawk from a handsaw," said the melancholy prince.

AS SAM ROSE TO BEGIN THE DEFENSE, I LET MYSELF PRETEND, FOR
a moment, that he was mine. I was his wife, curious and proud.

Then I pretended that I'd never met him, to see him as I
first saw him.

Finally, I looked at him as he truly was, as I truly was. He was
a young lawyer trying the biggest criminal case of his life without the support of his new love—because she was repulsive to
him. I was the writer who'd rather be anywhere on earth than
watching the man she had loved and admired and had driven away.

The sight of him made me physically sick with longing. I had to slip out to the washroom and lose my breakfast. How would I look at him every day for however many weeks this took? How would I bear it when he looked at me as though I were any other person in the room—or worse, let his gaze sweep past me as if I wasn't even there?

Sam got up, clutching a sheaf of notes. Then, as if this had just occurred to him, he put them back down on the table. He would speak extempore. He had once told me this was a trick to make the jury presume both his competence and his knowledge of the case—in the way that old-time advocates, to prove that they were erudite and devout, once picked up a Bible to search for a verse, only to say, *No matter, I can quote from memory.*

"Good people, thank you for taking time from your families and your busy lives to do your duty as citizens, in a case where the facts are difficult and painful at the very least. I will tell you a story that I believe in my heart of hearts to be true. Most of what my colleague and friend Israel Ronson has told you is true. Two men died cruelly. Two families are bereft. A young woman stands accused. Only one thing that Israel said is a lie. He said that Felicity Wild is a murderer. She is not.

"Can I prove this to you? I cannot. I didn't see what happened in Felicity's apartment or Cary Church's apartment. But I don't have to prove that Felicity is innocent. That is not how our justice system works. The defense does not have to prove that the accused didn't do it. Why? If that were the case, anybody could accuse someone of committing a serious crime and there would be no way to prove them wrong."

Sam pointed to the jury member closest to him. "I could say that you killed these men. Can you prove you did not? Do you remember exactly what you were doing last winter on the dates in question? If you were at a party, did you run to the store for a bottle of 7UP? Or did you murder a man instead? No? Can you prove it?"

Our judicial system protects the rights of the accused, he went on, by putting the burden on the prosecutor "to convince all of you that Felicity did exactly what he says she did. And he can't. He doesn't have that evidence. There is not one single speck of physical evidence that ties Felicity to this crime. I'm not saying that there is not one single speck of physical evidence that ties her to any crime. In fact, I will say right now, I believe she is guilty of the crime of moving a dead body. She is guilty of the crime of trying to cover up a death. These are serious crimes and if she is charged with them, and convicted, she could face three years in prison.

"But she's not charged with that crime today. She is charged with first-degree murder, intentionally causing the death of two men, which the evidence will show is not only untrue but impossible.

"Someone killed Emil Gardener. Someone killed Cary Church. But it was not my client, Felicity Wild."

Sam admitted that there might be times when attorneys, who are only human, tell a lie. They believe so strongly in their client's innocence, and they don't have the proof, so they make up what isn't there. He personally had never faced that choice. He didn't now. The joke he tried didn't entirely work. "You may have noticed that my last name ends in a vowel. I'm Italian. I want you to meet someone." Sam paused and extended his hand to Angela. "This is Angela Messina Damiano. Angie. She's managing partner of my firm. She's also my mother. Do attorneys tell lies? Sometimes they do. But I can tell you I'm not lying when I say that an Italian boy would never lie in front of his mother."

That drew a slight laugh, as Sam pivoted to a serious, doleful expression. "A trial is a moral event, a consideration of right and wrong. You could be tempted to think that a woman who made her living the way Felicity did is capable of anything. But we are not here to make a moral judgment on Felicity for engaging in sexual conduct for money even though that is a crime, a misdemeanor punishable with a fine, any more than we should judge the men who were killed because they made the choice to pay for sex, which is also a misdemeanor offense in this state."

No one, Sam said, could further prove that Felicity Wild was motivated to kill by money. "The same could be said of the wife and children of Cary Church. The same could be said of the wife and nieces and nephews of Emil Gardener." Sometimes, he said, we assume that if one event follows the other, then the first event must have caused the second. "It seems sensible, but it can be a trap. If she ever did think about how much she would benefit from the deaths of those men, and there is no evidence to suggest that she did, she did not act on it. And even if she told a friend, 'Oh, I would be rich if Emil or Cary died,' that still would not indicate that she had any part in those deaths."

Sam would only call two witnesses, a longtime friend of the family and a faculty adviser. He had told me that he would not call Felicity, believing that her composed demeanor would be seen as cold. Did the fact that she stood alone, without her family, make her seem unwanted and unloved? At that moment, I hated Rev. Wild and Ruth, for putting themselves and their own issues ahead of Felicity in her dark time. At least her aunt was there. I was there.

Sam was there.

He said he had no idea why Cary Church and Emil Gardener decided to provide for Felicity in the event of their deaths, except that, clearly, they cared about her. Clearly, those relationships met a need. "Perhaps the primary reason was loneliness, which is something everyone can understand," Sam said.

He proceeded quickly to refute Israel Ronson's assertions.

"When Emil Gardener died, Felicity Wild was with her family, a hundred miles away. When Cary Church's body was discovered, she was also with her family at a church service. Now, I know how ludicrous that sounds. The accused murderer, a known escort, was in church when the murders occurred. But Felicity Wild is the daughter of a minister and his wife, Ruth, a high school teacher and church secretary. Others in the congregation saw her. That is the first and most obvious exonerating fact."

When she discovered Emil Gardener's body, Sam said, "She did exactly the wrong thing. She assumed that no one would believe the truth. After all, she was a woman who sold sex for money. So in her fear, she called for help, and another man, who also loved her, came to help her. Cary Church came to help her. How did he later end up dead? Did he take his own life out of remorse, because he was the one who killed Mr. Gardener? Was his death accidental? Did someone kill him? One of those things happened. If she knew, Felicity would tell you, but she does not know.

"You may have heard the term Occam's razor. It's a way to explain that the most obvious answer is usually the correct answer. If you hear hoofbeats, you don't think of zebras, you think of horses. But even when the most obvious thing seems true, it is not always true. In this case, it's not."

Sam took a risk then, one I would think about for years, never entirely satisfied that the gamble was justified.

"We talked about morality. What would be the greater moral wrong? Would it be to send an innocent young woman to prison, to try to survive the rest of her life among hardened criminals? Or would it be to set a young woman free who committed a terrible crime? Would you be afraid that if she wasn't locked away, she would be a danger to society at large? You know the answer. In our society, we believe that it is better for a hundred guilty people to go free than to fail to protect one innocent person.

"You must answer just one question. Did Israel Ronson prove to your satisfaction that the person who killed Emil Gardener and Cary Church could be no one else but Felicity Wild? If you are not sure, then you must find my client, Felicity Wild, innocent of this crime. It is the right thing to do. It is your duty."

The first day concluded with police officer Michaela Doherty's account of the grisly discovery of Emil Gardener's body. She was small, shy, young, blonde, the kind of example that men several generations ago used to prove why women could not be police. "I'm a traffic cop," she said. "I was only working that night because I have low seniority and nobody else wants to work during the holidays. It was the first time I ever saw a dead body."

"But you went to the police academy," Israel Ronson prompted her.

"They didn't . . . The cadaver for our class didn't work out," she explained. "It didn't, um, last long enough."

"And you've never been to a funeral."

"No, I've never been to a funeral."

"So you were shocked by the sight of the deceased."

"Yes. You bet I was. He was just completely bashed around, all purple and blue, and swollen. And naked. Poor guy."

Several jurors began to look uncomfortable, as did Sam, but not because of the description. He well knew that his adversary was counting on the emotional impact of the officer's testimony; the more sympathy for the older man, the less for whoever put him there. When a crime-scene photo of the body was produced and distributed, Judge Martin had to declare a brief recess to excuse one juror, who, I later learned, threw up in the bathroom set aside for jury members.

"It was obvious that this wasn't a death by natural causes," Israel Ronson went on. Angela Damiano objected: Not only was this the first dead body that Officer Doherty had ever seen, but she also was not a pathologist.

"He looked like he had been run over by a truck," the young police officer said, and Angela seemed about to object again, but shook her head wearily instead.

I went home to Nell's house. Miranda was staying at a bed-and-breakfast inn, and had invited me to stay with her, but all I wanted to do was hole up like a denning animal, so Nell stayed with Mom. Alone in the kitchen, I ate a whole bag of taco chips and a whole carton of cottage cheese. I patted a sea mud mask on my face and, for five full hours, watched a British crime drama about a murderous pastry chef. Then I crept into my closet bedroom and slept nine hours straight. The junk food, the BBC, the excessive facial routine, and the sleep marathons would become the hallmarks of my life over the coming weeks.

In the morning came Dr. Moira McDermott, the Dane County medical examiner.

Sam had said that if the district attorney was wise, he would go straight to the screwup over Emil Gardener's cause of death. "Someone being found naked in a snowbank, that is already a suspicious death," he said.

Moira McDermott said, "Not necessarily." She talked about the odd phenomenon of paradoxical undressing that can happen with people near death from hypothermia who actually feel they are too hot, which has sometimes led to complications, including the belief that the deceased was sexually assaulted. "There wasn't necessarily any reason to think of foul play."

"And so," Israel Ronson went on, "it seemed to you that he died from the effects of exposure. And that the bruising . . . "

"It could have happened as a result of a fall or hitting his head, many reasons." The family had not requested an autopsy and the death seemed straightforward, despite the ghastly visual.

"And the conclusion was that Mr. Gardener died from cardiopulmonary arrest, correct?"

"Well, everybody dies of cardiopulmonary arrest," Dr. Mc-Dermott said with a sigh. "Your heart stops, you stop breathing, you die. It's what led to it."

The prosecutor led the medical examiner through the process of the discovery of the second victim, Felicity's involvement, the autopsy of the first victim, the discovery of the kind of tissue damage consistent with some kind of toxin. "Are you sure this damage was caused by some kind of poison?"

She said, "I'm reasonably sure. As to what kind, many poisons leave no chemical trace. The tissue analysis was inconclusive for that."

"What could it have been?"

"Objection. Speculation," Sam said.

"Overruled. I'll allow it," said Judge Martin. "Just please don't go too far afield, Dr. McDermott."

"Well, arsenic, for example, is used as an alloying agent in industrial procedures, in metallurgy, and in labs. It's used in some pharmaceutical applications. You could find it easily in a factory or in an engineering or chemistry lab at a university if you knew where to look and you had access to it."

"But you are not certain that it was arsenic."

"No."

"And what about Cary Church's death?"

"The same thing is true. A death caused by some kind of toxin is even more strongly indicated because Cary Church didn't present any apparent health risk factors. He was a healthy young man. And again, there was the way that the body was found, sitting in a bathtub, undressed."

"He could have been taking a bath," said Israel Ronson, "and let the water drain out."

"He could have been taking a bath and someone else drained the tub after he died. He could have been placed in the tub after death but before the effects of rigor mortis set in, while his body was still pliable," the medical examiner said.

Israel Ronson offered photographs of Cary Church's body. I glanced at the juror who had previously become queasy; she looked frightened, shivery and still.

The doctor continued, "There could have been a toxin in the water that he inhaled, or swallowed, or absorbed through his skin, although there was no forensic evidence of that scenario at the crime scene."

"Samples were taken, from the pipes, and so forth."

"Yes. It's impossible to know what happened specifically."

Just at that point, the queasy juror succumbed to nausea, and, after a short recess, Judge Martin said the juror was indisposed and court would be adjourned until the next morning.

In the corridor, I waited for the district attorney and displayed my press badge. "Mr. Ronson, I just have one quick question."

"That's fine. I'm happy to help," he said. He really was a genial guy who exuded easy confidence.

"What if that one poor juror keeps getting sick? How can you do this without showing the jury the evidence?"

"You can't, but that part of the proceeding is over. We can assure the jury that there won't be any more graphic images unless someone asks to see them again when they deliberate," he told me. "You're the girl from the fashion magazine, right? Who knows Miranda McClatchey?"

"Right. Who told you that?"

"Oh, you know Sally Zankow. She's the font of all wisdom."

"Yep," I said.

"Is Miranda covering this too?"

"She's just observing. She is my mother."

"You don't say," he said with a nod. "You don't say. Wouldn't have thought Miranda was old enough to have a daughter your age."

"Me either," I said. When I later told my mother this, she smiled, sweetly appreciative. I'd planned to have dinner that night with my mother at Aria, an old-style Italian restaurant that had been around since her reporter days. She asked if we should include Claire, Felicity's aunt. I didn't want to. I just wanted Miranda all to myself, as a mentor, but mostly, right now, as a mother.

I wanted to have a long and lingering conversation with Miranda, this time telling her all the details of how fast it all failed. I wanted my mother to comfort me. She'd never met Sam, but only seen him in court, so she would say that his sophisticated exterior hid a thug's heart. She would say, *He's not good enough for you.* She'd be wrong. But I could not tell her why he'd ended it. (Imagine telling my mother, or Patrick, about the reservoir! Then they could disown me too!)

So, of course, I did agree to ask Claire to join us for dinner.

When we arrived, the place smelled spicy and enticing, like the inside of a saucepot just lightly infused with citrus. We ordered a bottle of wine, and all I could drink was one sip, though I downed glass after glass of ice water and put an embarrassing dent in the loaf of home-baked French bread. Claire and my mother polished off the whole bottle of Barolo with gusto. I was glad I was the one driving. Unable to really talk about what was on all our minds, and unable to really talk about the reasons we couldn't talk about it, we sat there and picked at our manicotti, discussing how humid the day had been, in the way of true Midwesterners who never pass up a chance to analyze the weather.

Like a pitcher that filled and spilled and filled again, Claire couldn't stop crying. She and my mom were now best friends linked by empathy and eau-de-vie and would seemingly remain in touch forever (this turned out to be true), so my mother also shed tears. This cozy dinner out felt less like a respite and more like a punishment. As hungry as I was, eating seemingly nonstop, my reaction to stress, it felt like a gross indecency to swallow in Claire's presence.

My part of the dinner ended early, as I went back to Nell's. Wildly sad, unable to bear one more ping-pong game of what-if-he-this? and what-if-he-that?, I escaped into another ocean of sleep. I don't know what my mother and Claire did, but they certainly did not resemble daisies the next morning.

On cross-examination, Sam, in a rather gentle fashion, asked how the doctor felt about such a "mistake" as to certify Emil Gardener's death. Moira McDermott sighed again. "I am definitely not happy about it. But I am not guilt ridden either. This was an understandable mistake."

"Maybe," Sam said. "Understandable but not unavoidable."

"That's why we do autopsies."

"Does it mean that this death could have been accidental?" Sam asked. "It definitely could have been a suicide. It could have been a heart attack."

She said, "It could have been a heart attack. Mr. Gardener suffered from arteriosclerosis and had heart damage from a previous cardiac event. But other factors don't point to that."

"Such as what?"

"Such as the undressed state of the body. It's not consistent with a sudden heart event."

"But suicide?"

"Emil Gardener would have had to take off all his clothing and then swallow some kind of poisonous agent," the medical examiner said. "It's not done. It's not human nature. People who commit suicide are not unaware that somebody will find their remains. Even if it's an impulsive act, and it's always an impulsive act, even if it's planned, even if the person suffers from bipolar illness or some other illness. Especially for an older person, for a man, who was not affected by drugs or alcohol, this would be very unusual behavior."

"But you don't know, really, if Emil Gardener was inebriated or had used drugs. That is, with respect, one of the many things you don't know, even after an autopsy. He could have been drunk. He could have used drugs, correct?"

Dr. McDermott sighed again, gustily. "According to his family, Mr. Gardener was an abstainer. He never drank alcohol. He never had. He never used drugs. He never had. His daily prescription medication, a diuretic, a statin, an aspirin, that was all he used. He smoked a cigar once a year at Christmas."

"He could have been a secret smoker, though," Sam said. "He could have been a secret drinker."

"There was no evidence of that, in his lungs or his liver. Not at all."

The prosecution called Karen White, the first detective to interview Felicity. Israel Ronson played a portion of the videotaped interview. While not in tears, Felicity was visibly upset, removing her glasses to press her splayed fingers against her eyes, asking repeatedly for water. When the detective asked if Felicity wanted a lawyer present, and if she had one in mind, she said, "Why? I'm not a suspect, am I?"

"You haven't been charged with anything, Felicity."

"Do I need a lawyer?"

"This is just an informational interview. I'm just offering you the option of having someone here to look after your interests."

"Are you going to charge me with something?" Felicity said. "I know how this must look but really, I don't know how any of this happened."

She admitted to knowing both men and to asking for help from Cary Church to move Emil Gardener's body. As I watched, I could see Felicity's cloudless composure return, like that cloak of feathers she told me about so long ago that protected the goddess Freya from her enemies. Her voice no longer faltered. She answered each question clearly and concisely. After a while, she asked to make a phone call. Not long afterward, Sam showed up in the room.

How had she chosen Sam's firm? Was it because of her former boss, Jack Melodia? How would she have known about their connection, for she had no reason to know it? It was only because Felicity had a business card that had been tacked to a corkboard in the dressing room at Ophelia. She had not expected to ever need it, and had, until that moment, forgotten about it. She met Sam, and I met Sam, by mere chance, or perhaps kismet. Much later, when I saw some of her things laid out on a tabletop, I would notice how she had neatly laminated the card with a layer of clear tape. A long time afterward, Angela Damiano would say of this happenstance that the stars had aligned, and then hastily point out that she didn't believe in fate, astrology, or any of that claptrap—and that she believed only in saints, especially St. Catherine, not necessarily in God.

When the video clip ended, Sam called Marta Vincent, the older woman who'd known Felicity for so many years—who had, in fact, babysat for her when Felicity was a little child, even before I knew her. What was there to say? That she was cute and bright and polite? That she loved animals? That it was impossible to imagine this gentle girl growing up to harm anyone? The same could be said of most people. When his turn came, Israel Ronson seemed intent almost on reproving her. "You knew Felicity Wild as a child," he said.

"Yes, very well. I knew her family."

"But you did not know her as a grown woman?"

"No. I knew her mother. I saw Ruth occasionally."

"Well, you couldn't imagine Felicity ever growing up to hurt anyone. Could you have imagined the girl you knew growing up to become a stripper? Or a sex worker?"

"Of course not!" said the witness. "That would be impossible."

"And yet," said the prosecutor, as if wiping steam from a

mirror so that it would be possible to see the clearest reflection, "that is exactly what Felicity grew up to be. There's no contesting that. So, you cannot say for certain that she wouldn't also grow up to be someone capable of doing someone harm, isn't that true?"

Sam shook his head and raked his fingers through his hair, at first seeming about to speak but nearly visibly hauling that impulse down, like a kite by the tail.

"I guess I can't say for sure," Marta Vincent admitted.

The same scenario was set forth with Felicity's faculty adviser, but what could it possibly signify? Murder was a predictable destiny for no ordinary middle-class citizen. I supposed that it must be said, but to what end? It was not going to convert anyone. Something had provoked a change in Felicity. I thought back to my friend Ross's explanation of why people changed for the worse.

This was a trial that was serious, Angela Damiano would later say, but not complicated. There were not very many moving parts. I thought of it like removing an appendix, which could either be a relatively quick and effective operation or a mortal shit show. Both lawyers were excellent and prepared. The witnesses gave witness. All they could do was all they could do. As the final day approached, no one could call it.

Sally Zankow said, "This jury is going to have a lot to talk about. Get your popcorn. Prepare to camp out, folks."

Sam's final words with them helped me see why people in previous generations called a lawyer a "pleader." He wasn't simply practicing the lawyer's art; he was truly begging the jury.

"Now you know what I know about these circumstances, and maybe you know everything that anyone knows—except the killer of course. What you have heard over the course of this trial are two possible scenarios. One didn't happen. One did. What did happen was that a young woman who was desperate found the dead body of a man who had been her client, perhaps her friend, and she panicked. She thought she would be blamed. Maybe someone wanted her to be blamed. If Felicity would or could answer these questions, we would all have an easier time. What does it suggest to you, that she will not answer those questions? It suggests to me that she is either in peril for her own life or covering up for someone else. It is frustrating. It is maddening. But is it the same as being guilty of first-degree intentional homicide? It is not.

"Ladies and gentlemen, do you have the proof you need to find Felicity Wild guilty of murder? You know the answer. Should she go to prison for two life terms based on what you have heard? You know the answer to that question. Please. Listen to your conscience. Find the defendant, Felicity Claire Copeland Wild, innocent."

The next morning, looking like a much older man, a man who moved slower, like a man whose sleep had been scarce and shallow, Israel Ronson rose from his chair. "Here we are. No matter how this case ends, and I think I know how it will end, you will never forget this event." The jurors would experience happy times, sad times, achievements, and losses. Nothing they did in the future, however, would ever be more important.

"Sam is fighting for Felicity Wild's freedom. I am fighting for justice for two good men she killed. I must be their voice. You must be their advocates. Their deaths cannot go unpunished. If Wild finds herself here today, it is because she put herself here. The conditions for her arrest were met fairly. The allegations were proven. She had a fair trial.

"All kinds of things have been said to confuse you. Yes, of course the families of Mr. Church and Mr. Gardener also benefited financially from their deaths. Do you believe that these men's family members killed them? Or is this just another made-up obstacle?" Errors occurred, Ronson said. People are not always perfect. These things matter but do not change the truth.

"We know why," he said. "We know when. We know who.

"There is a single question. Did Felicity Wild kill Cary Church and Emil Gardener? There is a single right answer. Yes, she did. She took their lives and now you must take her freedom. I, too, would rather Miss Wild go free than to make a terrible mistake. But in this case, the grave and terrible mistake would be to let her go free. That mistake would haunt you for the rest of your life.

"She did this. She was caught. She must pay. We ask you to be brave and return a verdict of guilty."

The judge gave her instructions. The jury filed out. All of us filed out too. I felt the way you feel when you exit a movie theater and it's still daylight and there is a sort of guilty urgency about time whiled away that could have been better spent.

My mother wanted a nap. She wanted to call home and talk to my father, a reminder that not all the world was bleak and inexpertly balanced. Claire said she'd go to her bed-and-breakfast and do some reading, and they would meet later for a meal.

I couldn't sit still. I decided to drive to a place Felicity once told me about, to the Wisconsin River below the hydroelectric dam in Prairie du Sac, where eagles dipped and soared.

Not long before we broke up, I'd asked Sam, if Felicity didn't do it, who did? I remembered the conversation now, reliving, possibly because of the poignant pain of it, how interesting it had been just to talk to Sam.

He and his mother had talked about this often. She thought perhaps it was Ruth, a born-again Christian who lost her marbles and did this to free Felicity from sin. At the time, I'd scoffed. If Sam had ever met Ruth, he'd have known that nothing could have been further from the truth.

The theory, he went on, was that then she went on the lam because she thought the police would be after her. They'd given up on that idea as a little too convenient. The other top candidate was Jack, out of jealousy, but why then when this had been going on for a long time? Maybe Cary killed Emil and then himself. But the timing was wrong: Those insurance policies had been around for nearly a year.

Sam reached for my hand. "But none of those felt right. Felicity quit at the strip club long before any of this. Cary and Emil knew that she didn't have an exclusive relationship with either of them. They might indeed have been jealous, but why would it all detonate during Christmas break? These were family men. It didn't compute."

Sam's personal theory was that Felicity crossed somebody who was scary or crazy. He said he believed that it was some "nutter" who had a fantasy relationship with a woman he'd spoken to once, at a grocery store, or at a strip club. Both of us could see the merit of the other possibility: If Felicity wouldn't talk about it, it was because she was scared. Somebody threatened to kill her if she told—or her little brothers, or Ruth. Felicity knew that the likelihood of her being acquitted was good; Sam was shocked that she was even charged based on what they had, which was not much more than that she knew both men well. So, while she probably wouldn't go to prison, she would rather have faced prison, seven or eight years of her life before she could even apply for parole, than risk talking about whoever she believed was really responsible. That was what Sam sometimes believed. Other times, he thought she just genuinely had no idea.

I sat on a stone bench near the bridge watching the huge eagles ride the air, their great wings like shaggy old coats. I ate the ridiculously thick cheese-and-brown-bread sandwich I'd bought at one of Wisconsin's ubiquitous roadside cheese "cottages," along with two bags of taco chips.

Since Sam and I had broken up, I'd been drowning my sorrows in taco chips. Nell said I reminded her of our dad, who, when the bag got close to empty, would tip his head back and funnel chips into his open mouth. "Dad likes to get the chips out of the way," Nell would invariably say. I'd finally told Nell about what happened with me and Sam, pretending that he was just one of those men who was solitary by nature. She'd never met him but was as sympathetic as a good sister should be, her only qualm that she might have been able to wangle an internship from his firm. Thinking about my father and his chips made me long for him. I wished Patrick were here. I wasn't sure why. I wanted my dad.

That was when it started, a feeling of unease that crept over me, the premonitory sense that something was very near and very wrong. It churned my guts and made me grateful I'd purchased two stomach-settling Cokes, not one, although until today, I hadn't drunk a Coke for ten years.

Animals can tell where trouble is afoot. They don't have to think it over, although Felicity would have said that they do discuss it, sending warnings in their own tongue: look out, take cover, a storm, a hawk, beware. It doesn't always work; sometimes the threat is already upon them, but they are guided by instinct invariably, in the way humans have forgotten how to be. We have those instincts too, and experts on personal safety say that they are almost always right. Sometimes, we override those instincts. Always, when we do, it's a bad idea. Think of every time that you have done that . . . every ride you took with a sketchy guy because it was just so late and nobody else was around. Every time you decided to hit the snooze button because there was plenty of time before the exam. Every time you knew full well that you hadn't left yourself time and you ignored the weather. How did that work out? You look back on that time as a near miss, when you were lucky to pass the test, keep the job . . . keep your life.

That unease crawled on me as I ate the last bites of the sandwich and neatly folded the wrapping. There was a single white cloud above, the size of a continent, but white and benign. It did not portend a storm. I put one of the sweating Coke cans against my sun-basted forehead. I watched the eagles. They mated for life. They didn't get distracted by old tales or the tail feathers of new raptors. They were one-eagle kind of birds.

My phone rang then.

It was my mother. The jury was back. It had been not quite three hours. I was, of course, just a reporter and there was no way that the verdict would wait for me. So I asked Miranda to be my eyes and ears and she promised she would. As it turned out, everything had to wait on Israel Ronson, whose car broke down and who had to wait for an associate to pick him up on the beltway, which was suddenly clogged with traffic. Sam knew better than to go far. He didn't expect a verdict so soon, but had hunkered down with a book in a local coffee shop. His was a five-minute walk.

I would later hear that he told someone that it was a myth that a fast verdict was a guilty verdict. A jury coming back quickly often meant that the members understood everything and didn't have any questions.

Still, I ignored the speed limit, as I had that night in Chicago with the woman in labor. I wished I had a gumball to slap on the roof of the car. Barns and cows flashed past like images in a child's flip-book. When I was ten minutes out, my phone rang again: my mother. I couldn't bring myself to answer. Where would Felicity's arrow fly when she left the courtroom this evening? Would she go out for celebratory drinks with her stripper sisters, then back to her luxe condominium with the blue-tiled pool? Or would she be pointed toward a thousand other women as the occupant of her own eight-by-twelve cell at Manoomin Correctional Facility in Fond du Lac?

The sun had just begun its long summer descent over Lake Mendota when everyone again assembled in the courtroom. My mother and Claire held hands. Sam held Felicity's right hand and Angela held her left hand. I clasped my own hands together, scrutinizing my own emotions. Did I want her to go free if she had done this thing? I did. I did not. I whispered to Felicity with my mind: *Promise to be good*, I whispered. *Promise to walk the high path.*

Judge Martin addressed the jury forewoman, juror number eleven, a college track coach. "Madam, has the jury reached a verdict on which you all agree?"

"We have, Your Honor," said the forewoman, and I knew for sure when she reached out to grab a corner of the jury box and the woman next to her steadied her briefly by supporting her elbow.

"Please give me the verdict."

The bailiff handed the innocuous mustard-colored rectangle to the judge, who opened it.

"Miss Wild, please rise." Felicity stood, Sam and Angela pressing in beside her. "I will now read you the verdict." The forewoman closed her eyes. "On the first count, we, the jury, find the defendant, Felicity Claire Copeland Wild, guilty of first-degree intentional homicide as charged in the information. On the second count, we, the jury, find the defendant, Felicity Claire Copeland Wild, guilty of first-degree intentional homicide as charged in the information." The judge removed her reading glasses. "Do you understand this verdict, Miss Wild?"

"I . . . do . . . " Felicity stammered and then staggered against the table in front of her. Sam tried to put an arm around Felicity's shoulders but she struggled free. "Please no!" she cried out. "No! I didn't do this!" In a lower voice, choked with what I assumed were tears, because I could not see her face, she added, "Your honor, please listen. I may not be innocent, but I'm innocent of this!" Finally allowing Sam to take her elbow and hold her up, Felicity began to tremble violently, twisting her head wildly to the left and to the right. She called out, "Mom!" and "Reenie!"

Almost gently, the judge said, "Compose yourself, Miss Wild."

Now unsteady on my own legs, I reached for the back of the bench in front of me, my notebook and pen clattering to the floor. Sam flinched at the sound. I glanced over at my mother and my aunt. Miranda and Claire held each other close, their foreheads touching.

Then another of those things happened that you never believe in a novel, from the same deck as those many phony instances in which the beleaguered heroine curls her fingernails so tightly into her palms that her hands begin to bleed. I heard a voice calling "Wait! Wait! Just wait a minute!" and it honestly took me several seconds to realize that it was me. But I wasn't ejected from the courtroom for my disorderly outburst because it was all over. I caught a brief glimpse of Jack Melodia just as he turned away and left the courtroom through the main door. Then my mother came to my side and, with Claire trailing behind us, we walked down the stairs and out into the honeyed afternoon light, to the sidewalk where that absurdly blonde woman was saying, "This is Sally Zankow outside the Dane County courthouse, where former escort Felicity Wild has been found guilty in a swift verdict . . . the sensational trial of a gifted biology student who inexplicably gave up a bright future . . ."

I left my mother and ran into Sally on purpose, jostling her so hard that she nearly dropped her mic. I said, "Oh, I am so sorry." But I was not.

When, several weeks later, Felicity was sentenced to two consecutive terms of not less than twenty years each, I was not there.

I read the accounts and heard from Sally and others that she took it very well. She was composed. Her impassive exterior was back in place. Claire told me that she overheard Sam promise that he would come to see her right away to begin preparation for an appeal, but Felicity only thanked him and squeezed his forearm and wished him good luck before she turned away.

For the first time, I wondered if Felicity was actually mentally ill. Her composure wasn't simply unusual; it was eerie. Facing what she had to face, anyone else would have clutched for a lifeline, for any hope at all. Did her guilt so overwhelm her? Was her sense of justice so acute?

I wrote Felicity two letters, one right after she went to prison, the other a few weeks later. This time, my letters were not returned to me. One day, I received a letter from her. It was the only one she'd ever write to me from prison.

> *Dearest Reenie,*
>   *Thank you for the books. Your care and friendship mean a great deal to me. You have always been there. I know how hard all this has been for you to understand. I will never forget you or how brave and good you are.*
>   *With love, Felicity*

But I did not answer that letter.

I was confused.

A week went by as a question, one that had been in the water too long, washed up stinking on the shore of my consciousness. It was livid and ugly: Was Felicity ever who I had believed her to be? And if she was, had she changed so profoundly that no vestige of the girl she'd been was left?

When she first went to prison, I was in shock. I couldn't work the whole thing out. What was most on my mind was how horrified she must be, prison being worse by orders of magni-

tude than the eight often-empty cells at the Dane County jail.
I didn't want her to feel abandoned. But had her crime erased
my affection for her? Certainly, it would not have been the case
if the murders had been accidental. But how did I feel about a
cynical, pitiless plan? And what kind of person was fine with
having a murderer for a pen pal?

So I stopped writing.

Then, a week later, I saw Sam's number on my phone screen,
and my heart accelerated. At last. At last! But his text was only
to plead with me to write to Felicity. Felicity, Felicity, she was
the one who really mattered to him. When I didn't reply to that
text, he left me a phone message, which I listened to a dozen
times—not for the content but to hear his voice say my name.
Felicity could not eat or sleep and was finally hospitalized again.
She'd begun therapy, once a week when she was in crisis, later
once a month or less often. It seemed to be helping to a degree.
He thought I would want to know.

Poor sensitive girl. If she had such a delicate character, she
shouldn't have murdered two people. And Sam sent not a word
about him and me. How I reacted then confuses me now.

I would learn later, from Claire through my mother, that Felicity was adjusting. She still would not accept visits, even from
Sam, but spoke to him on the phone a few times. She sometimes
answered Claire's letters. It would take many months, and so many
things would have happened by then, before Claire would tell me
in passing that Felicity had completed her degree in biology, test-
ing out of many of the requirements. She'd started a book group
for her fellow prisoners and helped several women complete their
GEDs. Through a prison outreach program from the UW School
of Medicine, she traveled to a clinic to have laser surgery so she
no longer required eyeglasses. She became a vegetarian, ate her
meals alone, always, and, as time wore on, she was allowed to eat
in her cell or in the library. She was always in an individual cell.

She found comfort in prayer, spending an hour every evening in the chapel. Even the violent offenders and the stone crazies were compelled to respect her beauty and her reticence, Claire told me. She was never hurt or assaulted. Felicity never told me any of these things, and by the time I learned them, they no longer really signified anything, in Felicity's life or mine.

At first, when I was trying to forget her, I had to contend with the fact that, while Felicity might be out of my life, it would take time to excavate her from my psyche. My obsession with Felicity, for let's call it what it was, had towed me through a silty strait spiked with guilt and admiration (and joy and joy). I couldn't stop thinking of her in captivity, a bird of bright plumage in a cage.

At first, I dreamed of her every night.

Then less often.

Finally, not at all.

Then, one night, long after, when all the other shoes had dropped and my life had taken a decisive new turning, I had a vivid dream of Felicity, which would also, I would later decide, combine a kind of prophecy and a recovered memory.

She was standing outside, her arms thrust out and the sun spangling her dark hair. Around her head and along her arms, birds swirled and alighted, as if they were joyful to be near her.

At that time, I didn't know St. Francis of Assisi from Francis Ford Coppola. So I didn't understand until much later that this dream image of Felicity recalled the thirteenth-century Italian saint who was born the indulged son of a prosperous merchant but who grew up to be a humble friar who called all creatures his brothers and sisters. He preached even to the birds, and asked God to make him an instrument of His peace.

The next morning, I began to write to Felicity again, and I continued, every other day, a short letter or a long letter, letters she did not answer but which were not returned to me.

What should I say? I wondered.

My generation really has no idea how to write letters. There is generally no need. That was one of the things I mourned as a writer. In grad school, I'd been assigned to read the correspondence of the great children's editor Ursula Nordstrom, who worked with authors such as E. B. White on classics like *Charlotte's Web*. Her notes to friends and business associates were so revealing, so funny and brilliant and insightful, and I knew that Nordstrom was among the last generation of devout letter writers. Of course, people talked then too, but they didn't have the Satanic convenience of smartphones. What would anyone ever read from the most accomplished authors of my age? The collected text messages?

As time passed, and I became reconciled to the fact that this would be a one-sided effort, I began to treat the correspondence as a kind of journal—for my benefit as well as Felicity's. I wrote to her about my life, all that I was reading, what I was writing, the people I met, and my family. I wrote to her about politics and the environment, about movies and music, about fashion. I wrote to her about things we'd done and said long ago.

Through creating those letters, I unearthed my love for her, which was never really gone. There was still so much that I would never understand, but I considered that perhaps there had been a good reason for what she had done, if she had done it at all. Since I didn't know how to tell her that in words—and it seemed a kind of dangerous thing to write to a convicted murderer, I tried to show her. I am no artist, but (also paraphrasing St. Francis, who, unbeknownst to me, had advised doing a very few things but doing them well . . .) I decided to try to draw something for her. I kept working at it.

Prompted by my memory of the teenage Felicity crying as she tried to save a nest of orphaned birds, I kept at it until I could make a passable image of the humblest of all birds—a sparrow. How powerful that choice would be, how large it would loom, I had no idea.

THIRTEEN

Barn Swallow

Hirundo rustica. The vagabonds and acrobats of the air, barn swallows live much of their lives on the wing, drinking, feeding, courting, and even mating in midair. Aerobatic fliers, they perform twists, turns, swoops, and lunges, often just above the ground. They also face the longest journey of any bird on their annual winter sojourn from the Americas to the tropics, traveling in huge groups, up to six hundred miles a day, a pilgrimage that many say gave rise to the expression "snowbirds" to describe individuals who flee cold climates for sunny destinations. In African legend, swallows symbolize the need to start over. Shakespeare wrote that "True hope is swift, and flies with swallow's wings." But long before that, Aristotle warned, "One swallow does not make a summer, neither does one fine day; similarly one day or brief time of happiness does not make a person entirely happy."

IN THE WEEKS AFTER THE TRIAL, I SET ABOUT MAKING A NEW LIFE for myself.

They (they, whoever they are!) say that it takes twenty-one days to get over a breakup.

I could not count the two weeks of the trial, when my guts literally rebelled every time I saw Sam. But after it was over, I tacked one of those little calendars from the bank on the wall next to my bed. I didn't feel guilty about the tack; after all, it was a box room and a pin hole. Then I began to mark off the days. By the time I reached sixteen, my body's reaction to this loss had stabilized. I was no longer throwing up everything I ate. I still had fantasies in which Sam woke up and realized that he still loved me. I dreamed that he came to the door of my sister's house with a huge bouquet of yellow roses.

He did not, of course.

With my research completed and the basic shape of the story in mind, I turned my interview notes in to the transcriber at *Fuchsia* so that I would be ready to write when the time came. I requested the transcripts. The trial had lasted not nearly as long as I'd expected so I still had the luxury of time and expenses. I'd always been a fast writer. The actual composing of the story would probably take no more than two weeks, perhaps less than that.

I did new kinds of research.

I looked up strategies for emotional renewal, although I'd always made fun of anything that smacked of "self-help."

One particularly perky website suggested that the way to healing was to become your very best self. Learn new things. Develop new skills. Cultivate new sources for building your self-esteem. I'd already learned how to make a soufflé, even using Nell's geriatric oven. I'd mastered the brown-butter chocolate chip cookies that would make me a star at any holiday gathering for the rest of my life. Joining a travel group might be something I'd consider when I was forty. A book club? That was a definite possibility; I would post something at the library and the independent bookstores. The thought of going on a dating website filled me with terror and disgust: I was still too reminded of what "dates" meant in the world of escorts.

What I did decide to do before anything else was to get in the best physical shape of my life.

Every long walk I pounded my way through would exhaust

me past thinking. Every barre class I showed up for would banish Sam from my mind. I hiked for miles around Madison, circling the lake, rubbing blisters on my heels, trying to run a little and getting shin splints for my effort. I pedaled on my sister's stationary bike and read all the books that I'd ignored when they were assigned in school. I studied the classic crime and mental health reportage of Truman Capote, Emmanuel Carrère, Calvin Trillin, Bill Lichtenstein, Joe McGinniss, and Janet Malcolm.

The reward was that I fell into bed at night and slept like a tired child. There were times when I even fell fast asleep during the day.

Despite all that exercise, I didn't lose any weight, but I reasoned that muscle weighed more than fat, and, for the first time since I was an adolescent, I was seeing things on my body I hadn't seen—like biceps.

I signed up with a career counselor to see what other kinds of work I might do (maybe I could be a writer! Maybe I could teach . . . writing!). I took tests to determine where in the country, or even the world, I might find my destiny. (North Carolina was a strong contender . . .)

At last, I visited a therapist and told her the unvarnished truth. She looked surprised by the revelation of what I had done so long ago, but then she surprised me. "If there is love," she said, "everyone deserves a second chance."

My so-far-successful quest to avoid any place that I might set eyes on Sam backfired one night when I was trying out yet another life-enhancing strategy—dining out alone at a fine restaurant. Feeling like a show-off in my white crepe Alice + Olivia pants and vest, all yearny as I watched the cooing couples around me, I told myself to concentrate on the menu. When I finally made my choice and glanced up, there was Sam nervously looking back at me from a distance of about ten feet. Across from him was a very pretty woman about his age who seemed to be describing an art heist. She was one of those gesturers whose hands flew around like butterflies.

Of course, she could have been a client.

She could have been a new associate at the firm.

And I could have been a pterodactyl.

The waiter arrived with my artichoke risotto. Quietly and forcefully, I asked him please to box it up. "It doesn't travel well," he told me with the hauteur of someone who thought that, instead of waiting tables, he should really be in movies with Ryan Gosling.

"Okay," I said. "Then throw it out."

The waiter rolled his eyes and sighed, oblivious to how close he was at that moment to losing a finger. I gave him my card and studied the pattern of the tablecloth until the bill arrived, then grabbed my risotto and departed.

Once out in the street, I noticed that my anguish was undergoing a transformation. I was furious. I wanted to break windshields, trip passersby, kick over trash cans.

Granted, Sam didn't owe me any special allegiance. We'd now been apart much longer than we'd ever been together. I had told him something that would have blown anyone's mind. And yet, we didn't discuss it. I didn't get a chance to tell him about the solid year I went to therapy twice a week, the volunteer work I did at the animal sanctuary cleaning up after cats that had three legs and no sphincter, the meals I prepped at the domestic abuse shelter. I didn't get to tell him how I had learned to transform my abysmal opinion of my looks, the price for growing up alongside Nell, the American beauty, how I found the root of my anger and tore it out, how hard I had labored to see myself again as worthy.

I went back to my sister's house and tried to sleep.

But sleep would no longer come to me.

"The curse is come upon me, cried The Lady of Shalott."

I got up and pulled my sweatshirt on over my pajamas. I drove to Sam's house and strode up to the front steps.

"Sam!" I called. "Sam Damiano! Come out!" There was at first no response. Then the lights flicked on. I saw a shadow at his window. "You are a coward, Sam! You don't deserve to be a defense attorney because you don't believe in second chances! You don't really believe in redemption! You're a fraud! You don't deserve me!"

Sam appeared at the door, at the moment that the sky cracked open and a deluge of rain poured down.

"Reenie! For Pete's sake, just come inside!"

"I will not come inside. I hope the whole block hears me!"

Nobody would hear me. Rain was crashing down like a waterfall.

I turned and ran for my car. While Sam called my name from the porch, I got in and rattled out of the driveway, my wheels spinning in the river that was now coursing down the street. Back at Nell's house, I skinnied out of my wet clothes on the porch, sliding unseen and naked into my dark room. There I pulled on underpants from my suitcase, but my boxes were on the top tier and I was afraid of bringing them all crashing down on my head in the dark. Instead, I pulled on the first thing I could root out of one of the boxes marked with my sister's name, which happened to be a lacy patchwork cotton maxi-dress. I fell once again on the bed.

Was I glad that it was over, really, finally over? Only as glad as you can be when a death puts an end to suffering. There would be time to mourn, time and place, but I took some comfort in the notion of freedom, of turning a clean face to the future. I really could move to North Carolina. People were probably nicer there. I could do it right after I finished this story. I didn't need to be tied to the Midwest; my parents were going to be heading south in the near future anyhow.

Maybe I could even convince Ivy to let me work remotely, just visiting the office in Chicago once in a while. That was what more and more people with portable professions were doing.

I hadn't been asleep for more than an hour when I heard the pounding at the door. I got up and could see, through the windows, that although it was still pouring, the sky had lightened. If it was not morning, it was close to it.

The pounding continued, growing in volume and intensity.

From within the house, a voice slurred with sleep, not my sister's, called, "Who in the hell could be at the door? It's goddamn five in the morning!"

"I'm handling it!" I called and then addressed the door. "Hey, crazy person! Stop banging on the door! Leave whatever you have out there! We'll get it later, okay?" In response, the banging began again, louder and faster. Maybe someone was hurt and needed help. Maybe someone was out there with a gun. In a movie, I did the last thing you should do, the thing that would have the viewer screaming, *Don't! Stop!* I undid the locks and pulled the door open.

Drenched, Sam stood on the porch with a giant bouquet of yellow roses.

"What?" I said. "What is going on?"

"Reenie," he said. "Will you marry me?"

"What?"

"Will you marry me? You got me in trouble and now you have to marry me."

Nell came barreling down the stairs. "Jesus Christ! What's happening? Who's that? Why is he delivering flowers in the middle of the night?"

"Nell, this is Sam. I, ah, mentioned him. He just asked me to marry him."

Nell looked not one speck less annoyed. "I thought he broke up with you."

"I did," Sam said. "It was the worst mistake of my life."

"You don't deserve her," said my loyal sister. She ruffled her hair. "Well, make a decision because I don't have to get up for three more hours!"

I said, "I guess it depends on two things. One, how sorry you really are. And two, if I like the ring you pick out."

"I already have the ring. I've been carrying it around for weeks. It was my great-grandmother's. You can have the stone reset in any way you want."

"I'll never get back to sleep now," Nell said. "Let me have a look at that ring." It was a yellow diamond set about with pale blue sapphires in the basket-weave style of a hundred years ago. "You might as well get down on one knee. You already dripped all over the hardwood. Thanks a lot. I'm considering buying this house." She turned to me. "So, Irene?"

"I'm waiting for the other part of this."

"Reenie, I was afraid. I was afraid of the story you told me but mostly I guess, I was just afraid of the love I felt for you. I'm thirty-three years old and this is the first time I ever considered marrying anyone."

"This is the first time I ever considered getting married at all."

"Please give me another chance. Please say you'll forgive me."

"I do," I said. "And I will."

Sam kissed me once and again. He hugged Nell, and the flowers scattered. One by one, her roommates joined us in the hall, first annoyed, then applauding, except for Leslie, the beautiful and surly psychiatric social worker. She said, "I don't let strange people into the house. And I would appreciate it if you did not either. That's how single women get killed."

"Okay," I said. "I'm engaged now, to this stranger, for the past five minutes. Does that still count as being single?"

Leslie whirled and stomped back upstairs.

Nell then took a hard look at me and said, "That's my dress."

We drove up to see my parents, later that day.

On the way, I forced Sam to stop for taco chips. He gave me a quizzical look.

I told him about the dream I'd had, of the freezing shrimp-sized babies, and, as I had feared, he looked appalled. "You're not, are you? Pregnant? We're a little too old for that, aren't we?"

"You mean to have it be a mistake or at all?" I asked him. "Last I heard, I'm in prime time for the next fifteen years or more."

"To have it be a mistake," he said. "I think your roomie the social worker would say that is a pretty loaded dream."

"I agree with that, and pretty fear based. And no, I'm not pregnant."

"If you were, we'd deal with it," Sam said. "People always used to. People still do. It's just not the best way to start things off." I couldn't disagree, and my relief was mighty that he hadn't said any of the repugnant, atavistic things single men even older than he sometimes said, about how they didn't even know how to take care of themselves, much less a kid . . . I still wasn't sure I wanted a child, but I was sure that I didn't want to be with a man who didn't want a child—and that didn't pass the scratch test for common sense even to me.

After I got the taco chips out of the way, I told him, "We don't have to stay over, but they'll want us to. We can leave at the crack of dawn tomorrow. I can show you where Felicity lived, at Starbright Ministry."

"I don't want to bring Felicity into this, except I do have to call her and try to get a message to her."

I couldn't help myself: "Now of all times?" Perversely, I wanted this moment to be a closed circle of just two.

"Yes, now of all times. The last time I spoke to her she told me that you were the dearest and best person she ever knew and I was a fool to let you go."

I couldn't speak. This was my life to come, to be lived on

clean and unmarked land. There was no room for shadows. On the other hand, Felicity was the only reason I met Sam. Felicity was all alone. She would always be alone. The girl who had everything had nothing. No matter how hard I tried, she was part of me.

"'I am half-sick of shadows,'" I said.

"Finally a poem I know," Sam said. "We were forced to read it in eighth grade, the most depressing thing I ever read. She kills herself and then floats down to Camelot."

"I don't think she really killed herself. She died of a broken heart."

"Nobody really dies of a broken heart."

"They do in country-western songs," I told him. "And old poems. I'm named after that poem."

"I thought you were named after that old song."

I said, "Both. I'll explain someday."

Sam said, "We have plenty of time."

We talked about things we'd never discussed. He asked if I would want to stay home with a baby. I said it depended on the baby—that I hadn't really thought past peeing on the stick and getting presents. I asked him if he would, and he said absolutely. He told me his two youngest brothers were twins and that this ran in families. Then he pulled off at one of those rest stops frequented by long-haul truckers, a low-lying building complex that advertised Diner Showers Hookups.

"Do you think they mean electrical hookups or the other kind?" I asked. "Probably both, judging by the looks of that joint."

I waited while Sam made a phone call and left a message. "Guys, I am at a truck stop in Wisconsin. I just proposed. She said yes."

Miranda and Patrick were waiting on the porch swing. They came down to meet me.

Miranda said, "I was so surprised when you called. You

haven't been up here for a while. How long can you stay? Do you want something to drink? Come inside."

We all turned toward the porch, not even noticing Sam struggling to manage his satchel and mine. Finally, he said, "Wait a minute! I'm Sam Damiano, I'm a friend of Reenie's . . ."

"Sam is Felicity's defense lawyer," I said. "You remember. Well, Mom, you remember. Dad, you weren't there."

My mother said, "Of course. Hello."

Patrick put out his hand and they shook.

"That's a beautiful ring, Reenie," my mother said. "Is it new? Is it one of those new antiques they make?"

"It's a real antique. It belonged to Sam's grandmother. We . . . Well, Sam asked me to marry him, and I said yes."

Patrick said, "Is marrying the press required? For a solid defense?"

"It's required for me. I guess I didn't do too well with the defense. I did my best."

My father said, "I was kidding. In a clumsy way. I'm sure you did everything right, Sam."

"And want to be a good husband to Reenie, and a good father to our children. I hope you want that too."

Well done! I thought. *They will acquit!*

My mother said, "Reenie, are you . . . ?"

I said, "Nope." Then I went on, "Doesn't anyone want to say congratulations or when's the wedding? The answers are, thanks and we don't know, we've only been engaged for eight hours."

My mother hugged both of us, and then said, "I remember Angela from back when I was a reporter. She was a powerhouse. She got some of the worst people off . . ."

Sam said, "That she did! My mom is one of a kind."

Miranda said, "Wow."

Just then, Nell arrived. She'd left an hour after us but apparently driven much faster. She said, "Can you believe that someone is marrying Reenie on purpose?"

Patrick said, "I'm just about to tell Sam here about her dowry, the farm, the silver mine, the chalet in Zurich . . ."

"You can keep those," Sam said.

"Even the chalet?" Patrick asked. "I'm very partial to the chalet."

"I'll make dinner," Miranda said. "I don't know what I have around . . ."

"No, I will," Sam suggested. "Later on. I want to impress you." He said this not knowing anything about my mother's heartfelt but disastrous ways around a home-cooked meal. She eyed me a little skeptically, for we never scrupled to judge her cruelly because she could merely win Pulitzer Prizes and earn a healthy six figures in PR but could not whip up triple-chocolate oatmeal bars. I raised my hands palms out to protest my innocence.

Later that night, after we'd all eaten Pasticcio di Lasagna, which Sam made with a ridiculously velvety béchamel on top of the vodka sauce and double the amount of cheese, Patrick, his eyes misty with pleasure, said, "Okay, you have my permission to marry her. If she doesn't want to, we will adopt you. That was the best meal I ever had in my life." Patrick added, "I'll make coffee for us, if there are any takers . . ."

Nell said, "You have to agree to the coffee, otherwise you're a sissy. But I hope you have lots of activities planned because you won't be sleeping tonight."

My father said, "Irene told me she was going to show you the sights. That should take about fifteen minutes. I'm going to watch my old-time shows. Did Irene tell you about the deprivation she was subjected to as a child? That they weren't allowed to watch? She usually shares that with new people."

"Actually she didn't," Sam said. "When we were kids, my dad let us watch all the TV we wanted but we could only watch his shows. The effect was that we didn't end up watching too much because they were all old Westerns."

"Really?" said Patrick. He sensed a setup and glanced at me. "I like those myself. Did you know that Jodie Foster got her start on *Gunsmoke?*"

Sam returned the serve. "Did you know Ed Asner and Richard Dreyfuss did too? And that Bette Davis was in an episode or two?"

Patrick beamed. Here was a man a person could talk to.

My mother then said, "Sam, I don't want to spoil the mood but I hope you don't mind if I ask about Felicity. Is she . . . well?"

"I guess she's as well as can be expected. It's a big adjustment. A really terrible adjustment. We never saw this coming. I was confident."

"So you don't think that she did this," Miranda said.

"I don't," Sam said. "She hasn't told me who she thinks did it, and it's entirely possible that she doesn't even know."

"Do you always believe your clients?" Patrick asked. "Isn't it your job to defend them either way?"

"I don't always believe them. But I believe her."

Sam mentioned Felicity's illness, her severe dehydration and pneumonia and the fact that she had recently been hospitalized. My mother's expression shifted like a series of slides from compassion to consternation to confusion. There was the instinctive response to Felicity; there was the informed response. Sam finally switched topics by asking where to put the bags. We'd all forgotten that he'd never been there before.

There was some small and mostly comic concern about me and Sam sharing a bedroom. He couldn't believe that I'd never had a boyfriend stay over at my parents' house before, but that was true, and even Patrick agreed that it was okay since Sam had "put a ring on it," which phrase, I would like to be clear, he actually used. When we got ready to take a drive, my father said, "That coffee will come in handy! Sheboygan isn't exactly Las Vegas. Make her bring you back if it gets too boring. We can watch *Rawhide*. Did you know that Jimmy Stewart and Leonard Nimoy were—"

Miranda said, "Patrick, enough! Patrick is easily bored. Except by TV Westerns and blueprints and sparkling banter with the guy who does entablature."

But she said that with goodwill and affection. It was a statement made by someone who not only loved her husband but admired him. That I could say the same about Sam, who also did things and knew things that I didn't entirely understand, was a huge relief, while also suggesting that people whose marriages were founded on new relationships were lucky, since they would not run out of things to converse about for years.

In the long northern summer twilight, Sam and I took a drive past the house where Felicity had spent her childhood years, currently occupied by a couple who looked young enough to be in middle school. We parked on the former grounds of the Starbright Ministry and I explained Roman Wild's colorful shenanigans. "My mom and I walked over here last winter, and the place was a ghost town," I added.

It still was. There were signs of the construction intent on turning it into a municipal park, but most of the darkened buildings sat eyeless and moonlit, breathing what I imagined to be a kind of stone-tape despair. We walked down toward the lakeshore and saw how the paving-stone paths between the buildings were studded with commemorative plaques evidently endowed by former parishioners, each with a Bible verse: "Do everything in love." 1 Corinthians 16:14 Ann Wertz Garvin and family, and "You are the light of the world." Matthew 5:14 Katherine Furness Dooley and Peter Dooley.

"I know them!" I said. "They had eight kids a year apart."

"They must have decided on the couples option or they would have needed a way bigger stone," Sam said.

The plaques were beautiful. The landscaping was beautiful. No detail had been overlooked.

"I never saw inside these places," I said. "They're too dark to look in the windows." I tried the door of what seemed to be a dormitory of some kind and was shocked that it was open. We walked through the building, clean and tidy, with nice built-in bunks and desks, but as spooky as one of those abandoned insane asylums so beloved of fake-ghost documentaries. ("What was that? Did you hear that noise?" "It was Dave, he just texted that he dropped the boom mic . . ." "Dave, did you see something? Dave? He's not answering, we should get down there!" "He can't answer, he broke the mic.")

Finally, we came to the small chapel near the lake. Sam pushed the door open. By that time it was nearly dark and moonlight suddenly shot through the stained glass of St. Francis of Assisi. A quote was scrolled in gold: "Oh birds, my brothers and sisters, you have a great obligation to praise your Creator, who clothed you in feathers and gave you wings to fly . . ."

I had never seen this particular feature of the chapel before. It was as though Felicity was whispering in my ear.

"Birds," I said.

"Maybe her stepfather was trying to be kind to Felicity," Sam said.

"Probably he was," I agreed. "Probably at first, he tried. And you remember, he tried to visit her in jail."

"That's true. I know that he dumped her mom, but maybe he wasn't all bad."

"I don't think he was. Maybe he just got too ambitious. Sometimes, things just don't work out. He's not a minister anymore."

It was then that I remembered I'd had another recent dream

about Felicity. It came back to my mind, clear as film. I told Sam about a field trip Felicity and I had been part of when we were just kids, maybe in fifth grade, to Chicago museums and to the Brookfield Zoo. At the massive zoo, which I'd never seen, there was a program in the new aviary that allowed a few people at a time to stand among the birds in a re-creation of the rain forest. The docent explained that you could get bird poop on your head, and you could even get pecked, but probably not. Those revelations discouraged most of the girls, but not Felicity—and, since I couldn't show up as a coward, not me. You got a little bucket of seeds, which you held in your hands, and the birds would come to you. The way St. Francis looked in the stained glass was the way Felicity looked that day, in an ecstasy, as brown and orange and blue creatures alighted on her hands and arms and shoulders . . . but I was terrified; the birds seemed to be dive-bombing me, tiny assassins like in the Daphne du Maurier story, their little eyes fierce and unblinking, their wings pummeling the air.

I finally had to be ushered out of the space, Felicity's arm around my shoulders, and I now realized this was why I'd been frightened of birds, large and small, ever since. They really were not the merry little chubby-cheeked angel proxies of Disney movies but were instead like dinosaurs, cruel, coarse, combative creatures who would kill you in an instant over a crumb of suet if they didn't weigh only four ounces.

"They don't mean to scare you, Reenie," Felicity said and laughed, but not in an unkind way, when I said that indeed they did and if she liked them, she was stupid, because if she was studying birds in the desert and she fell and hit her head, they would pick her flesh until she was nothing but a skeleton bleaching in the sun.

"I think that window is creepy," I told Sam. "But I'm being like my very cynical father. Always looking for the worm in the apple."

"I like him."

"He liked you. My dad wouldn't put on a jolly front for the royal family if they came over. The way he treated you was the equivalent of a ticker-tape parade for Patrick."

"That's good. One less mountain to cross," Sam said, and then asked, "Do you want to get married in church?"

"Oh, Sam, I don't know. I'm not opposed, though I'm not any kind of believer, but my father would drop dead of a heart attack. Maybe we could get married outside? Maybe in a bowling alley? Maybe in this place. I like this place. We could convince Patrick that it's a municipal building."

"Okay. I, Samuel Anthony Messina Damiano, take you . . . What's your middle name?"

"It's stupid . . ."

"Okay, take you, Irene Stupid . . ."

"It's Tennyson."

"Ah, hence the very depressing 'The Lady of Shalott.' But really, that's a beautiful name. I, Samuel Anthony Messina Damiano, take you, Irene Tennyson Bigelow, to be my wife . . ."

"'My wedded wife,' I think it is, 'to love and to honor, to protect and cherish, to respect and defend, in good times and hard times, for all the days of our lives.'"

"Is that the usual way? It's a good way, I like it."

"I, Irene Tennyson Bigelow, take you, Samuel Anthony Massimo . . ."

"Messina . . ."

"Messina Damiano, to be my wedded husband, to love and to honor, to protect and cherish, to respect and defend, to share my stories and my silence, to be my friend, in good times and hard times, for all the days of our lives" I added then, "I promise never to be jealous of your work or your friends. I promise to tell you the truth except occasionally and never about anything important. I promise to idealize you and look up to you and never insult you in public. I'll stay up late with you and hire good people to clean the house. Most of all, I promise to try to make you laugh, even at my expense, even when my rear end is fat and my boobs sag and my ankles swell up if you insist on having a kid. I promise to love it too, although I can't imagine loving anyone more than I love you right now. If we have half of what my parents have and half of what your parents have, it will be enough. I promise these things in front of St. Francis and these ghosts who've probably been waiting a while for a great moment like this one."

Sam said, "What about obey? You left out obey."

I told him, "You can obey me all you want to."

Sam said, "Those were things I never thought of. They're things I never knew I needed. But now, I know. And you always knew." I kissed his cheek. "So can we just make a video of this? Do we have to do the other now? Invitations and fighting over the kind of cake?"

"We do, yes. We have to. I know exactly how to do this. All cake is good, if made by a professional. We could have a black-and-white wedding. It makes all the photos look good. And a black-and-white wedding cake, three layers, three different flavors, like chocolate, white, and coconut. Me, a fitted black lace bodice over a white tulle tulip skirt . . . the bridesmaids could carry white roses."

"I thought you never really thought about this."

"I thought about it for work, Sam! We had a wedding issue! And you know what they say, it's a public commitment. Got to show the flag!"

"Marriage is still the best legal framework to protect children, and with issues of property and inheritance and such. And families like it. There's only a fifty-fifty chance it will last, and I don't mean us, Reenie, because ours will last . . ."

"It's been months. My relationships aren't long on . . . on longevity. Months for me are like years for other people. So this has already stood the test of time."

"Well, families want to be on the side of hope. I think that's a good thing."

I added, "And so are presents. I really want the presents. I love presents."

"I thought we could say, please, no presents."

"No presents, no Irene. The real, real truth is, I want everyone to know that you love me. I want you to say it in front of everyone."

"We have to have a champagne fountain. I know how tacky that is but Italians require a champagne fountain and a live band. A live band that plays the tarantella. And a satin purse the bride carries that people put cash in when they dance with her."

"Like what the strippers had!" I said. "A little pocket on their bikini bottoms."

"My mother says back in the day, people used to stuff money right in the bride's garter. I thought that was kind of earthy."

"Too earthy for me!"

None of those things ever happened.

FOURTEEN

Red-Winged Blackbird

Agelaius phoeniceus. A beautiful bird with a distinctive
three-note trill, the red-winged blackbird lives almost everywhere
that suburban people do, in meadows, prairies, fields, and marshes,
but also suburban yards. And like those human dwellers, these birds
can be fiercely and even combatively territorial. A male red-winged
blackbird is polygamous, sometimes with more than a dozen
concurrent mates, but things are not always what they seem. In some
populations, half the chicks have a sire that is not the dominant
male. In folklore, red-winged blackbirds symbolize inner strength
even when faced with change, as well as a masterful blend of arts
and justice. Although they're not uncommon, the population of
red-winged blackbirds is decreasing, but as Lennon and McCartney
famously sang with the Beatles, they are also resilient creatures, all
their life, "waiting for this moment to arise." In the 1970s, cult leader
Charles Manson, who, coincidentally, was always surrounded by a
harem of young female followers, believed that this song was about
his murderous mission. In "Thirteen Ways of Looking at a Blackbird,"
the poet Wallace Stevens wrote, "A man and a woman are one/
A man and a woman and a blackbird are one."

I HAD LIED TO MY PARENTS.

Indeed, when Sam and I announced our engagement, I was
pregnant.

All through the trial, unawares, I'd carried a stowaway, my daughter, the unknown agent behind all those bags of taco chips. For more than four months, in a circumstance seemingly impossible for a modern woman, I had not noticed. Like a sixteen-year-old in denial, I'd let the chaotic days and weeks unspool without counting. Sam might have believed that all those birth-control slipups were so pre-2020s, and yet mistakes apparently still did happen—even when the window of opportunity, a single weekend, was opened only a crack. After employing diagnosis by Google, because I was so ravenous and yet felt so full, I finally saw a doctor because I feared that I had diabetes.

In fact, we had Cornelia Bigelow Damiano—a name whose initials, Sam helpfully noted, were the abbreviation CBD, or cannabidiol, one of the active ingredients in marijuana. I wanted to call her Claire, but Sam insisted that a clean break healed best and hurt least. His grandmother's name was Anna Cornelia Marie Messina, Granny Coco the namesake. We added "Frances" as a nod to that birdy chapel where we took our first vows.

There was no black-and-white wedding, although there were black-and-white cupcakes. No champagne fountain, but there were mimosas for everyone except the bride, who drank ginger ale with her orange juice and who never wanted to look at another mimosa. My parents hosted a brunch for a few dozen people, catered by Fair Alice, the premier local restaurant, and I thanked the universe because my mother would not be contributing any tried-and-terrifying culinary efforts.

Life is determined. Life strives against the odds to renew itself. It wasn't the best way to start things off, we agreed, until we saw her furious red face and assertive baby Mohawk. Then there was only Nelia, the very first firstborn, the light of the world.

My long story appeared in *Fuchsia*, a story that, I will say, boosted the profile and circulation of the magazine to new heights, encouraging more of the same kinds of long features. It wasn't true what I feared, that all my friends were going to be strangers. Instead, I heard applause from people who hadn't contacted me in years—former colleagues, professors, grad school classmates. I got two real job offers that were flattering if not tempting. The story was reprinted in countries around the world, probably as an example of American decadence, but that led to even more attention for me, and ultimately to a book contract for which I stipulated a very long deadline to delivery.

The story began this way:

Women on trial for murder don't wear pants.

In a simple navy blue shirtwaist dress, Felicity Wild walked into the courtroom, stopping only so police could remove the shackles around her wrists. Her dark hair expertly cut in an angled bob, huge turquoise glasses framing her strange amber eyes, Felicity looked like the homecoming queen she was once—not like an escort who killed two clients in cold blood.

Surreal is one of those words like *survivor*, too often said and too little understood. People throw it around when it doesn't even really pertain to the circumstances: *Oh, I was literally thinking about you at the moment you called! Surreal!*

This actually was surreal.

I was a couple of feet from Felicity, physically close enough to touch her, but unable to touch her—in a time and place that neither of us could ever have imagined growing up.

We were best friends. From the private history you share, a best friend knows what each of your eye rolls really means. Sometimes when you think something, you realize that the voice in your head is hers, not your own.

Writing that story was like a surgery for me.

I felt like I was betraying her, betraying myself, exploiting her, exploiting our friendship, like Nell said, because I could. But still, it needed to be finished, and once it was finished, I recognized that, like a surgery, it hurt badly at first. But in the end, even I could see that it had done me good.

Another year unspooled.

Sabrina Torres, my editor's mother and bankroller, evidently decided that, just as my old friend Marcus said, Florida was the new New York. She decided to move the magazine's base to Florida and to build the purple pavilion in all its glory. She would not be unmoved. So when Ivy was spirited away to become a TV *Fuchsianista*, always her first love, and I was tapped to take her place as editor of *Fuchsia*, I had mere weeks to decide, to create an expanded editorial plan, and then to organize my move.

I didn't want to uproot Sam or leave Sam even briefly. I didn't want to leave the Midwest. I didn't want to leave my family or my very few real friends—little though I saw them. There was a bid for me to teach writing at Sterling North College, a small liberal arts school in Madison, which I now decided to consider. It was a real job, a tenure-track job, and though I knew it might sometimes be dull, the duties sounded like money for nothing. If that didn't work out, I could try my hand at respectable PR jobs, finding something through my mother's vast and clean network.

Then Sabrina made me an offer I couldn't refuse, a figure more than twice the fictional salary I'd allowed my delighted, deluded parents to believe that I earned—back when I had fully seven hundred dollars in savings and got by only by regularly liberating cheese-and-mustard sandwiches from the office fridge. If I sold my little warehouse digs in Chicago to the subletter who kept pleading for it, I would be sitting "pretty

pretty," which had become a family catchphrase after a little girl used it to describe the white tulle overskirt with the forgiving waist that I wore to my courthouse wedding. When I played the Cornelia card, Sabrina stipulated a home office with a nanny stipend and an assistant. So I signed a four-year contract with bonuses that would be fulfilled no matter what the fate of the magazine.

In Florida with my folks that long-ago Christmas break, during the interval when Emil Gardener and Cary Church were murdered, I swore that, despite the fried grouper sandwiches, I would never live in that strange and tropical place, where the weather was extraordinary but also some of the people were extraordinary in a different way, like extraterrestrials, every second woman over the age of fifty with a face so blunted by Botox she looked like a Claymation figure.

Be careful what you don't wish for.

Now I would live my real life in vacationland, where thick-skinned fruit you knew from only the produce section could be pulled from a tree in your yard, where bugs that looked Jurassic never died but only grew and grew and grew. No more the harsh sun on crisp brown snowy prairie grass, the restless skeletal finger-snapping of black winter branches. I would always long for my Midwestern home, but it was not essential. What was essential would be there.

With reluctance that he took great pains to hide, Sam began looking for a job right away. Not two weeks had passed, however, before Angela Damiano decided that, this being Florida, where you could throw a coin in any parking lot and hit somebody who needed a defense lawyer, Damiano, Chen, and Damiano needed a satellite office there. Two of the firm's finest elected to join Sam, and he lured a young lawyer from Kelley and Hall who'd interned for him one summer, one Eleanor Bigelow.

Weeks passed, and while I had been terribly conflicted about living in a place I imagined populated only by drug dealers and senescent demagogues, the cartoon sunniness of the so-called Treasure Coast began to beguile me. It seemed to say, *You can rest here. You can be safe.*

That was the end of that. Or so it seemed. It was only the end of the beforemath.

FIFTEEN

Brown Pelican

Pelecanus occidentalis. A large, odd seabird, the
brown pelican is not quite as devoted a parent as was once believed:
Legend (not true) says the pelican pierced a hole in its own breast
to feed the blood to its chicks. But pelicans do fill their huge bill
pouch with fish to carry to their young. A large bird, three to five
feet long and weighing four to eleven pounds, with a wingspan
of nearly seven feet, brown pelicans dive from heights as steep as
fifty feet to hunt for prey. If a parent bird eats the fish first,
it always regurgitates part of the catch for the pelican chicks,
which are notoriously voracious. Because of the myth surrounding
their blood, pelicans are often associated in spiritual art with a
suffering Christ near the sea.

IN NARRATIVE, COINCIDENCE IS A JUVENILE STRATEGY ("WHAT
were the odds that the woman he crashed into on that crowded
ski slope in Utah would be his ex-wife, whom he hadn't seen
in ten years?").

In real life, though, stuff happens.

One Sunday, near their new condominium in Cocoa Beach,
my parents arranged a long-postponed brunch with one of Dad's
fraternity brothers, an engineer at the Kennedy Space Center.
Although they hadn't yet sold the house where we grew up, they
were gradually making the transition full-time to the land of

palm trees, pools, and pineapple plants. Their backyard was an almost sinisterly unchanging absinthe-colored Eden. Every couple of months, a gigantic storm came along and took out one of
their windows, but they were philosophical about it, even my father, who would have blown an aneurysm if this had happened
even a couple of years before. Dad had sold a half interest in his
business to a partner, who ran things ably in his absences—my
mother thought that this was proof of magic in the universe. She
had worked entirely remotely for several years.

Which brings me to the homily.

Buckle up, folks—this will be a ride to remember.

Patrick and Miranda decided to meet the old friend at this
nutty restaurant called Space Alley, where the servers all wore
silver Mylar outfits and the ceiling was a mosaic of spinning sau-
cers and flashing lights. Mom remembered later thinking that,
for somebody, it would be a seizure on a cracker.

As they waited for their Big Bang Burgers and Supernova
Shakes, Mom spotted a woman eating a modest salad alone in
a nearby booth. The woman glanced up, alerted by some psychic signal. My mother blinked, then swiftly snapped a picture
with her phone and sent it to me.

At that moment, I was floating in a pool on a big inflatable
chair in the shape of a whale, fittingly, as I was pregnant with our
twin boys (when I learned of this, I thought of Fay, so long ago,
saying "the requisite two boys"). I was wearing a bathing suit that
my sister called a BINO, or a Bikini In Name Only, because it
really was more the size of something you would attach to the
mast of a small sailboat. My phone, in a sturdy zip-sealed plastic
bag, was in the cupholder with my plastic bottle of lemonade. So
massive was I that it took me five minutes to flounder my way
out of the pool and get the bag open to study that photo.

It was Ruth Wild.

Though visibly older in ways that couldn't necessarily be accounted for by the passage of years, thinner, her hair entirely white, her expression sculpted downward by care, it was clearly Ruth, my old chemistry teacher, Felicity's mother. Given the location, you will have to forgive the allusion to the wrinkle on the space-time continuum, but it was not all that far-fetched to see her there. As I reminded Miranda when I texted back, Ruth's father, of whom she'd been enormously proud, had been a rocket scientist. He had worked on the first shuttle after the *Challenger* disaster. Ruth and her sisters had been born and raised nearby, and Ruth came north only for college, for a scholarship at Minnesota not very different from the one Felicity got to University of Wisconsin–Madison.

Why had I never considered that Ruth would return here to hide in plain sight? Florida was home to her. The truth was that, after Felicity was convicted, after I wrote the story, I scarcely thought of Ruth at all, except when I imagined the book I would write, which was on hold for the moment, but which would require revisiting old mysteries.

So much had detoured the plans I made.

What do they say? (And again, who are they, anyway?) Nothing comes with a greater guarantee of giving the gods the giggles (I still do like alliteration, a lot of alliteration . . .) than the huge hopes of humble human beings.

All the things I had wanted to happen, had happened— along with a few more. They had, however, all happened at the same time, which is what probably gave rise to that old aphorism about being careful what you wish for.

That Sunday, Sam was indoors, putting Nelia down for her nap. I yelled for him, and he came running with our naked two-year-old tucked under his arm in a football carry.

"My parents just saw Felicity's mother in a restaurant," I told him, as Nelia, who did not know fear, clambered onto Sam's shoulders and then leaped into my arms.

Sam said, "No way. They did not." I was about to show him the photo when I realized that Sam would not recognize her; he had never seen Ruth Wild. By the time he and Felicity met, Ruth was gone. "Are you going to try to talk to her?"

"It can't be her. But if it is her, I don't have any actual reason to talk to her."

"Aren't you curious?"

"Madly. But it's nothing to do with me."

"You should probably tell the aunts. Then they can follow up if they want to."

"True. I'll do that right away. I'll send them the picture."

I thought that over as I got Nelia settled for her nap. When I returned, Sam was asleep on a recliner, so I waited alone, pacing the pool deck with my big water bottle, for my parents to return and tell me the rest of what transpired over lunch. Sam was spent, crushed by his own work and parenthood but also trying to help my dad with a particularly gruesome stage of remodeling the vintage Spanish-style place we'd purchased while trying to ignore Patrick's muttering about romance versus common sense. My father had a point. We were swayed by the charm of the house before we realized that previous residents had included many generations of rodents and marsupials, not to mention the odd alligator strolling the neighborhood. When I found out about that, I wanted to leave. (How had I not realized this? Well, I was a Midwesterner! And who actually expects . . . alligators?) Sam pointed out that we would have to go to Missouri to entirely avoid them, so we installed a very tall vinyl picket fence with secure locks on the inside and the outside of the gate.

During that indefinite interval, we lived with my parents, who had four bedrooms and were gallant. Their place wasn't far from our base in Vero Beach and boasted perks including but not limited to that pristine and heated pool. I was sure that we would have a pool as well, by the time we started collecting social security. At my folks' house, I could be both mother and child. I got up at five, literally threw my toddler at my mother, sometimes worked from their house, sometimes drove an hour to work in the kind of traffic that made me wonder if all my fellow commuters had bathrooms in their cars, worked until six, by then so hungry that I actually relished whatever half-baked comestible Miranda provided, then fell into bed with Nelia tucked against my spine. We didn't even try to put her in a crib; she was too spoiled and we were too worn-out.

By the time my parents returned from their brunch, I had done too much thinking to keep up the pretense of nonchalance. I was ready to go out right then to search for Ruth, but Miranda and Patrick were adamant. Patrick, particularly, insisted that Ruth wasn't going anywhere, and although I didn't really believe that—for what if Ruth had seen my parents at the same moment they saw her?—I was too bulkily burdened to dispute them. Mom told me they'd asked the server if she knew the woman in the booth across and one back.

"She said, of course, that was Mrs. Copeland," Miranda told me. "I asked how she knew her and the server, who was just a kid, said she was a substitute teacher at the middle school and all the kids liked her. She came in a few times a week, always had the Cobb salad, always took half of it home in a poly clamshell for dinner. Then she said, 'She brings her little girl sometimes.' I said, 'Ruth's daughter is grown-up,' and, before you ask, I didn't say she's incarcerated. The server seemed confused. She said, 'You must be thinking of someone different. Mrs. Copeland, the science teacher?' I said, 'Right, I must be thinking of someone else.'"

"It can't be her then."

"It is her. You saw her yourself. Maybe she babysits for somebody. Maybe she had a baby."

"Ruth's sister said she wouldn't have any more children because she has a heart condition. That was one of the reasons the marriage broke up. But maybe she did."

I thought I would never have the patience to wait. I really did want to be able to deliver Ruth back to her sad sisters, now mourning not only her but Felicity as well. But a few days later, I learned anew how arresting it could be to give birth to nearly full-term twins, after twenty-three hours of labor, during which I couldn't feel pain because of an epidural, but I could feel a sensation like my midsection being dug up with a backhoe. I learned how awkward it could be to fall asleep nursing one baby with a book propped open in the crook of my unoccupied elbow and a two-year-old sprawled across my lap. As I sat up during the night, I remembered watching soap operas with my great-aunt Bridget, and how puzzled I was that these shows were just like real life: All people did was bicker, drink coffee, and go to restaurants. I wished they were still on.

I had not imagined that I would be a mother of three before my thirtieth birthday; if I had imagined it at all, I thought I would be freezing my eggs on the threshold of forty. Nelia was a Damiano in every feature, but Danny and Joey were both fair-haired but otherwise so unalike in appearance that they would grow up to tell people that they were just good friends. Unlike Nelia, the babies were good and learned how to sleep at night. The only aspect of being a new mother again that I didn't like was not enough presents. I still felt that Nelia's unplanned conception had robbed me of my life's allotment of crystal wine-glasses and candlesticks. Danny and Joey's double-header debut cheated me out of a baby shower. They would be wearing pink and yellow hand-me-downs until they could walk.

When the boys were eight weeks old, and Sam commenced his part of the parental leave, I finally called Fay and Claire. I did this against Sam's wishes. He was fearful that I might somehow step into some weird trap, although he could not imagine what that might be.

When I texted them the photo, they were elated and they were frightened. They arrived two days later, on the first flight they could book. Though they knew that their parents might never forgive them, they decided to hold off on telling two already brokenhearted very old people that their lost daughter might still be alive. For who knew what might happen?

My mother and Claire were happily reunited. Claire had brought along Yuri, one of her sons, who was recovering from a small but tricky dental surgery, and he got a kick out of seeing how he and his brother must have looked when they were baby twins. This big kid who could dive into pools was a source of fascination for Nelia, who followed him around like a puppy, sweetly offering him her Duplo blocks and her Beyoncé Barbie.

On the second day, my parents and Sam kept all the children so I could take Claire and Fay to Space Alley. It was massive and lustrous and noisy. There must have been twenty servers. We ate our Fusion Falafel and Sputnik Sweet Potato Fries. I could tell how impatient they were. Fay finally asked, "Which waitress was it?"

"I don't know," I told them. "I wasn't here."

"How are we going to find her then?"

All the young women looked the same, ponytailed milk-pale blondes, in the sunniest place in America.

"They're like carhops," Fay said. "Remember that fifties place Dad took us to when we were kids, where you ate in your car and the carhops were girls on roller skates? How did they carry big trays of burgers and shakes on roller skates?"

Claire said, "That was right around here."

Finally, I asked for the manager. When the woman approached, I said in a rush, "We're looking for someone who comes in here a lot, an old friend, she's a teacher at the middle school, Ruth Wild?

I mean, Ruth Copeland?" *Some old friend*, I thought. "We haven't seen her since she moved here and we wanted to surprise her."

"I know exactly who you mean," the manager told us. "But I don't know where she lives. Maybe you should ask at the middle school."

Claire and Fay stared at me, and I thought, *Yep, just good investigative reporting!*

"Is that far?" I asked. There had to be more than one middle school.

"About four blocks that way," the manager said.

On the way, we detoured to drive past the house where all of them grew up.

Fay said, "That was our room at the front on the second floor. It was a huge room, that went across the whole front of the house, with all these windows. Three beds, three closets, and our own bathroom. I have enough space to give my boys their own rooms, but I want them to share because it's better, you know? It makes you grow up closer to the only person who'll know you all your life."

"Imagine having siblings who weren't your friends," Claire put in. "Not that we always got along! I still have a bald spot the size of my pinky nail where Ruth pulled my hair out by the roots!"

Nell and I had separate rooms, but when she was little, she ended up every night in my bed. We'd experienced that rare thing, a happy childhood. Apparently, so had the Copeland sisters.

"She was a firecracker," Claire said softly. Each in her own way, we meditated on Ruth and what had broken her.

The middle school parking lot was packed. The parking space we finally found was three blocks away at the abandoned showroom of a furrier, with a ballroom dance studio on the second floor, a reminder that, however odd Florida was now, it had once been even odder, a sort of private club for the wealthy and oblivious. I was glad of the short walk, to summon my nerve. When we rang the buzzer and a voice asked if we had an appointment, I was able to say that yes, we had a meeting with Mrs. Copeland.

Inside, we followed a labyrinthine path to the office, green walls inexpertly adorned with daisies, porpoises, and peace signs. Claire and Fay sat down on a bench to wait while I, armed with my phone with the photo of Ruth, stood in line behind some burly students for my turn at the counter. Just as I got there, the secretary told me to wait, she would be right back, and disappeared into one of the glassed-in rooms that flanked the main space. When I turned to wave to Fay and Claire, to signal that I would be a moment, I saw her. She had come into the office and was standing just to my left, writing something in a huge ring binder that lay open on the surface.

I said, "Ruth?"

When she looked at me, I could tell that she was about to turn around and run away. Then her shoulders sagged. She said, "Reenie. How did you know to come here?"

"My parents saw you at that space restaurant, that big diner."

"How did your parents know to look for me there?"

"They were just having brunch, Ruth! They weren't looking for you! My folks have a place in Cocoa Beach now. But, Ruth, your sisters are here, right out there in the hall on that bench. They've been crazy worried about you. Your parents are so worried about you. Do you know that Felicity is in prison?"

"Not here," Ruth said. "Bring them around to the back entrance, down by the art rooms, and I'll meet you there."

"How do I know that you won't just take off?"

"Why would I tell you to go downstairs to the art rooms if I was going to just take off?"

"So you could take off quicker while we were stumbling around looking for the art rooms."

"I won't," she said. "You'd just find me again."

I still did not believe her.

"We can't just wander the school without permission, Ruth." I was proud of that inspiration. "I'll wait on the bench with your sisters." I left the office and sat down, not replying to Claire and Fay's urgent fusillade of questions. I watched Ruth through the glass window of the office as she completed whatever note she'd been making in that binder. I saw as she hesitated, glancing around her as if looking for the emergency exit. Then she walked out into the hall.

Claire cried, "Ruthie!" and rushed to her. Fay followed. Enclosed by those familiar arms, Ruth visibly allowed herself a moment of relief.

Then she said, "We'll go down into the sculpture studio. It's deserted. Nobody wants to pay for art anymore, so they stopped the program. It's quiet down there. We can talk."

We sat on high metal stools. There was a primitive-looking coffee station and a refrigerator. Ruth brought us cardboard cups of vile coffee with chemical sweetener. She reached into the fridge and took out a carton of apple juice and poured some into a cup for herself. No one knew how to begin.

Fay finally said, "We love you. We were afraid you were dead. I'm furious. I'm hurt. I don't want to waste time being upset but, Ruthie, how could you do this to us? And to Mom and Dad?"

Claire added, "And to Felicity? You weren't even there, Ruth. Do you know that Felicity is in prison now? Do you know she was convicted?"

Ruth didn't even glance at either sister, much less answer. She stared at the wall behind Claire's head. Whatever it was that Ruth was seeing, I hoped I would never see anything like it. Still without moving her eyes, she said to me, "Did you tell people where I am?"

"Just these people," I said, gesturing to her sisters. "And of course, my parents."

"Well, I suppose they told people." Her voice was harsh, almost sarcastic. It surprised me.

"I don't think they did, Ruth. There would be no reason for them to do that. They were just concerned, the way you would be for a friend. And your sisters were so scared that they called the police."

Ruth said, "Why?"

"Because they love you, that's why. And they love Felicity, no matter what. They think that there's been a terrible mistake."

Ruth says, "There has. This is all my fault."

Fay put her arms around Ruth, who still didn't look at her sister. "Don't go overboard, Ruthie. This is not your fault. You're a great mother. You always were."

"I'm not."

"You are," said Fay. "And you don't have to tell us why you took off if you don't want to."

"You wouldn't believe me if I did," Ruth said. "Trust me."

Fay continued, "You need to come home now, Ruthie. See Mom and Dad. If you're sick, we'll take care of you. You have nothing to be afraid of."

"I have everything to be afraid of. I can't ever go back there . . ."

Claire finally lost it. "For god's sake, Ruthie! What the hell is going on? Is this all about Roman and his bullshit? Is it about his new wife? What's her name? Faith? Is she so faithful and virtuous that she got involved with a married man, and a minister at that? When he wasn't even divorced? How is any of that your fault, Ruth?"

"He called her a harlot," Ruth said.

"I don't know if she's a harlot but she's not exactly a great role model of—"

"Not the new wife."

"What?"

"He called Felicity a harlot."

We all subsided into stillness. Strictly speaking, that was not an inaccurate description of Felicity, especially for someone of Roman's character—or, at least, his counterfeit character. That sense of a storm crept up my arms and my neck like electricity. Something else was coming. This was only the beforemath.

Ruth was saying, "At first, when she was a kid, she loved him. She thought that he would be a dad to her. She'd never had a dad. Her birth father, if you can call him that, was from Italy and I never saw him after I found out that I was pregnant. Roman said Felicity would turn out like me. He became obsessed with her, and he was the one . . ."

"He raped her?" Claire said.

"No! Not like that. He wanted her to be good. When she wasn't, he forced her to leave. She was seventeen, just graduating. She went to Madison. I helped her pack. I drove her . . ."

"What did you say to him, Ruth?" Fay asked.

"Say to him?"

"What did you say to stand up for Felicity?"

"What could I do? He was my husband. He was my pastor. I loved him. Jay and Guy were little. I had to submit . . ."

"You're a piece of shit, Ruthie," said Claire. "You should have defended your girl. You should have called us or Mom and Dad."

"Mom and Dad knew," said Ruth. "They already hated him before I found out about the other wife. I didn't want you to know the way he was toward her. It was all so bad . . ." Although she needed her parents and their support, Ruth had a hard time with their opinion of Roman, until she was forced to share that opinion. Even after she found out about Faith, she would have taken him back. She was ready to start over. For a long time, she adored him, no matter what he had done. Sometimes, she said softly, she still adored him.

"You're weak," Claire said.

"Stop it," Fay ordered Claire. "That doesn't matter. It's all in the past now."

I watched Ruth watching her sisters, not meeting their eyes but studying them whenever they looked away with widened eyes, black, nearly all pupils. Drugs? Adrenaline? When she spoke, her voice was flat, matter-of-fact.

Claire was wrong about Ruth. Ruth would indeed defend Felicity, and she would stop at nothing. Her sister had called Ruth a "firecracker," an unstoppable girl whose intuitive charm and intellectual might destined her for a future as more than a high school science teacher (here, Fay would have put in hastily, "Being a science teacher isn't nothing, but you know what I mean"). After that future was knocked out of her hands, Ruth must have made a decision. She would not be "poor Ruth." Her child would not be the woebegone proof of a book-smart girl's real-life naivete. Felicity would fulfill her own promise—and Ruth's. Ruth would cherish her nestling of bright plumage.

Or maybe I was being melodramatic.

Probably I was being melodramatic.

Still, that premonitory chill crept over me, that animal sense of something very wrong, the same thing I'd felt the day Felicity was convicted.

"Go outside now. Just for a moment," I said to Claire and Fay. "I want to talk to Ruth alone."

Claire muttered, "Nothing doing."

Fay agreed. "Come on, Reenie, don't you think we should hear this? Her own family?"

Ruth said nothing at all. She let her glance sweep over me as if I were a pair of rain boots or a houseplant. She seemed to be taking a break in another room, this one in her mind, a place where I couldn't follow.

"Please," I insisted to Fay and Claire, "I promise we'll come right out. This is getting out of control. Let me just have one last chance to try to make sense of it. That much, I owe Felicity."

A person doesn't confide to a crowd. A person wants to talk to a person, or so my mother always said. Even if there are millions of people watching, and millions more who'll hear about it later, the wildest revelations start with a conversation between two people.

I walked Claire and Fay to the exit and opened the door.

At the back of the parking lot, there was a bench with a little plaque, carefully set in the middle of a narrow horseshoe of colored stones. I was grateful that I was too far away to read the plaque, which, at a middle school, could only commemorate one of those rare, excruciating losses impossible to think about or ever forget. There came a snap of lightning, the passing sizzle of sulfur on the wind. Florida is the tropics and it rains almost every day. A storm was not far off.

Back in the sculpture room, I said to Ruth, "I have this feeling that you know everything about what happened that night with Emil Gardener."

"Well, your feeling is wrong."

"Ruth, come on. What did Felicity do? What did you do?"

Ruth jumped up and advanced toward me. Involuntarily, I stepped back, even though I had easily three inches of height and twenty pounds on her. "What did I do? I didn't even know those people. I didn't know what Felicity was getting up to. So how could I know anything about some man's death? That's ridiculous. I was at church. I had a special reading to do and I had to find space for two gigantic, stacked trays with ten dozen cookies each . . ." She hurried on with strange details about the church cat having kittens on Christmas Eve, about a broken coffee urn, about two women in their fifties in a loud argument about whether Backstreet Boys or NSYNC was the better boy band. It was just as Ross had described when people are lying—or when they feel as though they're lying, even if they're telling the truth. There was the elaborate, unnecessary detail, the active hands, the rounded eyes.

Ruth was lying and she knew she was lying.

She grew angrier by the moment, her face flushed, her breathing speeded up, her hands opened, then clenched into fists. "I think this is enough," she said.

"No, Ruth, it's not."

"You don't get to decide that."

"This goes way beyond a story. I need your help. Felicity needs your help. She needs you to tell the truth."

"I am telling you the truth. I am trying to do the right thing."

"I don't think you are."

"And of course, you would be able to tell, wouldn't you, Reenie?" Ruth shouted. I was sure people could hear her at the end of the hall or even a floor up. A security guard would come. Maybe other teachers. That didn't seem like a bad idea at all. "You're so deep. You're so perceptive. You're so smart. Do you know that Felicity would laugh at you? I had to warn her not to be so obvious. She didn't respect you. You were just convenient. The All-Purpose Sidekick. Miss Average."

"What an awful thing for you to say to me, Ruth."

"Well, here you are ruining my life, Reenie! Trying to take everything that is dear to me."

"Isn't Felicity dear to you?"

"Of course. What an awful, awful thing to say to me, Reenie."

I noticed then that she was still holding that small paper cup. She followed my gaze. Then with a sigh, she poured the juice into one of the metal sinks, then tossed the cup into the wastebasket, spilling some residue on the floor.

"What was that?" I asked her.

"Nothing," she said. "Just . . . Felicity doesn't deserve that on top of everything else."

The beforemath was nearly over.

I stepped out into the hall to a place where I could see Claire and Fay through a floor-to-ceiling window. The sisters huddled together on that stone bench as if they were cold. The rising breeze, news of the storm, lifted their hair. Their lives were about to change forever. So let them have this one last moment to believe that the worst that could happen had already happened. I wasn't completely sure of what would come next but I was sure it would be something that Fay and Claire would wish they never knew. Their parents would die in due course; there would be medical scares; children would say confounding things; a close friend would reveal herself to be an epic liar; their best professional achievement might combust right in front of them. All sorts of ordinary mishaps could knock them down, but this one was not ordinary. For them, the worst that could happen had already happened. They just didn't know about it yet. This was deeply personal for me, but it was not my own. Claire and Fay would be happy again, but never the way that it seemed they were once promised.

I took a deep breath and stepped back into the art room.

Ruth was gone.

I ran back to the door, thankfully remembering to jam my coffee cup in the opening so that it didn't close behind me and lock us all out.

"Where did she go?" I called to Fay and Claire. Claire held out both palms. Did she mean she didn't know where Ruth had gone or that she hadn't even seen Ruth? I jogged over to them. "Did you see where Ruth went?"

"Ruth left?" Fay said with a gasp. "See? We should have been in there."

"You're probably right." We circled the room, like nincompoops, opening the supply closets to see if she was hiding in one of them. "Where would she go?"

"To her house," Claire said. "Or to that restaurant. Although I can't imagine her having the appetite for a Cobb salad after all this. She's trying to get rid of us. Maybe she'll really take off. Like gone. This time for good."

But even Ruth didn't have superpowers. She couldn't simply disappear. She would need her clothing. Her medicines. Her passport. And she'd worked at this school for quite a while. Would she just take off without a word? She absolutely would. There was no sense trying to think about this as if the customary rules applied. The only rules were the ones Ruth was making up as she went along. I feared for the traffic cop who might try to pull Ruth over for speeding.

"Tell me how to get there," I said.

"We're all going this time, Reenie," Fay said firmly.

"But what if she comes back, Fay? She left all her stuff here, her backpack, her books . . ."

"Her phone," Claire said, emptying the backpack on a lab table and inspecting the contents.

"I'll call you the minute I find her, if I find her."

I glanced at the big gray aluminum trash can, at the paper cup in it and the residue. Bending to pick it up, I thought better of it.

"Don't touch that cup, you guys. Tell somebody to come and clean up the juice and then put the mop and cup and stuff in some big trash bag or something, okay?"

"Could there be something in it?" Claire asked.

"She acted like there was."

I grabbed the keys and looked up at the clock. It was high noon. Of course it was.

SIXTEEN

Roseate Spoonbill

Platalea ajaja. This large, bright pink wading bird is
gorgeous at a distance and bizarre up close. The roseate spoonbill
is common in coastal Florida, where they once were hunted
nearly to extinction for their beautiful rosy feathers, used in the
1800s to trim women's hats and make jewelry. That color comes
from their diet, mostly shrimp and crayfish, in the same way as
the color of flamingos. These birds forage in marshes, lagoons,
ponds, and saltwater wetlands, in a nearly lying-down position,
their bodies just above the water with head hanging down. The
roseate spoonbill is often seen as a symbol of harmony with
nature: Its population rebounded when hunting it was banned.
Spoonbills are very gregarious and interested in others of their
kind: When they spot a group of spoonbills flying overhead, they
stick their necks and bills straight up into the air in a posture
called sky gazing.

IF I READ IN A NOVEL ABOUT WHAT HAPPENED NEXT, I MIGHT LOWER
my eyelids and say, *Really?* But if it was a news account, I wouldn't
be disdainful. I would only feel sad and sorry for the people involved, grateful and guilty that this time, it was someone else's
problem, not mine. Except this time, it was my problem, because
I'd made it my problem. In real life, some things just crash the
imagination.

It was no big deal for me to follow Ruth's trail. It was a very short trail.

She had been living at her parents' Florida residence, where all three sisters and their families spent vacation weeks for their whole lives. Fay and Claire gave me turn-by-turn directions when I confided that my brain seized up when I looked at a map. Once I was seat-belted into the rental, I drove a block or two before stopping to compose myself. I used an old therapy trick, literally going through the motions of brushing off invisible cares with flicks of my fingertips. This time, though, the problems weren't just annoying mental lint but instead little imaginary flames, sucking up oxygen, getting brighter and bigger. Nightmares are dreams too.

It wasn't that hard.

I had no memory of a life that didn't include Ruth, not only as someone to say hello to, like the mothers of a dozen friends, but as someone I admired and trusted, someone I would drop by to visit even when Felicity wasn't around, whose food I ate, whose counsel I asked for. Parking the car on the other side of the street from the Copelands' rambling white stucco hacienda, I rolled down the window and, drowning in the heat, waited to see if anything moved before I even tried going to the door. Just then, as I watched, a car backed out of the garage and Ruth got out. Leaving the trunk open, she began tossing in duffels and totes. A little girl followed her in and out, handing Ruth a sleeping bag, then a miniature backpack.

Why was the little girl even there on a school day? Why was Ruth taking care of a kid even as she prepared to flee? I got out and, unnoticed, crossed the street.

The little girl called, "Granny, there's a lady here."

I looked hard at the girl's face. The reels on the slot machine spun: one heart, two hearts, three hearts. Alarms pounded, bells rang, and silver dollars poured down.

"Hi," I said to the little girl. "I'm a friend of your grandma."

Ruth came to the door. "Reenie, just let us go," she pleaded. "You don't understand."

I pretended to consider that. Finally, I said, "Well, it's true, I don't. So at least I'd like an explanation." Clearly frightened, the little girl with the wispy dark braid wrapped part of her shoulder under the hem of Ruth's sweater. It must have been eighty-five degrees, and Ruth, as ever, was shivering in her cardigan. Her pretty face was almost archaic, pale and fragile as a candle, as if from a photo taken a century ago.

Ruth said, "I don't have much time, Reenie."

I asked, "First introduce me to this girl?"

"This is my granddaughter, Sparrow. Felicity's little girl."

"Felicity's . . . what?"

"My granddaughter, Felicity's daughter. Sparrow Copeland."

"I never suspected this . . ."

"Well, how about that? I guess I fooled you, Reenie. Hard to fool you!" *Apparently not,* I thought. No wonder Felicity wouldn't say a thing. She was protecting more than Ruth. But why . . . ?

"Who was the boy? Was he at our school?"

Ruth wrung her hands as if they were a wet cloth, another novel trope that literally happens in real life. "Not a boy. That lawyer, Jack."

"Jack Melodia was the father? Is the father? But that was much later!"

"He came to talk to the school assembly about business and the environment, what the law could and couldn't do to protect animals."

"She was only sixteen when she met him?"

"Yes."

"He must have been thirty years old then, or more," I said. I thought back to Jack, unctuously telling me that he and Felicity never had any kind of intimate relationship. Why would I ever have accepted that bullshit, knowing, as I did through Sam and through Lily, what he might be capable of doing to keep what was his? Handsome, charming, powerful Jack, who could easily dazzle a girl with no experience of men, even a smart girl, especially one who never knew her own father. Jack, who seemed to care about the defenseless creatures in the way that Felicity did, who owned Ophelia, where Felicity went to work. How simple it would have been for him to manipulate her, when she was like a puzzle with missing key pieces in the center. "Did she start seeing him before she graduated high school?"

"She did but there was no . . . you know . . . "

"Sex," I said. "Until she was eighteen and in Madison." Felicity's manifest lack of interest in any high school boy, her periodic "birding" trips—all explained now.

Jack had taken Felicity everywhere, buying her the best binoculars and cameras (all of which she passed off to me as loaners). While most of the birdwatching that Jack did was watching one particular human bird in a bikini or a pair of ratty denim cutoffs and a man's shirt, he did care about wildlife of the animal variety. "Did he take her to other states? She was a minor, that would be illegal, wouldn't it?"

"He took her to other states and other countries," Ruth said. "First it was to the Everglades. Then Hawaii. Then Peru."

"How could he do that without her parent's permission?"

"Oh, she had my permission! I signed every slip, every health form, everything! She told me that it was a special extension program through the university and a great privilege for her, all expenses paid, and to some degree, it was, it was wonderful for her. And what could I do for her? I was dealing with my own grief. It sounded too good to be true and it was but . . . I wanted to believe that she would have at least those good memories from that time?" Ruth curled her lip, explaining how her sisters would be oh-so-shocked by this, Fay especially because she was so perfect. Fay would be saying how negligent Ruth was.

"But I bet that Fay doesn't even know the names of Cole's art teacher and his science teacher. I bet when she gets forms that say the kids are going on an overnight field trip to a Twins game and to the public museum, she doesn't call the police. She just signs the forms. And Fay would say that she would have been suspicious." With a neatly compact mother gesture, Ruth tucked some loose tendrils back into Sparrow's braid.

"I'm clearly not in Fay's league," Ruth said.

"But you had to know something was up."

Ruth looked down at her hands. She had wanted to believe it, so she did. And yet, how could Ruth have seen this level of duplicity and manipulation as anything but grooming? When Felicity left for Madison, she walked straight into Jack's velvet trap. No longer dazzled by him, Felicity later told her mother that she knew it was already probably over by then and thought she could end things any time she wanted—yet another example of Felicity's belief that people meant the things they said, because she did.

Ruth let slip the big backpack she'd hoisted onto one of her frail shoulders. Her lips were pale. She seemed to be reminding herself to breathe.

I said, "Ruth, we'd better go inside. I don't think this is good for you." And what I was thinking was here was the real Maleficent, not the cartoon one from Disney World, but a woman who saw the world in the same way—divided into people who got in her way and people who didn't. Ruth certainly hated my guts by then, although I presumed she wouldn't do anything to me because of Felicity's love for me. As I would learn, she had no particular feeling for Emil Gardener or Cary Church, but they really, really got in her way.

We stepped into a cool, vast white-and-yellow kitchen, like
the immaculate set for a cooking show on TV. Ruth gave me
iced tea from a pitcher in the fridge. I waited as Sparrow took
her first sip from the same batch, then drank a little of my own.
I was so thirsty that I could have downed six glasses of it; heat
and adrenaline had done their work.

As she talked, Ruth cruised back and forth along the marble
countertop, drumming her fingers as if playing a keyboard. Jack,
she told me, was attentive and gentle at first, but quickly began
to shorten Felicity's chain. She danced at Ophelia because Jack
wanted her to, because it was a kink for him to see other men
lusting after her. Her growing friendships with the other women
didn't please him nearly as much. And so, the moment she was
finished with work, he whisked her out of the club and back to
his apartment, or, occasionally, to her dorm. Felicity still managed
to find a kind of friendship with Lily and with Archangel . . . but
there would be no college-girl life for her, no pizza at the Union,
no sunbathing on the quad, no study group at the library, no football games, no silly social media photographs, no crop tops, no
new friends or old ones, not even me.

No youth for Felicity at all.

She might as well have been a newlywed Seventh Day Ad-
ventist. If she wanted to study in her dorm room, Jack might let
her go or he might lock her in his apartment and leave, sometimes
with nothing in the refrigerator except a jar of pickles and a can of
7UP. If she didn't want to have sex, he would hold her down and
rape her. If he got mad, he threw away her textbooks and she had
to apologize before he would purchase new ones. He came to her
classes and physically pulled her out, pretending to be her father.
She ran away but the police brought her back. When she tried to
be firm and say that she was too young for this kind of exclusive
relationship, Jack told her she had two choices—his way or no way.

Ruth stopped and gripped the lip of the countertop. "And

then, well, you can guess. At first she didn't even want to confirm the pregnancy. She played these fairy-tale mental games with herself about stress, although it was her young, healthy body sending signals."

Another month whirled past, and Felicity had to admit the only game she was playing was roulette. She showed Jack the test. He lifted her up and spun her around. "My little girl, my two little girls," he crooned. Felicity said the baby could be a boy. Jack went right out and bought an early gender prediction test. With 99 percent accuracy and a cutesy pink ribbon streak, it was Jack's dream, a girl after four sons.

Felicity didn't want to be a mother at nineteen. She didn't want to get married, even if Jack got divorced. No longer sure that she loved Jack, she was sure that she feared him. By the time she saw a doctor, there was no time to lose. But like so many other young women, when Felicity saw the somersaulting image of her unborn daughter on an ultrasound, she could no longer bring herself to stop that life.

She was going to be a mother. She wanted her own mother.

"So she ran from him," Ruth said. "There was no way she could stand up against him. He was rich. He was influential. He was a lawyer. But even more, he was a bad man."

"You mean, Felicity was afraid he would make her future impossible," I said.

"She was afraid he would kill her," said Ruth. "He said he would kill her if she had an abortion or a miscarriage."

Felicity had to think fast. She pretended a meltdown. She told Jack that her mother was suspicious and on the brink of coming to Madison to bring her home. She further appealed to his sympathies; she actually wanted to go home, for a little while. She wanted to give birth with her mother at her side—after all, Jack couldn't exactly tell his wife why he had to rush off to the hospital in the middle of the night, could he?

Later that night, Felicity confessed everything to Ruth.

"I went to Roman and said we could adopt the baby. We could raise her as our own. After all, he wanted more children, and this baby would be a part of me. He was furious. He was disgusted. He refused. He called her a harlot. He gave up on me then too, but he didn't tell me that. He kept up appearances, to seem like a couple holding to the vows we made when we promised for richer or for poorer. I didn't know about the . . . the . . . other wife."

The most Roman would agree to was for Ruth to help Felicity learn the ropes of parenthood, short-term, before she was out the door. The sooner the better.

Ruth tried to sift through the silt for the saving grace: Felicity had completed one year of school with distinction. Life was a journey not a race, right? She and her parents would help Felicity raise the baby, as in fact, they did, at first. When Sparrow was born, a surprisingly swift and easy delivery, Ruth was at Felicity's side. "I thought she was saying 'Cleo' and that was weird enough . . . but I got used to it. At least, the middle name is old-fashioned. Like mine."

"What is it?" I asked, not really wanting to know, irritated by her meandering around.

Clearly surprised, Ruth said, "It's Irene."

I did not know that.

"What did you tell Jack?"

"Felicity decided on that. She said I should call Jack and tell him that the baby died and Felicity nearly died as well."

"What? Didn't you think he'd check?"

"I did, but Felicity said, why would you think someone was lying about a thing like that, especially if you were talking to the girl's mother?"

I thought about it for a moment. "No reason, I guess. But that actually was a lie. She never lies."

"She never had this much reason to lie. And she had this sort of world view, about the visible world. She had to read Plato in high school, didn't you? In the ethics class? The world you don't see is just as real as the world you see? Maybe more important?"

"I have no idea what you're talking about. I didn't have that class. You mean Mr. Adi."

"Yes. Imari Adi. Such a nice man. He just took two years off to try to actually become a philosopher. The idea Felicity had was that you have to be strict with your mind to perfect your mind. It was like a dare—could you tell the truth all the time? She would have lied. To save Sparrow. She did a lot worse than that. And anyway, she didn't lie. She made me lie."

That seemed like splitting hairs. But evidently, it worked. Jack sent flowers and a check for ten thousand dollars. But he wasn't letting it drop.

A week later, Jack showed up on Ruth's porch, beautifully dressed and smiling, carrying roses and chocolates and jewelry boxes of robin's egg blue. He introduced himself and asked to see Felicity.

"I had no idea what to say. I just had to make it up. I said, oh wait, I said I would follow him to the hospital, because only family was supposed to be allowed to visit Felicity. But I was so glad he was there because he could be with her when they told her. And he said, told her what? I said, 'When they tell her that she can't ever have children anymore.'"

Ruth clearly had a gift. She told me that Jack's face blanked and he mumbled something about maybe he should wait to see her if she was still that sick. Ruth pretended like, no, no, it was a good idea to see her right then. Jack stalled. He made some comment about how attractive the rectory was and Ruth told him that Felicity's father was a very well-known minister with a huge congregation and a TV ministry. At that, the man literally began to back away toward his car, and Ruth started to breathe again.

Meanwhile, Felicity was upstairs, in a bedroom with the door closed, but had Sparrow begun to cry, it would have been all over.

Not long after, Felicity told Ruth that Jack sent his regrets that their "brief idyll" was over. It had been neither brief nor idyllic, but she was glad it was over. In time-honored fashion, Felicity was left holding the bag, in the home of a man she once wanted so much to be proud of her, but who now called her a disgrace. "He said Felicity took after me because I had a baby too, when I was only seventeen."

So sad, Ruth said, even if it was true.

I couldn't help but interrupt. "True? Did you think it was true as well? Was it both Roman and you who were ashamed of her? And him, lot of room to talk! Felicity was single, young, sort of naive. What was his excuse?"

Ruth shrugged. She . . . just shrugged. Every last drop of pity I might have had for Ruth dried up.

"So, Ruth, then what happened?"

"Before or after the winter break?"

"Before." I hit my phone with my thumb to text Claire and Fay, hoping Ruth didn't notice. She did not notice. She was long gone into the past.

When Sheboygan became unbearable, Felicity went back to Madison.

"Did you really think she was going back to school?" I asked. Ruth didn't answer. She turned and looked out at the backyard, where paths of white stonework were dotted with conical small trees so glossily green they appeared spray-painted. An orange tree and a grapefruit tree thrust out their heavy arms as if leaning on each other's shoulders. "Did you?"

"Why would you think I didn't?" Ruth nonanswered.

Of course, she was not. For Felicity, as she would later say, harlotry was a self-fulfilling prophecy. All she wanted was to fund her escape. She raked in money while Ruth and Ruth's parents cared for Sparrow. Jack Melodia would find out, and Felicity was perversely glad that being an escort would make her really damaged goods in his eyes. She would run from past deceptions and future disasters, from Jack and Roman and her own green gullibility. Ruth suggested Florida. It was home to her. Felicity suggested Hawaii. Hawaii was much farther away. And home was a four-letter word.

She and Felicity were mother-and-daughter misogyny magnets.

Ruth had some substantial savings. But when she took money out, Roman reminded her, in this house, the man controlled the money. Ruth pleaded, she still loved him, she could forgive him, but wasn't a mother's duty to save her child, even the black sheep? Roman said, well, yes and no. Her duty was to him. This wasn't a teaching of fundamentalist Christianity; it was a teaching of the Roman empire. The money would show his flock that Roman was a good man. He would repay the church with money he stole from Ruth. He'd wanted to ask her before, since she had to sign for funds to be withdrawn. It took a lot of nerve to use his wife's lifelong savings to help his reputation after the ruin he caused by cheating on his wife. But when he prayed about it, Roman received the word that not only should he keep the money, but, if she refused to obey, he should tell Jack where Felicity and the baby were. It was his opinion that Jack had the right to the little girl in any case, and it was wicked to deceive him.

I wished my father were there, for many reasons. Among them was the joy he would take in this parable of hypocrisy.

"And then what?"

Ruth struggled to take part in the Advent festivities at Starbright Ministry. Despair was never a moral option. During a final triumphant rehearsal, another choir member said that she had prayed on it and felt she must confide in Ruth about Faith, with a capital *F*, Roman's new beloved.

Now she was fully disgraced. Despair was right there waiting.

Ruth looked at me then, her eyes all pupils, the way her sister remembered from the night she told Roman Wild that she would pour boiling water on him and kill him. Again, I experienced that chill. Something bad was about to happen.

"You're saying you did this. How could you, Ruth?"

"Not me! It was just good luck for me that somebody else did it."

"Ruth, you know better."

Ruth began shrugging and nodding as if having an internal conversation with the two sides of her nature.

She looked so crazy. She was so crazy.

"Did you kill them, Ruth?"

She said softly, "What does it even matter?"

"Oh, Ruth."

"For Felicity," she said then. "It isn't that hard. You can't taste it. The old man, Emil, he used to have tea with her every time he came over. He wanted some tea, with just a little sugar, when I told him Felicity was running late. He didn't know I was her mother. So I gave him some tea. It was like he asked for it. Felicity didn't know until it was over."

"Oh, Ruth. The regret . . ."

"Not really," she said. "I had no choice."

"And the other guy?"

"He threatened her after they moved the body. I heard him. If she didn't stay with him, he would tell the police. He would tell them she did it. He said he was going to his apartment and then up to see his kids and he would come back the next day and she'd better make the right decision. Jack would have found out about the baby. The old man was going to die anyway."

"Ruth, we're all going to die anyway," I said.

I felt like a crone and sounded like a teenager.

"He was sick, sicker than I am. I had to help Felicity get away from Jack. We would have been on a beach somewhere. She might even get the money from the life insurance."

"Felicity went to prison."

"She thought I was too sick to stay alive in prison. She was sure she could not be convicted. She said it looked bad but there wasn't enough evidence to convict her. There was no other way," Ruth said, and took a long, quavering breath. "When it was all over, she thought maybe it was better, that this way nobody would find Sparrow. If Jack saw that Felicity was going to prison for murder, no way was he going to come within ten feet of her anyhow. Felicity said don't write, don't call. She said she would figure something out. She would find a way, a loophole, or something."

"Ruth, Felicity is innocent. We have to help her. And you need help . . ."

"You can't tell anyone."

"I have to, Ruth."

"No, Reenie. Please."

"Felicity can work something out with Jack. People mislead other people all the time. But later, they can be reasonable."

"I don't think so," said Ruth. She might have been right. No one will ever know.

"How old is she?" I asked. Ruth ignored my question. Sparrow was small and slight, but had to be nearly ten. "Where was she?"

"My parents had a nanny to take care of her. My sisters never knew. Sparrow was never there when they visited. I would go and stay with my parents all the time when she was a baby."

So much for those innocent old people we wanted to protect from finding out that their lost daughter was still alive. Did they know what else that daughter did? Were there no limits to deceit . . . or to love?

"Then they got older. She was an active little kid. It was time for her to go to school, so I came here. But there are lots of places I can take her. You'll never find her. Or me."

I played for time. "Ruth, calm down. There's no hurry. So Hal and Alice knew all the time? All of it?"

"Not about those men. The rest, yes. I'm sorry, Reenie. None of this should ever have happened."

I said, "Well," and I started to get up. At that moment Ruth spun around and punched me solidly on the jaw. I stumbled. This little woman, maybe just over a hundred pounds . . . she kicked me in the shins and pushed me against the refrigerator so hard that the next morning, I would have a bump on the back of my head the size of a Ping-Pong ball.

She grabbed Sparrow's arm. "Don't you dare follow me," she said. "I'll wreck the car if you do."

She ran for the door but stopped when there was a sharp knock.

"You little bitch," she said to me.

I half walked, half crawled to the door. Claire and Fay had brought the police.

They took my phone because I'd recorded everything Ruth said. I hated myself for it. But as she said, there was no other way. A child protection officer was summoned. Sparrow would have to spend at least the night in emergency foster care. That is, until Sam showed up, calm, competent, reassuring, armed with Felicity's fax naming him Sparrow's legal guardian. After she'd been examined by a pediatrician, the little girl was released into Sam's care. The day after tomorrow, he would travel to Wisconsin to secure Felicity's release from Manoomin Correctional Facility for Women.

I was not then nor am I now the kind of woman who weeps on her husband's shoulder. But that night, I did. I couldn't stop crying. My chin had swelled and purpled. Nelia kept pointing to it and saying, "Oh, poor ouchie!"

Nell went to the Brevard County Sheriff's Office to meet with Ruth. Sam offered to go with her, but Nell, although literally shaking, insisted on going on her own. She was Eleanor Bigelow for the defense, although she would not handle this case alone. We debated the question of Sparrow traveling to Wisconsin with Sam. She was so little. But Felicity had waited so long and had given up everything to keep her little girl safe— including that little girl.

"I want to come," I said.

"It's not a good idea. The children," said Sam. "I might be there for several days."

Later that night, Sam admitted he could not imagine going without me; he couldn't face the emotional back draft, although he didn't expect a media blitz. There were factors upon factors, some unknown, and he couldn't be sure even of the factors he knew about.

What if Miranda came along too, as the utility grandmother-in-law on-site? My father volunteered to look after the kids ("And if this doesn't prove the existence of God . . ." my mother said). He'd have the able help of Nell and Harper, my assistant with the parakeet-green hair and the pierced lip and nostrils. She had deferred her medical school entrance for a year; her appearance belied her bullet-train mind and gentle spirit. In the tradition of journalism and nepotism, the managing editor, one Gus Damiano, said, "Harper's bizarre."

Miranda introduced herself to Sparrow. "So I am happy to meet you. What is your name?"

"My name is Sparrow," she said. "I like Nelia. I'm ten, almost a teenager. But I like little kids still, even though I'm a big kid."

She was not, in fact, big; she was speck sized. That night, as I brushed tangles out of her wispy brown hair and put it into a braid, she began to cry.

"Sweetheart," I told her, "I know you must be so sad."

She said, "I really do want my Granny." I lay beside her and rubbed her small back, my mind unable to encompass how confused she must certainly feel, a little girl whose very circumspect world comprised of one older woman had burst into a cacophony of raucous kids and solicitous strangers.

I told her, "I know you are scared. For a long time, you were with Granny, but now you get to be with someone who's really nice too, maybe even nicer, who is your mommy but you didn't see her for a long time. Her name is Felicity."

"I know Felicity," said Sparrow. "I have her picture at my room."

"We will go on the airplane to see her. Did you ever go on an airplane?"

"When I was a baby. Of course, I don't remember. You don't have memories from when you were a baby."

"They'll give you nice food and maybe some candy."

"Oh dear," she said, and I had to stop myself from laughing. "I'm not allowed to have candy. They say it's very bad for you."

"Just once in a while it's okay. I'm a mom. I know."

"Will you come too?" said Sparrow. "Do you know Felicity?"

"Yes," I said. "She is . . . she is my best friend. I was her friend all my life, since we were little, like you."

"I am not little though. I told you that."

"When we were younger, like you. I'm sort of your aunt. Not really, but sort of." She seemed to think about that for a while. She certainly remembered it. She has called me "Auntie Mommy Reenie" most of the time, even as an adult.

That night, the next thing she asked was, "When can I see my Granny?"

"I don't know," I told her.

"Is my Granny bad?"

What could I tell her? "She did some very bad things, but she thought they were the right thing. She might have something wrong in her brain."

Ruth was under guard at Grace Hospital with significant chest pains. She would be transferred to Wisconsin for sentencing when she improved. Nell and Sam planned to plead Ruth not guilty by reason of a mental disease; all they could hope was that she would serve her time at Dawn Hill Hospital for Women operated by the Wisconsin Department of Corrections. At the police station, Ruth was chillingly nonchalant when she described such things as Emil Gardener's death throes and simply closing the bathroom door on Cary Church's final seizure. Ruth "didn't see any point" in describing how she got the man into the bathtub in the first place, beyond explaining that he was "initially reluctant," so Nell suspected there had been a knife, or even a gun. Ruth refused to talk about that. Her attitude was the very definition of "in cold blood."

Sparrow slept most of the way to Wisconsin. When we got into the airport, which now looked so small, she said, "I didn't get any candy at all. I feel sort of bad about that. I think I should go on another airplane." Sam and I bought her a big box of Dots, the kind you get in a movie theater, and a giant hot pretzel. The pretzel was a huge hit. Sparrow would ask for hot pretzels every time she saw me. I actually learned how to make them for her.

Sam and I decided that I would stay behind while he went to Fond du Lac to bring Felicity home. When she got there, my mother and I would take over.

Sam had so many details to work out while he was in Madison, and he needed at least to set the various wheels in motion. There was the matter of the insurance money: Felicity had not harmed either Emil Gardener or Cary Church, so she would ultimately receive the proceeds of their life insurance policies (Suzanne Church would attempt to sue her for those benefits but would have no grounds, as Cary Church could have chosen to leave life insurance benefits to a calico cat). Felicity offered to give money to both men's families but Sam put his foot down, saying that might open the door to speculation about a guilty mind. She also would receive a total of about one hundred thousand dollars from the state, county, and city for wrongful arrest and imprisonment.

In her direct way, Felicity had already decided she would leave the area as soon as it was possible. She thought she might build a house but wasn't sure where. Sam was stunned by her forward orientation. For her first days, we agreed that if she was comfortable with it, she would stay with Sam and me and Miranda in Sheboygan. It was not ideal, but it was a place she was used to, where she had spent many nights, long ago, and where she could have privacy.

What Sam had underestimated was the tidal wave of media interest in this bizarre reversal. Not only did press throng the car as Sam pulled out of the prison parking lot with Felicity, but reporters also tailed them to Sheboygan, filming and trumpeting a narrative about a "homecoming" and a "more innocent time."

By late afternoon, I had been up and down thirty times, scanning the windows, texting Sam, but, as they approached the neighborhood, I wanted to lock myself in my childhood bedroom. There was nothing I could say to Felicity, although, of course, I was mad with joy for her. But hadn't I doubted her? I had doubted everything.

Then, she was there, standing on the front walk.

Sam turned to the reporters. He said, "Please, have some dignity. Let Miss Wild see her daughter. You can't photograph a minor child anyway."

Somehow, commandeered by Sally Zankow, who told all present to "back the fuck off," it worked.

I held Sparrow's hand as we came out onto the front porch. She might be big, but she held on hard. When Sam and Felicity reached the bottom of the steps, they stopped, and I said, "This is your mommy that you didn't see for a long time, just like I told you."

Her eyes filling, her tone rigorously upbeat, Felicity said, "Hi, Sparrow. I sure did miss you! I won't try to hug you yet because you don't really know me."

Sparrow looked up at me. "This is Felicity? This is your best friend?"

I told her, "Yes."

Felicity said, "Oh, Reenie . . ." and stepped up and took me into her strong, skinny arms, while Sparrow hovered close and finally put her own arms around our waists. "This is all you," Felicity kept saying. "This is all your goodness, Reenie. You wouldn't give up."

And yet, how many times had I tried to do just that?

I finally said, "Wouldn't you have told the truth? Eventually?" Felicity shrugged. "But why not?"

"I guess I felt like I deserved to be punished. Maybe like I was doomed and all I could do was try to save the only good thing in my life."

Once Sparrow had an early dinner and quieted down, insisting that Felicity and I stay in the same room at least until she was asleep but preferably all night, we opened the adjoining door to what had been Nell's room and sat quietly, me sipping tea, Felicity a glass of Chardonnay. It was still light.

"That's a Carolina wren, that's a gray catbird, that's a pine warbler," Felicity said as the birds bombed the feeder in the fading light.

"You sound like my Grandpa McClatchey. He used to say, 'That's a Toyota Camry, that's a 1990 Mustang, that's a Buick Regal, they don't make them anymore.'"

We both laughed then. "I'm out of jail," Felicity said, softly, to me and to herself. "I'm free. I'm with my daughter. I'm having a glass of wine."

People don't ordinarily see those events as miracles. Maybe they should. "No one would blame you if you got hammered,"

I said. "You've been through a lifetime's worth of crazy in the past week."

"It's the crazy I'm used to," she said. "I'm the opposite of Occam's razor. With me, it's always zebras."

"Did you think you would get out of jail ever?"

She closed her eyes tight. "I really thought I would never get convicted. I know that's hard to believe. Then I thought I would get parole first try. But then I read about women forced to commit murder, like by cult leaders, at gunpoint. And they were never, ever going to get out! It was a double murder. A carefully planned double murder for profit. How could I prove that I was a good person who made one terrible mistake? That's true for most people who kill, by the way, except professionals or serial killers. I could do good for twenty years and maybe it wouldn't matter even then. And then, I thought that I'd tell Sam the truth when my mom died. But then Ruth got new medicine. And it worked. She's not even fifty. She could live twenty more years."

"All this is so strange and, if I can say this, not very well planned. For somebody like you?"

"Well, gee, Reenie, I really did never plan what I'd do if I was ever charged with a double murder . . . and then I was in a prison van!" Felicity shuddered. "It was so much worse, not just cold and dirty. I expected that. The people, they weren't just women who did wrong because of men. It wasn't *Anna Karenina*. Some of them were pathetic. But some were vicious women, child killers. Not everybody who has a hard life ends up bad." She went on, "I was bad, but I wasn't bad like that. Remember when we were kids and we used to say, he wasn't all bad, just middle-evil? That's what I was."

I tried to visualize Felicity, beautiful, neurotic, and refined, facing a ladle of beans, a slice of white bread, and a few strings of meat, repurposed from a previous meal, while across from a woman who wanted to eat her for dinner.

"They respected me for killing those poor men. I was their hero, a murderous hooker. They just wished that I'd gotten away with it. They wanted to be my friend; they wanted to have sex with me. They suggested all kinds of things even I'd never done."

I tried to smile. I don't think I managed. This was something I had not expected. The Felicity I knew was reticent, even with people she cared about. This Felicity was flayed bare.

"What did you do?"

"I pretended I was born-again. I pretended I was like a nun, always reading my Bible, always praying in the chapel. Either they thought I was holy or they thought I was nuts."

"How did you not actually go nuts?"

"I'm not sure I didn't," she said. She seemed to look down a dark corridor, into a cave, her eyes adjusting to what she saw. "I would wake up and forget where I was. The women laughed and screamed and fought and screwed all night long. They just never stopped. There was no silence. They wouldn't let me have earplugs. When somebody stole my headphones, they said I had to wait three months before I could get more because I was careless. If I really were a nun now? One of those people who could only speak once a week for the rest of her life? That would be okay with me."

"Why wouldn't you talk to Sam? Or anybody?"

She avoided Sam, fearful that any human kindness would crack her wide open. She was afraid that she would confess that she'd made it all up and that Ruth had done it and please, please save her. Some nights, she thought she was dying, and some nights, she wanted to die. Her brief encounters with the no-nonsense psychiatrist helped her.

That doctor was clearly down on his luck as well. He wasn't doing this because he was tired of a three-hundred-dollar-an-hour practice and wanted to serve humanity. He must have done something bad to end up in a nauseous green concrete window-less room at Manoomin, facing a woman whose ankles were chained to the floor. "Practice denial," he said, "until you can retreat into yourself and go to a meadow or a lake. Meditate. Do yoga. Take four naps a day. Do anything to give yourself some mental distance." Eventually, she got permission to eat alone in her cell or in the library. She wondered how many other "middle-evil" women were fighting for their sanity with small spoonfuls of privacy.

She lied to Sam.

She let him think that the conditions were tolerable.

The few clients of Sam's who'd been convicted of crimes were mostly white-bread people, corporate fraudsters, none of whom ended up in a maximum-security lockup. But even they complained of the degradation. So when Felicity sent him a single note, about starting a book club and learning to paint, he suspected that the big picture had big holes in it. He also suspected that Felicity's story had been suspicious from the jump.

When she ended up on IVs in the hospital, dehydrated to the point of collapse for the second time, Sam sat by her bed and grilled her: "What really happened, Felicity? What really happened? I promise that I won't betray your confidence. I just need to know the truth, Felicity . . ."

"But he couldn't really keep my confidence!" she said now. "He couldn't let me go to prison for life if he knew the truth!"

"What was it like?" I asked her finally. I wasn't sure that I'd ever again catch her in this mood, in a place where she felt at home, in a room so dark we couldn't see each other's faces. She knew I wasn't asking about prison.

"You mean, what was it like being an escort."

"Yes."

"Reenie! How dare you ask a thing like that?"

"I just do," I said. "I'm very daring. Fortune favors the brave." I could hear, rather than see, her grin.

"Well, I had very specific rules. I was never with a man I found repulsive. I was never with a man I found unkind. I wasn't attracted to any of them. Ever. But I could do it once a week for a lot of money." She drew in a deep breath and sketched in the subscription plan I already knew something about: six clients, one hour a week each, three weeks a month, pay whether or not you chose to play, all special requests double or triple the price. "One of them, we had sex twice in a year. One, we never did. He couldn't. He just really wanted . . ."

"A woman's total attention, right?"

"Right. Loneliness is the greatest aphrodisiac."

"That was one guy's theory. We don't have to talk about this forever, or even ever again. Just this one time about all of it. As if you were someone I was really investigating, not my friend. I want you to promise to answer every question I ask." She started to shake her head no, out of either reluctance or reserve, or both. "But you said this was down to me because I never gave up. You said that. Now you want me to give up?"

"I want to put it behind me and you want me to go back there." Her shadow ran fingers up through her tumult of dark hair, no longer the chaste, controlled court coif. "Okay. Quick, untraceable money. And revenge. I wanted men to pay me a ton of money to pretend I liked them. They would brag and strut and posture. They thought I was really impressed and just wished I could be with them all the time!" There was an unpleasant pleasure in her voice. "They were like him. The good reverend, the lying, cheating, stealing, preening, morally superior minister who took everything from Ruth and gave her nothing."

"Do you hate men, Felicity? I could get it if you did."

"No. I don't. I hate a couple of men. In prison, I thought, if I ever got out, I would find a good man of my own someday. Like you have. I want Sparrow to have a real father. Maybe I'd have another child."

"That must have been painful, that wish, at that time, I mean."

"Not really. I think it kept me going."

"Do you regret anything?"

"Sometimes, I regret everything." She sat there for a while, and then, suddenly, eerily, she took my hand. I liked the new Felicity, easy with hugs, generous with gestures, but I still wasn't used to her. "One thing I don't regret is Sparrow. Whatever I did, it was for Sparrow."

"But Ruth would say that what she did, she did for you?"

"Oh, Reenie, I hate Ruth for it." Something else was coming, though, and I counted backward, the way Nell and I used to do: three, two, one . . . "And still, there is a part of me that understands it. She gave up her spirit. Her science. Everything her own father taught her. She had to nod and smile, yes, of course, evolution was only a theory. She did it for love and he wiped his shoes on that love. She finally lost her mind. She thought she was saving me and Sparrow from men who could have whatever they wanted." Felicity asked me then, "Would you stop at anything to protect your children?"

"Yes," I said. "I would stop before I hurt someone."

In the next second, though, I realized that no, I would not stop. If I had to, I would do wrong. If anyone threatened Nelia or the twins, and if there was no other way, I would kill the person. I told Felicity as much and admitted that I'd then be no better than Ruth. In passing I wondered, what did Roman Wild think about all this? He probably felt lucky to still be alive. He easily could have been next.

Ruth's acts were monstrous. And yet, as Felicity reminded me when she asked about my own limits, what Ruth did, she did for love. Ruth, oh Ruth, why could you see no other way? And how was it that no one ever noticed as you imploded? Did no one care? Or was it simply too gradual? Ruth could not have been the first eccentric teacher ever to walk a pea-soup-colored hallway as her fine mind fell apart.

Hell is murky, I thought.

"And, okay, I never understood. Why didn't you say anything at the trial in your own defense? Didn't you think that made you look guilty?"

"I absolutely did not," she said.

What Sam said so long ago was correct. Until it was too late, Felicity literally put her faith in common sense. Hadn't she pleaded not guilty? She had. She was telling the truth. Would she say she was not guilty if she was, in fact, guilty? Hadn't she said that she wasn't there? She was telling the truth. Hadn't she already pointed out that she didn't know what happened? She was telling the truth. This was entirely in keeping with her personality. She was telling the truth. Why should she have to repeat it?

The way she saw it, it would look even more suspicious if she kept yammering on about her innocence. You couldn't prove you hadn't done something!

Sam pleaded with her.

Any other person, he said, would be in a plane dragging a banner that read, I Did Not Do It. But Felicity didn't know the rule of courtroom advocacy, which was to state your case, get other people to state your case for you, and finally, state your case again. How would she know? She didn't watch crime dramas or read them. She'd never done anything that needed a legal defense, including now.

As the trial proceeded, Felicity realized that the physical evidence or lack of it, all the mistakes, all the erroneous beliefs, all that reflected back on her. She could have called a halt right then. She could have asked for time to tell the whole truth. But even if she were believed, in that truth was danger, and not just for herself. So she was trapped. She said nothing.

Her eyes squeezed shut, Felicity whispered, "I was one hundred percent wrong. What a fool. What a fucking conceited fool I am. Oh, Reeno, when I let myself go there, I feel like

I'm dying. Because would it have made a difference? What if it would have changed one person's mind? I was trying not to make it worse.

"And afterward, I thought, what if I just said, 'Wait, wait, oh wait, I think I've given you the wrong impression. Because I actually don't know what happened. I just found him, that's all.' What if you were on a jury? Wouldn't you say, 'Well, this changes everything! All she did was stumble across this dead guy, and sure, she knew him, and sure, it was in her apartment . . . but gosh, Miss Wild, sorry for the mix-up'? If you were, say, a prosecutor, wouldn't you have believed me?"

Felicity had followed her misguided trust in fair play down a one-way street straight into a brick wall.

There was nothing more to discuss. I decided to say something wise and compassionate, but in keeping with the ways of human beings, settled for something selfish.

"Okay, this is crazy. I sound like I'm in sixth grade. Ruth told me that you used to laugh at me behind my back. She said you never respected me. I was just the neighbor, there when you needed her."

The last closed door between us slammed open. Felicity rested her forehead on her hands. For a moment, the only silence was our own. Together, we listened to a soundtrack of car alarms, barking dogs, a mother bellowing that this was the very last warning, the rumble of the ice machine, proof that so much of what happened all around us happened unobserved.

"Well, if I ever felt that way, you'd have known it." Felicity got up and faced away from me, her hands kneading her lower back. "I'm the one who relied on you, Reenie. You were my human credential. And that thing, that night at the reservoir? I did that because . . ."

"You did that because you are good."

"I did that because you are good," she said.

And there we were, events of the world having reshuffled the deck so that my former icon was my current acolyte. What I knew about human nature could have filled an eyedropper. And speaking of stupid and conceited, what kind of nutcase would step into the house with a murderer who could be in Puerto Rico by the time anyone found my body? This long and newsy chat between friends would not end with police cars and handcuffs. Every time I thought of Ruth, my mouth dried up and my heart raced like a rabbit.

Back when I asked Ross, did people really change, I never thought of Ruth.

Was Ruth the icy executioner always there, inside the Ruth I'd grown up with? What about the rest of us? Did we put on civilized behavior like a disguise to hide our claws?

Felicity walked back inside to check on Sparrow. I heard water running and a few muffled notes of conversation. Felicity came back outside, drying her hands. "She's reading *The Forbidden Library*. She says she picks out all her own books, mostly grown-up books. I wish I had been that kind of kid who picked out my own books when I was ten."

"You did," I reminded her. "You picked out mine, too."

Felicity sighed. "With the approval of Ruth and the good pastor."

Not too many minutes later, we'd run out of talk. We fell asleep side by side on the bed.

The next morning, we decided to go to a grocery store. Felicity whispered, "We have to make sure we have truly organic food. We can't give her frozen pizza again, I feel like I'm sinning against some sort of religious doctrine, and I don't mean the Starbright kind."

In the brassy dazzling light of a tropical morning, we drove a few blocks to one of those eerie grocery stores where oranges are the size of grapefruits and grapefruits are the size of melons and there are giant photos on banners of families prepping chopped pineapple and shredded coconuts for the sheer animal joy of it. Sparrow picked out hummus and carrots, all-organic mac and cheese with wheat pasta, raw almonds, and raisins, and she asked if she could have juice instead of water "just this time."

Felicity said, "She puts me to shame," and then told Sparrow, "You have to get chocolate-covered raisins."

With a glance of alarm, Sparrow asked, "Why?"

"Because chocolate has good . . . um, good magic in it," Felicity said. "And I like it. And it's unnatural for a little kid to not want chocolate." She whispered to me, "This is so weird. Here I am trying to deprogram my kid's healthy eating."

"I'd be grateful if I were you," I told Felicity. "Nelia only eats macaroni and cheese, and by only macaroni and cheese, I mean only macaroni and cheese, lunch and dinner. And it can't be homemade, it has to be from the yellow box. She counts the blueberries to make sure we don't give her too many."

With the slightest and fleeting upturn of her lips, Sparrow said, "Maybe yogurt on the raisins?"

Felicity said, "Nope, got to be chocolate."

As she made her way down the aisle five or six feet in front of us, I heard her murmur, "Okay . . . Mom." My breath snagged in my chest. I almost didn't dare to look at Felicity.

"I know," Felicity said. "She's been doing that. Almost like an experiment. Sometimes 'Mom,' sometimes 'Mommy.'" Catching up with Sparrow, Felicity took her small hand, interlacing their fingers. The translucent long-sleeved black shirt Felicity wore modestly showed only the vague outlines of her black bikini. She wore no makeup and her hair had grown, and a thick braid, the mama of Sparrow's baby one, danced against her golden shoulders. There were probably half a dozen prettier women just in that store alone. And yet, Felicity parted the shoppers like a seaplane landing in a quiet hidden lagoon. That ideal girl Lily Landry had described, long ago at the gentleman's club, cleaner and crisper and all-around classier than any real-life girl, the girl of special knowledge. Even if the people who could not take their eyes from her didn't realize it, there was something extra and indefinable about Felicity. There always would be.

We left the take-home food in the car and sat on benches on the boardwalk to eat a cold-dinner picnic straight from the grocery bag (another thing you start to do in Florida without anyone giving the slightest bit of a damn. In Sheboygan, even in July, passersby would have thought you were homeless or running from the law). I remember being a kid on vacation with Ross and his family and thinking that everyone who lived in Florida must be on vacation every day.

"Could I give some raisins to the birds?" Sparrow asked.

"Yes," Felicity said. "Wow, those birds, they do okay! Look how fat they are." Sparrow threw raisins into the air and gulls fought each other for the morsels like fighter bombers.

"People are driven by Satan to put chocolate on perfectly good fruit, you know."

"Well, sweetie, what I said about putting chocolate on fruit, that was just a joke. I was agreeing that the raisins were healthier without the chocolate . . ."

A car pulled over then, a big black Escalade. The tinted side windows purred down, and a young voice yelled, "Look, Mom! That little girl is a bird trainer!"

At the same moment, Felicity shouted, "No! Sparrow, come here right now!"

Her terror knocked the wind out of me. It took me a moment to say, "It was just a little kid. With her parents."

Felicity said nothing, crossing the thin horseshoe of sand to grab Sparrow's arm, none too gently.

"Stop!" Sparrow cried. And Felicity stopped, but still looking wildly around her with those darting-goldfish eyes I remembered from court. Then she apologized, leaning down to give Sparrow a kiss on the top of her head and half a stick of gum. Sparrow did not look convinced.

We walked all the way back to the car before Felicity said, "Reenie, you know why that happened? I saw that big black SUV and what do you think I thought?" I shrugged. I shook my head. "I thought, Jack Melodia. He's finally got us. He would grab the child and throw her in the back, and we would never catch up with him. The last thing I would see would be her little face crying in the back window, if I could even see through those windows."

What a heel I felt then. Felicity must feel this dread descend on her like sleet every time she stepped out into the sunny street with Sparrow. It waited for her on every sidewalk, beach, and playground, in the children's museum, the grocery store, the shoe shop, and the haircut salon. She must hear that threat in every slammed door, every broken shutter, every playful drunken argument between two frat boys at bar time. Everything was a menace. "I'm scared to death," she said.

She thought about it ten times a day.

Sometimes, a grave and simply dressed social worker with a no-nonsense French twist would come to the door. A simple DNA test, and Jack was established as the rightful biological father of Sparrow Irene Wild, a longed-for daughter whose lying slut of an ex-convict former prostitute mother had conspired with her own murderous mother to cause him anguish with a lie about the baby's supposed death. There would be a hearing. Felicity would be given supervised visitation, on the basis that she posed no physical threat to Sparrow. Then sometimes, she believed Jack would bypass the law. She would wake up one morning and Sparrow would simply be gone, the bright, star-embroidered curtains in her room gently billowing in the dawn breeze. And then, she sometimes thought that Jack would just chalk it up. He was no stranger to lies. He'd told his share. He was no stranger to cold treachery or cold pragmatism. Perhaps an all-out brawl over this little girl, conceived outside his marriage, risked the kind of attention even Jack Melodia could not manage or control, like the murder trial, with its appallingly appealing Lucrezia Borgia of an accused and its dozen hairpin plot turns.

So she was safe. It was all fine. She was just on edge. Paranoid! That's all it was.

She would lean into that assurance for two hours, sometimes three. And then she'd give herself a recovery lecture: Jack Melodia was not desperate. He was not reckless. So get a grip. Felicity, haven't you spent enough time in misery? Girl, learn how to be happy! Sparrow was happy!

So much could have gone wrong between Felicity and Sparrow, and yet, mostly they seemed enclosed by a protective circle of light. Felicity sometimes felt like the emotional equivalent of people who crawled out from under cars that had fallen on them. ("Miraculously, with only minor injuries!") Everything was just fine!

But it wouldn't take long for the central fear to snap a rubber band against her wrist . . . *Not so fast, my pretty, and yes, I do mean you!* There was always another mental movie to make about how Jack could destroy her.

Jack had been in love with her, for a long time. He once considered her his possession. He would consider Sparrow his possession. If he believed that Sparrow was his possession, he would never part willingly with her. Or had he parted with her already? Maybe he had.

Felicity would feel okay for a tiny window of time. And then she would think of a new scenario. "What can I do? Move to Italy? Walk around there by myself? Even though I survived the loneliest time in my life and the only thing in the world that makes me feel safe is to be around people I care about? There's nothing I can do." There was nothing she could do. Just listening to her, imagining a life like that, had given me the emotional equivalent of a migraine.

Felicity could hardly call the police to report that baby's bio-logical father might try to claim her. Well, right, no, he hadn't done anything to try to get her. And yes, he had every right to do that. He had no criminal record. He was a businessman. And unless you counted grooming and sleeping with a teenager . . . but you know, boys will be boys! . . . unless you counted that, he wasn't a bad guy in a way anybody could prove. Should Sam approach Jack with a plea for Felicity's custody of her child? Or not? Would doing that rock the boat? Would it rouse Jack to dev-astating action? For on the other hand (there were plenty of other hands) Jack could have taken steps to claim Sparrow, if he knew about Sparrow, at any point since Felicity got out of prison. He was a lawyer. He would know what to do. He hadn't taken that step. Did that mean something? Or would he draw that gun the moment that Felicity dropped her guard, breaking the bubble and stepping into the dreadful and lovely real world?

"Where's Ruth when we need her?" I asked, half kidding, then fully humiliated by what I'd just said, literally slapping my hand over my mouth. There were times when I had to remind myself that Ruth was Felicity's mother, as the rupture seemed too real and of such long standing. "Jesus, Felicity. I'm sorry. I'm an asshole for saying that."

"No, no, no. I know how you meant it, Reeno. How could anybody have those thoughts? But that's exactly what I think too. If he comes for me, if he comes for my child, what will I do?"

"We'll make a plan. We'll bring Sam in on it too. We'll find someone who's an expert in personal security. Also, he hasn't come anywhere near you yet. Let's not go looking for trouble," I said, sounding like Miranda.

That night, when Felicity and I again fell asleep talking, I had no energy to get up and find my own bed, much less seek out my husband or my mother or even change my clothes. Wasn't a sundress sort of like a nightgown anyhow? In the morning, I woke to Sparrow staring at me from a distance of about eight inches, her concentrated silence loud as a shout.

"You didn't put on your jammies," she said. "You must feel really ick."

"I was too tired."

"So will I have to take the airplane to my school? My friends miss me."

"What are their names?" I asked.

"Andre and Mary and Christopher and Sally Marie. I have a lot of friends."

"What is your school?"

"I go to Three C's. Cocoa Consolidated Christian. You don't have to be a Christian to go there. Andre is Jewish."

Felicity came in and sat down beside Sparrow on the foot of the bed. She asked, "Are you a Christian?"

"I don't know," Sparrow said. "I think so. We pray at school but only for one minute. And we sing a song. It's not that great a song usually. We get more vacation."

Practical girl.

I was hauling my bag down to the living room, having decided to lug a few of my old books and dolls back for Nelia. All of a sudden, Sparrow started to cry. "I want to go too. With your best friend."

Felicity asked me then, "I've been thinking. Can you wait until morning?"

"I wish, but the kids . . ."

"Just until morning. Then, we'll go with you."

"You can absolutely come! You could use the break! My dad would love to see you too . . ."

Felicity said, "No, I mean, we'll come to stay. Not to stay with you! At least, not for more than a week or something. Patrick will find a good house for us." She shrugged. "Florida is as good as anywhere, Reenie. Better. It's where you are, it's what Sparrow knows."

She would take her little girl to meet her great-grandparents today and then close this book. "I'd love to see my brothers, but that's a bridge I can't cross right now. There's nothing else left for me here, except memories, sweet and sour." Felicity was right. Even her beloved mother was lost to her. I knew that Felicity would visit Ruth, but it was hard to imagine what good could come of it.

She got out her one-day-old iPad and said, "Other people can sell my place. Other people can pack the four or five things I want to keep. I want to live where I won't be seen. I don't mean to hide. I mean where I won't be seen as something I'm not. I let men put things on me I never wanted." To Sparrow, Felicity said, "You want to go back with Reenie and Miranda? We can do that. We'll go to Disney World. Did Granny take you to Disney World?"

With her wide-eyed amber gaze, Sparrow was, for a moment, the image of her mother. She said, "There's a lot of sin at Disney World."

"Oh wait!" Felicity said. "Didn't you know that kids don't do sins? Not until they're like thirteen. And even after unless it's a really big thing."

Sparrow said, "Oh!"

"I thought they told you that. Kids do naughty stuff, but they just have to say sorry."

Sparrow said, "Oh!"

"Plus, they took all the sin out of Disney World a couple of years ago."

"Oh, that's good," said Sparrow. "I might like to go. Everybody I knew went except me." I had to turn away so Sparrow wouldn't see my face.

Like Sam, I admired Felicity's forward logic and her fearlessness. About everything except Jack Melodia, she seemed confident, even battle ready. When we turned to Sam, even he was short on ideas. It turned out that even as Sam stayed up late chewing on possible strategies, when it came to Jack, the universe had plans for his plan.

SEVENTEEN

Great Horned Owl

Bubo virginianus. The great horned owl, also known as the tiger owl or the hoot owl, is a large owl native to the Americas. It is an extremely adaptable bird with a vast range and is the most widely distributed true owl in the Americas. A fierce and strategic hunter, the great horned owl can be an intimidating sight with its short wide wings, massive claws, and staring yellow eyes. Its "horns" are tufts of soft feathers near its eyes. Male owls fear the larger females, often taking hours to approach during mating rituals. Owls have fourteen bones in their necks, compared with a human's seven bones, hence their ability to turn their heads nearly completely around. Silent in pursuit of prey, they eat even large birds such as hawks, also rodents and frogs. Their eyesight is so keen that it is the equivalent of humans seeing a mouse by the light of a match a mile away. Owls often live more than twenty years. In some cultures, the owl is considered the ruler of the night and the seer of souls, the guardian of those as they pass from the earthly plane to the realm of the spirit.

BEFORE SAM EVER GOT THE CHANCE TO APPROACH HIM, WE learned about Jack by chance. To this day, however, we aren't sure exactly what we learned.

Something none of us could explain happened once Nell visited Madison on behalf of Damiano, Chen, and Damiano. Little overachiever that she was, Nell had by then passed the bar in both states, and she sometimes acted as Sam's emissary when someone had to shuttle back and forth to wrap up small matters with cases at the base camp location of the firm. Nell had picked up her rental car and was headed for the office downtown when she passed my old workplace, Ophelia. On impulse, she circled back. She still had fond memories of the barroom brawl, a crazy that she still dined out on with friends.

When she ducked through the jingling curtain behind the front door, Nell noticed how dim and decadent it was, almost like a bordello, or like a haunted house. She had grown accustomed to Florida, where shopping centers in lime and coral stucco popped up overnight and were stocked within a week with shiny shoes and seventy-five-dollar T-shirts, if not a juice bar.

There were only two customers in that sleepy interval between lunch and the first show. As Nell waited for someone to appear behind the bar, she saw Archangel arrive, then Boston, then Rochelle. At last, Lily came out of the back room, adjusting the collar on her black button-down shirt. She looked right into Nell's eyes.

"Can I help you?" she said.

"I'm here to apply for the bartender job," Nell joked. She grinned. But Lily didn't crack a smile.

"We aren't hiring," she said flatly.

"Lily! It's Nell Bigelow. It's Reenie's sister."

"I'm sorry?" Lily said.

"Reenie's sister! Reenie Bigelow. The writer? Felicity's friend? You remember that Reenie came here to write about Felicity. You know that Felicity went to prison but she didn't . . ."

"I know that case, but I don't know any of those people," Lily said. "If you will excuse me, I have to get to work."

"But, Lily, remember the night of the big bar fight, when the owner showed up with the police . . ."

"There have been lots of fights," Lily said, not unkindly. "This is a strip club, not a . . ."

"Library," Nell finished for her. "My sister said."

Lily regarded my sister mildly and began to stock clean glassware. Nell knew that Lily recognized her, and that Lily was lying. She had no idea why.

Did Lily act that way because of Jack Melodia? Perhaps nobody will ever know. Lily certainly isn't saying.

She owns Ophelia now. Apparently, her agreement with Jack provided that if he should die or be otherwise incapacitated, she would assume full ownership responsibilities for the club for a period of three years, after which she would own it free and clear. I remember Archangel saying that Lily was the only one Jack ever really trusted. Did he trust her too much?

For Jack disappeared. That was how Lily described it when Sam finally went to see her. Sam had to try to negotiate some kind of visitation with Sparrow, if that was what Jack wanted and if his current marital status was expansive enough to accommodate the heretofore-unknown child of a former mistress. Grudgingly, Felicity knew she had no choice. She took Sam's advice to relocate before he gave even preliminary notice. If Felicity had still been in Madison, Jack could presumably have requested anything, even joint custody. He still could have.

But he had disappeared.

Lily shrugged when Sam pressed her about how to get a message to Jack. "I have no idea where he is," she said.

"When did he contact you last?"

"The last time I saw him." That had been last spring, she thought. Why hadn't she reported him missing? "Wasn't up to me," she said. "Maybe his wife did. I really don't know."

It was clear to Sam that she knew more than she was saying. Sitting in the midday dusk at Ophelia, Sam ventured something about how all this seemed pretty convenient, but Lily came back hard. "Convenient how? I get twenty questions a week about liability and facility depreciation and city permits that I have to figure out on my own. He's the one who knew that stuff."

And again, Sam had little doubt that Lily was literally unable to ask Jack for advice. Jack had overseen the financials of the club, separate from the accountants who handled the rest of his properties. Inherited from his godfather, it was a sort of passion project, Lily added. She gave Sam an ironic look that said she knew exactly how that sounded.

And yet, I had to consider Lily's unswerving loyalty to Felicity—and how the two of them, hiding in the back room that day, overheard Jack as he showed that man a photo. Of what? Of whom? Something or someone so dear to that guy that he was reduced to a blubbering, trembling, begging wreck of a creature . . . who knew Jack would do anything to keep what was his.

When Sam got back, I asked him if he ever had any news of Jack.

Sam said, "Not much." Before I could question him further, he added, "I'm not trying to find him. Nobody is trying to find him, I don't think."

"Do you think something happened to him?"

"I don't think about it," Sam said.

"Oh yeah, you do."

"When I do, I remind myself not to." He went back to the corner piece he was struggling to fit into the edge of our white subway tile kitchen backsplash. As he turned away, satisfied, the chip popped out like an imp. "Oh please, let's call a guy," Sam said. "This is an art form, and I clearly don't have what it takes. But I'll bet the guy I pay to do it couldn't make a closing argument either." Sam paused. "No, maybe he could." We stepped out onto the screen porch. We were nearly drunk on the blessed interval of aloneness because Claire was visiting, and she and Miranda and Felicity had taken the children on the long-promised sojourn to Magic Kingdom! We didn't know what to do first, go out to a fancy restaurant or get drunk or have noisy sex or simply turn off all the lights and sleep for nine hours. Or put all those things on hold to talk about things we didn't talk about during the ordinary run of life.

"Where do you think he went?" I asked Sam. "Come on!"

"Remember when we were first together, and I told you that you could ask me anything and I would give you an honest answer? But never to ask me a question you didn't really want to know the answer to? This falls under that heading. Because I am telling you the truth, Reenie. I really don't know, and I don't want to know."

"You think somebody whacked him?"

"I think those are great movies, Reenie," he answered. "He lives the kind of life that could put you in harm's way. So maybe. Maybe he went to Missoula."

"Would that be all bad?"

"I guess for his family."

"But not for mine," I finished, and my husband knew just who was included in "my family." As we lay in bed, I remembered that Lily used to be a police officer. If anyone knew how to make someone disappear and stay disappeared, it would be a cop.

Some months later, I wrote the real story. A murderer confessed her guilt. An innocent woman was freed. A businessman disappeared. All this happened in the name of love—all the fear, all the deception, and all the courage.

And that really was that.

The house that Felicity built was a lush little jewel box, everything in blue and gray except for a pop of gold here and there, with every amenity Patrick could dream up. In time, Sparrow began to call my parents Granny and Grandpa. In another year, Felicity decided, even if a prince did not come to break the spell, much less a familiar villain to try to ruin her life, she would try to have another child. The world to which she had returned, she said, was like a pair of running shoes she'd purchased but barely used—still practically new, worth another try.

Does it all sound so tidy and even sweet?

Parts of it were sweet and still are. Parts of it were not.

Shortly before her fiftieth birthday, Ruth died at Dawn Hill Hospital for Women. She was gardening with another inmate, another patient, and she simply lay down on the grassy verge and died with the sunlight on her face. The cause of death was cardiopulmonary arrest—as was true for everybody, as the medical examiner said in court years before. But though Ruth wasn't very old, the heart in her chest and the other heart, the one we think of as the seat of spirit, were too battered to last any longer. So was her ruined mind, once finely tuned and trained.

After she and Sparrow had moved to Florida, Felicity visited Ruth in the prison hospital only twice. Ruth's sisters went often, the hospital being not far from the Minnesota border. After her mother died, Felicity grieved hard for the Ruth who had raised her; but her feelings about her mother remained complicated, streaked with guilt, peppered with resentment. What makes someone change for the worse?

Felicity wondered what would have happened if Roman Wild had never come into their lives, especially since her adored younger brothers refused to see her. They'd chosen their remaining parent—wisely, Felicity thought—flawed as he was, rather than their wayward sister. Guy sometimes wrote to Felicity, asking to see pictures of Sparrow, asking if he could come to visit. Felicity always agreed. Guy never showed up. It was brave of him even to consider visiting, she said. She could imagine the stories he'd been told. Who wouldn't be ashamed of such a sister? Would Sparrow also be ashamed of her mom someday? Felicity asked me this on long afternoons at her pool. She jumped into the pool so that Sparrow, playing in the shallow end, might not realize her mother was crying.

The thing I knew from all those uncomfortable interviews was that the best way to make something bad worse was to not talk about it. Of course, Sparrow would find out about her mom's past. Of course, she would get over it. Felicity would tell Sparrow the simplest thing she could but not one sentence more.

Only a loving parent in the twenty-first century would ask that question. Children forgave their parents for joining Hitler Youth—because their parents admitted this and repented. Children forgave their parents for being part of the IRA—because their parents grew in understanding and repented. For years, Felicity had allowed Sparrow to live with a double murderer. She admitted this, and she repented.

One of the demerits of modern life is too much time to think.

Yes, we are all so consumed by career and family and so on and so on that our tender minds are shredded like cabbage for coleslaw. Still, we have so much time. We do not have to wash our clothes in the stream. We don't have to build the fire to boil our potatoes. Ordinary people have the kind of time that only philosophers used to have, to toss thoughts back and forth, yes to no, good to bad.

People forgive each other because they need each other. Unless the wrong is too great, the choice is simple, if not easy. This way lies independence. That way lies interdependence. Felicity could have taken Sparrow and vanished, but Sparrow needed us too. As time went on, we tried to help Sparrow see that most of the harm Felicity did was to her own dignity. We would all help Sparrow know that her mother was, on balance, good.

I would love to say that, restored to each other, Felicity and I had a relationship as placid as a day in May. That was mostly true. Once I told Felicity that good mothers didn't necessarily give their kids everything they asked for. Felicity didn't say anything right then, but she asked later, was I saying that Sparrow was a spoiled brat? No, I said, but even good mothers made mistakes sometimes.

Felicity said I had a point.

Later I apologized for sounding like a high-handed ass. After all, how could I blame her? Felicity was making up for lost time and of course, she was afraid that Sparrow wouldn't love her. No, Felicity said, not a big deal.

A moment later, she added, "Bitch." For an instant, I was shocked. Then we cracked up.

A couple of months later, I asked her if she realized that Sam had once been attracted to her. She said, "Duh. He's only human."

I agreed. Then I added, "Bitch."

We went on. We tried to live the life as friends we might have lived. Of course, the past is never really past. We did our best.

ALL OF THOSE EVENTS HAPPENED BACK WHEN PEOPLE WERE STILL trying to figure out how they would refer to dates that came after 2020. (Didn't the "twenty twenties" sound weird? Like a vision prescription?)

Sparrow was a little kid then and now she's a very mouthy but also cuddly young woman, not quite a young adult but nearly. She can do roundoffs and backflips. She can dive off the high board. She wears green nail polish. She reads only mysteries. Nelia is still little enough that she considers Sparrow the equivalent of a movie star she has the privilege of hanging out with.

Felicity has had two or three promising dates. But she's holding out for a combination of Sam Damiano, Sam Claflin, and Samuel Adams—the signer of the Declaration, not the beer. She's not holding out to wait for another child; she's already begun that clinical process. Anyone who falls in love with Felicity will have to consider Sparrow and a player to be named later as value added. Anyone who falls in love with Felicity will have to understand that she has a past, including but not limited to an erroneous conviction for murder.

It really did take years for me to think of ordinary life, each day not so very different from the day before or the day after, as something it was possible to trust. The first big story I wrote may always be the biggest story I ever do. And you know what? That is 100 percent okay with me.

When I set out to be a journalist, I wanted to change the world. But, as Leo Tolstoy (remember him?) said, "Everyone thinks of changing the world, but no one thinks of changing himself."

Without meaning to, I changed myself by changing a very small part of the world, helping out a few people, people who were my world. It turned out to be enough.

When we were children, Nell and I made parachutes from the sheets that our mother dried outside on a spinning rack. We had a dryer. But perhaps our busy working mom wanted to give us a memory of another mother, who paid attention to such small details. We would tie the corners together, slip our arms through these makeshift sleeves, and then jump from a tree or from the roof of the shed, and we never doubted, even after Nell chipped a tooth and I cracked my collarbone, that these parachutes would bear us safely to earth.

I still drag my parachute of the past behind me, and in it are the people I have met and made and loved—Sam, my parents, Nelia, Joey, Danny, Sparrow, Ruth Wild, Nell, Lily Landry, Archangel, and Felicity, Felicity, Felicity—and as long as I drag that parachute and my heart keeps pumping, I believe that it will somehow bear me safely to earth wherever I land.

The parachute is love.

For what is this life? Comforting, confounding, besmirched, and bedazzling life? What does it all mean? It means the people we carry. They are our hell, as the philosopher said, but also our heaven.

They follow us everywhere. They become our home.

Acknowledgments

This story was suggested by one of the first criminal trials I covered long ago, as a young newspaper reporter. The young woman on whom I based the character of Felicity Wild was accused of a crime not too much different from the one in this story, and I watched her be convicted. What stayed with me over decades was not the case so much as the riddle: What compels gifted people with good choices to make awful choices instead? I want to thank the doctors and lawyers who gave me advice; the smart and tireless author friends—especially my Annie—who helped me search until I found the one small middle piece that would make the jigsaw puzzle into a picture; my book club sisters; my daughters and my sons; my helper, Sara, faithful and true; my brother and my sister; my patient spouse and my even-more-patient agent; and an editor friend with an old-fashioned first name not unlike Irene's who knows who she is. Thank you, MIRA HarperCollins, for believing in a story of mine, one more time. Everything except the birds in this book is made up, every street, every park and restaurant. But just because all of it is fiction doesn't mean it isn't true. I must add that I am sure that there are many errors in this novel, and all of them are mine. One more thing: as I promised, Merit, I'm going to take three weeks off. Maybe two.